Banner O'Brien

**Center Point
Large Print**

**This Large Print Book carries the
Seal of Approval of N.A.V.H.**

ॐ श्री गणेशाय नमः

Banner O'Brien

Linda Lael Miller

Center Point Publishing
Thorndike, Maine USA

Compass Press
British Commonwealth

This Center Point Large Print edition
is published in the year 2001 by arrangement with
Pocket Books, a division of Simon & Schuster, Inc.

This Compass Press edition is published in the year 2001 by
Bolinda Publishing Pty Ltd., Tullamarine, Victoria, Australia by arrangement with
Pocket Books, a division of Simon & Schuster, Inc.

The text of this Large Print edition is unabridged.
In other aspects, this book may vary from the original edition. Printed in Thailand.
Set in 16-point Times New Roman type by Bill Coskrey.

US ISBN 1-58547-118-6
BC ISBN 1-74030-496-9

Library of Congress Cataloging-in-Publication Data

Miller, Linda Lael
    Banner O'Brien / Linda Lael Miller. -- Center Point large print ed.
    p. cm.
    ISBN 1-58547-118-6 (lib. bdg. : alk. paper)
    1. Large type books. I. Title.

PS3563.I41373
[B36 2001]
813'.54--dc21

                                                          00-069482

Australian Cataloguing-in-Publication Data

Miller, Linda Lael.
Banner O'Brien / Linda Lael Miller.
ISBN 1740304969
    1. Large print books.
    2. United States - History - 1865-1898 - Fiction.
    3. Historical fiction.
    4. Love stories.
I. Title
813.54

British Cataloguing-in-Publication is available from the British Library.

For Kate Duffy and Linda Marrow,
who swung open a door when I knocked.

Chapter One

Washington Territory
December 15, 1886

The lights of Port Hastings winked and sparkled through a veil of snow as the steamboat drew alongside a long, wooden wharf and was made fast to the pilings. Hurdy-gurdy music swelled out of the darkness, raucous and merry, and Banner O'Brien bent forward at the ice-crusted railing, trying to discern its source.

At her side, Mr. Temple Royce gestured toward shore and muttered, "Here it is—Little Sodom and Gomorrah."

Banner's chin lifted. Little Sodom and Gomorrah, was it? And why had Mr. Royce spoken of this town in only the most glowing terms until now, when it was too late to retreat?

Before she could give voice to her questions, he caught her arm in a suave, somewhat proprietory motion and ushered her toward the boarding ramp. "We need you here," he said, as though that settled everything.

The music grew louder still as they made their way down the slippery ramp to the wharf, and Temple was quick to reach a waiting carriage and help Banner inside.

She peered through the uncovered window as the vehicle made its cautious way up a steep, stony hillside and onto a street lined with weathered saloons and brothels. Here, prostitutes called out coarse invitations and sailors reeled, already drunken, from one seedy establishment to another.

"Water Street," allowed Temple Royce in a bored tone.

"Please don't judge the whole community by this place."

Banner drew in her head and sat back in the tufted leather seat, her hands buried in the warm folds of her fraying, blue woolen cloak. At the moment, she almost wished that she'd stayed in Portland, where she had had a clean, warm room and the kind of starvation practice that kept a doctor humble.

She sat up very straight and took herself in hand. Sean was in Portland—she'd seen him there with her own eyes—and that decided the matter.

"You are very beautiful," observed Mr. Royce in an off-hand fashion. He was a good-looking man, of medium height and weight, and his hair and eyes were a dark caramel color of exactly the same shade. He was about thirty, by Banner's reckoning, and his fine linen shirt and obviously tailor-made suit indicated that he was well-to-do, if not downright wealthy. "How did you happen to become a physician?"

Banner was too tired and too unnerved to go into the details. She was here to take over another doctor's practice while he recovered from an injury, not to bare her soul to a man she barely knew. "You have reviewed my qualifications, Mr. Royce," she said with dignity. "I have shown you my letters of recommendation and my diploma. It would seem to me that the manner in which I obtained them is irrelevant."

A grin quirked the corner of Royce's mouth, and his voice was like sugared brandy when he spoke. "That cinnamon-colored hair, those green, green eyes—why hasn't someone married you, Miss O'Brien?"

"*Doctor* O'Brien," corrected Banner, as a small, insistent headache began to throb between her temples. One man *had* married her, and sorely regretted it, but that was none of Temple Royce's concern.

He nodded a suave concession. "Dr. O'Brien," he repeated. "How old are you?"

Banner sighed. "I am twenty-six. How old are you?"

He chuckled, though annoyance flashed in his caramel eyes. "You are quite impudent, Dr. O'Brien," he said. "And to answer your question, I'm thirty-two."

"How was Dr. Henderson injured?" she asked, referring to the man Mr. Royce had persuaded her to replace.

"It happened during a consultation with your competition, Dr. O'Brien. Poor Stewart dared to venture a contrary opinion, you see, and our Dr. Corbin took immediate issue."

"You don't mean—"

"Oh, but I do. Adam Corbin is a violent, opinionated man. Those who disagree with him run a grave risk."

Banner shuddered, appalled that a doctor would behave in such a manner, but offered no response.

"I dare say that Adam will be beating at your door as soon as he learns that you've taken over Stewart's practice. If you'd rather not stay alone—"

Color pulsed in Banner's face. She wasn't afraid of any man, save Sean Malloy, and she had no plans to cower under Temple Royce's smoothly offered wing like a frightened chick. "I'll stay in Dr. Henderson's house," she said coldly. "As you assured me I could."

"As you wish," said Royce with a shrug.

They were well out of Water Street now, Banner saw, and again peering out through the swirling snow, she made

9

out a bank, a general store, and an impressive brick court-house before the cold wind buffeted away her breath and she had to give up.

Not wanting to talk, she huddled deeper into the half-warmth of her inadequate cloak and closed her eyes to reflect. She had been rash—there was no doubt of that—in taking Mr. Temple Royce at his word and traveling such a distance in his company just because he said that his town had need of another doctor, but desperation had driven her to accept. Not two hours before Royce had entered her cramped, storefront office, she'd gone to Port-land's waterfront to look in on a patient and seen Sean there, among a group of longshoremen entering a tavern.

The offer of a position in Port Hastings, though extended by a total stranger, had seemed a godsend.

Dr. Henderson's house, now abandoned since he'd gone to recuperate in the home of his sister, was a small, sturdy structure with a picket fence and a holly tree growing at the end of the front walk.

A light burned in a front window, and smoke curled from a brick chimney. The scent of it gave Banner a cozy, welcome feeling, as did the tenuous smile of the young Indian woman who met her at the door.

"Where is husband?" she wanted to know, looking past Banner and seeing only Mr. Royce and the carriage driver, who were unloading the few belongings Banner had taken the time to pack.

Used to such questions, Banner smiled and stepped around the woman to enter the small house. It was a sparsely furnished place, very clean, and a tea tray had been set beside the brick fireplace in the parlor. "I don't have a husband," she answered, shedding her cloak, bonnet, and gloves. "I'm Dr. Banner O'Brien. What is your name?"

The woman gaped at Banner for a few moments before stating that she was called Jenny Lind.

It was Banner's turn to gape. "Jenny Lind?" she echoed, just as Mr. Royce and his driver brought in her trunk and the two crates that contained her books and medical supplies.

Temple laughed. "Jenny's Klallum name is virtually unpronounceable, so we gave her one we could manage."

Banner recovered herself and poured tea from the pot the world-famous singer's namesake had prepared. It was a pity, she thought, that the white man had taken not only the Indian lands, but their names in the bargain.

Royce's brown eyes swept over Jenny. "What are you doing here, anyway? This isn't—"

Jenny drew nearer to Banner, as though she'd sensed her sympathetic thoughts. "House was very dirty," she broke in in a tremulous voice.

Temple considered her answer and made a visible decision not to pursue the point. He favored Banner with a few more pleasantries and then took his leave.

Jenny was clearly relieved, and Banner yawned and fell into a comfortable chair to sip at her tea and enjoy the fire. Saints in heaven but she was tired, and the shock of almost encountering Sean was heavy within her.

Jenny came to stand beside the chair and touch Banner's snow-dampened hair with a chubby, nutbrown hand. "Doctor Firehair," she mused, in a wondering tone.

Banner had lived in the West for nearly a year, and she

liked to think that she had some understanding of Indian ways. They were quick, these people, to touch whatever drew their interest, and it was common for them to walk into a private home without knocking. While some were affronted by this direct approach, Banner was not.

"Do you work for Dr. Henderson?"

The girl drew back as though the cinnamon-red tresses had burned her. Her brown eyes widened, and her waist-length, blue-ebony hair glinted in the firelight as she shook her head. "No!" she replied, with spirit.

At a loss, Banner simply watched Jenny, her teacup poised between her lap and her mouth.

"Dr. Adam tell me come here. Clean house good."

A tremor of alarm invaded Banner's weariness. "Dr. Adam?"

Jenny's rich hair shimmered as she nodded.

"Is he the man who hurt Dr. Henderson?"

Jenny lowered her eyes and her mouth worked. "Yes," she said. "But—"

At that moment, a cold draft suddenly filled the room and made the brave little fire undulate eerily on the hearth. The sense of a third personality was palpable, and Banner looked up to see a tall, dark-haired man, probably some-where in his mid-thirties, raking Jenny's squat little frame with mocking navy blue eyes.

"You promised," he drawled, folding his arms.

A golden glow appeared in Jenny's cheeks, and she lowered her head. "I'm sorry, Adam," she said, in perfectly accented English.

The indigo gaze swung back to Banner, assessing her swiftly and coming to rest on her face. "She's been doing

12

her rendition of the Ignorant Savage again, hasn't she?"

Banner was so overwhelmed by the effrontery of this man's unannounced entrance and the impact of his presence that she couldn't speak.

The tall man was unperturbed by this; his teeth flashed in a pearlescent smile, and he bowed slightly. "Dr. Adam Corbin," he said, in crisp introduction.

Banner stood, knowing that her response would unbalance this man and relishing the fact for some reason that was quite beyond her. "Dr. Banner O'Brien," she said, with a corresponding nod.

The impact of her words was in no way disappointing. The rakishly handsome brute paled slightly, his eyes scraped her, and his jaw hardened. "What?"

"You came here to intimidate the new doctor, didn't you?" Banner retorted, determined not to let the fate of her predecessor quell her hard-won bravado. "Well, Dr. Corbin, here I am!"

He ran one hand through his dark, unruly hair and squinted at Banner as though he didn't trust his vision. "My God—a woman—is this a joke?"

Banner drew herself up to her full if unprepossessing height. "I assure you that it is not. I am here to replace the man you brutalized—doctor."

"*Brutalized?*" The word was only whispered, and yet it seemed to rock, the small house like an explosion. "Who told you that? Temple?"

Jenny stepped between Banner and the giant, a plump diplomat clad in buckskin. "Jiggers, Adam, will you relax? Of *course* it was Temple!"

"What did he say?" Adam demanded, his impossibly

13

blue eyes searing Banner's face.

Banner sank back into her chair, fresh out of courage, and her hands trembled as she set aside her endangered teacup. "He told me that you are 'violent and opinionated,' Dr. Corbin, and that disagreeing with you is a risky proposition."

"I see."

"Furthermore," Banner went on, rising on a swell of irritation and fatigue, "this is my home, for the time being, and I will thank you not to walk in without knocking ever again. Is that clear, doctor?"

The response was a raw, jarring burst of amusement. "I stand corrected," he said, with another bow—this one more impudent than the first.

Banner O'Brien was far too overwrought to deal with the likes of Dr. Adam Corbin. She wanted him to go and take his overwhelming personality, his broad shoulders, and the keen intelligence pulsing in his eyes with him. "Good night," she said pointedly, taking up her teacup again.

But Adam stood fast, his arms folded across his chest. For the first time, Banner noticed that he wasn't wearing a suitcoat, as cold as it was outside. His trousers, linen shirt, and half-buttoned vest fitted to his muscular frame with an easy perfection, as though they would not dare do otherwise, and the fabrics, while rumpled and snow-dampened, were of the finest quality.

The silence lengthened, and then Jenny broke it with a nervous giggle and a sympathetic glance at Banner. "Shall I get you something to eat?"

Banner was wildly hungry, for she hadn't had a full meal

14

since Portland, but she found the prospect of being alone with this strange man unsettling indeed. "N-No," she sputtered quickly. "Thank you, b-but I'll fix something for myself later."

Adam's indigo eyes sliced to the young Indian woman, and some almost imperceptible signal was given. Jenny scampered toward the back of the house without another word.

"How do I know you're really a doctor?" Adam intoned, his arms still folded.

"I guess you'll just have to trust me," Banner retorted.

The magnificent head moved in a slow denial. "Oh, no," came the gravelly response. "Henderson did enough damage as it was. I'll be damned if I'm going to turn another quack loose on the people of this town."

Banner was insulted, and her headache had taken on a marked tempo—that of her pounding heart. "You speak with such authority, doctor," she said coldly. "Almost as though I needed your permission to practice."

A mirthless grin curved his lips. "Perhaps you do," he replied.

Banner shot to her feet and then swayed precariously as her hungry, exhausted body protested.

Adam Corbin caught her shoulders in his hands, to steady her, and a fearsome, inexplicable jolt went through her. "Sit," he said, pressing her back into her chair.

She was on the verge of tears now, and she could still feel the weight of Adam's hands, even though he had promptly withdrawn them. "I am not a 'quack,'" she said. "I studied with Dr. Emily Blackwell, at the New York Infirmary for—"

He was crouching before her in a most distracting fashion, and his powerful hands gripped the arms of Banner's chair, thus imprisoning her. "Dr. Blackwell," he mused. "That is august company. August company indeed."

"Yes," breathed Banner, because she could manage nothing more. Why was she looking at the sprinkling of glossy black hair revealed by his open collar?

"I would like to see your diploma."

Every nasty word Banner knew surged into her throat, each tangling with its fellows, and she swallowed them all. "You are insufferable," she said through her teeth.

"Yes," he confessed, and his eyes danced with an odd mischief. "The diploma, please."

She almost directed him to her medical bag, which was sitting on top of her trunk, but she stopped herself in time. There were other papers in there, papers she didn't want this man or anyone else to know about "You'll have to move, sir, if you expect me to comply."

He subsided, rising to his feet in a fluid motion. With his left hand he gestured, and his dark brows were arched, as if to say, "Get on with it."

With dignity that was completely feigned, Banner lifted her small frame from the chair and made her way to her bag. She extracted her credentials and extended them to Dr. Corbin briskly.

He unfolded the documents and read them with a solemn, tolerant expression. Then he surveyed Banner briefly and read the papers again. "Banner could be a man's name," he mused, after a long time. "What if you stole these documents, say, from a father—a brother—a husband?"

Banner colored. "I most certainly did not! I *earned* them, and I assure you, it wasn't easy, considering that I had to deal with so many arrogant buffoons to do it!"

Though Adam's lips were grim, laughter flashed in his eyes. His shoulders moved in an insolent shrug. "Are you calling me an arrogant buffoon, Miss—Dr. O'Brien?"

"I am."

A chuckle erupted from the depths of him, but then he went on as though she hadn't spoken. "I'll take you on rounds with me tomorrow, and we'll soon see if you're a doctor or not."

Crimson flags unfurled in Banner's cheeks at his presumption, but she knew she could not refuse to accompany him, no matter how badly she wanted to do so. He would not stop harassing her until she proved herself, and the only way to do that was to demonstrate her knowledge of medicine firsthand. "I will be ready," she said.

"Good," he replied. "I'll come for you at seven."

"Seven," Banner confirmed.

Apparently satisfied, for the moment, at least, Adam Corbin left the house. Glad as she was to see him go, the place seemed strangely unreal without him.

Banner was still pondering this paradoxical fact when Jenny returned, carrying an empty tray. She put the tea things and Banner's cup onto it and smiled with infuriating understanding.

"There is only one Adam," she remarked.

"That is, indeed, a mercy," said Banner.

Jenny looked offended. "You are wrong, Dr. O'Brien," she answered. And then she walked haughtily off, the tray

17

in her hands, leaving Banner no choice but to follow.

The journey ended in a small kitchen with a wood-burning cookstove and open shelves for cupboards. A bowl of fragrant soup steamed on the round table, and a plate of fresh bread rested beside it.

"Your supper," said Jenny coolly, setting the tray down beside a cast iron sink and pumping water to fill the cup and the teapot.

Ravenous, Banner sank into a chair and began to eat. The barley soup was delicious, as was the bread, and the food brought relief from the spinning dizziness in her head and the weakness in her knees.

During the meal, Jenny managed to stay busy at the sink, keeping her back to Banner, and the mood in that cozy little kitchen was a stiff and forbidding one.

"You like Dr. Corbin a lot, don't you?" Banner ventured, once her hunger had been brought under control.

Jenny turned, and her wide brown eyes were quietly fierce. "He is a good man. Too good, maybe."

"Good?" Banner countered, with gentleness, "Jenny, how can you say he's good when he—"

"When he broke Stewart Henderson's jaw?" finished Jenny, a golden blush rising in her round cheeks.

Banner felt herself go pale. "Good Lord! He broke the poor man's *jaw?*"

Jenny took up a red-and-white-checked dishtowel and then flung it down again. "Yes!"

"Why?" persisted Banner, stricken.

Jenny's chin jutted out, and she folded her arms. "Adam caught Henderson doing surgery on Water Street," she said in level tones. "Stewart gave the patient opium instead of

18

ether, and the woman woke up before the operation was over."

Banner closed her eyes against the image, and sickness scalded in her throat. "Saints in heaven—"

"The woman died," Jenny summarized, "screaming."

Banner shuddered and grasped the table edge until she had recovered herself a little. She could well imagine the rage such a situation would stir in a responsible physician.

Jenny squared her shoulders and started across the kitchen again. "I'll show you to your room," she said.

Still horror-stricken, Banner rose shakily from her chair and followed Jenny through the kitchen and into a tiny room off the parlor.

There was a brass bed spread with a bright quilt there, along with a wooden bureau and a washstand. On this stand was a china pitcher filled with steaming water, a mismatched basin, and a scratchy white towel.

Banner did her best to be grateful for these items, though she yearned for a long, luxurious bath. She was just shedding her sensible woolen dress when Jenny slipped out and closed the door behind her.

Alone, she poured water into the chipped basin and, shivering in her thin underthings, began to wash. When that task had been completed, she took the pins from her dark auburn hair; and it fell in a bright cascade to her waist.

Banner hadn't unpacked a hairbrush, any more than she'd gotten out a nightgown, but none of that mattered on this curious and disturbing night. Her head was spinning, and she didn't know what to think of Adam Corbin or Dr. Henderson or the incident on Water Street that had prompted one man to assault the other. She did puzzle a bit as to why Dr. Corbin would engage Jenny to clean the house of a man he so obviously disliked.

She slid between the sheets of the narrow bed and found that they were impossibly cold. She moved about, trying to heat them with the friction of her body, and then fell into a fitful sleep where a woman was bleeding to death and screaming and Adam Corbin's handsome face was contorted with a killing rage.

Then the dream woman became Banner herself, and Adam became Sean. The screams brought Jenny running on bare red feet.

"Friends?"

Jenny smiled as she filled Banner's cup with fresh coffee and sat down across from her at the kitchen table. "Friends," she confirmed.

It was twenty minutes before seven by the watch pinned carefully to the bodice of Banner's heavy broadcloth dress, and a gentle snowfall sifted past the window over the sink to glisten on the spiky-green leaves of a nearby holly tree.

"I'm sorry I awakened you last night, Jenny."

Jenny took a contemplative sip from her coffee cup. "Do you have a lot of bad dreams?" she asked.

Only one, Banner thought to herself, but her words were calculated to close the dangerous subject. "I was very tired," she said.

"Who is Sean?" pressed Jenny.

Banner was saved from answering by a thunderous knocking at the front door. Bless him, Dr. Adam Corbin was not only prompt, but early to boot.

"O'Brien!" he bellowed irritably, as Banner raced to

20

admit him.

He was standing on the small porch, his blue eyes dark with some secret annoyance. Today, he looked more like a member of the English gentry than a country doctor about to make rounds: his trousers were of some soft, fawn-colored fabric that clung to his muscular thighs and tapered into the tops of a pair of glistening black riding boots. Over his crisply tailored white shirt he wore a snow-dusted coat of some fine tweed, and seeing him up close, Banner realized that his hair was not really black at all, but a very dark brown threaded through with strands of dark gold and chestnut.

"Is something wrong, O'Brien?" he demanded.

Banner blushed to think of the overt way she'd inspected his person and managed a valiant little smile. "No—no, of course not."

His jaw knotted. "Well, then?"

Banner had laid out her warmest cloak and her medical bag, and she turned to fetch them so rapidly that she caught the toe of her right shoe in the hem of her skirts and very nearly fell.

She knew that embarrassment was blooming in her cheeks when she gathered her things and forced herself to face Adam again.

His features had softened a little, and there was a twitch of amusement at the corner of his mouth.

"I'm ready now," she said, just to break the silence.

"Your eyes are just the color of shamrock," he responded, somewhat distractedly.

Banner decided to ignore the remark, though propriety would have her challenge it. "Shall we leave?"

21

Adam chuckled and indicated the horse and buggy waiting beyond the picket fence and the holly tree. "After you," he said.

This was Banner's first opportunity for a good look at Port Hastings, and it was easy to let her curiosity over-shadow the strange, nameless emotions this man engendered in her.

She settled happily into the buggy seat and peered through the thickening snow as Adam joined her and took up the reins. "Do they really call this town Little Sodom and Gomorrah?" she asked.

Adam laughed. "That and other things. The term does bring Water Street to mind."

Banner was reminded of the woman Jenny said had died on that street, and some of her joy in the crisp splendor of the morning drained away.

In an attempt to divert her thoughts, she drew a mental map and placed Port Hastings on the Strait of Juan de Fuca, the waterway that separated Puget Sound from the Pacific. No doubt ships from every part of the world dropped anchor here to pay duty on their cargoes and give foreign passengers an opportunity to show their papers to customs officials.

The distant, keening shrieks of mill saws indicated that there was a thriving timber industry, and as the buggy was drawn out of the quiet street and into the main part of the town itself, she sighted the framework of a half-constructed clipper in the shipyard fronting the water.

There were wooden sidewalks edging Center Street, and snow mounded on the square tops of kerosene-fed street-lamps. Housewives and millworkers and rough-looking

22

sailors intermingled with the occasional Indian or Chinese.

A bell was ringing somewhere on a side street, and well-dressed children and urchins alike scrambled after the sound, some more willingly than others.

With Christmas just over a week away, there were evergreen boughs arranged in the windows of shops and offices, and almost every door boasted a beribboned holly wreath.

Banner was enthralled by the raucous vitality of that town. It was obvious that Port Hastings had aspirations to be more than it was.

They rounded a corner, and Adam drew back the reins and wrenched the brake lever into place. "I'll be back in a minute," he said.

Banner eyed the steamy windows of Wung Lo's Laundry and Savory Tea Shop suspiciously. Adam had promised to take her on rounds with him. Was he actually planning to leave her sitting in his buggy while he saw patients?

He seemed to read the question in her face, and it made him laugh as he stepped down to the ground, which appeared to be a rutted mixture of snow, mud, and sawdust.

"I'm only picking up my shirts, Shamrock," he assured her.

Banner felt very foolish indeed, and she averted her eyes and folded her hands and sat rigid until she knew Adam had gone inside the store.

Moments after that, a tiny Chinaman came out of the establishment, balancing an enormous stack of neatly wrapped parcels on his shoulders. He wore loose garments of black silk, and a queue reached well down his back.

Banner looked at the man's feet, which were shod only in wooden sandals, and ached to think how cold he must be.

He had gone only a dozen yards or so when half a dozen schoolchildren encircled him, linking their hands. Their voices were the crueler for their chimelike innocence as they chanted,

Ching Chong, Chinaman
Have you any fish?
Snip off yur pigtail
Make a wish!

The little man raged at them in swift, high-pitched, bird-call words, but they were undaunted. The stack of laundry teetered precariously on the Chinaman's shoulders, and Banner was about to break up the game with a memorable invective when an Indian man came out of an alleyway, looking fierce in his buckskins and braids and clapping his hands angrily.

"*Klatawah! Klatawah!*" he scolded, and the imps scurried away in every direction, calling taunts over their shoulders and then running in earnest when the Indian poised himself to give chase.

The Chinaman flung one baleful look at his rescuer, realigned the incredible burden on his back, and scampered on about his business.

Shortly, Adam came out of Wung Lo's establishment with a package only slightly less cumbersome than the Chinaman's and dropped it behind the buggy seat. The whole vehicle shifted as he climbed in and took up the reins, and Banner was unaccountably conscious of the hard line of his thigh pressing against her own.

She shivered involuntarily, even though there was a strange, drunken warmth surging through her system.

Adam studied her, one dark eyebrow arched, and the snow-and-soap scent of his clothes and hair made her even more uncomfortable than his gaze.

"Cold?" he asked.

"No," Banner croaked.

Adam didn't seem to believe her, and the molten humor in his eyes made her want to double up both fists and pummel his chest. "I should have brought a lap rug," he said.

The idea of being cosseted under a warm covering with this particular man was blatantly disturbing. "Your patients are waiting," she said stiffly.

He laughed that alarming laugh and slapped the reins down on the horse's back and the buggy was moving again, jolting and shifting over the rutted road. The winter wind stung Banner through her coat and her dress, but not for all the tea in Wung Lo's shop would she have admitted it.

Their first call was routine; they visited a man who had fallen from a scaffold in the shipyard and broken his ankle. The patient was obsequious with Adam and openly curious about Banner.

The second stop was sobering. Adam drew the buggy to a halt behind the merchantile, and they climbed steep, slippery wooden steps to reach a modest apartment where a woman lay groaning on a narrow bed that had been wedged between an iron cookstove and an unfinished wall.

Two small boys in shabby knee pants and untucked shirts hovered at the foot of the cot, their eyes wide and frightened.

Adam ruffled their hair in turn and drew two peppermint sticks from the pocket of his tweed coat. "I haven't had time to eat these," he said, with a serious expression that flailed against Banner's heart like the wing of a trapped bird. "How about some help?"

The children were eager to solve the dilemma, and they retreated to a pallet in the opposite corner of the room, whispering and measuring one stick of candy against the other.

Banner's attention swung to the woman on the cot. She was so thin that her hipbones were clearly visible even through her blanket. Her eyes were sunken and shadowed, and her lackluster brown hair was matted.

Adam's tone was gentle when he spoke. "Hildie, this is Dr. O'Brien. Will you please let her examine you?"

Hildie's pain-haunted eyes assessed the healthy, neatly dressed woman standing nearby, then shifted back to Adam. "If you'll go outside, I will," she said. "My Fitz don't want—"

Adam held up both hands in a concessionary gesture. "I know," he broke in. "Your husband doesn't want any man to see you without your clothes."

"It ain't decent," muttered Hildie.

Adam made an exasperated sound, and for all its softness, it startled Banner. She'd been trying to identify the familiar, cloying odor that underlined the ordinary smells

26

of cooking, tobacco smoke, and an unrinsed chamberpot.

"I'll take the boys downstairs for a while," he said.

Hildie half-rose from her dingy, coverless pillow. "Don't you buy them nothin', Doc, like you did the last time."

Adam's jaw tightened, but he drew the two children to the door with him with an eloquent motion of one hand. Only a moment later he was gone, the stale air of the room stirred by the brief admission of the outdoors.

Banner and Hildie were alone, and the nature of the smell Banner had been chasing through her mind came home to her with dismal clarity.

"Open your nightgown, please," she said, cloaking her despair in brisk professionalism.

Hildie hesitated, then grudgingly complied. "How'd you ever get to be a doctor?" she demanded.

"It wasn't easy," said Banner, keeping her features under strict control even though bile was rising in her throat like acid. Hildie's right breast was eaten away by disease.

"My Ma's leg got just this way," confided Hildie, in hushed, shaky tones that betrayed her fear. "She went blind, Ma did. And then she died."

Banner closed her eyes for a moment and longed for a breath of the crisp, bracing winter air outside. She cleaned the infected area with an alcohol solution and gave Hildie a stiff dose of laudenum.

When this had been accomplished, Banner helped herself to water from a kettle on the stove and scoured her hands with the lye soap she carried in her bag.

That done, she went to the door and opened it and swallowed great gulps of clean air.

Adam had been waiting at the base of the stairs, though Hildie's children were nowhere in sight, and he looked up at her with eyes that betrayed an ache to match her own.

They met in the middle of the stairway, but Banner could not manage a medical consultation at the moment. She covered her mouth with one hand, made a strangling sound, and rushed down the steps to vomit into a pristine snowbank at their base.

Adam was ready with a clean handkerchief when the spasm of illness passed. "Cancer?" he ventured, like a teacher quizzing a slow child.

Banner shook her head and took clean snow from the stair railing, putting it into her mouth and then unceremoniously spewing it out. "Diabetes," she said, and the word was a soblike rasp. "Her breast—there's gangrene—"

Respect mingled with the sympathy in Adam's blue eyes. "I know."

"How?" croaked Banner. "How did you know, if she wouldn't let you examine her?"

"The smell."

Banner nodded distractedly. "She should be hospitalized."

"Yes." Adam paused, grinding his teeth and assessing the sky as though it had offended him. Snowflakes glistened in his thick hair and gathered on his eyelashes. "But—"

"But 'her Fitz' won't allow it."

"Right. He's convinced that I merely want to get her alone so I can have my way with her."

Frustration swelled in Banner's mind, crowding worthy thoughts into shadowed corners. She had thought she'd

28

encountered every form of ignorance during her training and her brief practice in Portland, but this was a new aspect. "She'll die."

"Yes."

"And she must be in wretched pain."

Adam only nodded, but his exasperation was visible in the set of his jaw and his shoulders.

It was then that Hildie's boys appeared, laughing and flinging handfuls of powdery snow at each other, exulting in the weather and the brief escape from the grim quarters at the top of the stairs.

"What will happen to them?" Banner whispered.

Adam sighed. "God knows. Right now, Hildie is my main concern. I'll have another talk with Fitz tonight and try to persuade him to bring her to the hospital."

Banner had not dared to dream that there actually was a real hospital in Port Hastings. For all its vigor, it was a relatively small town, and most such communities considered hospitals an extravagance.

Despite the weight of what they both knew would befall Hildie, Adam smiled. Again, it seemed, he'd read her thoughts. "Would you like to see my hospital, O'Brien?"

"*Your* hospital?"

He nodded. "Since I run it myself, I tend to think of it as mine, yes,"

The idea engendered depths of weariness Banner had never felt before, even during the grueling days of her training. "By yourself?" she marveled.

Adam's shoulders stiffened under the tweed coat. "I haven't had much choice," he said. "Henderson is the only other doctor within twenty-five miles, and I wouldn't let

29

that butcher near my horses, let alone my patients."

Having imparted this information, Adam left Banner to go back to Hildie's room and reclaim the cloak and medical bag she had left behind.

One of the little boys approached Banner, gnawing philosophically on the strip of dried beef Adam had been forbidden to buy. "You sure do got red hair till hell won't have it, missus," he said.

Before Banner could come up with a suitable response, Adam reappeared, carrying her things. Somewhere between herself and Hildie, he had shed his frustration and his anger, or hidden them, and he was again the unflappable country doctor.

Banner wasn't certain whether to mourn or feel relieved.

Chapter Two

The hill leading from Port Hastings proper to Adam's hospital was a steep one—so steep that Banner knew moments of alarm. At times, it seemed that the lightweight buggy would slide backward, all the way to the harbor, dragging the stoic little horse with it.

To distract herself from this image, Banner turned her attention to the houses rising on each side of the road.

They were sizable places with widow's walks along their waterward sides and fashionable scrollwork edging their roofs and windows. Each house had a yard, and each a picket fence. The pruned rosebushes, in their traceries of snow, stirred a nostalgia for a vanished summer within Banner.

At the crest of the hill was an elegant two-story brick

house with many chimneys and dozens of glistening windows. Ivy vines, netted with snow, cossetted one end of the building like a gentle hand. At the other, a long, covered walkway annexed a one-story wing.

Banner thought surely they would pass the place by, but the horse drew the rig into the cobbled drive without any perceptible urging from Adam.

"This is your hospital?" Banner asked, thunderstruck.

He laughed, but the sound was mirthless, and his blue eyes were fixed not on the magnificent building or on Banner but on the mountain rising beyond. He seemed to see something there besides the countless evergreens in their lacy snow chemises. Something he prized.

After a second or so, however, Adam turned to Banner, and he was seeing her. Smiling. "This is my house," he said. "Or, I should say, my mother's house. That wing over there holds the hospital, my office, all that. "

Banner was impressed. "Such a big house," she breathed. Was there a woman living behind those thick walls, a woman who wore Adam's band on her finger? She had not considered that possibility before, and now, as it edged into her mind on sticky shoes, she found it distinctly unpleasant. "I suppose you have lots of children," she said.

Adam laughed again, drawing the reins back and wrenching the brake lever into place in front of a small stone porch. Above this were massive, brass-handled doors. "I would like nothing better," he said, "but propriety dictates that I take a wife first."

Wild relief brought swiftness to Banner's breath and color to her cheeks—color that had no connection at all to the biting December wind. "Are you such a respector of propriety, doctor?" she ventured, her eyes sparkling.

He chuckled. "Not normally. In most respects, in fact, I'm an unconscionable rake. However, when it comes to children, I have very provincial ideas."

Banner felt an odd quickening in her womb, as though it were preparing itself to nurture and cherish this man's child. Reprimanding herself for having such a fanciful and untoward thought, she bit her lower lip and squared her small shoulders. "It is quite cold," she said stiffly.

The lie was so brazen that she thought Adam would surely challenge it; despite the weather, there was an unaccountable warmth under the black leather bonnet of that buggy. His face had drawn very near to hers, and for one wild moment she was certain that he meant to kiss her.

Before the quandary could be resolved, however, one of the two doors at the front of the house swung open and a pretty young girl appeared in the chasm, one arm looped through the center of the biggest holly wreath Banner had ever seen.

The sprite had wide, crystal blue eyes and hair as dark as Adam's, and her face was alight at the sight of the buggy.

"Adam!" the woman-child whooped in unceremonious joy, bounding over the snowy steps in a tomboyish leap and scurrying toward the buggy.

Adam turned from Banner and, to her deep annoyance, climbed out of the rig to embrace the elfin enchantress and whirl her around, red-berried, prickly wreath and all, in exuberant greeting.

Banner felt the first real jealousy she had ever known, though she forced a patient smile to her mouth. After all, it wasn't as though she herself had any claim to this man's affections, and though he had said he was unmarried, he had *not* said that there was no one he cared for.

The girl's eyes were on Banner the moment Adam had set her down, but no challenge leaped in their blue, blue depths. Only a sort of mischievous speculation. "Who is this?" she chimed, letting the huge wreath rest against the skirts of her soft azure dress.

Adam held out one arm in a dashing gesture of introduction. "Melissa, meet Dr. Banner O'Brien. O'Brien, my sister, Melissa."

Relief sang through Banner's system, and her assumed smile became genuine. "Hello," she said, as Adam helped her down.

Melissa's delighted gaze swung from Banner to her brother, and an unspoken "Ah-ha!" rang in the air.

Adam tossed a look of mock sternness in his sister's direction and then tucked Banner's hand into the crook of his elbow before starting toward the open door of the house.

"When did you get back?" he asked of Melissa, who hesitated on the step to hang the wreath on a waiting hook.

"Why, Adam, how nice, of you to ask!" retorted Melissa. "You were supposed to meet the steamer, remember?"

A look of exaggerated chagrin moved in Adam's face and his broad shoulders as Melissa joined them in the entryway. "You're here," he observed expansively, "So I don't see the problem."

"You wouldn't," drawled the girl—Banner guessed she was about seventeen years old—rubbing her hands together as though the holly wreath might have left dust on them. "If it hadn't been for Jeff, I would have had to walk."

"Horrors," said Adam, and his hand came up to touch Banner's hand, where it still rested in the crook of his arm.

Melissa took pointed interest in the gesture and studied Banner with mischievous eyes. "Are you really a doctor?" she wanted to know.

Adam's eyes linked with Banner's as he guided her out of the entryway, with its black-and-white-tiled floor and its tall clock. "Yes," he said, in a voice that made his colleague's heart cavort wildly between her throat and her midsection. "Shamrock is really a doctor."

So he had accepted her, then. Inwardly, Banner rejoiced. "Could we see the hospital now?"

Adam nodded, ushering her through a massive dining room that boasted mahogany-paneled walls, a crystal chandelier that must have measured at least six feet across, and a fireplace big enough for three or four men to stand up in. The furniture here was heavy, but not ornate, and the overall impression was one of easy, longstanding wealth.

"Before Papa built this house," Melissa announced, "he and Mama lived in a cabin right on this very spot." She tapped the long, highly polished table with the knuckles of one hand. "He used to say that my brothers were all born right where Maggie sets the mashed potatoes."

Adam paused, and gave his sister a dour look. "Speaking of Maggie, why don't you find her and tell her that Dr. O'Brien and I will want something to eat when we get back from the hospital."

Melissa looked as though she was going to argue—she would obviously have preferred to tag along after her brother—but then her aquamarine eyes registered understanding and she turned, in a whirl of finely sewn skirts, to prance off toward a door on the other side of the room.

Grinning, Adam led Banner through an archway and onto the covered walk she'd seen from outside. It had glass walls and a smooth wooden floor, and snow whispered past on both sides.

At the end was a broad room boasting eight empty, immaculately made beds and a huge iron heating stove.

"This is the infirmary itself," Adam said. "Usually, there are half a dozen patients here."

Banner looked around, both impressed and puzzled. "Is there just the one ward?"

Adam's eyes were as merry as the big wreath Melissa had hung on the front door. "You're wondering whether or not women patients have to share the ward with men," he guessed, quite accurately.

"Do they?"

He chuckled. "Of course not, Shamrock. We get very few female patients, given the backward attitudes of their husbands and fathers. When a woman is brought here, I usually put her in one of the guestrooms on the other side of the house."

"That must be most inconvenient."

"Not really. Maggie—that's our housekeeper—takes care of them and comes to me if there's a problem."

They left the ward to enter a cluttered office. Here, the walls were lined with hundreds of books, except for one, where a startling array of diplomas hung, framed. According to these august parchments, Adam Corbin had attended the prestigious University of Scotland, in

Glasgow, and taken special courses in such places as Vienna, Berlin, and Stockholm.

Banner, thinking of her four years at the New York Infirmary, her courses squeezed in between the menial hospital tasks that paid her way, felt intimidated. No wonder Adam had been so suspicious of her education.

"You are well trained," she admitted, with a slight lift of her chin.

"Thank you," he said, pulling her past a very messy desk and into a larger outer office, where there were chairs and benches to accommodate patients waiting for treatment.

At a neat desk beside the outmost door sat a girl about Melissa's age, her long fingers poised over the keys of a typewriting machine. Her hair glistened around her face in hundreds of appealing little taffy-colored curls, and her dark brown eyes assessed Banner with tart dispatch. "Hello," she said.

Adam was all gentlemanly grace. "Francelle, this is Dr. O'Brien. O'Brien, Miss Francelle Mayhugh."

"Francelle," Banner nodded cordially.

But Miss Mayhugh was done with pleasantries; she harumphed and went back to her work with frightening energy.

"There are two examining rooms," Adam said, pulling Banner unceremoniously into one of them and closing the door.

Banner's heart was doing crazy things again, and she braced herself against one examining table and cast an uneasy glance toward the closed door. "I don't think Francelle likes me," she said, though that was the last thing she was really concerned about.

Adam laughed and came nearer. So near that Banner could feel the warmth of his breath on the bridge of her slightly upturned Irish nose. The hard, lean length of his body sent primitive signals to the softness of hers as he imprisoned her by bracing himself against the table, one hand on each side of her. "Who cares?" he said.

Banner trembled. Her knees were weak and the pit of her stomach was spinning and there was a strange melting sensation somewhere in the depths of her pelvis. She had never felt this way before, with Sean. What was happening?

Adam's lips came down to taste hers, tantalizingly. "Shamrock," he breathed.

Banner ordered her hands to come up to his impervious chest and push him away, but they were bloodless, without muscle or bone. She wanted Adam Corbin to kiss her.

He caught her lower lip between his lips and a jolt went through her. His thighs were hard against hers as he drew her nearer still and claimed her mouth fully.

All five of Banner O'Brien's senses sang in wanton harmony as he compelled her to surrender, and confusion whirled in her mind. How was it that he could make her feel such things, when her own husband's kisses had engendered only fear? What was the medical basis for this?

She was gasping when Adam drew back, swept her face once with those impudent indigo eyes, and kissed her again.

Banner's riotous response was quelled by the brisk opening of the examining room door.

"Well," said Francelle coldly. "Is this a consultation?

37

I'm sorry I interrupted."

Adam swore and turned to face the girl squarely, though Banner could not have done so for anything. She lowered her head, embarrassed.

"What do you want?" Adam snapped.

"I was going to ask about the Christmas party," Francelle answered, with a dignity calculated to sting for days. "Will you be there, or do you plan to disappear again and come back in a black rage, as usual?"

"Couldn't this have waited?" Adam drawled, and through the thick fringe of her lashes Banner watched as his jawline tightened and a muscle twitched at the side of his neck.

"I didn't expect to find you and the—lady—so engaged, Adam. You must forgive me."

"Must I? Get out, Francelle."

"To be sure," she replied, and promptly closed the door behind her.

Adam stood at a little distance from Banner now, and his powerful shoulders slackened as he ran one hand through his hair. "I'm sorry, Shamrock," he said in gruff tones, though he did not meet her eyes. "I shouldn't have done that. Francelle will have your reputation shredded by nightfall."

Banner had no doubt of that. Female doctors tended to engender gossip as it was—especially in small towns. But she didn't regret the kisses, though she knew she should have. "Do you really disappear at Christmas and then return in an ugly state of mind?" she asked, to change the subject.

This she did regret, and instantly. Adam's eyes were

fierce when they sliced to her face, and a white line edged his jaw.

"I only kissed you, O'Brien," he said. "I did not offer to unveil my soul."

He could not have humiliated Banner any more deeply even if he had made a conscious effort. She felt cheap and presumptuous, and her eyes shifted from the strange menace in his gaze.

To her surprise, Adam sighed raggedly and caught her shoulders in strong hands. "Shamrock, look at me," he muttered.

She could not, for there were tears brimming in her eyes and her fierce pride demanded that she hide them.

Not to be dissuaded, Adam caught her chin in a hand that felt rough and smelled of antiseptic and forced her to obey his order. "I'm sorry," he told her, and the pain in his face made it easier for her to reveal her own.

She sniffled. He'd seen the tears, and there was nothing for it. "There is no need to apologize," she said.

"There is," he insisted. "I was rude and I'm sorry."

Banner did not know what to say to that, and besides, she'd already set aside her own hurt feelings to wonder what it was that pained him so much. "Adam—"

He laid an index finger to her lips. "Don't ask me," he said. And then he stepped back and released his hold on Banner's chin and she felt bereft, as though a great distance had risen up between them.

At the door of the examining room he paused, his hand on the knob. "Will you work with me, O'Brien?" he asked.

Banner was agape. Dear heaven, what a mercurial man he was, one moment kissing her as though he would consume her, the next wounding her with words, and the *next* asking her to work with him! "I—I don't understand," she said.

Adam arched one eyebrow and spread his gifted, healing hands wide in a gesture of gentle impatience. "I'm asking you to share my practice, O'Brien."

"But, Dr. Henderson—"

"Henderson," he scoffed. "If you're worrying about how you'll look after his patients, don't. He doesn't have any."

"But—Mr. Royce expressly told me—"

"Mr. Royce, O'Brien, doesn't give a damn whether you tend Henderson's 'patients' or not. Knowing him, he took one look at you and decided that courting you would be an enjoyable diversion. Of one thing you can be certain, Shamrock: he brought you here because he found you appealing, not because he has any stirring need to provide medical care in Port Hastings."

Banner felt a myriad of things—confusion, anger, disbelief. "You're lying! He said Dr. Henderson's patients needed me—he said—"

Adam looked maddeningly smug. "No doubt he said you were beautiful, too, didn't he?"

She was deflated by the truth in his words. Temple *had* remarked on her looks as they were leaving the waterfront in his carriage the night before.

"I thought so," Adam said, aptly reading the look on Banner's face. "Don't be naive, Shamrock. I'm offering you a job. A real job. Do you want it or not?"

Banner was undecided. The idea of working in such a spacious, well-equipped place was attractive, on a professional level, and she knew that she would learn much from Adam. Still, how did she know that he was telling the truth? How could she be certain that he wasn't doing exactly what he had accused Temple Royce of doing?

"Where would I live?" she asked, reasonably.

"This is a big house, O'Brien. You could live here."

The prospect was alarming. Banner O'Brien was a woman of principle and upright morality, but how long would these qualities last if there were more kisses like those just shared? Heaven help her, she'd shrunk from Sean's kisses, and he with a legal right to them, but Adam's were of a different ilk entirely. They stirred longings for the thing she had most hated in marriage.

"I don't think that would be a good idea," she said.

Adam shrugged. "Whatever you say, O'Brien," he tossed back as he opened the door and strode out, leaving Banner the bitter choice of following after him or staying behind and looking just as much the fool.

She followed grudgingly, avoiding Francelle's eyes, only to feel their scorching glare on her back as she left the office.

Adam's strides were long and furious as he traversed the long walkway back to the main house, and Banner scrambled after him angrily, her face flushed, her heart bruised. Damn you, she thought, with tender malice.

As if he'd heard the words, Adam turned his head and grinned. "Well, O'Brien," he wheedled, as they entered the dining room again. "What's your answer?"

"Yes," intruded another masculine voice. "What's your answer?"

Banner whirled and was greeted by the benign amusement of Melissa and the tall, pirate-handsome man beside her.

He had glossy, butternut-colored hair, this man, and his shirt had flowing sleeves and was open at the throat. His laughing eyes were the same impossibly dark blue as Adam's, and his teeth were perfect.

"Hello, Jeff," said Adam, in somewhat weary tones.

"Some greeting, after six months," retorted Jeff, with mock indignation. He turned and looked down into Melissa's bright eyes. "Don't you think that's a shame? My own brother—"

Melissa tried to look just as annoyed. "I'm not surprised. He didn't even bother to meet my steamer. What do you suppose he'll do when Keith and Mama get here? Yawn?"

Adam laughed. "Stop it, you two. You'll have O'Brien thinking I'm without family loyalty."

Jeff's blue eyes came with gentle humor to Banner's face. " 'O'Brien'? Trust my elder brother to address a beautiful woman as though she were a lumberjack. Tell me your given name, my lovely, for I do perish to know it."

Adam made a rude sound.

Banner laughed and executed a curtsy befitting Jeff's playfully formal remark. "My name is Banner," she said.

Adam was quietly furious. *My name is Banner,* he mimicked, in his mind. Damn it all to hell, he hadn't yet dared to call her by her first name, even after those two ill-advised but patently delicious kisses stolen in the examining room, and here she was offering it to Jeff in a way that could only be called coquettish.

Suddenly, he couldn't bear the way she was looking at his brother—he had to have her attention. "Shamrock," he said crisply. "Shall we eat? We aren't finished with our rounds and—"

Jeff swung a knowing smirk in his direction and broke off his words by taking one of Banner's hands in his, bending slightly, and kissing it.

Adam seethed.

"We're having an all-day skating party the day before Christmas," said Jeff smoothly, ignoring his brother. "After that, we'll trim the tree and enjoy one of Maggie's magnificent dinners. Won't you join us, Banner?"

Banner's clover green eyes were bright as she looked up at Jeff and nodded shyly. "I don't have skates, though," she said.

Melissa was quick to leap in with, "Don't worry, Banner, I have an extra pair. Maybe they'd fit you—let's go up to my room and see."

Incredibly, O'Brien readily agreed and dashed off after Melissa as though she weren't a doctor with patients to see. Adam ground his teeth and glared after them.

Jeff's laugh was low and entirely too knowing. "Where did you find that one?" he asked, folding his arms.

Adam's gaze sliced to his brother's face. "Never mind where I found her," he growled. "What the hell do you mean, kissing her hand and—"

Jeff grinned. "And liking her? She's the best-looking woman I've ever seen."

"Leave her alone."

Jeff arched one eyebrow. "Shall we discuss this further?"

"Yes."

"Outside?"

Adam nodded. "Outside."

They strode to the front doors and faced each other in the yard, just as they had on a thousand other occasions, throughout the tumultous years of their childhoods.

They were about evenly matched, equal in size and weight and prowess, and a fight between them, Adam knew, could go either way. At the moment, he didn't give a damn. Stupid as it seemed, he was ready to tangle with this brother of his, this brother he loved and respected.

Jeff planted his booted feet wide apart and refolded his arms. "If you feel something for the lady, Adam, why don't you just say so?"

Adam didn't know what he felt, beyond a crazy, consuming sort of desire. He wanted O'Brien—he had since the moment he'd walked into Henderson's house and seen her—but he wasn't sure how deep the feeling went, or how permanent it would be. Was it love? He couldn't answer that question, either, since he'd never truly known what it was to love a woman.

Jeff grinned. "Well?" he prodded.

Adam swore. God, how he wanted, needed to throw a hard punch. "I don't know," he confessed lamely.

Jeff whistled, and his blue eyes danced. "Oh, my God, it's for real. You're in love!"

Adam gave a crazy whoop of frustration and turned his back. "No," he said, after a long silence.

"No?" Jeff mocked. "This is your brother you're talking to, Adam. The person who knows you better than anyone else in the world does. I invited the lady to a skating party and kissed her hand, and admit it, you're ready to cut my throat."

Adam lowered his head, and snow gathered, cold, on the back of his neck. Was he losing his mind? He *had* wanted to hurt Jeff, he still did. *Jeff,* his brother. His best friend!

"I'm sorry."

"Adam, if you love her, it's all right. I'll leave her alone."

"I met her last night," Adam said, drawing deep breaths that did nothing to clear his mind. "*Last night.* How the hell can I be 'in love' with her?"

"Stranger things have happened," Jeff replied. "Besides, she's so beautiful—*I* only met her about five minutes ago, and I'm a little in love myself."

Adam whirled, his fists clenched, his reason displaced.

Jeff laughed and stepped back, holding up both his hands in a conciliatory gesture. "Adam, Adam—for God's sake, it's almost Christmas. What will Mama say if she comes home from Olympia and finds me, her favorite son, a mass of bruises and cuts?"

Adam relaxed his hands. "Am I insane?"

"Yes," replied Jeff. "But that's nothing new. And there isn't any medicine for the fever you've got now, brother—believe me."

Adam made a bellowing sound, strode over to the nearest snowbank, and fell into it face first. He was almost surprised that the ground didn't sizzle.

Jeff's laughter rang toward the sky, and then he reached down and helped his brother to his feet and they went into the house, each with an arm around the other.

Banner learned much while she was trying on Melissa's spare skates—with two extra pairs of stockings, they fit

45

her feet perfectly—about the Corbin family.

There were three brothers, all born within a year of each other, Adam first, Jeff second, and Keith third. The youngest brother had been thirteen when Melissa came along, but despite her late arrival, she was very close to all three of her siblings.

Her mother's name was Katherine, and from Melissa's description Banner discerned that she was both beautiful and formidable. She traveled almost constantly, making speeches in support of woman suffrage, and wrote articles that were printed in highly respected periodicals.

"What about your father?" Banner ventured, as she sat tugging her high-button shoes back onto her feet.

Melissa's expression made her instantly contrite. "He died five years ago," she said.

"I'm sorry—I shouldn't have asked."

Melissa went to stand at the window nearest the fireplace, where a pleasant blaze was crackling, and stood looking out, one lace curtain crumpled in her hand. "There was an accident, out on the water—P-Papa and Adam were salmon fishing in Papa's boat. The Indians saved Adam, but they couldn't find Papa."

Banner swallowed hard. "Oh, Melissa."

The girl turned to face Banner, and her crystalline eyes were glistening. "It was terrible for Adam. I think he blamed himself. He still broods about it, and sometimes he disappears for a whole day or even longer."

Banner spoke gently. "Why are you telling me this?"

"Because Adam likes you—I know he does. Maybe you're exactly the person we've all been hoping he'd find." She paused, searched the shadowed ceiling of her bedroom, and sighed. "Please, Banner, don't hurt him. He's been through so much."

Banner recalled his reaction to her question in the examining room, a question that had only echoed Francelle's. "The girl in his office," she mused. "She asked him if he meant to come to the Christmas party or if he would disappear again. Is that what you mean?"

Melissa nodded miserably. "Holidays are harder for Adam. He stays away as long as he can, and when he gets back, he's impossible."

"Maybe he just doesn't enjoy celebrations," offered Banner lamely, wishing that she could say something that would reassure the girl.

But Melissa shook her head. "Before Papa died, he loved them."

Banner ached to think of what Adam might be suffering, of how he might be burdened with guilt because he'd lived after the accident and his father hadn't. There seemed nothing to do but change the subject.

"You've told me that Jeff is captain of a clipper ship— the *Sea Mistress,* wasn't it—and that Keith is in charge of the family's apple orchards over beyond the mountains. What about you, Melissa? What do you do?"

Melissa's pinched little face brightened, and she lifted her chin proudly. "I attend the territorial university, in Seattle. I want to be a journalist, like Mama."

"That's wonderful! What kind of pieces do you write?"

Mischief frolicked in the beautiful blue eyes. "I'll show you, if you *promise* never to tell a soul! My brothers would—would—well, it doesn't bear thinking about, that's all." She was opening a chest at the foot of her bed, rummaging through it. After a moment or so, she drew out a publication with a lurid cover that showed a scantily clad woman being carried by a bearded mountain man. The title read, "Tenacia's Adventures in the Wild West."

Banner was aghast for a moment, but she recovered herself quickly. The byline was that of a man named Marshall S. Whidbine. "You—you drew this picture?" she asked, hopefully.

"Heavens, no," said Melissa, sitting down beside Banner on the bed. "I'm Marshall Whidbine!"

Banner's mouth fell open, much to Melissa's uproarious delight.

"Remember, Banner," she chided, between giggles, "You promised to keep my secret! Besides, the stories aren't really like the pictures lead one to believe."

"I certainly hope not," breathed Banner. "Why do you do this, Melissa? You surely don't need the money—"

Melissa spread her hands in a Corbinish gesture that was becoming very familiar to Banner. "I do it for practice, for experience. The same way you probably visited hospitals when you were still a student."

Banner's hands trembled a little as she handed the dime novel back to its very young author. "Why don't you write a—a real book?"

Melissa smiled and touched the cover of her work with a tender hand. "I will, when I know enough. Would you read this for me, Banner, and tell me what you think? What you honestly think?"

Banner had been meaning to buy a copy at the first opportunity, but she took the volume Melissa offered eagerly. "I'd love to read it," she said in all sincerity.

"Good," replied Melissa in a delighted whisper. "But be sure you don't tell. Adam stopped spanking me years ago, but if he found out about this, he'd probably take it up again!"

Banner laughed all the way down the stairs, but Melissa's novel was tucked safely into her cloak pocket, and she would have died before betraying the secret.

She and Adam shared a rather stiff luncheon, alone in the big, brick-floored kitchen, and then left the house again.

They were settled in the buggy, this time with a heavy bearskin lap rug to cover their legs, before Adam spoke of what was on his mind.

"Will you join my practice, Banner?"

She smiled at his use of her first name, welcoming it. "Yes," she said. "But I'd best go on living in Dr. Henderson's house—just until I find a place of my own."

For a moment Adam looked as though he might protest this last, but in the end, he didn't. "Thank you," he said. "Did the skates fit?"

Banner smiled. "Yes."

He frowned, keeping his eyes carefully on the road, which the horse seemed to know well enough for both of them. "You're coming to the party, then?"

The prospect of a Christmas spent alone paled beside one passed with such fun-loving sorts as Melissa and the charming and handsome Jeff. "Of course," she answered. "Don't you want me to?"

A muscle flexed in his angular jaw then relaxed again. "O'Brien, as long as you take care of my patients, I don't care what you do with your free time."

Banner sank back against the cold leather seat, feeling as though she'd been slapped. "I see."

"Good."

"Are you going skating, Dr. C—Adam?"

He flung one unpleasant, wondering look in her direction. "I never do stupid things, O'Brien. My brother—no doubt, *both* of my brothers—will look after you, so don't give me another thought."

Banner again felt the need to strike this man, to strike him and strike him until he stopped hiding behind that wall of hostility.

Instead, she watched the tugs and cutters and clipper ships interweaving on the stormy water.

She wondered about the accident that had claimed Adam's father's life and the affect it had had on the one who had survived. She suspected that there was more to the incident than anyone had guessed—much more. For as brief a time as she had been acquainted with Dr. Adam Corbin, she knew that such a thing, however terrible, could not do such lasting damage to him on its own.

He disappeared, Melissa had said, especially around holidays. And he was always in a nasty temper when he rejoined his family.

Banner sat bolt upright as a most disturbing possibility struck her. Suppose Adam had another family hidden away somewhere, perhaps an Indian woman and several children? Many men did this, she knew. Some of them were even married to a white woman in the bargain.

A feeling of desolation swept over her, and she closed her eyes, only to see visions of Adam making love with a beautiful, coppery-skinned woman. She even heard the cries that had seemed so ugly coming from Sean—the hoarse, beautiful cries that Adam would utter when his joy became too great to bear.

One tear trickled down Banner's cold cheek to shimmer in the folds of her cloak.

"What the hell is the matter now, O'Brien?"

She opened her eyes, looked into Adam's arrogant, insolent face, and put out her tongue.

He laughed as they reached the bottom of the hill and turned the buggy toward Water Street. "I'm sorry I asked," he said, with a shrug.

And I'm sorry I ever met you, mourned Banner, who had thought that she would never want a man again, after all she'd suffered with Sean Malloy.

But she wanted this man, and she cared for him, too. Worse, one day she might even love him.

A shudder rocked her, and Adam reached out, impatiently, to pull the lap rug up around her waist. The contact made that strange melting sensation start up again, and Banner was so annoyed by this that she slapped away his hand and barked, "Don't touch me!"

Adam stared at her, shook his head, and passed all the brothels and saloons Banner had noticed the night before to drive the buggy down over a hill, toward the water.

Her eyes popped open when she saw the beached clipper ship there. It had been put into dry dock, and there were steps leading up its side to the decks. At its ornately carved bow was the legend, *Silver Shadow.*

Along the railings of the vessel, prostitutes lounged, looking down at the approaching buggy or gazing off into the snowy skies. Somewhere on board a tinny piano was playing and exuberant voices were singing, "God Rest Ye Merry Gentlemen."

A brown-haired, lushly curved woman near the bow smiled, patted her outlandishly styled locks, and shrilled, "Hey, Doc, did you bring Bessie her Christmas present?"

Adam laughed and shook his head as he halted the rig and tossed back the lap robe to alight. For a moment, it seemed that he'd forgotten Banner existed, and no wonder. "Not now, Bess," he called back. "Can't you see I've got a lady with me?"

Bess pouted. "Mind you don't give her *my* present, sweetness."

Banner reddened and her back stiffened and she would not have gotten out of that buggy at all if Adam hadn't rounded it, taken her arm, and forced her to step down.

"You wanted to practice medicine, O'Brien," he said out of the corner of his mouth, "so stop acting like an offended missionary wading into the heathens."

"D-Do you *visit* that awful woman?" Banner whispered back furiously, and though she pulled with all her might, her arm would not come free of his hand.

He flung a look of evil mirth at Banner. "What the devil do you care?" he retorted.

"I don't!" lied Banner with spirit.

"Good. The sweet young thing in room four has a boil on her backside. You go and lance that while I—er—while I examine another patient."

"Bessie, for example?"

The perfect white teeth flashed in another dazzling smile. "O'Brien, O'Brien," he breathed. "When will you learn? When I want a woman, I don't have to pay."

For weeks afterward, everyone on Water Street talked about the way one doctor had slapped the other, right in the middle of the *Silver Shadow's* boarding ramp.

Chapter Three

The decks of the *Silver Shadow* were slippery with snow and the spittle of tobacco-chewing patrons, and Banner held her skirts above them, curling her upper lip.

"People get sick everywhere, O'Brien," Adam reminded her dryly in a crisp undertone. "Even in nasty places like this."

Banner stiffened. She'd been in worse places during her training—tenements and shanties where rats roamed free and broken windows were stopped up with wads of damp newspaper. Hospitals where alleged physicians smoked cigars over open wounds and sported a coating of horse manure on their shoes. "Thank you very much for that enlightening remark," she retorted.

Bessie, the prostitute, was sidling toward them with well-oiled hips, her thin taffeta dress leaving much of her body bare to the biting cold. She patted her hair again and dragged slumberous eyes from the toes of Adam's boots to the top of his head, pausing once, with sympathy, at the flaming mark Banner's hand had left on his face.

Adam thrust an appalled Banner forward, in introduction. "This is my colleague, Dr. O'Brien," he said. "Will you show her where Lou's room is, please?"

Bessie tossed her head and looked Banner over with tolerance. "This way, Red," she said, after a long and rather unsettling silence.

Too proud to look back at Adam, Banner followed Bessie down an inside hallway lined with numbered doors. Room four was at the far end, and the prostitute rapped at it with unsympathetic vigor.

"Lou!" she shrilled. "Hey, Lou! You decent? You got company."

"Come in," wailed a pitiful voice.

After drawing one deep, preparatory breath, Banner clasped the knob and turned it. The room was surprisingly clean, though dimly lit, and it smelled of some flowery perfume.

On the bed, in a tumble of pink satin, her patient waited. The woman—in this light, she hardly looked older than Melissa—was crouched on her knees and elbows, with her plump, lawn-covered posterior pointing heavenward.

Bessie muttered something and left, closing the door behind her.

"I understand you have a boil," Banner said, setting her bag down on a bedside table littered with crystal atomizers, pleated bon bon papers, and copies of dime novels like Melissa's. Amid all this were printed business cards that read, *Miss Lou, Room 4, Silver Shadow. Always a gentle welcome.*

"Who are you?" whined the enterprising Lou, turning her head to peer at Banner with miserable lavendar eyes.

"My name is Dr. O'Brien. May I see the boil, please?"

Lou hiked up her nightdress and lowered beribboned drawers. "Are—"

"Yes," Banner broke in crisply, bending to examine the offending lesion. It looked sore indeed, and the flesh surrounding it was inflamed. "I really am a doctor."

With the inevitable question answered, Lou was somewhat at a loss. "Where's Adam?"

Banner bit her lower lip and turned away to open her bag and rummage through for cotton, alcohol, a scalpel, and carbolic acid. "Dr. Corbin is aboard somewhere. Would you like to see him?"

"No!" Lou cried quickly. "At least, not like this. It's kind of nice to have a woman tend me."

Banner suppressed a smile and turned to look at the washstand on the far side of the room. There was a pitcher there, along with a basin and soap, but she doubted that the water would be hot.

She took her own bar of soap from its wrapping of cheesecloth, after setting aside the items she would need for Lou's actual treatment, and crossed the room to wash her hands.

That done, she cleaned the scalpel carefully, with carbolic acid, and gave the boil a thorough dabbing with alcohol. "This will hurt a little," she warned in a kindly voice.

Lou's bright purple eyes were squeezed shut in preparation. "I'm ready, Doc!"

As gently as possible, Banner lanced the boil, drained and cleaned it, and then applied a clean bandage. While she disposed of the cloths she'd used, washed her hands, and then gave the scalpel another dousing with carbolic acid, Lou continuously bemoaned the fact that she couldn't very well work with a bunch of gauze stuck to her backside.

Banner's lips were quivering with barely concealed amusement. "I would think a little rest would be welcome," she observed.

Lou stretched out flat, winced a little, and arched her tiny, featherlike eyebrows. "I'll get lonesome, lying in here all alone. How long will it be till I'm better?"

"A few days," replied Banner, closing her bag with an authoritive click. "And don't you try to—to work before that wound is healed. If you think having the boil lanced was unpleasant, just let yourself get an infection."

Glumly, Lou promised to refrain from enterprise.

"I'll come by again in a couple of days," Banner told her patient in parting. She was only a little surprised to find Adam waiting in the hallway, his back braced against the wall, his arms folded.

Banner immediately noticed that he wasn't wearing his suitcoat. "My patient is doing fine," she said stiffly. "How about yours?"

Adam's mouth twitched, just at one corner, and he straightened. "Recovery is imminent."

Banner yearned to slap him again, just as she had on the boarding ramp, but she didn't dare. She sensed that, although he had endured it once, he would take firm issue with a second attack. "Shall we go?"

His blue eyes laughed at her, and he came to strict attention. "Let's," he said, as the voices inside the strange ship's window-lined saloon struck up a rousing rendition of "Good King Wenceslas."

On the deck another prostitute waited, clad in a blue satin garment that covered little more than her torso. She wore stockings of black net, a lace garter, and a smile, and she tossed Adam's suitcoat to him with a practiced flourish.

56

Adam caught the coat and shrugged into it, never noticing that Banner O'Brien's face was the color of holly berries. "Thanks," he said.

"Thank *you*," purred the half-naked creature before turning away to join the celebrants in the saloon.

Adam offered his arm and looked only mildly confused when Banner proudly refused it and stomped down the boarding ramp on her own.

They were inside the buggy and climbing back toward Water Street before he spoke. "What's the matter, O'Brien?"

She would not look at him, but fixed her eyes on the saloons and brothels ahead. They had a certain festive innocence, those buildings, in the cloaking of pristine snow. "Nothing is the matter—Corbin," she replied.

He gave an unsettling shout of laughter. "Good God, you think I was availing myself to the pleasures of the flesh back there, don't you?"

"I certainly don't care, one way or the other."

"Yes, you do. Why don't you admit it?"

Banner took a stubborn interest in the evergreen wreath hanging from the door of a ramshackle card palace. A silent interest.

"O'Brien."

"What?"

"Look at me."

"I will not."

"Why?"

"Because you disgust me, that's why. You're supposed to be a responsible physician and here you were—"

"There I was, examining Hermione's tonsils."

57

Banner gave a little cry of exasperation and contempt. "Her tonsils! Do you think me an utter idiot? One hardly needs to disrobe in order to look at another person's tonsils!"

Adam laughed again. "The coat," he said, in the tone of one experiencing glowing revelation. "Shamrock, I took off my coat because I was too hot. That's all I took off, for your information."

"I don't want to hear this."

She felt his shrug rather than saw it. "Fine."

"Her tonsils!" railed Banner, under her breath.

"If you went around dressed like that, O'Brien, you'd have sore tonsils, too. Not only that, but—"

Before he could finish, a saloonkeeper dashed out into the road, waving his arms. "Adam!" the man shouted, "Adam, stop!"

Adam immediately complied and was standing on the ground before Banner had even managed to toss back the lap rug. "What is it?" he asked, reaching to the floor of the buggy for his bag, finding it with unerring ease.

"Somethin' awful's happened!" whined the barkeeper, slipping and sliding back toward the swinging doors of his establishment in his haste. "Get in here quick!"

Banner took up her own bag and scrambled into the saloon behind Adam. As her eyes adjusted to the almost nonexistent light, she was aware of a circle of people crowding around one of the tables.

There was spittle-strewn sawdust on the floor, and the walls were lined with curtained booths. Over the scratched and battered bar hung a gaudy portrait of a simpering, overweight nude.

Men, thought Banner.

"Damn it, get out of the way!" raged the barkeeper, elbowing his way through the muttering group around the table. "Let the doc through!"

Banner was quick to step into the narrow swath that had been opened for Adam, but when her eyes fell on the subject of all the fuss, she devoutly wished that she'd run the other way.

A young, fair-haired man sat at the table, his right hand pinioned to the surface with a pearl-handled knife. His face was pale with shock and pain, and spittle gathered at the corners of his mouth. His eyes rose to Adam's face, imploring, but he couldn't seem to manage a word.

"Jesus," Adam breathed. And then he grabbed the hilt of the knife with both hands and drew it out in a quick, clean motion.

As blood spouted from the narrow slit in his hand, the young man fell forward in a faint.

At last, the spectators moved back, away from the table, mumbling among themselves. Banner took bandages and alcohol from her bag as Adam used the bloody knife to cut away the young man's coat sleeve. He was applying a tourniquet when she began cleaning and binding the wound.

Adam gave the rapidly saturated bandage a skeptical glance. "He'll need stitches," he said.

"I know that," Banner retorted, though the truth was that she'd been so overwhelmed by the horror and brutality of the situation that she'd forgotten.

"Give him something for the pain," Adam ordered, as he edged Banner aside and began unwrapping the wound.

The boy was stirring now, moaning, low in his throat, like an injured animal.

Stricken, not so sure of herself as she had been, Banner stared at the half-conscious boy and the doctor who tended him. "Laudenum?"

"Morphine, O'Brien. He's going to need stitches on both sides of his hand, and the wound probably hurts like hell as it is."

Chagrined, Banner helped herself to a syringe and vial from Adam's bag, as she had no such items in her own. Her hands trembled as she filled the syringe and held it to the lamplight, pressing the bubbles out of the fluid with a pumping motion.

Satisfied, apparently, with the decreased blood flow, Adam was loosening the tourniquet. "Alcohol first, Banner," he said.

Banner colored at the reminder of something so elemental. Then, holding the syringe in one hand, she struggled to cleanse the boy's inside forearm with the other.

Adam made an exasperated sound and wrenched the cotton out of her hand, soaking it thoroughly in alcohol before wiping a space over the protruding veins just under the patient's elbow. That done, he claimed the morphine and administered the injection.

Adam's indigo eyes were ruthless as they shot to Banner's face. "I trust you're capable of sterilizing a needle?" he growled.

Banner battled tears of humiliation and nodded, but she found the required needle, cleaned it with carbolic acid, threaded it with catgut, and handed it to Adam.

"What the hell happened here?" he demanded of the

general populace as he sutured the wound with deft, practiced flashes of the needle.

No one answered, and it was obvious that no one was going to own up to the deed, either. Or point out the culprit.

Adam tied off the stitches on one side of the hand and turned it over to close the gash in the other. The boy awakened, stared at the needle, and fainted again.

Finally, Adam was finished. He put aside the needle, cleaned both wounds once more, and applied a thick bandage.

The mood in the saloon was suddenly vocal again; it was as though everyone had let out their breath at once.

"Who's the pretty lady, Doc?" one man wanted to know.

"She your new nurse?" demanded another.

A third man assessed Banner's womanly bosom with infuriating dispatch. "I'd like her to nurse me," he said, and everyone in that place of degradation and ugliness laughed except Adam and Banner herself.

Adam straightened, his work finished, and swung his eyes from one grizzled, dissolute face to another.

A new silence fell.

"We was just funnin', Doc," drawled a middle-aged sailor who was lounging against the bar and looking anything but contrite.

Adam caught Banner's elbow in one hand and thrust her toward the saloon's swinging wooden doors. "Wait in the rig," he said.

She stopped, planting her feet, mortally afraid of what might happen to Adam if he dared to challenge so many tough-looking men alone.

"No," she said.

Adam turned toward her in an ominous motion centered in his muscular waist. "*Damn* it, O'Brien—"

She remained where she was.

Adam scanned the room once more, swore under his breath, and helped the half-conscious fellow at the table onto his feet. Together, he and Banner squired him out into the fresh air and the snow and hoisted him into the buggy.

He lolled between them, looking befuddled, as they drove back up the hill to the magnificent house and its adjoining hospital.

The patient had been undressed and settled into one of the ward beds before Adam turned a scathing, now-you're-in-trouble gaze on Banner.

She stumbled backward as he advanced upon her between the two rows of beds, his hands on his hips.

"O'Brien," he simmered in deadly tones, still approaching, "the men in that saloon back there were not gentlemen, waiting to scribble their names in your dance-book! Why didn't you leave when I told you to?"

Banner reached the far wall, beside the stove, and could go no further. "I was only—I didn't want—"

"When I give you an order, obey it!"

Rage surged into Banner's face, staining it a hot battle-red. "Who are you to give me orders?"

Adam was only a few feet from her then, and he looked so furious that Banner was certain that he would lunge forward and do her bodily harm. She was never to find out, however, because a feminine voice intruded at the crucial moment, ringing from the houseward end of the ward like a rescue bell.

"Adam? Is this Banner? Introduce me at once!"

Adam's massive shoulders slackened, and his hands relaxed at his sides. Banner watched him assume a thin smile before turning to face the slender blond woman behind him.

"Hello, Mama," he said gravelly, as the beauty embraced him.

Banner was amazed that such a wonderous creature could be the mother of four grown children, but the clear Corbin-blue of her eyes gave further evidence that she was. She bent around her son's forbidding shoulder and peered winningly at the woman he'd been about to throttle.

"Jeff and Melissa were right—you are lovely!" she chimed. "And a doctor in the bargain. My, my, my—I'll bet that nettles *you,* doesn't it?" She shifted her gaze to Adam, and it was instantly imbued with a sporting sort of tenderness. "Mercy," she added as an afterthought.

Adam laughed. "I was about to strangle her, as a matter of fact. Mother, Dr. Banner O'Brien, Banner, my mother, Katherine."

Katherine extended a small, stately hand in greeting. "He wouldn't really strangle you, you know," she said, her wide blue eyes sparkling. "He knows I'd have him horse-whipped."

Relief and the warmth of this woman's personality combined to make Banner laugh. "How do you do, Mrs. Corbin?" she asked.

"Quite well, thank you," replied the lady, taking Banner's arm and ushering her away from Adam and through the ward, toward the main part of the house, "But you must call me Katherine. Tell me all about yourself,

Banner O'Brien."

Jenny not only had dinner waiting that night, but she'd heated water for a bath, too.

After eating, Banner hurried into the small bedroom, took off her clothes, and sank gratefully into the tub of steaming hot water.

"I imagine you've had a long day," remarked Jenny, who was standing at the bureau, her back to Banner, arranging and rearranging the brush and comb set she'd unpacked, along with a few other things.

"That is an understatement," sighed Dr. O'Brien, as the pulsing soreness in all her muscles began to ease a little. "By the way, Jenny. How did you come to be here, in this house?"

"Adam hired me," Jenny answered without turning around. "He said that, since the rooster was away, it would be a good time to clean the chicken coop."

Banner grinned. She could well imagine Adam, in his dislike for Dr. Henderson, saying such a thing. "I'm grateful to you for all your work," she said. "And for your company, too."

Jenny shrugged, offered no answer.

"How long have you known Adam?"

Jenny went to sit on the edge of Banner's bed, eyes politely averted, and smoothed her poplin skirts. "All my life. Why?"

"He puzzles me," mused Banner, squeezing a shower of deliciously warm water out of a sponge and onto her left arm.

Jenny laughed. "He puzzles everybody."

"Melissa tells me that he has black moods."

Jenny looked a little uncomfortable. "Doesn't everybody?" she parried.

"He has a secret," Banner insisted.

The Indian girl's knuckles turned a pale honey shade as her hands entwined in her lap. "No," she said.

"Yes," countered Banner. "He disappears, you know. Especially around holidays."

"He's a doctor. If he disappears, it is because he has patients to visit."

Banner sighed. Jenny was hedging and she knew it, but there was no way to make the girl talk. "I think he has a woman somewhere," she said, and the thought made all the various and sundry aches in her body grind into prominence again.

"Do you?" replied Jenny in a tremulous voice.

And then, apparently not expecting an answer, she stood up and walked out of the room.

Banner finished her bath, berating herself all the while for being so insufferably nosy in the first place, and climbed out of the tub. For some unaccountable reason, tears were slipping down her face.

After taking five minutes of excruciating pleasure in one of the booths, the sailor laid a few coins on the bar to settle his bill and walked outside. Blast, it was cold, with that wind howling in from the sound and that snow to sting a man's bones.

At the swinging doors, he looked back at the table where the barkeep was trying to scour away bloodstains. He smiled and felt the pearl handle of his knife. They'd all remember not to accuse Mike O'Hurlehey of cheating at a game of cards, that they would.

In the street, O'Hurlehey listened for the bell of his ship, the *Jonathan Lee,* and heard it. His pace was rapid as he strode toward the wharves; no sense in angering the captain by getting himself left behind.

There was a run up to Canada tonight, and Mike wanted his share of the loot even more than he wanted to stay in Temple Royce's good graces, which was one and the same thing, for all accounts.

But even as he scrambled to board the clipper before she set sail, he thought of that little redheaded scrap that had come into the saloon with the doctor. What he wouldn't have given to get *her* behind the curtains of one of those booths for five minutes!

O'Brien, that was her name. He ruminated, piecing the rest of it together from what the doctor had called her. Yes, it was O'Brien—Banner O'Brien.

O'Hurlehey laughed to himself as he dashed down the wharf to the snow-powdered boarding ramp of the *Jonathan Lee.* What a hell of a yarn he could spin of her and the knifing and the dark-haired doctor, once he got to Portland. He might even spice the thing up a little and say the doctor—spoiling for a fight, he'd been, had that one—had taken Miss Banner O'Brien into one of the booths and had a time with her there.

Maybe he'd claim that he'd had a turn at her himself. Hell, nobody would know the difference, way down in Oregon, and thinking about it was damn near as good as doing it.

Talking would be better yet.

Adam was standing at the parlor windows, a drink in his hand, looking out at a mountain he couldn't possibly see for the darkness and the storm.

Jeff studied his brother in silence, wondering.

Adam sensed his presence and turned, only briefly, to rake him with one glance. Then, his attention was on the invisible mountain again. "Is Keith home yet?"

Jeff sank into a chair near the fire and stretched his long legs out on the attending hassock. "No. Mama thinks he'll be here sometime tomorrow."

Adam lifted his glass to his mouth, lowered it again without drinking. Damn it, what did he see out there?

"He'll like Banner," Jeff said, to fill the silence.

His brother's imposing shoulders stiffened beneath his shirt. "Why should he be different?"

Jeff sighed. "Good Lord, are we back to that again? I'm sorry I mentioned her, Adam."

"So am I."

Jeff emitted a soft, furious breath and scrambled out of his chair to make a drink of his own. These brooding silences of Adam's always nettled him, though he wasn't sure why. Perhaps it was the distance they spawned between the two of them. Or the annoying idea that Adam might know something he didn't.

Crystal clinked against crystal as Jeff filled a glass with imported brandy. "What are you thinking about?"

Adam chuckled rawly but did not turn around. "Papa," he said.

Jeff regretted prodding him now. Five years had passed since the accident, but Adam had been there, seen their father die. "It wasn't your fault," he said, going back to his chair. "Why torture yourself?"

Adam offered no answer to that, but his face looked ravaged when he finally turned away from the window and strode to the sidetable to add bourbon to his glass.

Jeff felt the pain that he saw in his brother, shared it, and the fact infuriated him. "Christ, Adam, it's been years! Grief is grief, but—"

"Shut up," snarled Adam. "You don't know what the hell you're talking about. You don't know what I'm thinking or what I'm feeling, so—"

Jeff's face reddened as he bolted out of the chair again. "Poor Adam!" he boomed. "Let's all weep for what he's suffered! And heaven forbid, that any of us should *enjoy* anything!"

Something terrible moved in Adam's strained features. He dropped his glass to the floor and lunged at Jeff with a soul-numbing bellow.

"*Mama!*" shrieked Melissa from somewhere in the pounding blur.

The noise was horrific, and Melissa's screams did lend a certain drama.

Katherine Corbin took her fabled buggywhip from its rack behind her desk and advanced on the parlor, prepared to use it. Lord, trying to persuade the territorial legislature to grant women the vote was nothing compared to keeping peace between her own sons.

Entering the war zone, she found Adam and Jeff rolling on the rug like two ruffians, and it was hard to tell where one brute left off and the other began.

No matter. Katherine unfurled the buggywhip and gave

it one warning crack.

Instantly, the battle abated and her sons got to their feet, looking shame-faced and wan and still angry, all of a piece. Adam's lower lip was bleeding, and Jeff had the beginnings of a black eye.

"If you must fight," their mother said succinctly, "kindly go outside."

One after the other, their hard breathing metering the motions of their Daniel-like shoulders, they bowed. Then, after exchanging vicious looks, they made their way toward the front doors.

Katherine shook her head as the fight resumed in the dooryard, gave an anxious Melissa a reassuring look, and went back to the study to work on the speech she meant to make when the Senate was back in session.

Keith Corbin was tired and cold, and the last welcome he'd expected was a bare-knuckle fisticuff in the petunia patch.

He paused on the walk, watching in silence as Jeff went hurtling past him, backward, to make hard contact with the trunk of a holly tree.

Probably revived from the inevitable daze by the shower of snow that was dislodged from the festive plummage of the tree, Jeff bellowed, lowered his head, and charged into Adam's midsection like a bull.

Adam's breath was expelled from his lungs in a whooshing grunt, and he landed roughly where next year's tulips and irises would grow.

Keith spread his hands in reverendly grace and shouted, "I'm home!"

69

Both of his brothers staggered forth to greet him.

There had been more snow during the night, though the flakes were no longer falling, and Banner O'Brien thought it a pity that Adam was about to get out of his buggy and spoil the perfect, diamond-strewn counterpane that quilted the front yard of Dr. Henderson's house.

Her first sight of his face set her fanciful ideas to rest, however, for his lower lip was split at one side and swollen, and his right eye was blacked.

Adam seemed to sense her perusal as he strode up the walk, and he lifted his eyes to favor her with a somewhat sheepish glare.

Banner went to the door and pulled it open, aghast. Had he gone back to that stupid, smelly saloon after all and ended up in a brawl? If he had, she'd black his other eye!

"Adam Corbin—"

He lifted one hand to silence her. "Don't start, O'Brien," he warned.

Jenny squeezed into the doorway beside Banner and whistled appreciatively. "Jeff must be home from the seven seas!"

"Shut up," he grumbled.

Jenny gave a whoop that made him wince. "You lost!"

Adam scowled at her, for all the world like a small boy. "I did not," he argued.

Banner bit her lower lip to keep from grinning and caught Adam's coat sleeve in one hand. "Come in and let me have a look at you," she said.

His eyes assessed her crisp black sateen skirt and white pleated shirtwaist with grudging approval, and he permitted Banner to pull him past a giggling Jenny and into the kitchen, where the light was good.

There she settled Adam into a chair and examined his battered lip. "You should have had stitches," she scolded, frowning.

Adam stiffened. "If you think I'm going to let you near me with a needle, O'Brien—"

"It's too late now," Banner broke in, stung by his inference that she wasn't competent enough to suture a simple wound. No doubt he was reminding her how badly she'd bungled the treatment of the stabbing victim in the saloon the day before.

"I wonder what Jeff looks like this morning," sang Jenny.

"Considerably worse than I do, believe me," glared Adam.

"I don't," said Jenny, but she filled a cup with coffee and set it before him in an easy gesture of friendship. "I'm surprised Mrs. Corbin didn't break up the row with her buggywhip."

"She did," said Adam, trying to suppress a grin. "Being sensible sorts, my brother and I removed hither."

Banner tried to picture this man's elegant mother wielding such a weapon and failed miserably. "Why on earth were you fighting with Jeff?"

An unreadable look passed between Adam and Jenny; after it he shrugged and she looked quickly away.

Banner was annoyed, and she tugged at the cuffs of her prim white shirtwaist to disguise the fact. "Who do we visit first today?" she asked. "Hildie?"

Adam shifted his gaze to his coffee cup, and Jenny

71

slipped out of the kitchen to busy herself in another part of the house.

"Adam?" Banner prodded.

He stood up, faced her squarely. "I just left Hildie, Banner," he said. "She died while I was there."

Banner swayed a little. Though she knew Hildie's passing was a mercy, she was always stricken by the death of a patient. It made her feel as though she'd worked and studied all those years for nothing.

Adam took her shoulders in his hands and pressed her into a chair. "She was glad to go," he said, but the gruffness of the tones betrayed the fact that he felt Hildie's loss, too.

Banner nodded, swallowed. "The boys—what will happen to them?"

Adam dropped into his chair and sighed. "Fitz has a new wife in mind—Miss Mamie Robbins. He's marrying the lady as soon as Hildie's been properly buried."

Banner was horrified, even though she knew that a stepmother was probably just what Hildie's boys needed.

Adam grinned tenderly, caught her hand in his, made her sit down beside him. "Close your mouth, O'Brien," he said. "These things happen all the time."

Anger moved through her, anger that was not meant for Adam but for Sean. For Hildie's Fitz. For all men who were so concerned with their own comforts that human decency fell by the wayside.

Adam touched the tip of her nose with an index finger. "The boys will have a good home with Mamie Robbins, Banner. And Hildie isn't suffering anymore. What else matters?"

Banner lowered her eyes to hide the unprofessional tears that smarted there. "It just seems so callous, that's all. Poor Hildie—will no one mourn her?"

Adam's finger traced the outline of her lips, stirring feelings that had no place in the mood of the moment. "I think someone is mourning her right now," he said.

Banner stood up again, quickly, because she didn't know what she would do if Adam kept on touching her like that and speaking in that tender tone of voice. "Well, there are other patients," she replied, with a brightness she didn't feel. "Shouldn't we see to them?"

Incredibly, Adam shook his head. "I'll make the rounds myself today, O'Brien. I'd like you to stay at the hospital and look after our wounded gambler."

Banner's emotions spun about in her heart in an illogical tangle. "Maggie could do that," she argued, fearing that he'd only invited her to join his practice so that he could keep her away from his patients. Next he'd be saying that she had to stay in the hospital every day, whether it was occupied or not, in case someone came there seeking treatment!

Adam shook his head. "Maggie is getting ready for Christmas," he reminded her.

Banner's shoulders sank. She would stay with the patient today, but tomorrow was another matter. She wanted to make house calls; the day before, for all its rigors and heartbreak, had convinced her of that.

"I won't stay behind every day," she said firmly as she found her cloak.

"I know," Adam answered as they went out, respoiling the glorious snow as they walked toward the buggy.

73

"Tomorrow we visit the Klallum camp."

Banner's face was alight as her colleague helped her into the buggy seat and came around to join her and take up the reins. "A real Indian village?" she beamed, delighted.

"Complete with fleas, dogfish oil, and noble savages," he grinned.

The gambler's name was Clarence King, and he fell in love with Banner the moment she walked into the ward and smiled at him, it seemed to Adam. Maybe he could skip rounds today, and just stay around the hospital. . . .

He caught himself up in stern professionalism. What the hell was the matter with him? Last night he'd brutalized a brother he loved, and today he was actually thinking of forsaking people who depended on him.

Adam glanced at King, who was beaming up at an attentive Banner, regaling her with accounts of his youth on the Columbia River, where his father had a ferryboat. His youth! Why, the kid was closer to Melissa's age than Banner's.

Maybe I'll stay for the Christmas party, he thought. But then Adam remembered the mountain and the promise he'd made. The reminder sobered him and gave him the impetus to leave Banner here with Jeff and this rounder—who obviously adored her.

Smiling to himself, Keith Corbin approached Adam's new partner, who sat near the heat stove in the ward, her feet resting on its chrome railing, immersed in a dime novel.

As the woman read, her cheeks turned a fetching apricot

pink, and her green eyes darkened to a shade resembling that of summer clover. No wonder he'd come home and found his brothers bludgeoning each other in the snow the night before.

"Hello," he said, his eyes diplomatically averted from the novel. "I'm Keith."

She looked up at him with dazed eyes, smiled falteringly, and turned the book title-side down on her lap. Then her gaze caught at his clerical collar and she blushed. "H-Hello—"

He laughed. "You're Banner O'Brien, aren't you? And no, I'm not a priest."

She laughed with him and made room by the stove as he found another chair and drew it close. "If you're not a priest, what are you?" she asked, with a forthrightness that delighted him.

"I'm an orchardist and—despite me dandy Irish Catholic family—a Methodist minister."

Banner stared at him, and a ray of rare winter sunshine flamed in her dark auburn hair. "Good heavens!"

Keith grinned and took her hand in his, and she did not draw back from him. They talked as giant flakes of snow whispered past the windows, as Francelle came and went, as the gambler slept a healing sleep.

Keith did not release Banner's hand until he heard a distant door open and knew that Adam was home.

Chapter Four

"Were you really meaning to strangle me the other day in the hospital ward?"

Adam was fitting the buggy harness into place, his movements strong and sure, and his teeth flashed in a grin. "What do you think, O'Brien?" he countered.

The stable was only dimly lit, due to the snow flurries that shrouded the sun, and it smelled of stored hay, grain, and old leather, among other things. Banner stood in the wide doorway and shrugged. "You definitely looked murderous."

"I definitely *felt* murderous. That was a dangerous situation, Shamrock, and you should have left when I told you to."

Banner looked down at her gray woolen dress, with its short overjacket and black corded trim, and smoothed the skirts. She hoped the garment was suitable for a visit to an Indian village. "I was afraid those men would hurt you," she said as an aside.

Adam left the horse and the rig to come and stand before her, searching her face. "What?"

"I said I—"

He stopped her by lifting his hands to her shoulders. "What am I going to do with you, O'Brien?" he asked in a soft, amused voice. "In case you haven't noticed, I'm a grown man, and I can take care of myself."

Banner was stricken, as always, by his touch, by the sweetly alarming proximity of his body to hers. "Of course," she replied in a mocking tone engineered to hide her reactions. "That must be why your lip is split and your eye is blackened."

Adam laughed. "You've seen Jeff. Did I really do so badly?"

His mouth was too close to hers, entirely too close. She

could almost feel the soft, searching warmth of his lips on her own, and his breath, like a stone cast into calm waters, sent tremulous ripples into the very depths of her spirit.

Out of self-defense, Banner recalled Jeff's swollen jaw and lacerated forehead, and the image generated the anger she needed to step back out of Adam's spell.

"Is that what you were going to do to me, before your mother interrupted?" she snapped.

"You know the answer to that, O'Brien."

"Do I?"

He turned back to the horse and gripped its harness, leading the animal toward the doorway where Banner stood. The small rig rattled after.

"If you must know," he said dryly, through the curtain of briskly falling snow, "I intended to turn you across my knee."

Banner was insulted, and it was this that made her tremble, rather than the crisp December weather. "In that case, I'm very glad your mother came in when she did. I would have had to have you arrested."

Adam laughed, caught hold of her arm, and propelled her toward her side of the buggy. "Arrested, is it? The marshal would have chuckled over that for days, O'Brien." He lifted her easily into the seat and planted her on it with a thump. Then he just stood there, the snow making a striking contrast to his dark hair, his blue eyes bright with enjoyment. "Arrested," he repeated after a long interval. Then he shook his head, rounded the buggy, and got in to adjust the lap rug and take up the reins.

Banner squared her shoulders and folded her gloved hands, looking straight ahead. She remembered the day

77

Sean was arrested. How could she forget when she'd been the one to summon the police, the one to accept their reward?

Hearing the dreadful things he'd shouted, across the years, she trembled.

Adam cast one quick look in her direction, but then he brought down the reins with a crisp motion of his hands and the buggy was moving.

Instead of taking the road that would lead down to Port Hastings, Adam guided the animal around the stables and into a tree-lined clearing beyond.

The snow was deep there and undisturbed, except for the tracks of an occasional deer, but the horse trudged through it without apparent difficulty, its breath forming scalloped cones in the air.

"How far is it to the camp?" Banner asked, in an attempt to make sane conversation.

"Six or seven miles, I guess," replied Adam, without looking at her. The amusement was gone from his features, leaving behind a quiet puzzlement.

They passed through the clearing and into a dense stand of Douglas fir. Skeletal blackberry vines clawed at the spokes of the wheels and the bonnet of the buggy itself.

Spotting an oblong basket hanging in the boughs of a tall pine tree, Banner again broke the silence.

"What is that?"

Adam flung one look at the basket and scowled. "That," he informed her flatly, "is the final resting place of an Indian child."

Banner shivered and drew her cloak more tightly around her. "But the animals might—"

"No animal could reach it, O'Brien. Too high."

Banner swallowed, closed her eyes for a moment. "Do the Klallum dispose of adults that way, too?"

Adam frowned. "Sometimes. Most often they put them adrift in canoes, on the sound. There is usually another canoe on top, upside down, of course, and they attach clam shells and things to that, hoping that the racket will scare away *tamanous*."

"An evil spirit?"

He nodded. "In this case, yes. Actually, a *tamanous* can be a good spirit, too, or an indifferent one, for that matter. The term encompasses their whole religion."

Banner suddenly felt indignant. "Why can't they just bury their dead, like everyone else?"

Adam gave her a look that was not wholly friendly. "They consider that a barbaric custom," he said. "Indians like to stay between the grass and the sky, and I can't say I blame them."

Subdued, Banner looked down at her hands, which rested atop the furry lap rug. "We're not so different, I guess—we Irish—with our banshee and our little people."

Adam startled her with an appreciative laugh. "So ye believe in the wee mischiefmakers, then?" he teased in a remarkably authentic brogue.

The basket in the tree, the canoe-graves, the *tamanous*—all of it was instantly in perspective, and Banner was comforted, cheered. With this man beside her, she was safe from all specters, real or imagined, and there was peace in the knowledge.

The laughter lingered in Adam's eyes as he drew the buggy to a stop beneath a storm-stirred, hidden sky and turned to face her. "O'Brien," he said, and then he kissed her.

Banner trembled under the sweet assault but was powerless to resist. Beneath the lap rug, Adam's hand kneaded her waist, rose to slide along her rib cage and then caress the outer rounding of her breast.

This time, there were no thoughts of Sean Malloy, no comparisons. There was only the wind and the cold and the fire within her that would not be cooled by any earthly element.

But suddenly Adam drew back, swearing under his breath, and he did not meet Banner's eyes as he took up the reins again and urged the horse forward, causing the buggy to lurch.

Banner was too proud to ask what was wrong. What, after all, did one say under such circumstances? Pardon me, sir, but why didn't you make love to me on the seat of your buggy?

Feeling both dejected and wildly embarrassed, she took a new interest in the surrounding countryside.

"I'm sorry," Adam said after they'd traveled some distance.

Banner still could not look at him. "For what?" she asked, giving the words a levity that she hoped would disguise her interest in his answer.

He was stubbornly silent.

And it was then, of all times, that Banner realized the pitiful entirety of her problem.

She loved Adam Corbin.

For a time she tried to deny it. She hadn't known him long enough. It was unreasonable. It was impossible; it was hopeless. She'd been hurt too badly in love to wander witlessly into its net again—hadn't she?

The buggy shifted and rolled onward, and Banner grew quietly desperate with the need to escape it, to escape the way gravity kept thrusting this man's rock-hard frame against her own.

Tears smarted in her eyes, and she turned her head away so that Adam would not see them. The forest passed in a fragrant green and white blur.

Presently the rig came to another stop, and Banner was jolted out of her reflective misery by a pungent stench composed predominantly of fish oil and human waste.

She wrinkled her nose.

Adam arched one eyebrow and indicated the Indian village below the ridge on which they sat. "Pleasant, isn't it?" he drawled. "Would you like to wait here?"

Nausea welled, scalding, into Banner's throat, but she shook her head. Bad smells were something one got used to, and for all her revulsion, she was wildly curious about the Klallum village and its people.

From their vantage point she could see a series of long wooden buildings constructed of unpainted cedar or pine. Between them, quick red children frolicked in the snow. Squaws in buckskin shifts or ill-fitting discards from the wardrobes of white women tended fires, wove baskets, and dug for clams along the shore beyond the camp.

The braves sat in circles, talking and engaging in what appeared to be games of chance.

Banner looked again at the lodges, feeling a little disappointed that there were no teepees.

Adam secured the buggy's brake and jumped to the

ground, his bag in one hand. "Come on, O'Brien," he said, walking away.

Banner scrambled after him with such haste that, had he not caught her arm and steadied her, she would probably have rolled down the slanting face of the ridge in a ball of gray woolen and ruffled muslin petticoats.

The tribe was aware of them now, and the children came forward first, dancing around Adam as though he were a piper and shouting questions in a mixture of English and Chinook, the jargon that had begun as a method of inter-tribal communication, long before the advent of the whites.

A small boy caught at Adam's hand, his dark eyes shining. "*Kloochman?*" he cried eagerly, indicating Banner. "Big Doctor's *kloochman?*"

Adam laughed and shook his head.

"What was he saying?" demanded Banner, in a whisper.

Adam looked at her with mischief and something resembling tenderness. "Never mind, O'Brien. I'll explain it later."

"*Ub-ran!*" shouted the child in triumph.

"What is an *ub-ran?*" Banner insisted, as the braves and squaws began to gravitate toward them in unnerving numbers.

"It's you, Shamrock," he replied. "The boy was trying to say 'O'Brien.'"

Feeling foolish, Banner eyed the horde of approaching Indians. "Are they dangerous?"

"Only if you accept a luncheon invitation."

"They're not cannibals!" cried Banner, who wasn't so sure.

Adam chuckled. "No, but they're terrible cooks. Step it up, Ub-ran. The glamorous practice of frontier medicine awaits."

The masses had reached them, and a man Banner would have sworn she'd met or seen before stepped forward and caught at her cloak with a semi-clean hand. "*Kloochman?*" he beamed, peering up into Adam's face as he spoke.

Adam laughed again, this time throwing back his head in the force of his amusement, and the sound pleased the savage, as did his reply. "God forbid!"

Banner was not to be put off again. "What is a *kloochman?*" she whispered tersely.

"A wife," replied Adam, without so much as glancing at her.

Banner stiffened, but even her outraged pride could not have coerced her to leave the questionable safety of Dr. Corbin's side. "May I say that I find the idea of being your wife just as reprehensible as you do?" she responded with biting dignity.

Adam chuckled and shook his head and immediately became embroiled in an incomprehensible exchange with the Indian—Banner now remembered him as the man who had driven away the children that were tormenting the small Chinaman in Port Hastings—and she found herself wishing that she understood Chinook rather than just its history.

To distract herself, Banner looked upon the children, many of whom were nearly naked in that bitter cold, and shivered. As they were propelled toward the center of the village in a red swell of humanity, she ventured, "How do they bear going almost without clothing in this weather?"

"They've had centuries of practice," responded Adam. "And if you can't speak decent Chinook, kindly keep your very lovely mouth shut. It is impolite to converse in a language your hosts do not understand."

"You did."

"When?"

"Just a moment ago. You said 'God forbid' and the man understood!"

"He doesn't know the half of it. Be quiet, Shamrock, or I'll trade you for two goats and a berry basket."

Banner blushed and bit her lower lip, temporarily defeated.

As they approached the doorway of one of the lodges, which had only a bearskin curtain to keep out the cold wind, a younger man approached, authoritative in his buckskins and braids, and spoke to Adam in swift, quelling Chinook.

Adam listened soberly and answered in kind. Again the word for "wife" was mentioned, again, Adam vigorously denied the assertion.

The Indian gave Banner a speculative look, his dark eyes lingering long at her fiery hair, and spoke again.

Adam turned to her and grinned. "I've just been offered four dried salmon and a cedar canoe for you," he said. "What's your counter offer?"

Banner reddened and drew nearer to Adam, even though she was certain, now, that she hated him. "I beg your pardon?"

"What will you give me to keep you?"

"Bastard," replied Banner.

Battling to suppress his amusement, Adam turned his

blue gaze back to the Indian and spoke words of apologetic tone.

The brave looked disappointed and stomped away.

But the other tribesmen were eager to talk with Adam, and they drew him inside the lodge, leaving Banner to stand, befuddled, among the women.

Quickly enough they surrounded her, touching her clothes, smiling gapped smiles, showing her the baskets of which they were justifiably proud.

Banner felt herself warming to them for, after all, they were Jenny's people and their culture was an ancient one, deserving of respect.

After a time, though, Banner began to grow impatient. There was much laughter, inside the log walls of the lodge, and Adam did not come out.

Why were they here, if not to treat patients?

Her medical bag heavy in one hand, Banner wandered toward a stone hut near the water. "What's this?"

Several of the women offered answers, but only one was in English.

"My people use to drive out sickness—bad *tamanous*," offered an older woman who wore an outsized brown sateen dress and a patched paisley shawl.

The *tamanous* again. Banner shivered and went to the hut's arched doorway to peer inside.

The voice at her side startled her. "They heat stones and drop them into cold water inside the hut," Adam said. "And when the patient has been properly cooked by the steam, they carry him down to the shore and drop him into the sound."

Banner was horrified, though she did feel a measure of

relief that Adam was no longer secreted away in that masculine stronghold, the lodge. "Saints in heaven!"

Adam looked at the hut as though he'd like to tear it apart, stone by heavy, rounded stone. "They rarely use it unless there's an outbreak of smallpox. Shall we go, Shamrock?"

The idea was appealing, even though visiting the Klallum camp had been a memorable adventure. "No one is sick?"

He smiled and reached out to catch her hand in his, and the innocent contact gave Banner a certain sweet, piercing pleasure. "No one is sick," he confirmed, and then they were on the way back to the horse and buggy that awaited them on the ridge.

"Did they really offer you fish and a boat for me?" she asked when they were on their way again.

Adam grinned. "Yes. The bargaining got pretty interesting inside the lodge, as a matter of fact."

"How interesting?"

"Two of their women, a horse, and all the canoes I could ever want."

Banner suppressed a smile. "Why didn't you trade?"

Suddenly, Adam's eyes were serious. "For the same reason I didn't press my advantage when we stopped on the way," he said.

"And what reason was that?" Banner blurted out, before she could stop herself.

He held the reins in one hand, caressed Banner's cold-pinkened cheek with the other. "I didn't have the right," he answered hoarsely.

Banner lowered her eyes, but he only forced her to look

at him again.

"Did you think I didn't want you?" he asked.

Color pounded in Banner's cheeks at her own brazen reply. "Yes," she said.

"You were wrong, O'Brien. So very wrong."

Banner was still confused, though the knowledge that he had wanted her was soothing. Had he restrained himself out of respect for their professional relationship, or because he thought she was a virgin?

And what was she wondering such scandalous things for anyway?

Banner had a sudden need to tell Adam about Sean—all about Sean. About the beatings and the heartbreak and the terrible fear. "Adam, I—"

But his hand fell away from her face and his eyes were suddenly very faraway. Was he thinking of the woman she was certain he kept somewhere nearby, remembering that she loved him and trusted him to be faithful?

Banner swallowed a cluster of tears, and neither of them spoke until they had reached the Corbin house again.

Even there they were drawn into the boisterous celebration of the midday meal, and the few words they exchanged were polite, superficial ones.

It was foggy on Puget Sound, and the masts creaked in rhythm with the tide. The great sails of the Jonathan Lee were useless.

Temple Royce grasped the railing and swore. Where the hell was the wind?

The first mate was peering through the shifting gloom of snow and murk. "That's a cutter, all right," he said. "We're in dutch, Cap'n, if they catch us with all them Chinks below decks. And what about the rum and them bolts of wool cloth?"

What, indeed. "You're sure that's a revenue cutter?" Temple asked, wondering how the man could recognize any craft in that weather.

"I've been runnin' one kind of smuggle or another for forty years," replied the mate. "And yes, sir, that's a cutter for certain."

Temple sighed. His head ached and sickness churned in his stomach, rising and falling like foam on an unsettled sea. "Tell the men to dump the cargo," he whispered.

"All of it?"

"All of it. And be quick, damn it." With that, Temple hurried into his cabin and shut the door tight.

Even so, he could hear the shrieks as the Chinamen were flung overboard, into the swallowing, frigid waters of the sound.

Trying to console himself with the fact that some of the men would make it to shore, despite all odds, Temple found a bottle, opened it, and drank deeply. If there really was a hell, he thought, it would not consist of fire and brimstone. No, it would be a place where he was forced to relive this day, over and over again.

Stewart Henderson returned first thing Sunday morning. He was a small, plump, avid-looking man with moons of grime under his fingernails and a complicated system of wires holding his jaw in place.

Because of this appliance, he spoke in a mumbling monotone. "You're more than welcome to stay right here, little lady."

Banner drew back, her hand at her throat, and then recovered herself enough to smile. "I couldn't do that," she said reasonably.

Dr. Henderson stomped the snow from his boots before stepping into the house, and his colorless eyes assessed Banner briefly, then scanned the spotless little parlor. "Somebody really cleaned the place good."

Jenny had vanished at the first appearance of Dr. Henderson's buggy, and some instinct warned Banner not to mention her. Since she couldn't very well take credit for the appearance of the house, she said nothing at all.

Henderson sank into a chair before the fire, where Banner had been sitting reading Melissa's epic adventure only moments before. With a grunt, he kicked off his boots and settled himself.

Immediately a dense, cloying odor filled the room, and Banner stepped back, her oversensitive nose twitching.

He smiled at her in a familiar way. "You're a pretty one," he must have suffered to say, considering his wiring. "Prettiest sawbones *I* ever seen."

Something within Banner rebelled at saying the expected "thank you." She clasped her hands together and wondered when the boor had last changed his stockings. "I—I was given to understand that you would be away for some time," she ventured.

Henderson touched the wires along his jaw and tried to laugh, and the effort was painful to watch. "Takes more'n a little set-to with a whippersnapper like Corbin to run *me* off," he said.

Odious as this man was, irresponsible and even criminal

as it had been to attempt surgery using opium as an anesthetic, Banner could not countenance the violence Adam had done him. "I've met Dr. Corbin," she said, unwilling to express her private opinion.

"I don't wonder. Ain't much happens in this town that he don't know about." Henderson tried to look gallant. "He didn't bother you, did he?"

"No," lied Banner. "He didn't bother me."

Henderson shook his balding head. "He's got a wicked soul, that Adam Corbin. Wicked and hateful."

Banner knew better, but she refrained, of course, from saying so. And something inside her was overjoyed at the prospect of shocking this man. "I've agreed to join Adam's practice," she said.

The little man glared at her. "That's a mistake," he said, after a rather disturbing interval.

"I don't think so," argued Banner in moderate tones as she took her cloak down from a peg on the wall and put it on. That done, she found her bag and started for the door. "I'll send someone for my things," she said, and then she was, blessedly, outside, where the air was fresh and yet another snowfall was beginning.

She hurried toward the center of town, on foot, mentally counting and recounting the few dollars hidden away in the bottom of her medical bag. They would be enough, she hoped, to rent a decent room.

It was the very worst of luck that Banner fairly collided with Jeff Corbin in the doorway of the town's one hotel. "Banner?" he breathed, squinting at her.

Banner wondered distractedly if this dashing sea captain needed spectacles. "Hello, Jeff," she said, trying to make her way around him and inside.

He would not permit her to pass. "What are you doing here?" he demanded with typical Corbin directness.

Banner lowered her eyes. "I plan to live here," she said. "If there is a room available, that is."

Jeff caught her elbow in a grasp reminiscent of his brother's and tugged her a little way down the board sidewalk, where those coming to have Sunday breakfasts in the hotel dining room would not overhear their conversation. "Here? I thought you lived—"

Banner was wildly impatient. It seemed that she was always being dragged about or propelled these days—by a Corbin. "Dr. Henderson is back," she snapped in a furious whisper. "Do you expect me to stay in his house with him there?"

"Of course not. That's ridiculous. Our house—"

Banner shook her head. "No, Jeff. I can't stay at your house."

"Why not? You work there, don't you—in the hospital, I mean?"

Honesty seemed the only viable course, though Banner would, under the circumstances, have preferred to lie. "Adam is there," she reminded him miserably.

Understanding registered in Jeff's bruised face, along with a certain quiet pain. Still, he was obviously reluctant to give ground. "Let's go inside and talk—please?"

The hotel's dining room was a modest place overlooking the water, and the tablecloths and implements were clean. Banner breathed a little sigh as a waiter set heavy mugs of coffee before them.

"Banner," Jeff began gently, his hand coming to close

91

over hers in a brotherly fashion, "do you love Adam?"

She took distracted note of the scrapes on his knuckles and then forced herself to meet the ink-blue eyes. Eyes like Adam's. "I don't know," she hedged.

"But?"

She blushed. For heaven's sake, what did the man want her to say? "There are problems."

Jeff's grin was rueful and totally disarming. "With Adam, there always are," he said. "But he's a good man, Banner."

She took in his injuries with pointed interest. "Look what he did to you, Jeff. For that matter, look what he did to Dr. Henderson."

Jeff smiled and the greenish-yellow flesh on his battered cheekbone nearly eclipsed his right eye. "It isn't Adam's temper that worries you, is it, Banner?" he asked with uncanny insight. "You must know that all brothers fight sometimes, and you're a doctor yourself, so you surely understand how he felt, seeing someone die in terrible pain because of blatant ignorance."

"It's the woman," mourned Banner, unaccountably.

"What woman?"

Heat throbbed in Banner's face. What had she *said?* Her suspicions that Adam had a woman and perhaps even children tucked away somewhere were woven of fancy and hearsay, not fact. And even if her guesses were correct, what right did she have, after knowing Adam not quite five days, to consider such things at all?

"Banner," Jeff prodded gently.

To her mortification, she began to cry. "Please—I'm sorry—I had no right—"

"You do love him," said Jeff in gentle, decisive tones. "I'll be a—"

Ever conscious of her dignity, Banner took up a red-and-white-checked table napkin and dried her tears. "I am an utter fool," she lamented, more to herself than to Jeff.

He chuckled. "No."

"I was always so practical!"

His broad shoulders moved in a shrug. "Loving Adam changes that?"

"Yes. I don't seem to know what I think about anything anymore. I feel one thing and then I feel another—"

"And you think he has a woman."

Banner searched her mind for something to say and found nothing. In the end, she only nodded.

Jeff's eyes were faraway, seeming to see through the ceaseless snow to something beyond. Perhaps he was remembering the accident that had taken his father, and perhaps he was trying to frame the words to tell Banner that Adam did care for someone else.

She was never to know, for before he could speak, Adam, himself suddenly loomed at the table side.

"This is enlightening," he said, and the look on his face was quietly ferocious.

Jeff's eyes met his brother's intrepidly. "Don't make an idiot of yourself, Adam," he said. "Banner was thinking of moving here, now that Henderson's back from his travels, and I've been trying to talk her out of it."

The odd and awesome tension in Adam's wide shoulders eased, and he sank heavily into a chair at their table. "Jenny told me about Henderson," he admitted, having the grace to look a bit sheepish now.

Banner was bracing herself for an argument. He would maintain that the hotel was too far from her work, or somehow unsafe, or—

"I think she should stay here."

The announcement struck Banner O'Brien's confused heart like a stone, and she was speechless.

Jeff suffered no such difficulty. "What?"

Adam shrugged with exaggerated nonchalance, his eyes avoiding Banner's. "Most of the time, you and Mama and Melissa are gone. I live alone, except for Maggie. What would the townspeople say about Shamrock if she moved in?"

The logic was unassailable. Banner had used it herself in deciding to take a room at the hotel. Still, the cool matter-of-factness of his words was a wounding thing.

With remarkable dignity, Banner gathered her spinning emotions, excused herself from the table, and went to inquire about a room.

Half an hour later, her trunk was delivered, and she was just feeling free to sit down on her bumpy iron bed and cry when Jenny arrived.

"You belong with Adam," the girl said flatly, slipping out of her oversized woolen coat and carrying it with her as she paced the rough board floor.

Banner sat down on the bed and slowly, sadly shook her head. "Where will you go now, Jenny?"

Jenny smiled and shrugged her plump shoulders. "Back to Miss Callie Maitland's house, of course. I work for her."

To her shame, Banner had not thought to ask about Jenny's life—where she worked, what she did, what she hoped for and regretted. The girl had simply been a friend, there when she was needed.

Jenny's intuition was in full play. "You thought Adam just conjured me up, didn't you?" she teased gently. "Like a *tamanous.*"

"I didn't think at all. Jenny, I'm so sorry!"

The girl came to sit beside Banner. "Everything will be all right, you know," she said reasonably.

Nothing had been all right since the moment she'd met Adam Corbin, but Banner didn't say so. There was no point in burdening her friend with her low spirits. "Yes," she echoed. "Everything will be all right."

Jenny stood up and put on her coat again. "Miss Callie lives on Harbor Street," she said quietly. "Number 5 Harbor Street. Will you come and visit me sometime soon, Banner?"

Banner squeezed Jenny's strong, nutbrown hand. "Of course I will."

A moment later, the door closed behind Jenny with a soft click.

Melissa was walking back and forth, the heels of her shoes clicking on the hard and splintery floor of Banner's room. "Did you really like my writing, Banner?" she trilled. "You're not just saying that so I'll keep trying, are you?"

The child was a restorative; her energy was contagious. "I wouldn't lie to you, Melissa," Banner answered. "I think you're very talented."

Like quicksilver, Melissa moved on to another subject. "You're not really going to live here, are you?"

"I have to live somewhere."

"Live at our house. Jiggers, we could put up an army in

that place!"

Banner shook her head, though there was a part of her that constantly reached for that very special house at the top of the hill. "It wouldn't be proper."

"Proper!" scoffed Melissa.

"Yes, proper," insisted Banner firmly. "May I remind you that, once the holidays have passed, your brother and I would be alone there?"

"Maggie is always around."

Again Banner shook her head.

"What a prig you are, Dr. Banner O'Brien! How is romance supposed to blossom if you and Adam are never by yourselves?"

Banner shrugged in a so-be-it sort of way.

Melissa looked very disappointed, but she brightened as an inspiration struck her. "I know! You could just stay until we all leave again! You could sleep in my room and—"

"Melissa."

"Won't you at least come to supper? Keith is waiting downstairs to drive us home, and Mama is so hoping you'll come."

There seemed to be no point in refusing just to avoid Adam. After all, she would be working with him on a regular basis in the coming days.

Besides, she felt lonely and cold in that little room, as though she'd been exiled to it.

"All right," Banner said, and her heart gave a joyous little leap, just as though she, like Melissa, was going home.

Francelle's father sat directly across from Banner, at the

Corbin table, and smiled his senator's smile.

"A lady doctor!" he boomed. "Well, well. Francelle told me, but I confess that I didn't believe her."

Banner felt like a carnival freak. A bearded lady! Well, well. Francelle told me, but I confess that I didn't believe her.

Katherine had been badgering the dictrict's representative to the territorial legislature about one thing or another throughout the meal. Now, she smiled at Banner and then Adam and then the senator. "Don't you think it strange, Thomas, that a woman can practice medicine in this territory yet be refused the vote?"

Thomas Mayhugh looked pained, and one of his chubby hands went nervously to the watch chain stretched across his stomach. "Now, Katherine, I've told you before. I myself presented an amendment that would grant suffrage to women and—women and—"

Katherine leaned forward in her chair. "Women and half-breeds, Thomas."

Senator Mayhugh's rescue was brought about by his daughter, who flashed a venomous look in Banner's direction and said, "I think women should keep houses and have babies. Why should we bother to vote when our husbands would dictate our choices anyway."

When no one spoke, Francelle shifted her gaze from Banner to Adam. "What do you think, Adam? Should women vote?"

Adam smiled. "Some women," he said, in tones of sweet acid. "Furthermore, since I have to live in this house, that wasn't a fair question."

Katherine was watching her son with interest—and a

measure of wry humor. "You've missed your calling, dear," she said. "Anyone who can utter so many words and still say nothing belongs in politics, not medicine."

Adam lifted his wineglass in an amused salute.

Chapter Five

The ride down the hill to Port Hastings seemed more perilous than ever that night, especially with Adam Corbin at the reins of the buggy. Typically, Banner made conversation to distract herself.

"Mrs. Corbin was right, you know," she ventured. "You didn't actually say whether or not you think women should vote."

He looked at her—she knew that by the motion of his head—but his expression was hidden in shadow. "I'm not against suffrage, O'Brien," he replied.

"But you're not exactly in favor of it, either, are you?"

Adam appeared to be concentrating on navigating the steep hill. "Since women are held accountable under the law, I think they should enjoy the rights it provides."

Banner frowned. "Most men don't feel that way, though. Why is that, Adam?"

He was watching her again. "The issue is linked with prohibition. They probably envision an army of Carrie Nations converging on the polls, hatchets in hand. And when liquor is outlawed, prostitution won't be far behind."

Banner fell silent, and she huddled deeper under the lap rug as a snow-flecked wind howled around the bonnet of the buggy. How dearly men regarded their two favorite pleasures, she thought to herself.

"Talk to me, O'Brien," Adam said as they reached the bottom of the hill and turned in the direction of the business district. Banner's hotel was only about a block ahead.

"I was just thinking how selfish men can be," she replied honestly. "Imagine denying adult people simple, basic rights just to drink rum and—"

Adam laughed and drew the buggy to a stop under a spill of golden light coming from the streetlamp in front of the hotel. "And what?"

She colored in anger and then realized, too late, how deftly he had baited her. And she had risen to the hook. "You know *what!*" she hissed.

Buggy reins draped between his right thumb and index finger, he lifted his hands in comical surrender. "Don't shoot, O'Brien. Have pity. 'And what' seems to come into my mind a lot when I'm around you."

Banner hurled back the lap rug and scrambled unceremoniously out of the buggy. "Go home!" she cried.

"Come with me," he answered.

Banner went crimson, whirled, and stormed toward the warm sanction of the hotel, Adam's laughter following after her.

The snow grew deeper with each passing day until the roofs of houses were groaning under its weight, children were kept home from school, and ships were neither leaving nor arriving in Port Hastings.

Banner, for all that she was very busy with patients at the hospital and the occasional house call with Adam, felt uneasy. It was as though something was bearing down on her, something that would crush her the way the snow was

99

crushing outhouses and chicken coops.

By contrast, the mood in the Corbin house was boisterously festive. Secrets were kept, holly boughs and evergreens were gathered, songs were sung. It turned out that Clarence King, the gambler who'd had a knife thrust through his hand, was possessed of a rousing baritone.

It was to escape this that Banner went to Maggie's kitchen that stormy afternoon of December twenty-third.

A sturdy woman with merry eyes and unruly gray hair, Maggie McQuire was rolling out pie dough at a worktable near the fire and humming a yuletide hymn.

"No smile for old Maggie?" she asked, breaking off her humming to grin at Banner.

Banner helped herself to coffee at the stove and then went to sit disconsolately on the bench closest to the hearth. The warmth of the crackling, busy fire seemed to exist only on the other side of some invisible barrior. "I'm afraid I don't feel much like smiling," she said.

"Missing your folks?"

There were no folks to miss; Banner barely remembered her parents, and her grandmother, who had raised her, had died long before her marriage to Sean. "Isn't it ever going to stop snowing?" she whispered, neatly skirting Maggie's question and frowning at the white-trimmed windows.

"Yes," said Maggie, going on with her work but lending Banner a gruff sort of comfort as she spoke. "It'll stop and the sun will come out."

The double meaning lifted Banner's spirits a little.

"You've been cooking for days," she observed. "Don't you get tired?"

"I'm planning to be tired the day after Christmas,"

quipped Maggie. "Until then, I don't dare stop to draw breath." Her plump shoulders moved in a shrug. "I kind of like having all of the family around. Wouldn't be Christmas if I didn't have to chase one of those boys away from my blackberry cobbler every few minutes."

Banner smiled, and it was a real smile, without effort, feeling good on her face. "You love, them very much, don't you?"

Maggie nodded. "Melissa, too, 'course. But the boys are real special to me—especially Adam. We've had a time with that one right from the first. Near starved to death when he was a baby, Adam did. Guess that's why I like to cook for him now."

"Starved to death?" Banner repeated, staring.

Maggie nodded. "Mother's milk didn't set well with him, and we didn't think Adam'd last through his first year. Probably wouldn't have if it hadn't been for old Martha Washington."

Martha Washington? Banner was about to voice her confusion when she remembered the custom of giving Indians the names of famous white people. "What did she do?"

"She came right up to the cabin door one day and said as how she'd heard we had a sick baby. Miss Katie was in tears and Daniel was away somewheres—that's why I was around so much, though I had myself a husband then—and Adam was squallin' fit to rouse the dead.

"Old Martha took him right in hand, she did. Once she found out that he wouldn't take the breast, she boiled up a batch of fresh clams and gave him the broth. Lived on it until he was ten months old."

Banner pictured the small cabin and the beleaguered young mother and thought how much things had changed since then. "Daniel was Mrs. Corbin's husband?"

Maggie nodded. "He was a handsome one, if something of a rake, and he had himself a knack for makin' money. Time Keith was born, Daniel had four ships sailin' the seas and the beginnings of the boatyard and the mill. They built this house right up around the cabin."

Banner was still framing a response when the door leading from the dining room swung open and Adam came in. He spared one grin for his associate and then descended on Maggie's peach pie filling, one finger curved to dip.

"You touch that and I'll whack you!" Maggie threatened, brandishing the floury rolling pin in both hands.

Adam leaped back in comical alarm and then subsided to sit on the bench, beside Banner. "Shirking again, O'Brien?" he drawled.

Banner elbowed him in the ribs. "Shirking, is it? I, Dr. Corbin, have been in the hospital all morning, treating patients and cleaning instruments. You, on the other hand—"

Adam laughed. "It isn't my fault that Jeff and Keith had to look at every pine between here and Portland before they could agree on a Christmas tree."

"Speaking of that," Maggie broke in, and there was irritation in her face and in the movements of her arms as she rolled out yet another circle of dough. "Are you going to be here tomorrow, or are you going to traipse off by yourself again?"

Instantly the festive humor was gone from Adam's eyes. "I'll leave in the morning, as usual," he said sharply, rising

102

to his feet and ignoring Banner. "Have the food ready."

Maggie's annoyance seemed to equal his, but she only nodded and vented her anger on the pie dough.

Adam turned and strode out of the kitchen, leaving Banner to draw her own conclusions about his plans for Christmas.

When she next encountered him, in the ward, he was examining Clarence King's hand for infection. Having done this repeatedly herself, Banner knew that the wound was healing cleanly. In fact, now that he was over the shock of being stabbed, Clarence could have been released and sent on his way. Probably Adam was only keeping him because it was Christmas and the young man had nowhere else to go.

Banner went to the front windows of the ward, which overlooked Port Hastings and the now quiet harbor, too proud to approach Adam and strike up a conversation.

Francelle and Melissa were in the yard, laughing and flinging balls of snow at each other, and their voices were like songs rising on the wintery air. For all their commotion, Banner barely saw or heard them. She was thinking of the woman Adam would visit tomorrow, the woman he would take food to. Was she beautiful? Did he love her?

Banner's eyes stung, and she bit her lower lip. She must be very special, Adam's woman, whoever she was, if he would leave such a wonderful home and family at Christmastide to spend time with her.

In the snowy distance, a steam whistle blew, and the sound mingled with the joyous laughter of Francelle and Melissa, all of it combining to make Banner feel lonesome.

She lifted her chin, however, and thought of Adam's

woman again. I will take him from you, she vowed. She, Banner O'Brien, who had never wanted another man to come into her life, let alone coveted someone else's love.

"Shamrock?"

She turned, slowly, not wanting to face Adam now but knowing that she must. "How is Clarence's hand?" she asked, quite unnecessarily.

Adam grinned and folded his arms across his broad chest, his head tilted to one side. "It's mending nicely," he answered, and his dark blue eyes caressed her with a sort of quiet humor. Had he somehow guessed what she was thinking?

Banner blushed a little, praying that he hadn't. "It's still snowing," she observed with an inanity that made her hate herself before the words were out of her mouth.

The indigo eyes laughed at her, but gently. "Yes, Shamrock, it is indeed still snowing." He reached into the inside pocket of his gray silk vest and withdrew an envelope. "Here. It's a month's salary."

Banner's eyes widened as she took the envelope; it was thick with currency. "I haven't worked a month," she reminded him, but her heart was stirring within her. After all, Christmas was but two days away and she would spend it here with this family and she had been despairing because she couldn't bring even the smallest remembrance to show her caring for them.

Adam shrugged. "I think I can trust you not to run off before a month is out, can't I, O'Brien?"

Banner tallied the money tucked into the envelope with as much subtlety as possible. There were five twenty-dollar bills—a hundred dollars! Merciful heavens, she'd have been lucky to earn that much in a year working on her own. "Isn't this rather a lot, just for a month?"

Adam's grin eased to a half-smile. "Not really, considering the rigors of a practice like this one. It's been easy so far, O'Brien, but the first time this ward is filled and we've got patients howling in the outer office, you'll be demanding a raise."

Banner looked down at the money and thought of the pretty lace handkerchief she'd seen in the window of the general store—that would be perfect for Mrs. Corbin—and of the beautiful, leatherbound book of days she wanted to buy for Melissa. Suddenly, her low spirits were dispelled.

"Take a few hours off," Adam said, and this time she knew that he *was* reading her mind. "Jeff is around somewhere—I'm sure he could be persuaded to take you down to town."

Banner rushed to get her cloak with such eagerness that Adam laughed. She turned at the opening of the walkway leading into the main part of the house, her color high. "Thank you," she said.

Adam shrugged and turned away.

Jeff was in the parlor, supervising the placement of the towering, fragrant Christmas tree. A movement inside the lush boughs indicated the presence of someone else, too—Keith?

"The windows, damn it—in front of the *windows!*" barked Katherine Corbin's second son.

Deliciously scented pine boughs moved, and Keith's voice was recognizable, if muffled. "I can't *see* the windows!" he retorted. "Will you just say 'left' or 'right'?"

105

"Starboard," instructed Jeff, with terse impatience.

The twelve-foot tree paused, then sidled a few inches to the right. "*Starboard,*" muttered the voice within. "This is the parlor, you idiot, not the decks of the *Sea Mistress!*"

Banner had been enjoying the scene too much to betray her presence in the doorway, but a giggle escaped her and Jeff turned, grinning, his hands on his hips.

"Hello, Dr. O'Brien."

"Am I in front of the blasted windows or not?" demanded the tree.

Banner laughed out loud, and her weary spirit soared. Somehow this simple spectacle had brought the joy of the season home to her. "Just a little to the left," she said.

Obediently, the massive tree slid to the left, filling the huge, gracious room with its pitchy, festive scent as it went.

"Now?" implored Keith in baleful tones.

"Now," confirmed Banner.

The tree rustled again as Keith came out, looking rumpled and patently annoyed. At the sight of Banner's joy-flushed face, however, he flung a grin at Jeff and muttered, "Have you ever noticed that Adam always gets the best presents?"

Jeff nodded and just for a moment his Corbin-blue eyes were wistful.

Banner was puzzled by the cryptic exchange, but she didn't explore the feeling. She wanted nothing to spoil the bright glow of the day. "Your brother told me," she began, addressing Jeff, "that you might be willing to drive me to town. I want to do some shopping."

Jeff executed a sweeping bow. "At your service, milady,

I'll have the carriage brought around."

"The buggy would do," said Banner, who was not accustomed to luxury.

"Not for you," replied Jeff in a rumbling vibrato, as he caught her hand and suavely kissed it.

Keith rolled his eyes and then his gaze swung, warmly mischievous, to Banner. "Excuse my brother, please," he enjoined her. "You see, Jeff sometimes gets his centuries confused. He changes, before our very eyes, from the captain of a modern ship to a swashbuckling pirate. Some of us even suspect that he swings from the rigging and stands at the end of the gangplank, brandishing a sword."

"Go tend to your flock or something," retorted Jeff out of the side of his mouth, his eyes never leaving Banner's face. "There is a price, Dr. O'Brien, for my escorting you today."

Banner knew better than to be alarmed; there was no danger in this man. At least, not to her. "And what is that?" she asked archly.

"You must let me buy your supper."

"Done," she agreed.

Keith elbowed his brother in the ribs as he passed. "I hope you've led a long and full life," he told him mysteriously, and then he was gone.

Barely a quarter of an hour later, Banner was settled comfortably inside the family carriage, a bright plaid lap rug covering her legs. Jeff sat easily in the seat opposite hers, though the small space should have cramped him, considering his size.

They went first to Banner's hotel, where she collected her best dress—a pale blue taffeta that had been packed away too long and needed pressing. When they had dropped the garment off at Wung Lo's busy establishment, they went on to the general store.

Guessing, perhaps, that Banner wanted to shop alone, Jeff went off on business of his own.

The mercantile was well stocked, and heat radiated from a sizable stove in the back. The scents of spices, peppermint candy, saddle soap, and soot filled the place. On the yardage counter were bolts of bright silks mixed in among serviceable woolens, cambrics, and calicos. Enormous green pickles were sold from a barrel near the counter, and elegant dolls with china heads nodded between toy firewagons and tiny wicker baby carriages. Occasionally, a St. Nicholas dressed in the rough-spun clothing of a farmer or a millhand would come in to purchase one or two of the toys.

Banner explored at her leisure, dropping the planned handkerchief and the book of days into the basket slung over her arm, pondering an array of modestly priced perfumes until she found one she thought Maggie would like. After that, she selected books for Jeff and Keith and, following much study of the stock available, a pretty satin sachet for Jenny.

That left Adam.

Banner went back to the books, but none of them seemed right. Besides, she wondered if it was fitting to give Dr. Corbin a gift at all, considering the way she felt about him.

But she had to, of course, if she was going to buy presents for all the others. Frowning, Banner traversed one aisle and then another, picking things up, putting them down.

"Problems?" interceded a masculine voice at her side as she paused before a display of toy Indian drums.

Banner turned, still musing, to look into the handsome, smiling face of Temple Royce. "Hello," she said.

"Dr. Henderson tells me that you've joined Adam Corbin's practice," remarked Mr. Royce, and though he was still smiling, something disturbing lurked in the depths of his childlike brown eyes. "I must say, I was surprised to hear that."

"Why?" asked Banner distractedly, wondering if a box of chocolates would be too intimate a gift for Adam, given the fact that such presents were usually exchanged by lovers.

"Adam isn't an easy man to work with," supplied Mr. Royce, raising one eyebrow.

Banner smiled. "No, he certainly isn't. But he is a very good doctor, and I expect to learn rather a lot from him."

A tiny muscle in Royce's smooth-shaven cheek tightened, relaxed again. "Yes," he said, after a long and rather unsettling pause. He turned his fine beaver hat in gloved hands and somehow managed to look elegant and uncomfortable, both at once.

"Is something wrong?" Banner asked.

There it was again, that discomforting smile. "No—of course not—it's just that—well—"

"Yes?"

Mr. Royce assessed the sleeves of his tailored coat for snowflakes that had long since melted to glistening beads. "I would feel responsible, having brought you to Port Hastings myself, if anything—er—happened."

"Such as?" prodded Banner, feeling slightly insulted but

not knowing why.

Before the man could frame any sort of answer, halting or otherwise, Jeff returned, his powerful hands wedged into the pockets of his blue sea-captain coat. His collar was turned up and snow shimmered on his imposing shoulders and his eyes were angrily vigilant as they swept Banner's companion.

"Royce," he said, and whether the word was a greeting or a threat, Banner could not tell.

Temple smiled nervously. "Jeff," he replied, with a nod of his head.

Jeff's gaze swept to Banner's face and softened. "Are you finished?" he asked.

Banner was careful to tilt her shopping basket so that he couldn't see inside. She wanted his present to be a surprise. "Not yet. Could I have just a minute more?"

The great shoulders moved in a good-natured shrug. "I'll wait," he said, and as Banner walked away, she heard him speak, in a heated undertone, to Mr. Royce.

It was something she should have thought about, she knew, this thinly veiled hostility between her friend and the man who had persuaded her to come to Port Hastings in the first place, but with Adam's gift still to be chosen, she had enough to consider.

Her attention was drawn back to the display of toy drums eventually, and in a rush of delicious daring, Banner selected the most colorful one for Adam, to commemorate the day they'd visited the Klallum camp.

Temple Royce had left the store, and Jeff remained at a discreet distance until Banner had made her purchases and the storekeeper had wrapped them all together in a length of heavy brown paper tied with twine.

While she waited just inside the front door, watching the snowfall and the brisk foot and wagon traffic in the road, Jeff made a purchase of his own. After tucking something into the pocket of his coat, he joined her.

It was but mid-afternoon, but Jeff gestured toward a dining establishment across the street as they went out. "Hungry?"

Banner was hungry since she hadn't had lunch, but she was intent on claiming her taffeta dress from Wung Lo's first. The next day, after the skating, there was to be a party, and she wanted to look nice, even though Adam wasn't going to be there. Being a doctor, Banner knew that an emergency could come up at any moment and leave her with no time to recover her gown.

"I would like to stop at Wung Lo's first, please," she said.

Jeff nodded and offered his arm. "How well do you know Temple Royce?" he asked lightly as they made their way over the slick, crowded walks in the direction of the laundry.

"Not well, actually," replied Banner, recalling the animosity she'd sensed between Jeff and Mr. Royce, back in the store. "You don't like him, do you?"

"That is an understatement," said Jeff, affably enough. He looked like an overgrown boy, with the snow gathering in his polished-honey hair. "Do you like him, Banner?"

She considered. "I hadn't really thought about it, one way or the other. I'm indifferent, I guess."

Banner had not realized that Jeff was tense. Now, as his body relaxed visibly, she did. "Good," he said, and then they were at the door of Wung Lo's and he was opening it for her.

The inside of that laundry was a cluttered, starch-scented delight. Steam billowed from the washing vats behind the counter, and a machine for grinding rice made a great, festive clatter. On the shelves were packages of exotic tea, bags of rice, and bundles of clean, carefully wrapped laundry.

Wung Lo himself greeted Banner, grinning and chattering apologetically. She couldn't understand most of what he said, but the gist of it was that her gown had not yet been pressed.

As Banner and Jeff watched, the Chinaman found the dress and spread it out carefully on a padded board. Then, simultaneously reaching for a flat iron heating on the stove and filling his mouth with water, he spewed the liquid over the skirts of Banner's cherished gown and began to press it.

Jeff chortled at the look of horror on Banner's face. "Startling," he observed, in an undertone, "But very effective all the same."

Banner's eyes widened as the Chinaman repeatedly filled his mouth and spat water onto her dress. His tiny hands moved rapidly, however, and, when he was finished, the garment looked almost new.

"Me bling to missy's house?" Wung Lo asked, beaming.

Banner wanted the dress immediately, but she was considering the mechanics of getting it home without rumpling it somehow. She and Jeff still had to eat, and how would the garment fare in the snowfall outside? If it survived that, would it be crushed in the carriage?

"Bring it to Corbin House, please," Jeff said smoothly, laying several coins on the counter top. "Today."

"Today," confirmed Wung Lo with a nod.

On the street again, Banner grappled with her package of Christmas gifts, meaning to repay Jeff for the coins he'd given Wung Lo.

Jeff took the parcel and shook his head. "Never mind the money," he said firmly.

They were settled in the restaurant when she took the proper number of coins from her handbag and laid them on the table.

Jeff ignored them all through the meal, which was delicious. Banner had never tasted anything like the thick-crusted chicken pies they were served; in fact, she consumed hers with such relish that Jeff offered to order another.

Banner refused, but only after giving herself a silent lecture on ladylike behavior. There was still the cider to drink—it was hot, spicey stuff with a cinnamon stick floating on top—and she savored that.

"You seem to be enjoying yourself," Jeff observed, as their empty dishes were taken away by a rather flustered young waitress.

Banner smiled. "You are good company, Captain Corbin. Good company indeed."

He looked a little sad, even as he returned her smile. "Am I?"

Banner was quick to assure him that he was.

Jeff touched her hand briefly and then drew back, having thought better of the gesture, it seemed. "I hope you didn't mind my telling Wung Lo to take the dress to

113

our house. Mama and Melissa are hoping you'll spend the night there."

Since Melissa had already broached this subject, in her tenacious fashion, and extracted a promise that Banner would share her room until Christmas Day, she nodded. It was good to know that, for however brief a time, she would not have to return to her hotel.

There was a short silence, which Banner broke with a gasp.

"What is it?" Jeff asked, concerned.

"I forgot to buy Clarence a present!"

He chuckled and shook his head. "We can't have that. What will you buy for our dashing young gambler, Banner?"

She had already decided on a copy of Melissa's zesty dime novel, but she couldn't say that, of course, the girl's writing career being a guarded secret, so she simply shrugged and changed the subject.

When they had left the pleasant restaurant, they went back to the general store, where Banner purchased the intended book. After that, Jeff instructed the carriage driver to take them to the waterfront, where the *Sea Mistress* rode at anchor.

Sensing that Jeff was as proud of that sleek clipper ship as any father would be of a child, Banner enthused over it and asked a number of questions. Her interest was not feigned; she was filled with wonder just to think of all the places Jeff must have visited and all the strange, exotic sights he'd surely seen. He had even been to Hawaii once, he said, his father sailing with him.

"Six months later," he went on, as they walked back up

a wooden wharf toward the waiting carriage and driver, "Papa drowned in the accident."

Banner linked her arm through Jeff's and spoke softly into the quiet of his grief. "Then it's good that you and he made that voyage together, isn't it?"

Jeff nodded and moved as if to touch her hair, then stopped himself. With a sigh, he helped Banner into the carriage and joined her.

Since he seemed to be in a reflective mood, Banner did not attempt further conversation as the carriage made its way back up the hill to the house.

Adam paced the ward from one end to the other, his strides metered by the snores of Clarence King. Good Lord, any minute it would be dark. Where was O'Brien, anyway? Had she taken her month's salary and skipped town after all?

"Adam."

He stopped at the sound of his youngest brother's voice and turned, his hands clenched at his sides.

Keith laughed. "Trying to figure out how long the ward is?"

Adam waved one hand in an impatient gesture but said nothing.

Bracing himself against the framework of the door, Keith folded his arms across his chest and surveyed his brother calmly. Though he had Katherine's fair hair and blue eyes, it seemed to Adam that he resembled their father. He was always so calm, damn him, and so sure of things.

"Jeff asked Banner to have supper with him, Adam.

That's why they're not back yet."

"Who says I was wondering?"

"I do." Keith's blue eyes moved to the sleeping patient nearby. "The boy looks all right. How about leaving him long enough to let me beat you at chess?"

Adam laughed. "You do have faith, pastor."

Keith shrugged and raised one eyebrow. "Faith nothing, big brother. I've been practicing since the harvest. Besides, you have a habit of leaving your queen unguarded."

The remark made Adam think of O'Brien and his brother, and he grimaced. Supper, was it? Damn it all to hell, he hadn't given her time off so she could go gala-vanting off to *supper*—especially with Jeff.

"Stop worrying," admonished Keith, as they started, single file, into the walkway.

"Supper," grumbled Adam, half to himself and half to his brother. "Good Lord, don't we have enough food here?"

Keith chuckled. "What a romantic soul you are," he chided, over one shoulder. "Women like to go out once in a while, Adam."

"Thank you very much, reverend, for that sage observa-tion, but the fact is that O'Brien works for me and she had no business—"

The door joining the walkway to the dining room opened with a gentle shove of Keith's hands. "No business liking Jeff?" he finished.

Adam sighed in exasperation. "Are we going to play chess or not?" he snapped.

Keith indicated the parlor beyond with a slight bow and a sweeping motion of one hand. "After you. Did you buy

Banner a Christmas gift?"

"What if I did?"

They reached the parlor, where the tree stood in its wooden stand waiting to be adorned. In the middle of the rug, Melissa knelt, plundering through a huge box of geegaws with both hands.

She looked up, beaming, as her brothers entered. "This is the best tree ever!"

Adam scowled at the tall, lush pine. His feet were still cold from stomping around in the snow that morning; he'd thought Keith and Jeff would never agree. A whole damned forest to choose from, and they'd acted as though they were looking for the proverbial needle in a haystack.

"It's a fire hazard," he said flatly, as Keith brought the ivory chessmen in their familiar leather case from a drawer in the desk.

Melissa put out her tongue and went back to her rummaging.

"You are a charming fellow today," Keith mocked, as he set the chess pieces atop an ebony-and-brass-inlaid table near the fire.

Adam drew up a chair, sat down heavily, and began to put his pawns in place. He wondered where Banner and Jeff were having supper and what they had ordered to eat.

Presently, when the game was well underway, he glanced at the windows. Even through the green-needled boughs of the Christmas tree, he could see that the snow was still falling. The weather was cold, and the ice on the pond behind the house would be hard and smooth tomorrow—no chance that the traditional skating party would be canceled.

Adam wondered how he would get up the mountain and whether or not they would understand if he was delayed, if he didn't bring the food until the day after.

He moved a bishop out of immediate peril. O'Brien would be a sight, flashing around that frozen pond on her borrowed skates. Maybe her cinnamon hair would fall from its pins and tumble down around her shoulders and her—

On the mantelpiece, the clock made a whirring sound and then pounded out five ponderous chimes. Five o'clock. How long had Jeff and Banner been gone now? Two hours? Three? If Jeff tried to kiss her, would she let him?

Adam gave himself a mental shake and tried to concentrate on the game. What did he care if O'Brien let his brother kiss her?

"Adam."

He looked up, met Keith's knowing blue gaze. "What?"

Keith smiled benignly. "Checkmate," he said.

Banner hid her gifts away in Melissa's room before going over to the hospital in search of Adam. It would have been fun to wrap the presents in the pretty paper and ribbon she'd bought, but there was no time for that now—she'd been gone much too long.

Adam was nowhere in sight when she reached the ward, but Clarence was sitting up in his bed, his bandaged hand resting in his lap, his eyes brooding and faraway.

Banner touched his forehead briefly and smiled, thinking how young he was to be living such a dissolute life. What would his mother say if she knew he'd been stabbed through the hand in a seedy boxhouse?

"Feeling better?"

His answering smile was forced. "My hand don't hurt," he said.

"I think your heart hurts a little, though, doesn't it?" Banner ventured, in a voice crisp enough not to offend his dignity. "Are you missing your family?"

Clarence nodded and averted his eyes. "They've likely been gettin' ready for Christmas since October," he brooded.

Before Banner could offer comment, Melissa waltzed in, pulling Jeff along behind her. "We're all having supper in the parlor tonight," she announced, her smile lingering on an obviously bedazzled Clarence. "You're strong enough to join us, aren't you, Mr. King? Maggie made oyster stew, like always, and after we eat, we're going to trim the tree."

Over Melissa's dark head, Jeff's gaze linked with Banner's and he smiled. Apparently he'd been recruited to assist Clarence to the other side of the house, should that be necessary.

Clarence looked pleasantly befuddled. "Well, I—I mean—"

Banner patted her patient's shoulder. Sometimes, she thought to herself, the best medicines didn't come in bottles or powders at all, but were contained in people. "I'm sure Miss Corbin will be very disappointed if you don't join in," she said.

Clarence's heretofore wan face was shining now. "I'd like to," he said shyly, but then he looked down at his nightshirt and robe and colored. "I can't go like this!"

"Nonsense," said Melissa warmly.

At that, Jeff helped Clarence out of bed, and then Melissa caught his arm in one hand and escorted her guest out of the ward, leaving Banner and Jeff alone.

Banner busied herself with the remaking of Clarence's bed, her own cheeks pink. "You'll be late for supper," she said.

His voice was low. "I've eaten. Remember?"

She nodded, glanced at him, saw that he was leaning against the wall, just inside the walkway door, his arms folded.

"I'm going to have to resign myself to being brotherly where you're concerned, aren't I, Banner?"

Banner bit her lower lip and nodded again. Jeff was so handsome and so funny and so wonderful to be with, but he wasn't Adam and there was no changing that, no matter how much simpler it would have been to love this brother rather than the other.

He turned and walked away, and when Banner went in to watch the trimming of the tree, Jeff wasn't there with the others.

Chapter Six

The morning of December twenty-fourth dawned—still and bright, and the world lay like a slumbering maiden beneath a counterpane of white. Adam Corbin turned from the line of windows at one side of the kitchen and yawned.

"Damn fool," muttered Maggie, angrily stuffing two jars of crabapple preserves into an enormous covered basket.

Adam laughed ruefully and strode to the stove, where hot coffee and a shimmering mirage of heat awaited him. "Did you tell Jim to have the sleigh ready?"

Maggie wrapped two pies in checkered napkins and put them into the basket along with the crabapples and a small roast goose, among other things. "Yes," she snapped.

"Thank you!" Adam snapped back, though his anger was only a mockery and Maggie's was real. She didn't like it when he or any other member of the family kept secrets from her.

In truth, Adam would have liked to confide in Maggie—she was a sensible sort and the burden would be lightened if someone else shared it—but he didn't dare take the chance. Too many people would suffer if word got out.

"You got a squaw up there somewhere?" Maggie demanded, as she did every time he prepared for the journey up the mountain.

Adam took a thoughtful sip from his coffee and brought one booted foot to rest on the bench in front of the fireplace. "Think whatever you like, Maggie."

A cagey look crossed the woman's plain face. "Too bad you won't be around to look after Dr. Banner."

Adam was annoyed. "Jeff and Keith will do that."

"That's what I mean. She's a pretty bit, that one. Every man at the party will be scramblin' to lace her skates and fetch her hot chocolate."

Adam flung his coffee into the fire, sizzling as it sizzled.

Maggie laughed in appreciation. "Don't you lie to me and say you don't care, neither, Adam Corbin, 'cause I know you do. If you want that woman for your own, you'd best stop running up the mountain every three weeks, and

121

tend to your courtin'." There was a short pause, for effect, before she added, "Jeff has an eye for the lass, you know, and *he's* got the good sense to go after what he wants."

Adam lifted his empty mug in an impudent salute. "I wish him every success," he lied. "O'Brien, you see, is everything I never wanted in a woman."

Maggie quivered with indignation and slammed the lid of the basket. "You'd better put on them spectacles you wear for readin' and take another look at her, that's what you'd better do! She's beautiful, that one, and no woman could be better suited to you than she is!"

"She's a born rabblerouser, like Mama," Adam argued quietly. Calmly, he hoped. "The woman I marry—*if* I marry—will be a resident wife, sleeping in my bed at night and sitting at my table in the morning. What she will not do is spend half the year in Olympia, pestering the legislature."

"Or practicing medicine in Port Hastings?" prodded Maggie, who could be very perceptive at times. "I'm surprised at you, Adam. Seems to me that Banner O'Brien would be a real helpmate."

That and more, thought Adam, wondering how much longer he could be around that fiery little Irish minx without forceably bedding her. *Forceably.*

He shook his head in furious despair. What the hell was he thinking thoughts like that for, when he'd never used force with a woman in his life? Damn, he'd never even had to pay a whore, let alone resort to rape.

Muttering to himself, Adam wrenched his coat from a peg near the back door, took up the heavy basket Maggie had packed, however grudgingly, and left without another word.

The sleigh awaited him in front of the stables, hitched to two of the sturdiest horses available. The usual supplies—coffee, flour, sugar, warm clothes—had been loaded behind the seat.

He was just taking up the reins when Jeff rode in on his sorrel gelding. The sight of his brother made Adam laugh in spite of everything—his shirt was open almost to his waist, weather notwithstanding, and he wore no coat. His hair was rumpled and there were smudges of red lip rouge on his chin and just beneath his right nipple.

Jeff looked the sleigh over and slid from his saddle. "Another mysterious journey?" he drawled, and there was anger in his gaze, along with a certain broken satisfaction.

Adam ignored the question. This was ground they had covered before, and much as he would have liked to tell Jeff everything, he couldn't. Especially not Jeff. "You look like you've been held prisoner in a brothel for the last two weeks," he jibed, instead.

Jeff grinned as a stable hand came to lead his horse into the barn. "Actually, it was only about half an hour," he retorted. "Before that, I was willing."

Adam laughed again and brought down the reins with a determined motion. Beneath his amusement was the conviction that if he got to pondering the circumstances that had driven his brother to spend the night on the *Silver Shadow* there would be a loud argument.

Happily, Banner pronounced Clarence King well enough to get dressed and spend the day at the pond with everyone else. "No skating, though," she added, wagging an index finger in warning. "If you fell, you could reopen your wounds."

Clarence promised that he wouldn't skate and was joyfully flinging back his covers to dress when Banner left the ward for the outer office.

Francelle was there, at her infernal typewriting machine, looking quietly vicious. "Adam isn't here!" she snarled before Banner had a chance to speak at all.

"I know that," Dr. O'Brien retorted, though she had, until then, nursed a certain foolish hope that Adam might have changed his mind and stayed. "Are there any appointments scheduled today?"

"No," answered Francelle, bristling. "After all, the skating party starts at ten."

Banner drew a deep breath. "Francelle, people do hurt themselves and fall ill, even when there is a party going on."

Francelle shrugged. "Everyone will know to look for you at the pond, even if you don't write where you are on the slateboard outside," she said, in tones that betrayed a profound hope that Dr. O'Brien would be called away.

"You don't like me very much, do you, Francelle?"

Long fingers poised over the typewriting keys, the girl shook her head. "Actually, no."

"Why not?"

"I saw Adam kissing you."

Banner blushed a little, remembering. "And?"

"And I knew him first. I love Adam."

"I see. And does he return the sentiment?"

Despair shimmered in Francelle's velvet-brown eyes. "He thinks I'm a child—a *child,* and I'm seventeen! Papa said the best way to suit myself for marriage to a doctor

124

was to work in his office, but—"

Banner suddenly felt sorry for Francelle, but because she knew the girl would not welcome her sympathy, she disguised it. "I'm glad the snow stopped."

Francelle didn't even glance at the window, with its tracery of frost, and she clearly wasn't going to be diverted from the subject at hand. "He has a woman, you know. Nobody knows who she is, but he visits her once a month, no matter what."

Banner forced herself to smile, to look as if she didn't care. "So?"

"So don't you feel kind of—well—*cheap,* going around kissing somebody else's fellow?"

Fury sang in Banner's veins and she stiffened, but before she could answer back Melissa came in, her dark curls glistening around a flushed, animated face.

"Breakfast is ready!" she sang out. "And then we skate!"

"I've eaten," said Francelle in lofty tones, turning back to her machine.

Melissa caught hold of Banner's arm and fairly dragged her out through the ward and the long walkway. "Don't mind Francelle," she whispered. "She wants Adam in the worst way, and he's so oblivious to her that he'd probably hang his coat on her if she stood still long enough."

Banner's laugh was thin, for Francelle's words were still ringing in her mind. *He has a woman—nobody knows who she is—he visits her once a month.*

The skating pond was hidden away in the woods in back of the house, and there was already a giant bonfire going at its edge when Banner and Melissa arrived.

Several dozen people were there, the women watching and calling out encouragement, the men sweeping away the snow that covered the ice. Soon enough, the first skaters were venturing out.

Pure glee swelled in Banner O'Brien's throat at the thought of skating again—it was a pleasure she hadn't enjoyed since her childhood. She sat down on a pine log, beside Melissa, and began undoing her shoes.

But the thick gloves she was wearing made her fingers awkward, and she was still struggling with the last buttons on her shoes when Jeff suddenly appeared before her. "Allow me," he said.

Banner extended one foot in queenly acquiescence, while Melissa bounded off the log and made her way toward the pond, eager to skate.

Jeff's hands were deft, and he had Banner's shoes off and her skates on and laced in no time. Rising from his haunches, he suavely offered his arm.

The ice was bumpy in places, and Banner was wobbly, not having skated in so long a time, but Jeff managed to hold her up until her muscles remembered the mechanics of the sport and came into play.

All around, other skaters whizzed by, like colorful etchings from a picture book, and the sky above was a pearlescent blue. The crackling bonfire and the scent of the surrounding pine trees added to the festive nature of the scene.

"Do you have a party like this every Christmas?" asked Banner, smiling up into Jeff's slightly wan face.

He nodded, handsome in his woolly brown coat and

dark trousers. "If it's cold enough, yes."

Just then Katherine flashed by, laughing, her arm linked through that of Francelle's father, the senator.

"I didn't think she liked him," Banner remarked in a whisper.

Jeff grinned. "She says he's pompous and unbending," he confided conspiratorially. "But she wants to make sure that the suffrage bill gets proper consideration in the legislature."

"Will it?"

He considered. "I suppose. Even if it becomes law, though, it will still have to withstand the inevitable public outrage."

Banner frowned, sorry she'd pursued the subject but unable to give up the chase. "I honestly do not understand why anyone should be outraged, as you put it. After all—"

Jeff held up one finger. "Wait. You don't need to convince me, Banner. Believe me, I'm on your side."

They were stopped now, facing each other in the flood of happy skaters. "Even though liquor and brothels might be outlawed as a result of granting suffrage?"

Almost imperceptibly, Jeff winced. "Liquor can be smuggled into the country," he said after a moment. "And a man wouldn't need to go to a brothel if he—"

Banner blushed and skated away.

"If he had a wife!" Jeff yelled after her, and in seconds he was beside her again, laughing at her with his eyes, guiding her hand through the crook of his elbow.

Banner tried to ignore the amused glances of the other skaters. "Lots of those men have wives," she whispered

127

furiously. Given her experiences with Sean, she was in a position to know. "And they still go to brothels!"

"When I have a wife, I'll be faithful to her," he said.

"You say that now," Banner scoffed, and a part of her spirit, untroubled in the years since Sean had gone to jail, pulsed in rhythm with an old pain.

Jeff stopped her again, forced her to face him. "Someone hurt you very badly, didn't they, Banner?"

She swallowed hard and nodded her head.

"Who?"

"I can't tell you that," she whispered miserably. "Not now, anyway. Please, Jeff."

He touched her cheek with a gloved hand and nodded. "All right, Banner—all right."

"Thank you."

"Banner!" Melissa came to an impressive stop inches away, her cheeks glowing, her eyes bright. "Come with me—I need you."

"What's the matter?"

Melissa flung an eloquent look at her brother and grimaced. "Jiggers, do I have to explain it now? I just need you, that's all!"

Banner followed her young friend off the ice and then trudged awkwardly after her until they were well into the dense woods. "What—"

Melissa stepped behind a hazelnut bush and crouched.

"Couldn't you have done this alone?" Banner demanded, annoyed.

"Of course not," chimed Melissa. "It would have been a violation of the code of womanhood."

"Good Lord."

128

Melissa was righting her drawers and arranging her red woolen skirts. "Do you like Jeff?"

Banner rolled her eyes. "Yes. Don't you?"

Melissa giggled. "I have to, goose—he's my brother. Do you like him enough to kiss him and things like that?"

"No!"

"Good."

"What do you mean, 'good'?"

They were making their way back toward the pond now, shaky on their skates.

"I want you to marry Adam," Melissa announced, by way of an answer, and she was so matter of fact that Banner laughed out loud.

"I see."

Melissa frowned prettily. "I wonder if he'd stop calling you O'Brien all the time, if you were his wife."

"Yes," answered Banner, warm and kind of achy at the thought of being Adam's wife. "He'd probably start calling me Corbin."

Melissa laughed. "You're right," she said, and then, reaching the pond's edge again, the little scamp blithely skated away, leaving Banner on her own.

"Hello, again," said Temple Royce from beside Banner.

Taken aback, Banner said nothing. It was surprising to encounter Mr. Royce here, considering the attitude Jeff had taken toward him the day before during the shopping expedition.

Mr. Royce spread his elegantly gloved hands. Somehow he had divined Banner's thoughts. "Mrs. Corbin invites the entire community to events like this. Since they're always held outdoors, she doesn't have to count the silverware afterward."

Banner was embarrassed and changed the subject. "How is Dr. Henderson?"

"He's recovering. How are you?"

Banner gave some inane answer and then spotted Jeff out of the corner of one eye. He was approaching rapidly. To avoid the confrontation she knew was coming, she muttered a polite farewell to Mr. Royce and skated toward her friend.

"What did he want?" Jeff scowled.

Banner bridled a little. "For heaven's sake, he was just passing the time of day!"

Jeff subsided, but only grudgingly. "I'm sorry," he said, at great length.

Banner smiled at him. "Could we go and stand by the fire awhile? I'm cold."

At the fireside, Banner talked with Jenny while Jeff went off in search of hot chocolate. But Dr. O'Brien's heart was far, far away, on the mountain where Adam was visiting his mistress.

At midday, Adam stopped the sleigh. The mountain was silent around him, except for the snorting of the tired horses and the occasional whisper of snow dropping from a tree bough.

He shouted, and his breath made a white plume in the air. There was no answer.

A familiar fear rose within him, but he fought it down. They were around somewhere, watching. Waiting. Knowing.

Adam found a tin cup and the metal bottle of coffee

Maggie always sent along. After two sips, he drew the flask from the inside pocket of his coat and added a stiff shot of brandy.

Fifteen or twenty minutes later he gave the horses the feed he'd brought along and shouted again.

This time, his greeting was returned.

He set aside his coffee and began unloading the sleigh, stacking everything on a patch of snowless, needle-softened ground under a Douglas fir. The loamy scent of this little speck of earth soothed him, reminded him that spring would come eventually.

When the food and clothing and supplies had all been carried to the base of the tree, he settled back against the rough trunk to wait. Sometimes they came; sometimes they didn't.

This time, they didn't. After waiting over half an hour longer, Adam scanned the mountainside one final time, muttered angrily, and got back into the sleigh. The jingling of the harness bells made him think of O'Brien, made him long for her with an intensity that bordered on pain.

Added to this was his despair. He opened the flask again and drank directly from it this time, swallowing brandy in searing gulps that gradually eased the knowing, the hurting.

When the pain came back, he endured it.

The Corbin Christmas tree was a shimmering thing, though there were no candles in its boughs. It was covered with intricate, fragile ornaments and shiny spirals of gold and silver foil. Ribbons graced it, as did the magnificent star at its top.

Banner tucked her carefully wrapped gifts into the branches, with the others that were already hidden there and stepped back to admire the effect. It felt good to celebrate the holy birth again, to have someone to give presents to.

"Have your toes thawed out yet? Mine haven't."

Banner started. She'd thought that she was alone in the parlor, but now she saw Keith sitting in a chair near, the fireplace, his bare feet stretched out toward the blaze.

She smiled. The house was very quiet, now that the party was over and the family had gone off to hear midnight mass. "I'm quite warm, thank you."

He stood in a mannerly fashion and then sat down again, indicating the chair next to his with a gesture of invitation.

Banner took the chair and folded her hands in her lap.

"Why didn't you go to church with everyone else, Dr. O'Brien?"

Even though she ached inside—no matter how she tried not to notice, Adam wasn't back from the mountain yet—Banner shrugged offhandedly.

"Are you an infidel, like me?"

Banner considered her divorce from Sean. "I guess I am," she said.

"Aren't you going to ask how I managed to grow up in a fine Catholic family and end up as a Methodist?"

Banner smiled. "I'm sure it's none of my business. Why is it that there are no candles on your Christmas tree?"

Keith laughed at the deft change of subject. "Adam won't allow it. Too much danger of fire."

Adam. Now, how had *he* gotten into this conversation, when she had been trying so hard not to think about him?

"Does he always dictate such things?"

"Usually. Despite her modern thinking, Mama often defers to him. For all intents and purposes, he's the head of the family."

"Adam is something of a tyrant, I think," Banner said gently, her mind straying up the mountain again, in search of her heart.

"I've never heard anyone condemned so tenderly," observed Keith. "What do you really think of him, Banner?"

"You won't tell?"

"You know I won't, Banner."

"I think I love Adam."

Keith gave a startling shout of joy and bounded out of his chair to face Banner. "If he asked you to marry him, would you accept?"

Banner blushed. She'd never intended to love again, let alone marry, but she hadn't counted on Adam Corbin, either. "Yes," she said miserably.

Keith shouted again and then bent to kiss her forehead soundly. "Tell Adam how you feel, Banner."

"I couldn't!"

"Why not?"

"It would be *fast!* And suppose he said—"

"You might be surprised at what he'd say, Banner. Adam cares for you."

"But it's only been a week since we met!"

Keith turned away, took a small package from the mantelpiece. After a glance at the clock there, he came and placed the gift in Banner's lap. "Adam asked me to give you this if he wasn't back by now."

Banner's heart surged into her throat and thumped a mad cadence there. Her fingers trembled as she undid the narrow ribbon and the tissue paper, and tears burned in her eyes when she lifted the lid of the wooden box inside and saw the pendant.

It was a shamrock formed of gold filligree and suspended from a delicate chain.

Keith kissed the top of her bowed head and discreetly left the room.

For a time, Banner was too overcome to rise out of her chair. Presently, however, a distant metallic clamor brought her out of her dreamy state.

After clasping the beautiful pendant around her neck, the skirts of her blue taffeta dress rustling musically, Banner made her way through the house to the walkway. There, she quickened her step, for she heard another clatter followed by a thundering, continuous crash.

Clarence was snoring in his bed, undisturbed, so Banner hurried on.

She found Adam in one of the examining rooms, and the sight of him made her forget the lovely shamrock at her throat. His shirt was open to his midsection, his hair was rumpled, and there was a stubble of new beard darkening his face.

He weaved unsteadily and grinned. "Hello, O'Brien," he said, in the singular slur of the hopelessly inebriated, "and Happy Christmas to you."

Banner looked at the variety of surgical instruments scattered over the floor. "What happened?"

Adam shrugged. "Spilled the damn things. Will you sleep with me tonight, O'Brien?"

Banner was grateful for the task of gathering the instruments; it gave her a means of hiding her flaming face. "No, I will not."

With rather a lot of difficulty, Adam knelt, facing her. Had it not been for the pain shifting in his ink-blue eyes, she would have been furious.

"Why not?"

"We aren't married," replied Banner, setting instruments on the tray that had obviously been dropped with them.

He caught his hand under her chin, forced her to meet his gaze. "Is that your price, O'Brien? Marriage?"

Banner wanted to cry, but instead she nodded her head, knowing all the while that she should have said she didn't have a price.

The awful truth was that, where this man was concerned, she did.

Adam gripped her shoulders and pulled her to her feet. "O'Brien, I need you. I—"

Banner closed her eyes, but the words she had hoped to hear were not spoken. After a time, and against her better judgment, she lifted her hands to his face. "You need coffee, Adam. And sleep."

"Marry me."

Banner sighed. "You're drunk. We can't—"

Adam's powerful shoulders moved in a disjointed looking shrug. "Why not? Do you already have a husband, O'Brien?"

She stood on tiptoe, kissed the beard-roughened cleft in his chin. "No, I don't have a husband. But I did once, Adam. His name was Sean."

Adam swayed, looking benignly puzzled. "Sean?"

135

Banner nodded. "I'm divorced, Adam."

"I don't care."

"But, the church would. They wouldn't recognize a marriage between you and me."

"I don't care," he repeated.

"You will when you're sober."

He shuddered, and a soft, soblike sound escaped him. "Hold me, O'Brien," he said.

Banner held him, longed to draw the pain from him, into herself. "I love you," she whispered.

"Then marry me."

Banner could only hope that the cold night air would sober him. "All right, Adam. All right. But where is this marriage to take place? We haven't a license, or—"

Adam found his suitcoat, which smelled of brandy and pine pitch, and draped it over her shoulders. "Stop worrying, O'Brien," he said. Then he dragged her out into that cold, snowy night.

"Adam—"

He was holding her hand, dragging her toward the stables. There, he hitched up a horse and buggy with surprising dexterity, considering his state of drunkenness.

This done, he lifted a wide-eyed Banner into the buggy seat and scrambled up beside her.

It didn't look as though the night air was helping.

"Adam, please," she pleaded as they started down the slippery, rutted hill. "We can't do this! You're drunk."

He belched.

Banner sank back in the seat and knitted her fingers together. What if Adam didn't sober up before they reached their destination, whatever it was? What would

136

she do then?

"Suppose I say I won't marry you after all?" she asked, testing the waters.

Adam shrugged and his white teeth flashed in a grin. "Then I'll take you anyway, O'Brien. Right here in the buggy."

Banner blushed with fury and a scandalous measure of anticipation. "You wouldn't."

He moved to draw the buggy to a stop alongside the road. "Want me to prove that I would?"

"No!"

"Then you'd better marry me."

It was then that Banner O'Brien faced the distasteful facts. She hadn't been hoping that Adam would get sober at all. Insane as it was, she did want to marry him, to share his life and his bed, to bear his children.

She said nothing until she realized that they were headed into Water Street. "Wait a minute! Where—"

Adam laughed. "You can tell our grandchildren that we were married in a brothel, O'Brien."

"A *brothel?*"

The buggy was jostling down over the hillside that led to the *Silver Shadow.* The converted ship's many windows were merrily alight in the snowstorm, flinging soft-edged golden squares onto the ground, and the raucous voices aboard rose in an exuberant rendering of a carol.

"Adam!" Desperately, Banner caught his unshaven face in her hands. "Adam Corbin, are you listening to me? No. Do you hear me? No!"

He climbed out of the rig and dragged her after him, and she struggled as he carried her up the boarding ramp. Onto the decks of Water Street's finest bordello.

"Adam!"

He nuzzled her neck, nibbled at her earlobe. "One way or another, O'Brien," he vowed, "I'll have you tonight. You might as well have the paper to make it legal."

Banner was dizzy; her head swam and her blood sang and her womb was melting within her. She'd tried to reason with Adam, hadn't she? She'd told him about her previous marriage, she'd pointed out his drunken state. What more could she do?

He carried her to the end of a long, dark hallway and set her on her feet. She trembled as one of his hands came to cup brazenly over her right breast.

A low chuckle rose from Adam's throat and rumbled in the cold, dark air. He pushed back the suitcoat he'd put over her shoulders and tugged at the front of her good blue taffeta dress. Her nipples hardened as he drew down her camisole, baring her.

"Make your choice, O'Brien. Marry me, or I'll take you here." He bent his head, tormented one distended nipple with warm lips.

She should have struggled, she knew that. But she couldn't, for Banner's wanting was as great or greater than his. She arched her back and gasped with delight as he made a banquet of her swollen breast.

And Adam was pressing against her; she could feel the hardness of him. He turned to plunder the other breast while caressing the first with his hand.

Banner whimpered. Would he take her here, as he'd threatened, against the wall?

She must have spoken the question aloud, for he left his

feast to nibble at her earlobe again. "Here," he said.

Banner was in agony—sweet, tumultuous, irrational agony that drove her on toward something she didn't understand, for all her learning. Something she had never experienced before.

Adam bent again, slowly, and softly kissed each of her pleading nipples. Then he pulled the camisole back into place, along with the upper part of her dress, and knocked on the door that was inches away.

"Who's there?" demanded a raspy, aged voice.

Adam yelled his name, causing Banner to wince.

"Come in then," came the brusque answer.

Inside the spacious, well-lit room, a grizzled old man sat at a table with a tassled cloth, playing a solitary game of cards. He wore a frayed suit and spectacles, and his hair was combed to cover a bald spot.

"Well?" barked the elderly gentleman.

"I want to marry this woman," Adam replied flatly.

The old man took in Banner's mussed hair and rumpled dress and grinned, revealing two gold teeth.

"Looks like you'd better. All right—you fill out the paper, and I'll say the words."

Adam and Banner both signed a remarkably ornate form that even had places for their photographs, should they wish to add them.

"Who is that man?" Banner whispered, as the fellow went out to recruit the necessary witnesses.

Adam smiled fondly. "He's a justice of the peace. Usually, he marries sailors to prostitutes."

"Wonderful," wailed Banner, who was having second thoughts now that her blood was almost back to its normal temperature and her insides were solid again. "Adam, we can't do this."

He lifted one ebony eyebrow. "Must I convince you again, Shamrock?"

Banner had no doubt that he would, there and then. "I'm convinced!" she said quickly.

The justice returned, followed by a prostitute and a man wearing a ruffled shirt and a diamond ring. After clearing his throat and marshaling everyone into position, he opened his black book and began the ceremony.

Within five minutes, it was over.

Adam grasped Banner's hand and strode out, dragging her along the hallway and out onto the deck. There, he swung her up into his arms again and carried her down the ramp to the buggy.

Banner didn't open her eyes until he thrust her onto the seat. She looked up at the *Silver Shadow* and down at her ringless hand and wondered what had possessed her to do such a stupid and impetuous thing.

The drive back to the dark, slumbering house on the hill was passed in a daze. Banner alternately rejoiced and despaired, smiled and wept.

Inside the stables, Adam lifted her from the buggy and drew her close. Again, she felt the warm granite of his need, the power of his thighs. Within minutes, perhaps, he would be moving upon her, claiming her as his wife.

He kissed her at leisure, his hands cupping her bottom, pressing her to him.

At last, however, Adam broke away and unhitched the horse. When the animal had been led to its stall and fed, he gripped Banner's elbow and propelled her out of the stables, across the snow-swept expanse of the backyard, and into the kitchen.

They traversed that room and the back stairway in silence and, on the second floor, Adam again lifted her off her feet. Without preamble, he carried his wife into his bedroom and thrust the door shut with one heel.

A fire had been lit on the hearth, but there was no other light in the room. Shadows danced on Adam's face as Banner looked up at him, and he might have been either an angel or a devil, this husband of hers.

Adam's hands came to remove the suitcoat she wore; it floated silently to the floor.

He undid the catches at the back of her taffeta dress, reaching around her to do so, and she let her head fall back in wanton surrender, felt the heat of his gaze through her camisole as the dress slid away. The undergarment came gently over her head, the pins were pulled from her heavy hair.

She heard him groan as the mane tumbled to her waist, and she reveled in this small power that was hers.

With gentle hands, Adam smoothed her hair back over her shoulders and caressed her cheeks, her upper arms, her breasts. And while he touched her, he spoke softly, wickedly, of all the places and all the ways in which he would pleasure her.

Banner shuddered and, of her own accord, untied the strings that held her drawers in place. Easily, she stepped out of them, standing before her husband, naked now, except for the shamrock pendant at her throat.

Adam touched the necklace with the tip of one finger, went on to touch the rosy gems beneath.

Banner gasped as he bent to suckle at one breast.

He savored that one nubbin as though it were a sweet morsel, and the warmth penetrated Banner's flesh and mingled with the blood pounding through her veins. "Have me," she pleaded shamelessly.

He chuckled. "Oh, no—not yet. Not—yet."

Banner trembled and arched her back, silently offering herself to him.

Adam flicked at her with his tongue, ruthlessly taking what she gave. And when he had plundered both breasts, he knelt.

He parted the nest of silken curls with cautious fingers, found its sheltered secret with his tongue. Banner groaned.

"No—oh, Adam—"

He punctuated his answer with soft, wicked kisses. "You—are—mine now."

Banner cried out softly as his lips caught at her, taking full and inexorable possession, driving her and yet offering a fierce sort of comfort, too.

Adam drew on her with gentle ferocity, pressing her legs apart, kneading the yielding flesh on her buttocks. He pulled her down and down, until she was kneeling over him, writhing in search of a freedom she had no desire to find.

His strong hands came to her hips, forcing her to give the strange, sweet nectar he sought so mercilessly.

Banner's breath grew rapid and harsh, and beneath it coursed a low, primitive whine. Sweat shimmered on her upper lip and between her breasts, and then a sundering heat exploded inside her like a sunburst, centering in the nubbin Adam was still tormenting with his tongue and spreading to reverberate against the insides of her hip-bones. From there, it streamed down into her thighs and up into her weighted, pulsing breasts.

In the molten glory of her release, Banner sobbed out Adam's name. He brought her gently down from the crimson skies with treacherous kisses—kisses that would soon send her soaring again.

Chapter Seven

Banner could not recall being lifted and placed on the bed; it seemed, rather, that she had floated there. A singular satisfaction permeated her flesh and her spirit, and her breathing was still rapid.

She was a doctor. She should have understood human anatomy and the pleasures that could be wrought by skillful kisses and caresses, but she hadn't. Never, for all the times she'd suffered beneath Sean Malloy's heavy, straining frame, had she felt this fierce yet delicate fire that Adam had ignited within her.

He undressed quietly in the darkness, joined her on the bed. His fingers played over her breasts, her rib cage, her satiny stomach. He had drained her of every essence and he had yet to take her fully.

"P-please," she managed. "Now?"

Adam withdrew his hand to light a lamp at the bedside, and there were dark blue, smoldering embers in his eyes as he savored her nakedness. "I want to see you, Banner," he said, in a voice so low that she almost thought she'd imagined it. "I want to know that I'm pleasing you."

Banner shuddered as his great, gentle hands came back

to her breasts, whimpered as he plucked the nipples into readiness with his finger. "I—oooooh . . ."

Adam chuckled as he released the pebble-hard morsels to take pillows from the head of the bed and fit them under Banner's hips. She was more vulnerable than ever now, raised to him like an offering, and the sensations this stirred in her were woundingly beautiful.

She closed her eyes in a daze of passion as he began to stroke her again, circling her nectar-laden breasts with magical fingers, making patterns of fire on her middle, lifting her knees high so that she was spread for him, a tender banquet.

But Adam did not come to feast. Instead, he plied the quivering rosebud of flesh with his thumb, delighting in her soft, eager whimpers.

Everything within Banner leaped when his fingers sheathed themselves in her pulsing warmth, and her hips began to rise and fall with the thrusts of his hand.

She tried to draw her knees together—this pleasure was too keen, too fierce to be borne—but he would not allow her this defense or any other. No, he knelt between her legs, blocking one knee with his body and holding the other at bay with his free hand.

And still Adam plundered her sacred depths with tender savagery, smiling as she tossed her head back and forth in frenzy and thrust her hips ever upward, wanting more of him and still more.

Tears brimmed in her lashes and spilled down her cheeks as the passion grew to intolerable proportions. "Adam—oh, my God—"

"Let it happen, Banner," he said, over her gasping cries.

"It's right, it's good—let it happen."

Banner's entire being buckled now, in rhythm with the ceaseless, searing motions of his hand. A haze blurred her vision and an inferno raged within her and then she was sent spinning into the night skies, free of her body.

Adam brought her back to earth with kisses, pagan kisses that branded the spoils of their battle, the insides of her knees, the glowing smoothness of her belly. How much more of this could she bear?

In self-defense, Banner grasped the heated, imposing shaft that was his manhood in both hands. He groaned and fell away, still on his knees, and she somehow found the strength to lift herself from her prone position and plot vengeance.

Operating on instinct, she bent her head and nibbled at him, and her reward was a gutteral groan that seemed to rise from the darkest depths of him. As he had shown no mercy, she was ruthless with him, tormenting even as he pleaded.

Finally, in desperation, Adam thrust her backward and entered her. She had expected pain—there had always been pain with Sean—but even after the glories she'd already experienced that night, Adam's conquering was a surprise.

This pleasure was the most ferocious of all.

Their bodies were one, woven together like the strands of a rope tossing and buckling in the wind. Frantic, Banner wrapped her legs around Adam and held on as the sun flew apart and the moon splintered and all the universe trembled with the resulting shocks.

They slept for a time, as one, exhausted, then awakened

to love again. Now, Banner sat astride her husband, facing him, suckling dark nipples hidden in a carpet of ebony down.

Banner's name was torn from Adam in a hoarse cry, and he grew within her until she feared she could not contain him. She pressed him backward until he was prone and rode him wildly, professions of her love for him falling from her lips like a fevered litany.

And when their triumph came, in a sizzling, brutal fusion, their separate cries blended into one.

Adam opened his eyes to the insistent dawn, saw that Banner was sleeping beside him, one hip curved beneath the blankets, one delectable nipple peeking at him over the edge of the sheet.

He groaned and spread his legs slightly to accommodate the inevitable response. His tongue was thick and his head pounded.

God, he'd been drunk, and he'd seduced O'Brien in the bargain. What could he say to her? And how the hell was he going to explain this to his family?

Banner stirred beside him, and the one bare nipple taunted him, puckering in the chill air. Unable to resist such an inviting tidbit, he lifted himself onto one elbow and circled the pink confection with the tip of his tongue.

O'Brien whimpered and opened her wide, shamrock green eyes. Then she cupped one hand under the plump breast to offer it.

Adam nursed at his leisure, clinging to the sweet nubbin even as Banner sat up. He was cradled in her arms now, like an infant, but he didn't care. He craved the intangible nourishment he drew from her.

Banner's hand moved gently in his hair, pressing him close, and little cries of soft surrender came from her as he took his pleasure. After a long time, she guided him to the other breast and brushed his lips with the hardened nipple until he groaned and took it hungrily.

His gentle greed made her gasp and arch her back, then croon with soft contentment.

When Adam had taken his fill at her breast, he wanted more. While she watched him, wide-eyed but trusting, he lifted her legs, one by one, to drape them over his shoulders.

Adam kissed his way into the silken, sanctioned place, and his spirit soared when she cried out a fevered welcome. He looked down the length of her, watching the passion play in her beautiful face.

And to intensify this, he lapped at her, the way a kitten might lap at sweet cream. She squirmed and chanted his name, and her eyes were glazed emeralds, pleading a cause of their own.

Adam chuckled and ceased the lapping to nibble.

Banner's hips seemed to take wing; her hands knotted into fists and pounded at the bedding as she rode the forbidden pleasure. When she pleaded, he suckled until her small body quivered with release.

She fell from him, shuddering, and welcomed him when he came to her for final solace.

As he moved upon her, sheathed in her warmth, forever marked by her fire, he realized that he loved her.

It might, Adam thought, as his mind and soul collided.

147

within him, be a good thing if he married O'Brien.

"What?" Adam rasped, staring at Banner from across the wide, rumpled bed.

She swallowed. He didn't remember! She drew the blankets up under her chin with one hand and reached for the certificate, which she had found sometime during the night and placed on the bedside table.

The document sailed through space and wafted down onto his naked, imperious chest.

Scowling, Adam took it up and read it. "Is this a joke, O'Brien?"

Hot tears welled in Banner's eyes. She'd known this would happen all along, but that didn't make it any easier to bear.

"We w-were married on the *Silver Shadow*. D-don't you remember?"

Adam flung the proof aside. "I remember three things," he growled, glaring up at the ceiling. "One: I was drunk. Two: we made love. Three: you weren't a virgin, O'Brien."

Color ached in Banner's cheeks. "I told you, Adam—I explained about—"

In a sudden, terrifying motion, Adam hurled back the blankets and shot out of bed. "About your sordid past?" he snarled, wrenching on his clothes.

Banner couldn't have been hurt more cruelly if he had struck her. She'd told him about Sean and her divorce—she'd told him. It wasn't her fault that he'd refused to hear!

"Damn you to hell, Adam Corbin!" she whispered. "I—"

But he was at the door now, his clothes on but in disarray, his hand on the knob. "You ought to have cards printed, O'Brien," he rasped. *"Always a gentle welcome."*

Banner shrieked, in her outrage and her pain, and he strode suddenly toward the bed. In one terrifying grab, he caught the filligree shamrock in his hand.

"Until now," he whispered savagely, "I've prided myself on the fact that I'd never paid a woman for what you just gave." He let the pendant fall, cold and oddly heavy, against her stinging flesh. "Now it appears that I have, doesn't it, O'Brien?"

Banner flung herself at him, fists flying, wild in her injury, but he subdued her easily, his hands biting into the delicate skin of her wrists.

"You wanted to be a wife so badly that you would trick me into marriage," he went on in a brutal undertone. "Well, it's a wife you'll be, Shamrock."

Banner's throat thickened, and she stared at him, aghast. "W-What do you mean?"

"I mean, you little sorceress, that I intend to get full satisfaction from this marriage, when and where I want it. And let me assure you, dearest, that there is no end to my imagination. Do you understand me?"

Furious, Banner broke away from his hold and began gathering up her own clothes. She understood all too well, but she wasn't going to give him the victory by saying so—she'd die first.

Adam grabbed the drawers from her hands and ripped them asunder in one vicious motion. "You won't need these," he said in a hissing growl, and then he flung the pieces of the garment into the crimson embers on the hearth.

Banner trembled with impotent rage, and her heart beat not in her chest, as it should, but in her face. Words eluded her, and her husband had stormed out of the bedroom, slamming the door behind him, long before she could move from where she stood.

Adam avoided the front of the house, realizing that it was Christmas morning and members of his family would no doubt already be gathering there. He was relieved to find the kitchen empty when he entered it by the back stairway.

He went to the windows and looked out at the snowy countryside and the mountain. Why in hell had he treated O'Brien that way when he loved her? Was he insane?

In the distance, he heard Melissa laughing. The sound was soothing, though it did not prompt him to face his family and make the necessary announcement.

I married O'Brien last night, he imagined himself saying. Of course, I don't remember proposing or saying the binding words, but she has the license, so it must be true.

Memories wriggled in his mind like fingers: O'Brien with snow on her nose. O'Brien sharing his bed, touching him in more ways than just the physical, ways he had not begun to imagine before that. O'Brien pleasuring him until he was half-blind with the need of her.

O'Brien, O'Brien, O'Brien.

And who had had her first? Who was the man who had taught her to love like that, so fiercely and so well?

Again, Adam lifted his eyes to the mountain. There was someone he had to see, had to talk with—if he expected to retain his sanity.

For the first time in his career, Adam Corbin walked away from his duties without once looking back, without leaving word of his whereabouts or making provisions for his patients.

Heedless of his uncombed hair and unshaven face, he grabbed a coat from the pegs near the door and left the house.

Christmas was a mockery for Banner Corbin. She gave gifts, she accepted them, she ate sumptuous food that lay like sawdust in the pit of her stomach.

Adam was gone, and while his family didn't seem particularly concerned, Banner grieved.

Once in a while during that hectic day, she considered standing up and saying that she was Adam's wife now, but she couldn't bring herself to do it. If *he'd* thought the marriage a trick and a sham and all but called her a prostitute, what would their reaction be?

Jeff was annoyed. Blast it all, it was Christmas and Banner was downstairs looking like someone had drawn her soul out through her great, green eyes.

Where in blazes was Adam?

Pausing outside his brother's bedroom door, Jeff sighed. Adam would have to decide, once and for, all, whether he wanted Banner O'Brien or not. If he didn't, his younger brother was more than willing to step into the breach.

After drawing one deep breath, Jeff rapped at the heavy door with the knuckles of his left hand. There was no answer, but that didn't mean anything—Adam often

151

ignored such things, especially when he was brooding.

Prepared for a surly objection, Jeff opened the door and stepped inside. Adam wasn't there, but he had been. The bedclothes were churned into knots, the pillows were on the floor. . . .

Jeff surveyed the wreckage uneasily. He scanned the room again, and that was when he saw the certificate, lying forgotten on the rug nearest the bed.

A muscle strained in the base of his stomach as he bent to take the document into his hand. It seemed to weigh a thousand pounds, that gaudy bit of paper, and a small eternity passed between the time Jeff picked it up and the time he read it: "This will certify that Dr. Adam Corbin and Miss Banner O'Brien were joined in marriage, this twenty-fourth day of December . . ."

Jeff closed his eyes, crumpled the certificate without knowing that he did so. She'd said she loved Adam, and he'd felt the fire between Banner and his brother.

Why, then, was it such a brutal surprise to know that they were married?

Muttering, Jeff Corbin flung the wadded marriage license onto the bed and turned away from this most wounding proof of his brother's victory.

Closing the door of Adam's room with a gentleness that was totally foreign to everything he was feeling, he decided that, weather permitting, the *Sea Mistress* would set sail that very day.

Banner lifted the snow-glass and turned it upside down and then right side up again, so that the little specks of white inside showered down around a miniature unicorn with silver hooves.

"That's pretty," said Katherine, in a soft voice that invited confidences.

Banner smiled wanly. "Jeff gave it to me."

Katherine helped herself to a cup of hot chocolate from the china pot resting on a sidetable and sat down beside Banner, her eyes fixed on the quiet splendor of the Christmas tree. "I'm rather a good secret keeper, you know," she remarked. "Is there anything you would like to tell me?"

Banner's vision blurred, and she set the lovely snow-glass aside with a thump. "It's Christmas," she said. "I wouldn't want to spoil it."

"You couldn't do that, Banner. Even with Adam away, it was a grand day."

Banner's throat was thick with unshed tears. Adam hated her, and he was probably on the mountain, with his woman, at that very minute. As far as she was concerned, the day had been an unqualified disaster.

Katherine's hand came to rest on hers, gentle and reassuring. "He'll be back, Banner."

A surge of anger went through Banner, despite her tender grief. "I hate him!" she blurted. "I hate Adam and I don't care if he never comes back!"

Having made this foolish announcement, Banner Corbin burst into tears.

Katherine set aside her chocolate and drew the younger woman into a motherly embrace. "There, there—you don't hate him at all, and that's the problem, isn't it?"

"Yes!" wailed Banner.

"I declare," breathed Katherine, her arms still around the

woman she didn't know was her son's own wife, "I love my Adam with every speck and fiber in me, but sometimes I'd like nothing better than to take a buggywhip to him!"

Banner sobbed harder, and at the windows, a drizzling rain washed away the scalloped trimming of snow.

By morning, the world was an ugly place, dressed in mud and the occasional tatter of dirty snow. Jeff had gone the day before, without so much as a fare-thee-well, and Melissa was packing to board a steamer for Seattle, where she would stay with friends and attend a dizzying round of holiday parties. Keith planned to leave within an hour of his sister, though he was bound for Tacoma, where he could catch a train over the mountains to Wenatchee.

Katherine would remain in the house until after New Year's Day, and then she, too, would be gone. There was much lobbying to do in Olympia, and after that she was scheduled to tour the territory with several other staunch advocates of suffrage, to make speeches and hold rallies.

Just the thought of that house being empty made Banner feel bereft.

Adam had not returned the night before—she could imagine why—and the corridors of Banner's spirit echoed with the beat of his absence.

Few patients came to the hospital, and those who did were suffering more from overindulgence than any compelling malady.

At midday, the marshal arrived, in search of Adam. Four bodies had washed ashore near the Klallum camp, he said, and even though they were "only Chinks," Dr. Corbin was county coroner and he had to view the remains and make a report.

Banner had been all but suffocating in the quiet despair that surrounded her, but examining the bodies of four drowning victims was hardly the respite she'd been hoping for.

"If you're the doc's assistant," the marshal allowed, his hat in his hands, his gaze baleful, "I reckon you'd do. I got the corpses in one of my cells, and the papers gotta be signed before I can get rid of 'em."

Banner shuddered, even as she gathered up her cloak. Distasteful as the task was, she would have to do it—the rules of professionalism dictated that much.

The bodies were all Chinese, just as the marshal had said. They were bloated and bits of their flesh had been eaten away by the fish.

After covering them with their shared tarp again and signing the necessary papers, Banner walked out of the courthouse with brisk dignity and quietly vomited in the alleyway.

Once she'd recovered herself, she climbed into the buggy she had imposed upon one of the Corbin stable hands to hitch for her and took up the reins. To keep her mind off the horrors she'd just viewed, she concentrated on her outrage.

The marshal's attitude toward those poor men had been insufferable. Again and again, he'd referred to them as "Chinks" and said the town was better off that they'd drowned. Finding out why they'd died was the furthest thing from his mind.

When Banner had pressed him he had speculated that

the men might have been smuggled in from Canada, as hundreds of them were every year, now that strict limits had been set on their immigration, and dumped into the sound at the approach of a government ship.

Those who survived the journey were absorbed into the Chinese community and rarely, if ever, deported.

When Banner reached the Corbin house again, and the stables in back, there was no one around to help her unhitch the horse and buggy, so she performed the task herself.

After hanging the lightweight harness on a wall peg, as she had seen Adam do, she led the horse back to its stall, where grain and fresh water already awaited it. She was just closing the stall door and working the metal catch to secure it when a devastatingly familiar voice demanded.

"O'Brien!"

"I'm here," she answered, in tones that were neither pleasant nor sharp, as she stepped out of the shadows.

Banner was prepared to be indignant, but Adam looked so haggard that she felt tenderness shafting through her instead, like rays of strained sunlight. His clothes were rumpled, and his hair needed washing and a beard of several days' growth shadowed his face.

"How was your woman?" she asked, to keep from flinging herself at him in a fit of despairing welcome.

The powerful but now slightly stooped shoulders moved in a shrug. "I don't know, Shamrock. How was she?"

Banner had no idea how to reply to this, so she didn't. She simply folded her arms across her chest and waited.

All around, horses nickered companionably, and the scent of stored hay was pungent in the air. The light, filtered through the sieve of a winter sky, made it difficult for Banner to read her husband's expression.

"I'm sorry," Adam said, finally, in a low, hoarse tone.

"That is undeniable," Banner retorted.

He laughed, though whether the sound was one of amusement or resignation, Banner could not discern. "Did you tell my family about our—marriage?"

Color ached at Banner's cheekbones. "Of course not. Under the circumstances, it hardly seemed appropriate."

Adam came one step nearer, paused uncertainly. "O'Brien—"

Banner retreated. "What?"

"How the hell am I supposed to apologize if you keep backing away? I treated you very badly and I'm sorry." Adam folded his arms, assessed her with shadow-veiled eyes. "Are you wearing drawers?"

Banner swallowed a shriek of rage. "Yes I am, Adam Corbin, and don't you dare come one single step closer!"

There was a white flash of a grin, followed by, "May I remind you that you are my wife?"

"That doesn't give you the right to order me not to wear undergarments or fling me down wherever—"

A weary chuckle escaped him. "I know, O'Brien. I know. I said I was sorry, didn't I?"

Banner fought back tears. Wasn't that the way with all men? They would say awful, dreadful things to a person, leave them alone at Christmas, not knowing whether they were a wife or what, and then come back expecting to make things right with a simple "I'm sorry"!

"Bastard," she said.

Adam spread his hands, as if to concede the point.

And Banner was so annoyed that she strode across the small space that separated them and slapped Adam's face as hard as she could.

He turned his head slightly, then caught her shoulders in his hands. For a moment she knew wild, fathomless fear, but this passed when she saw the broken, defeated expression in his eyes.

"Don't be afraid of me, Shamrock," he pleaded softly. "I'll never hurt you. Never."

From a physical standpoint, Banner knew this to be true; Adam was not the sort to beat a woman. But she was so very vulnerable to him in other ways, and the agony of the night and day just past was proof of that.

She lifted her chin, too proud to let him know how she had already suffered. "We could annul the marriage," she suggested.

Adam shook his head. "Oh, no. For one thing, it's been consummated—deliciously so. And for another, I have absolutely no intention of giving you up."

Banner's tired heart leaped within her, in a dance of hope, and then sank again. Adam had not once said he loved her; his reasons for refusing the annulment were not so romantic. By marrying Banner, he had acquired not only a partner for his practice but a bedmate. She was a convenience.

"Where have you been?" Banner demanded, with a bravado designed to hide her broken heart.

Adam's fingers were kneading her shoulders, stirring paradoxical needs within her. "I can't explain that, Shamrock. Not now, at least. Were there any medical disasters while I was gone?"

It was a moment before Banner could assemble the dignity to speak. "One. Some Chinese men were drowned—four of them. The marshal said the Klallum found the bodies."

"My God—Royce again."

Banner searched Adam's face. "Temple Royce? You mean, you think he had something to do with—"

Suddenly he released her, turned away. "*Damn* that son-of-a-bitch—"

Banner caught hold of one of his arms, afraid and confused. "Adam?"

Her husband faced her, ran one hand through his hair. "Did Marshal Peters have any idea what happened?"

"He said that they were probably smuggled in from Canada—the Chinese men, I mean—and dumped overboard when a government ship came. D-Do you think Mr. Royce—"

"I *know* it was Royce."

"If he's a smuggler, and a murderer, why hasn't he been arrested?"

Adam made a bitter, exasperated sound. "His money is good, O'Brien. By laying it across the right palms and throwing the occasional load of contraband overboard, he gets by."

Distractedly, Banner lifted an index finger to trace the stubbled outline of her husband's jaw. "Why on earth do the Chinese take such a risk? Why would they even board a ship when—"

Adam caught her hand, caressed the inside of her wrist with a gentle thumb. "They're desperate, O'Brien. They want to work in the territories, join their families. They not only take the chance that they'll be flung into the sound, they pay a hundred dollars and more for the privilege."

Banner tugged, trying to free her hand, but the effort was gently forestalled. "You aren't going to tell me where you've been, are you?"

"No."

"Fine." If he wasn't going to talk about his woman, she wasn't going to explain about Sean and her divorce again. Let Adam wonder, as she wondered. "You need a bath."

Adam laughed and pulled and Banner found herself imprisoned against the lean, forbidding length of him. "I know. You'll help me, won't you—Mrs. Corbin?"

Mrs. Corbin. Was he mocking her? "Of course I won't help you. You're a grown man, perfectly capable of—"

He silenced her with a hungry, consuming kiss.

Banner's traitorous heart quickened within her, and her blood raced through her veins like lava. Damn him for daring to do this, she thought wildly. Damn him for turning to her after a rendezvous with his mountain woman!

But was she, herself, any better? The awful truth was that she wasn't. She not only wasn't resisting him, she was enjoying this fierce, quiet travesty of her pride.

She even helped him unhitch the team from his wagon.

The steam rose up around Adam's bathtub in clouds not quite dense enough to hide his blatantly masculine frame—or Banner's blush.

He laughed at her, first with his eyes and then with his mouth. One long foot was propped on the rim of the tub, toes wriggling.

"Why don't you join me, O'Brien?"

160

Banner did not know why she remained in the bathing room, his towel clutched to her bosom. It would have been easy to flee and he could hardly have given chase. "My name is not O'Brien," she reminded him.

"You will always be O'Brien to me, Shamrock."

Wounded, Banner lowered her eyes. "I-I hope you don't mind, but I signed the papers, so that Marshal Peters could have those poor men buried."

Suddenly Adam stiffened. Water spilled over the sides of the stationary bathtub, with its complicated system of pipes and faucets and its steam-operated boiler. "Good God," he breathed, rising like a phoenix and sending water everywhere. "You didn't view the bodies?!"

The reminder made bile scald in the back of Banner's throat. She, covered her mouth with one hand, just for a moment, and then lowered it again and squared her shoulders. She didn't know what was more alarming—Adam's anger or his naked, wonderously sculpted body.

"I am a doctor," she said, in a shaky voice. "And you weren't here to do it."

There was a barb hidden in Banner's words, and it caught on Adam and deflated him so that he sank back into the steamy tub, glaring at either his big toe or the spigot that allowed water to flow in from the black, kettlelike boiler.

"It really wasn't so bad," she lied. "After all, in medical school, we had to—"

Adam grimaced and held up one hand. "Enough, O'Brien. Enough."

"That is a remarkable bathtub."

He leaned back and laughed, loving her with his eyes if

161

not his heart. "It is, isn't it? Jeff brought it back from one of his voyages. Pirate's plunder from some brothel, no doubt."

Frowning, forgetting the peril of such a move, Banner drew nearer, peering between Adam's feet into the soapy depths of the water. "How do you empty it?"

Adam grinned and reached to pull a plug from somewhere in the floor of the heavy iron vat. There was a loud gurgling sound, and then a rush of water traversing pipes. The waterline was getting dangerously low.

Banner leaped backward, but not quickly enough. Adam wrapped strong, unerring fingers around her outer thigh and drew her back. She toppled unceremoniously over the side of the tub and into what remained of the water.

Infuriated, she flailed and fought, but his muscle-roped forearms closed around her and, his mouth nibbled at the rage-pinkened shell of her right ear.

Banner trembled and then gave one more valiant, if quite hopeless, struggle.

Adam's tongue flicked at the inside of her ear, sending all sorts of tempestuous feelings from that point to her breasts and her abdomen and the secret place. Her dress and shoes were soaked and he was hard beneath her. Ready.

Banner struggled again, only to be easily restrained. In a swift movement, he was suddenly above her, astraddle of her hips, his eyes smoldering with laughter and passion.

"Now, we'll see," he said cryptically.

"See what?" snapped Banner, who was outraged and embarrassed and all too willing to surrender.

Adam delayed his answer, opening the buttons of her

saturated dress, unlacing the small blue ribbons that held her new camisole—a gift from Melissa—in place. Almost reverently, though he was still smiling, he bent to greet each bared breast with a kiss.

Banner moaned. "S-See what?" she insisted.

"Whether or not you're wearing drawers, Mrs. Corbin," he answered, pulling her dress down over her hips.

Banner squeezed her eyes shut, and her face flamed at the soft chafing of his laughter.

"So," he said, in gruff triumph, "there is some wifely obedience in you after all, Little Rebel."

Had passion not sustained her, Banner Corbin would have died of mortification.

She was sleeping, still naked, still glowing from the warmth of their joining and the shared bath that followed. Tenderly, Adam covered Banner and then bent to kiss the cinnamon wisp at her temple.

"I love you," he said.

She stirred slightly, but did not awaken.

Turning away, Adam dressed and then added wood to the fire on the hearth. He was brushing his hair when he spotted the crumpled wad of paper half-hidden behind the foot of a chair leg.

Frowning, he bent, retrieved the paper, smoothed it with his hands. It was the marriage certificate.

With a pang, Adam glanced at the sweetly curved creature sleeping so peacefully in his bed. Judging by the condition of that document of matrimony, she had not been without doubts herself.

He shrugged, read the words that would bind them to

each other for always, as far as he was concerned, and smiled. They would make a life together, despite their differences, building on fire and passion if not reason and logic.

It wouldn't be the first such union, nor the last—but it would be among the best.

Banner sat up with a start, alone in the shadowy mixture of night and firelight. Adam's side of the bed was cool and empty.

Slowly, full cognizance returned. Adam was home from the mountain. They'd made love in the bathtub and again, here in the bed—

She sank back to the pillows, pulled the covers up to her chin, and sighed. Several hours must have passed since their furious joinings, but she still felt sated and warm.

Banner stretched, like a contented, feline creature, and then marveled that her breasts still remembered the magical ravaging of Adam's mouth. Cupping her hands behind her head, she allowed the sleep-warmed, passion-plundered globes to rise free of the blankets, their tips straining. Adam, she thought. Adam.

As if in answer to her unspoken cry, the bedroom door creaked open. "Shamrock?"

She lay still as he entered the room, lit the lamp at the bedside, drew in his breath at the sight of her bounty.

The bed shifted as Adam sat down. He was fully dressed, his hair and skin fragrant with some muted, musky cologne, his blue eyes possessing the breasts and their crests with quiet greed.

One of his hands rose to gently pull Banner's hands

164

from beneath her head and stretch them high, imprisoning them against the pillows.

She whimpered as he lowered his head to one reaching confection while tormenting the other with caresses and a plucking motion of his fingers.

This was a rite as old as mankind; Banner knew that. But it seemed so special, so new, because it had never been good before. Now, oh, now, it was excruciatingly, deliciously, wonderously good.

Banner writhed as he enjoyed a banquet freely served, crooning his name, feeling and reveling in the rising, savage need of his fulfillment and her own.

Between greedy spates of suckling and tantalizingly slow samplings, he drove her into a fevered, mindless state with words. He ordered her to leave her drawers behind again and gruffly detailed the reasons why.

The warm scandal of it drove Banner's hips to rise and fall with the meter of her reeling pulse. He drew back from her breasts but did not release her hands.

"Come to me," she pleaded, without pride or shame.

Slowly, his blue eyes plundering her breasts just as his mouth had done, Adam shook his head. "I'm not getting undressed, O'Brien," he said. "Dinner is in five minutes and I'm hungry."

With his right hand, he tugged the blankets down, until Banner was completely revealed to him, her wrists still caught together high above her head. He touched her knee, his fingers doing a fire dance from there to the curve of her thigh and then the silky nest that veiled a pulsing, aching bud.

"Yes," she breathed, as his fingers questioned her.

165

Banner's back arched of its own accord as he claimed her. Her breath came in raspy whimpers, and her teeth were bared in a fierce and primitive surrender.

Having no choice, she gave herself up to the business of passion.

Chapter Eight

Katherine Corbin lowered her lashes and hid her smile behind the rim of her teacup. It was no great mental feat discerning what had delayed dinner. Banner was glowing and Adam frowned at the food spread on the table as though he resented it for existing.

There was an expectant silence as the two approached the gathering. Melissa set her own cup down with a nervous rattle and Keith sat back in his chair, lips curved into a grin, arms folded across his chest. Even Clarence King, who was going back to Oregon in the morning, stopped staring at his plate to look up.

They paused, and then Adam put one gently possessive hand to Banner's elbow and announced, in comically formal tones, "Ladies and gentlemen—my wife."

A communal shout of glee went up, seeming to ring in the teardrop crystals of the chandelier over the table, and then there was a riot of hugs, kisses, and handshakes.

Katherine joined in with exuberance.

Sean Malloy paused outside the south entrance to Erickson's Bar, mentally counting the coins resting in the mended pocket of his coat. A snowy wind stung his ears and ate its way through his boots to his toes.

Inside the famous saloon there was music, warmth, free food, whiskey. Out of work since the day his ship had docked in Portland, Sean hungered for all those things and more.

He stepped inside, awed. Completely outlining the enormous room was a mahogany bar, polished to an impossible shine. A painting as tall as Sean himself showed plump, nude women being ravaged by legions of Roman soldiers.

Sean scowled. Thanks to Banner, it had been long enough since he'd tossed up a skirt, and that was a fact.

His attention was drawn to an ornate concert stage, which was edged with gas footlights and graced with an orchestra composed of eight buxom women. They were sedately playing a tune Sean didn't recognize.

"Buy you a drink, mate?"

Sean turned, suspicious, and glared into the face of a brown-eyed dandy.

The man laughed and held up hands that had never done a day's work, from the look of them. "Don't get excited— I'm as much a man as you are, my friend."

Sean relaxed. He'd been in jail too long, gotten too cautious. All the same, he allowed his eyes to rise to the mezzanine, where a bevy of soiled doves lounged, trying to lure a customer or two. When he met the dandy's gaze again, he saw amusement there.

"Sean Malloy," he said, offering one calloused hand.

"Temple Royce," replied the dandy, ready with a hand of his own. "Are you a longshoreman, Mr. Malloy?" "Aye, when I can get the work."

They were at the bar then. Sean brought a two-bit piece

from his pocket and asked for whiskey. Two shots were set before him.

"I offered to buy your drink," Royce reminded him.

Sean assessed the man beside him, wondered what the bloke was after. "I'll buy me own till I know what you're wanting, then," he replied.

Royce shrugged and a half-smile curved his lips. "Very well. You're a big man, Malloy. Have you ever worked aboard a ship?"

Sean emitted a bitter, raspy chuckle. "Aye. All the way around the Horn. You hirin' a crew, Mr. Royce?"

"I am."

"Bound for where?" demanded Sean, downing one shot and taking up the other. He needed work—he'd already been thrown out of his room and God knew what he would have to eat once the coins in his pocket were gone, but he liked the feel of land beneath his feet and the idea that he could have himself a woman now and then.

"Canada," Royce answered, at length.

Sean gazed at his own reflection in the mirror behind the bar. He was a good-looking man, if he did say so himself, but who could tell it to see him now? His light brown hair, usually curly, was matted to his head. His hazel eyes were sunken into his face, and a scruffy beard hid the strong lines of his jaw.

If he accepted the job Royce seemed to be offering, he could probably get some of his wages in advance, buy himself a meal and a bath and a romp with one of those buxom little trollops upstairs.

"Canada," he said, considering aloud.

"Yes."

"After that?"

"Seattle. Port Hastings. Back here, eventually."

"Port Hastings? Where the hell is that?"

Royce smiled. "On the Strait of Juan de Fuca—Washington Territory. Little Sodom and Gomorrah, they call it."

Sean was intrigued. "Does it deserve its name, then?"

"Absolutely. I'm offering fifty dollars for the Canadian run; half now and half when we dock in Port Hastings. Do we have an agreement, Mr. Malloy?"

"We do, I'm thinking. When do we sail?"

"First thing in the morning. The ship is the *Jonathan Lee*. Know where she's anchored?"

"Aye," answered Sean, who had seen the clipper among a dozen others.

Royce counted out the promised wage. "Be aboard by dawn—we sail at high tide."

Sean took the money, folded it, tucked it into his shirt pocket. "I'll be there."

"See that you are."

So there was some steel under all that fine frippery after all. Sean was pleased. "You have me word."

Royce nodded, and then he was gone.

There was some kind of stir on the mezzanine. Sean looked up to see a tall, light-haired man fielding the advances of two separate women.

"Shit," remarked the old swabbie next to Sean at the bar. "He don't even have to pay 'em, that one. Some say they pay *him*."

Sean ordered two more shots of whiskey. "Who is he, then?"

The sailor turned a pearl-handled knife in his hands,

sheathed it at a warning look from one of the bartenders. "That's Jeff Corbin. He skippers the *Sea Mistress*."

The name Corbin meant nothing to Sean, nor did the man's obvious prowess with women. He'd only been making idle conversation.

"Scuttlebutt is that the cap'n got his heart broken by a redheaded lady doctor."

Sean stiffened, flung a furtive glance at the captain, who was making his way down the stairs now, doing up the polished brass buttons on his coat as he went.

"You know her name? This lady doctor, I mean?"

"I'd never forget it—met her once, I did."

For just a moment, that crowded, noisy bar seemed to buckle and shift around Sean like a ship run onto a reef. She'd talked about becoming a doctor, Banner had—dreamed about it and fair driven Sean into a state with her chatter. Could she have done that—perhaps on the money she'd gotten for selling his hide to the law?

"Banner O'Brien," he said, reflectively. She wouldn't be calling herself Malloy, now would she? Not after what she'd done to him.

The old seaman looked disappointed. "Now, how the devil did you know that?"

Without troubling to answer, Sean whirled away from the bar, forgetting his plans for dinner and a bath and a woman. He followed Captain Corbin out of the bar, hailed him in the street.

Corbin turned, his eyes as blue as the North Sea and hollow-looking. He stood beneath a streetlamp, his hands wedged into his coat pockets, the snow gathering in his hair. "Yes?"

Sean feared few men, but this one stirred a certain wariness in him. There was a quiet control about the bloke, a sureness that said more than all the boasting in the world could have done.

"Good evenin'," said the Irishman politely.

The captain only nodded, his eyes watchful now.

"There was a man in there—" Sean grinned engagingly and tossed his head toward the golden billow of light that was Erickson's south door. "He said you know my sister."

Corbin made no reply, but he didn't walk away either. Probably, with those archangel looks of his, he was often confronted by the brothers of women he'd trifled with. "Her name would be Banner," Sean went on cautiously.

Something moved in the ink-blue eyes. Recognition? Pain? Sean couldn't tell.

And Corbin still didn't speak.

"She might be usin' her grandmother's name— O'Brien," prompted Sean, feeling his way, still sensing an unusual need for caution.

Corbin's neck corded, and his mouth looked hard. "If Banner is your sister, it seems to me that you would know what name she goes by."

Triumph and hatred met within Sean in a surging rush. His fingers and palms ached and sweat prickled between his shoulder blades, but he smiled. "Aye and that I should. But we had a tiff, me sister and I, and we didn't part friends. It's makin' that up to her I'll be, once I find her."

"Good luck," allowed the captain.

"Is she well, then?" Sean blurted quickly. If the blue-eyed giant decided to walk away, there wouldn't be much he could do to stop him.

The answer was a terse nod and, "She's well."

And she's done a jig on your innards, mate. That she has, Sean realized. "She's a pretty bit, me sister. Please— tell me where to find her."

The captain considered. "How do I know you're really Banner's brother? And even if you are, how do I know she would want to see you?"

"You'll have to take me word, I guess."

"Give me your name," Corbin parried. "And when I see Banner again, I'll tell her you're here."

Christ. If she heard his name, she'd run like a rabbit and he'd never find her. It had only been luck that he'd come this close. "Will you see her soon then?"

"Probably not."

Sean's smile threatened to come unfixed. He was getting nowhere with this one, and chances were he was not only wasting his time but risking a broken bone or two. "Tell Banner that Robert sends his love," he said, and then he turned away and went back inside the saloon.

The old sailor was still at the bar—the one who'd said he'd met Banner. The bloke looked thirsty.

Sean worked up another smile and approached him.

Day by day, as December became January, the ragged snow melted, seeping into the ground. The resultant mud tugged at Banner's shoes and made buggy travel a horror.

The weather was deceptively mild; gentle winds blew up the strait from the sea, warm and springlike, and the sky was a polished, tender blue. Whenever Banner looked up at it, she felt a bittersweet tug in her heart.

She was happier than she'd ever been, though being

172

married to Adam Corbin was an arduous thing. In the day-time he was a taskmaster, dragging Banner from one house call to another, lecturing her when she made a mistake. But at night he was a tender and inventive lover, and it was this that made the rest bearable.

Often, of course, Banner and Adam were called out at night—more babies deigned to be born then, and there were always brawls on Water Street to generate business.

If life had gone on at this even, if hectic, keel, Banner would never have complained. But of course, it did not.

Three weeks after Christmas, Adam disappeared again.

When he returned, after one full day and night, he was not contrite, but surly and uncommunicative.

"He has a woman," mourned Banner, who stood before the kitchen fireplace, staring into the flames.

"Maybe," said Maggie, paring vegetables for a stew. "If he were my man, I'd be about finding out."

Banner turned from the fire, her fingers intertwined. There was a lace of frost at the windows, an eiderdown tracery of fans and curliques, and the sky was gray with a burden of snow.

"I've asked him."

"Asked him!" scoffed Maggie. "Ain't we all?"

Banner's throat ached. "What do you suggest?"

"Follow him. He'll take off again, in three weeks, sure as summer comes after spring. When he does, you get yourself a horse and—"

"I couldn't! Maggie, he would be furious."

"Are you scared of him?"

"Of course not!"

"Well, then?"

Banner was saved from answering by the clatter of boots on the back stairway.

"O'Brien!"

Banner sighed, met Maggie's angry gaze momentarily, looked away. "What?"

Adam came into the kitchen blithely, as though he hadn't been away for twenty-four hours, as though he hadn't betrayed his wife. His clothes were fresh, his hair was still damp from a very recent bath, and his smile was mischievous, if weary, "Did I miss breakfast?"

Banner wanted to slap him, but somehow she restrained herself. As she sidestepped a kiss aimed at her forehead, Maggie left the room.

Adam visibly braced himself for a confrontation, but his words belied the action. "Did you miss me, O'Brien?"

"No more than I would miss the grippe."

He laughed, but it was a broken, weary sound. "There is no woman, O'Brien."

Tears brimmed in Banner's eyes, she turned away to hide them. "Tell me where you've been, then," she said, with a lift of her chin.

"Tell me who had you before I did," he replied.

Banner whirled and slapped his face with all her might, restraint be damned.

He smiled at her with an insolence that made her want to shriek and stomp her feet. "There, you see, we both have our little secrets, don't we, O'Brien?"

"Only I told you mine!" Banner cried. "You were just too drunk to listen!"

"So tell me again. Believe me, I'm sober."

"I'll be damned if I will, you bastard!"

Adam's hands were at her waist now, easily working their accursed magic. They traveled up her rib cage, to the rounding of her breasts, and she trembled, hating herself for needing this man.

"Take your hands off me!"

Slowly, maddeningly, Adam shook his head. "We've discussed this before, haven't we, O'Brien? Whenever. Wherever. Remember?"

His palms moved full on her breasts now, brazen and strong, causing traitorous nipples to strain beneath her clothing. Damn him, damn him, she hated him, she loved him, she could have killed him but would have given her own life to protect him. What spell had he cast over her?

"I missed you, O'Brien."

The skirt of her dress was riding up now, inch by scandalous inch. "Stop—Maggie might—"

The hem reached her calves, her knees, the firm flesh of her bare thighs. Why hadn't she worn drawers? Now he would laugh at her again. Now he would know that he had won long before the battle had even begun.

"I h-hate you!"

Adam's hand had found its mark; he was stroking her, igniting a fierce and savage flame. "Um-hmm," he answered.

"Wasn't your woman e-enough?"

He was plundering her shamelessly now; she couldn't breathe or think. Dear Lord, he was going to take her here, in the *kitchen,* and she couldn't seem to muster the internal forces to stop him!

"I never get enough—of you." He sank to the bench in front of the fireplace, but his hold on Banner was

175

unbroken. "Come here."

Banner's heart was pounding and her vision was blurred and she moved with him only because he drew her. "Why?"

"Because I want you."

"Here?!"

"Here." He had been preparing himself; he drew Banner to him, pressed her downward, so that she sat astraddle of his lap and of the bench. His entry was swift and searing.

With his hands, Adam lifted her, lowered her, lifted her again. It was a delicious torment, savage in its ancient meter, and Banner soon took over the process herself.

When she did, her husband fell back along the length of the bench, groaning, the powerful thrusts of his hips almost unseating her. But Banner clung to him, impaled on a pillar of fire, and thrust her legs out wide when the moment of spinning insanity came.

Only seconds later, Adam stiffened beneath her, then arched his back with such force that she clasped his sides with both hands to keep from being flung to the ceiling.

And inside her, Banner could feel Adam's flesh rippling against her own, filling her with his seed, claiming and conquering and worshiping, all at once.

Banner cried out with the shock of a second, unexpected release.

After a long time, Adam sat up. He was still a part of her, a soft part that was slowly growing hard again.

"Dessert," he said, opening the first button of her dress.

Flushed with satisfaction and scandal, Banner flailed at his hands. "No—oh, no—Maggie might come in—"

"She wouldn't dare," he said, opening another button.

"Adam, please."

He chuckled and finished the task of baring her. "You needn't beg, O'Brien. I promise full satisfaction."

"Why, you—"

Adam's mouth closed suddenly over one waiting nipple; his hands came to Banner's hips, turned her from side to side, like a wheel mounted on a hub.

And all the things she'd meant to say wafted away on a soft moan.

Discreetly, Maggie McQuire turned away from the kitchen door. Time enough to set the stew boiling later, she thought with a smile, for there was something else boiling now.

And wouldn't it be a fine thing if there was a brand new Corbin baby to look after one of these days?

Maggie's smile spread to a grin. From what she'd heard through that door, things were off to a promising start.

It was sheer luxury, soaking in that hot, scented water. With a sigh, Banner Corbin sank to her chin.

The thought of Adam and what he'd done to her—what they'd done together—brought fierce color to her cheeks. Good Lord, he'd taken her in a kitchen, and in broad daylight!

A small smile curved her lips. She supposed the kitchen was tame compared to some of the other places where he'd chosen to enjoy her—in his buggy, for example. Over an examining table in the middle of a busy workday. And once, the night before he went away this last time, behind a screen in the parlor.

Her smile faded, though, as she imagined Adam with his woman. Could *she* make him groan and cry out, in beautiful vulnerability, the way Banner could? Did she fight with him and nurse him at her breasts?

Tenderness and rage mingled within Banner, and one tear slid down her face to lose itself in the bathwater. She loved Adam fiercely, hopelessly, but sharing him was a brutal blow to her pride.

A soft, ragged sob tore itself from her throat.

The door of the bathing room creaked. "Shamrock?"

She tried to stop crying, but another sob followed the first and then the torrent was unstoppable.

Adam came to the side of the tub, knelt. "Banner—please—don't cry."

She looked at him and thought how she was trapped inside her love for him like a bird inside a jar, and she howled at the agony and the injustice of it.

Tenderly, Adam drew her up out of the water, dried her with one towel, wrapped her in another. Speaking softly, he carried her to their bed and placed her there, covering her, making no demands.

"Sleep," he whispered, brushing her hair back from her face, smoothing the grief from her lips with an index finger. "You're exhausted."

Banner was not sobbing now—she was too tired—but humiliating little hiccoughs and sniffles still plagued her. "The patients—"

"It's my turn to take care of them, O'Brien. Sleep now. And sweetheart?"

She sniffled again. "What?"

"There isn't anybody—*anybody*—besides you."

Because she was so tired, because she loved this man and needed him, because even now his child might be growing within her, she believed him.

And believing him, she slept.

When Adam came downstairs, Maggie was in the kitchen, rolling out biscuit dough. The stew simmered on the stove.

"You're a lot like your papa," the housekeeper teased.

For the first time in his memory, Adam blushed. Too late, he orchestrated a shrug. "I don't know what you mean."

"The hell you don't. Where is Banner, by the way?"

"Sleeping. I'll be on rounds for the rest of the morning. Don't bother my wife unless there's an emergency."

Maggie executed a brisk salute, and Adam laughed.

It was going to be a very good day.

The rap at the bedroom door was not Adam's; it was too tentative, too soft.

Banner snuggled under the covers and yawned, sleepily observing to herself that Adam wouldn't have knocked at all. "Come in."

The door opened and the scent of a familiar perfume wafted into the room. "I've brought your dinner," said Katherine.

Banner turned quickly and sat up, the blankets under her chin. For a moment she was wildly embarrassed to be found in Adam's bed, but the feeling passed when she remembered that she had the right. "You're home!"

Katherine smiled at this weighty observation and set a

tray across Banner's lap. "I am, indeed. And I have wonderful news."

Banner yawned again and then began eating from the bowl of stew on her tray. There were biscuits, too, fragrant and dripping with butter. "What news? I thought you were going to lecture about suffrage—"

Katherine sat down on the foot of the bed, beaming. "Today the legislature passed a bill making it legal for women to vote, Banner."

Banner's eyes widened and her heart leaped inside her. She had not dared to hope, despite the promises of Francelle's father and others like him. "That *is* wonderful news!"

"Isn't it?"

"Have you told Adam?"

Katherine nodded. "I think he was pleased, but he did warn me to be prepared for a fight."

"A fight? Could they overturn the decision?"

"Oh, yes," Katherine sighed, smoothing her crisp skirts, studying the fire crackling on the hearth. "He could well be right. We had the vote once before and it was taken away. Men are frightened of surrendering any sort of control, Banner—I think they're afraid we'll legislate them right out of their beloved supremacy."

"No more brothels, no more whiskey."

"Their worst phobia, couched in six simple words," agreed Katherine. "And how have you been, Banner? Are you happy?"

Banner's throat ached; she was happy—she was. But now, in wakefulness, in the presence of this sensible woman, she felt foolish for accepting Adam's vow of fidelity so readily. After all, if he didn't have a mistress somewhere, why did he disappear every three weeks? Why did he refuse to explain the absences? And why was he always in such a wretched temper when he got back?

"Banner? What is it?"

Banner lowered her eyes to the stew. Suddenly, it didn't seem so savory anymore. "Nothing," she lied.

The marshal flung back the tarp, revealing the small, battered body to Adam's gaze.

"Jesus," he breathed. "What happened?"

Peters shrugged. "You know how it is. She probably tried to steal some sailor's purse. . . ."

Adam turned away, sickened. After drawing a few deep breaths, though, he turned back again. "She was a prostitute?"

Marshal Peters nodded. "Yeah. She was working on Water Street, as far as I know. That's where they found her anyway."

Adam assessed the flowing red hair, closed the staring green eyes that still reflected bewilderment and horror. "What was her name?"

"Dunno."

Adam's heart constricted within him; he covered the girl again. She'd been sixteen years old, at the most—not even as old as Melissa—and something about her made him feel a primitive, stalking sort of fear.

He went into the little room behind the marshal's office and scoured his hands until the flesh between his fingers burned like fire. Red hair—green eyes—Banner.

Adam straightened, dried his hands with a rough towel.

She'd looked a little like Banner, that girl—that was what was bothering him. But there was no connection—how could there be?

An inspiration overtook him; he drew out his watch and frowned. If he hurried, there might be time.

Banner stared at the gold band; it glistened in the light of the lamp and the fire. Adam let it fall from his fingers to his palm and reached for his wife's hand.

He put the ring in its proper place and sanctioned it with a soft kiss. "O'Brien," he said, "I love you."

Banner flung her arms around him, and he held her fiercely, almost as though he expected her to disintegrate within his embrace.

"I love you," he said again, in a low, desperate rasp. "I love you."

She drew back, watching his wan, ravaged face tenderly. "Adam, what is it?" she whispered.

But he only drew her close, and it was a very long time before he let her go again.

In the morning, the telegraph message was delivered. Francelle brought it grudgingly into the office that Adam and Banner now shared and snapped, "Here!"

The missive was brief: "Banner. I saw Robert in Portland a few weeks ago. He sends his love. Jeff."

Banner frowned. Robert? She didn't know anyone named Robert—did she?

She read the message again, and a spark of fear danced up and down her spine and then pirouetted in her throat. Banner swallowed it, only to have it sniggle under the lining of her stomach and lodge there.

Briskly, Banner crumpled the message and discarded it. She had no time for vague and fanciful fears.

That night, she dreamed that Sean was standing at the foot of the bed, watching her, hating her.

Banner awakened with a brutal start and a cry that left her throat raw.

Adam stiffed beside her, sat up. "Banner?"

"Hold me," she whispered.

He drew her into his arms. She was safe there, warm. There was no Sean, no woman on the mountain, no monster crouching in the shadows at the foot of the bed.

"Adam?"

Her husband's hand came to entangle itself in her hair. "Ummmm?"

"I was married before."

"Ummmm."

Banner sighed and snuggled closer to her husband. She would explain everything in the morning, tell the whole truth about Sean and take the consequences.

But Adam was already out of the house when Banner came downstairs the next morning, and Francelle was in a perfect dither, certain that the first patient of the day meant to give birth in the waiting room.

With money in his pockets, Sean Malloy found it easier to bide his time. He took a room on Water Street and worked aboard the *Jonathan Lee* whenever she ran smuggle in from Canada.

He was certain now that Banner lived in Port Hastings—he could almost catch the spicy, defiant scent of her—but he'd had no glimpse of the imp, and no word, for he hadn't dared to ask.

Of course, there had been that problem when he'd *thought* he'd found her. He'd gone into a blind rage, seeing her standing in the street like that, offering herself to every man who passed.

Sean had caught her arm and dragged her into an alleyway, meaning to exert his husbandly rights before he dealt with her past sins. But she'd stated her price and something inside him had splintered—by the time he'd realized that the trollop wasn't Banner at all, he'd crushed in her throat.

He'd been more careful after that, avoiding trouble, taking his pleasures in the boxhouses, where there was light. There was little privacy, of course, but that didn't bother Sean—he liked having his whiskey and his women in the same curtained booth.

On the morning of February third, however, Sean made a mistake. He drank a little too much and got mean with one of the whores on the *Silver Shadow,* and when he did, she brought a brass lamp down over the top of his head, drawing more blood than he would have thought one man could hold.

And if that wasn't bad enough, he got himself arrested in the bargain.

Banner paced the parlor, preparing herself. She had put it off long enough, telling Adam about Sean, and out of simple stubbornness, too.

She hadn't meant to deceive him, not really. It was just

that it had taken all her stamina just to keep up during the days, and at night he had loved her so ferociously that she had neither the breath nor the courage to talk.

Now, on this snowy evening, the time had come. Maggie was away visiting her sister, Francelle had gone home for the night, and Katherine was away in Olympia. There were simply no more excuses.

But when Adam came into the parlor, he was obviously not feeling receptive to confidences from his wife. He carried his bag in one hand, and Banner's new, fur-lined cloak was draped over his arm.

"Marshal Peters was just here," he said. "He's got some brawler bleeding all over his best cell. Coming?"

Banner drew a deep breath. Perhaps it would be better, safer, to tell Adam in a more public place. "Yes—of course. Is the injury serious?"

Adam shrugged; it was clear that his mind was far away. On the mountain perhaps? He helped Banner into the buggy waiting at the side door and they were off.

"Will you be leaving again soon?" she dared, as they made their way down the hill.

Beside her, Adam stiffened. "Tomorrow."

Banner's guilt over her own secrets was suddenly evaporating. She might have had a past, but she was faithful *now,* when it counted. She didn't go off to visit some mysterious lover whenever the mood struck. "I want to go with you," she announced.

"No."

"Why not?"

"Because it wouldn't be safe, that's why."

"I'll follow you, then."

He turned, gave her a scorching, sidelong glance. "You do that, O'Brien, and I'll paddle your delightful little backside!"

"Will you now?" bluffed Banner, who knew very well that he would, if pushed far enough. "I wouldn't advise it, you pompous ass, because I would be forced to have you jailed!"

The answer was a howl of laughter. "Jailed? O'Brien, I'll have you know that under the laws of this territory I could hang you from a streetlamp by your thumbs if I so wished."

"That is disgusting!"

"But, nonetheless, true. As far as the government is concerned, my cherished darling, I own you."

Banner made a face. "The laws are changing!"

Adam arched one eyebrow, navigating the treacherous hill easily, almost as an aside. "Are they, O'Brien? All hell is breaking loose over that last amendment, and there is a movement afoot to retract it. Why do you think my mother raced off to Olympia the way she did?"

Banner was angry, not just with Adam but with all men. "And you would be pleased, wouldn't you, to see women lose the vote?"

"Not pleased. But not surprised either."

Banner shivered, even though she was warm in her heavy cloak. "Do you think, by chance, that my sex is inferior to yours?"

Adam grinned—there was definitely an obnoxious quality to the curve of his lips—as they rounded a corner and entered Main Street. "On the contrary. The female gender is probably superior. Close your mouth, O'Brien—

186

it'll be full of snow in a minute."

Superior! What game was he playing? "You don't really believe that!"

"Oh, but I do. Women are generally more rational than men—they have a long-range view of things. They can bear more pain, stand up under more abuse—"

"Only because they're forced to! Women are the same as men, Adam!"

"God forbid."

"Just what do you mean by that?"

Adam drew the buggy to a stop in front of the brick building where Banner had come to view the Chinese and sign their death certificates. He pulled the brake lever into place, wrapped the reins around it, and grinned again. "Were you sleeping in anatomy class, O'Brien? Women and men are definitely not the same. I'll be happy to demonstrate the theory later."

"You wretch," Banner hissed, leaping down to the ground before he could round the buggy and help her. "That wasn't what I meant, and you know it!"

They were still arguing when they reached the row of sturdy cells in the courthouse basement.

"Shut up," Adam said companionably as the marshal approached with a ring of keys.

Banner looked around, oppressed by the dark, dank misery of that place. At the end of the hallway, there was a chair, complete with leather arm restraints and a billyclub resting on the seat.

Perhaps because Banner was looking at that and wondering if the marshal used brutal methods when he questioned a prisoner, she was inside the first cell before she remembered the patient they'd come to see.

He was a burly brute of a man, too long for the cot he rested upon, and his curly, light brown hair was blood-soaked—

Banner fell back against the cold barrior of the bars. *No!* screamed something hidden deep inside her. *No!*

"I need more light," snapped Adam, oblivious to her terror, to everything but the half-conscious man lying on the cot. "O'Brien—"

Banner wanted to seep through the bars, like so much smoke, and dissipate into nothing. Her head moved back and forth, back and forth, in a fevered denial of what she knew to be true.

The marshal carried a lamp, and he struck a match to the wick. "Is it bad, Doc?"

Adam's eyes were on Banner, puzzled and impatient. "Not necessarily—head wounds often bleed like this. Get me a basin of hot water, Peters, and some clean cloth."

Banner was inching toward the cell door as it opened; the process was unbearably slow, and progress was gained bar by bar. Peters slammed the escapeway just before she reached it.

And Sean turned on the cot, dragged his eyes over Banner's trembling frame, and smiled.

"Hello, darlin'," he said.

Chapter Nine

Banner's knuckles ached, so tight was her grasp on the bars behind her, and her throat worked convulsively, making speech impossible.

Adam came to her, caught her forearms in his hands. At his touch, she quietly fainted.

When Banner awakened, only minutes later, the world was spinning helter-skelter through space, off its axis, out of its proper orbit. She was lying on a cot and someone was waving smelling salts under her nose.

Sputtering and sick, she bolted upright, only to be pressed down again. "You just rest, Mrs. Corbin," enjoined the marshal gruffly. "Your husband's busy just now, stitchin' up that fool Irishman's head."

Banner closed her eyes. She could hear Sean's voice, and Adam's—they were close, only a cell away, and yet their words seemed to be echoing through a long tunnel.

"Pretty piece, ain't she now?"

"I think so," replied Adam evenly. Banner didn't need to see him to know that he was concentrating on the cleaning of Sean's wound or already stitching it closed.

"She workin' for you, or warmin' your bed of a night?"

"Banner is my wife," Adam responded. "And how would you like your earlobes stitched to the tip of your nose?"

"Is she your wife, now? That's odd, that is—real odd." There was a long silence, a silence during which Banner's blood congealed in her veins. "Considerin' that she's already married to me."

There was another silence, but this one was thunderous, like the stillness between violent earth tremors.

Sean laughed; the sound was low and weary, rumbling in the close, uncirculated air of the jail. "Thought you were the first to spread her thighs, did you? Well, you ain't, mate, and that's the truth of it."

Adam said nothing, nothing at all. And, in a way, that was worse than any rage.

Banner sat up, made a conscious effort not to lose her supper. She would explain—Adam would understand when she had explained. . . .

Her husband finished his work, collected her in scathing silence from the cell where she'd been recovering from her shock. His face was cold and the expression in his eyes was colder still, and Banner wanted to die.

Outside, in the crisp, snowy night air, Adam lifted her by the waist and fairly flung her into the buggy.

"It's true, isn't it?" he rasped, without looking at Banner, as the rig lurched into motion.

Banner lowered her eyes, and a tear fell to the lush fox muff that warmed her hands. All the reasonable, sensible things she'd planned to say rose into her throat and lodged there, in an impassible tangle.

Adam said nothing until they'd reached the stables, until he'd surrendered the horse and buggy to the man who tended them.

"Start talking, O'Brien," he growled, grasping Banner's arm and half flinging, half propelling her toward the house. "Right now!"

Banner swallowed, stumbled. Adam's grip was almost bruising as he righted her and thrust her onward. The waiting room was dark and shadowy and monsters were lurking there. "I—I told you—"

"Damn it all to hell, O'Brien, I don't *remember* what you told me and you know it!" Adam exploded, throwing in his lot with the monsters. "Are you my wife or his?"

"Yours!"

190

"Thank you very much. So why does he call you darlin'
and claim you're married to him?"

Banner bit her lower lip, closed her eyes. "He p-prob-
ably thinks we're still married."

"Wonderful. Keep talking."

"I-I was very young when we were wed—I didn't really
know Sean. He—he beat me and there w-were other
women. One n-night there was a fight, in a tavern, and a
man was killed. He was rich, this m-man, and his family
offered a reward—"

Adam's hands came to Banner's shoulders, whether to
reassure her or hold her at a distance she did not know.
"Go on," he whispered.

"I was afraid of Sean and I-I knew that he'd been the one
to b-beat that man—he'd boasted about it, Adam! He'd
·boasted—"

"Yes?"

"I told. I went to the police, Adam, and I t-told. They
f-found proof against Sean and—and they came for him.
Wh-When he saw them in the street, he knew what I'd
done and he hit me and hit me—"

Adam drew her very close, held her in the warm circle
of his arms.

"I was taken to a hospital," she went on, her face buried
in his shoulder. "They took care of me there. And a-after I
was well, I stayed, using the r-reward money to pay for my
books and courses. When that ran out, I worked for my
tuition."

"And the divorce?"

"The people at the hospital helped me get that. When
w-we heard that Sean might be released from prison, s-some

191

of the women on Dr. Blackwell's faculty got together and—and gave me the train fare to come West."

"Why *did* they release him from prison, Banner?"

"I don't know, Adam—I suppose they decided that that man had p-provoked Sean or something. I h-had my degree, so I bought a train ticket and left."

His embrace tightened. "I won't let Sean or anyone else hurt you, Shamrock," he vowed, in a hoarse whisper.

But Banner trembled, fearing not for herself now, but for Adam. "Sean's vicious—he won't stop until—"

Adam lifted her gently into his arms, cradling her like a child. "I can handle him, Banner," he said. "In the meantime, you're not to leave this house alone, under any circumstances. Do you understand me?"

Banner sighed, too exhausted to argue. But inside she knew that nothing short of death itself would stop Sean Malloy from taking his vengeance now. And there was only one way to make sure that Adam stayed safe.

The stitches stung, and so did the knowledge that Banner was sharing another man's bed. Sean cursed and sat up on the cot, and the room swayed and shifted around him.

He wondered if she liked spreading herself for that doctor—some niggling thing at the base of his mind believed that she did.

Sean cursed again. She'd hated it when he touched her, stiffened when he took her. And him her own husband!

He considered the doctor. By his clothes and his manner, he was a wealthy man, that one, raised to the best of everything. And now he fancied himself Banner's husband.

Sean wondered if the slut did things for the rich man that

she'd never done for him, and fury surged through him, forcing him to his feet.

A slow smile spread over Sean's face. He'd found her. At last, at last, he'd found her. And she'd pay, the little she-Judas, for selling him to the law the way she had.

Hoarsely, Malloy laughed. Aye. And he'd put her through her paces before it was over—she'd do every trick she knew and a few that he meant to teach her.

And as for her "husband," well, he'd watch, the bastard. And he'd die with the image in his mind.

"No!" Banner cried, heat throbbing in her face.

"Yes," replied Adam, who was sipping coffee at the kitchen table and implacably reading a newspaper. "And that's the end of it, O'Brien, so pack your clothes."

Banner cast an imploring look at Maggie, but it seemed that the woman had contracted a sudden case of deafness. "Wenatchee is so far away!"

Adam turned a page and frowned at something headed with a complicated drawing. "That's the idea."

Banner stumbled to the bench, fell to it, her back to Adam and Maggie, her face to the fire. She'd meant to run away, just as she had run away from New York when she'd been awarded her diploma. She'd meant to lose herself, forever, to draw Sean away from Adam and his family.

But by going to Wenatchee, as Adam insisted, she would endanger Keith.

Maggie came, squeezed Banner's shoulder in wordless commiseration, and left the room.

There was a short silence, and then Adam came to sit beside her, his indigo gaze fixed on the crackling, crimson fire. Banner wondered if he was remembering the day they'd made love on this very bench, and she blushed.

"Just let me leave entirely, Adam—let me leave this town and the territory before Sean kills you."

Adam smiled, but his face was wan and there was no humor in the expression. "He isn't going to kill me, Banner. And you're not going to leave me. At least, not permanently."

"Don't you see that Sean will follow me? And if you believe that he'd hesitate to kill Keith—"

Adam's hand closed over one of hers, drew it upward, to his lips. "Don't worry about Keith. He prays a lot, but he's meaner than all hell in a fight."

Banner shook her head, despondent. "This wouldn't be a front-yard row between brothers who love each other, Adam. Sean is strong, and he's ruthless."

"*Thank* you," Adam mocked. "In that case, I'll hide under my bed and tell my brothers to do the same. We'll just cower there, among the dustballs, while Malloy rapes and kills one of our women!"

"That's it!" Banner cried, her face alight. "I could hide on the mountain, with your woman! He'd never look for me there!"

Now it was Adam who shook his head, Adam who marveled. "That would be a great idea, O'Brien—except for one small hitch. I don't have a goddamned woman on the *goddamned* mountain!"

"And the moon doesn't have craters!"

Adam's massive shoulders stooped as he gave a long, ragged sigh. "God almighty," he breathed. "I've been *faithful* to you, do you hear me? Faithful! Can you get that

194

through your head or do I have to write it on a rock and *beat* it in?"

"Sure," scoffed Banner, because if she didn't argue she would most certainly cry and plead and make all manner of a fool of herself. "I'm not enough for you, and you go to her!"

"On the contrary, Shamrock—even if I was inclined to take a mistress, I wouldn't have the goddamned energy to do anything about it. You use up everything I've got, wife-of-mine, and more."

Banner blushed, hoping that what he said was true, praying that it was. "Please don't send me to Keith."

"Give me a pen and a flat rock, O'Brien."

"You're impossible—do you know that?"

Adam nodded. "And you're on your way to Wenatchee," he countered. He bent, nipped at her lips with his. "And O'Brien?"

"What?"

"Wear your drawers."

It was a surprise when Katherine Corbin came storming down the wharf, her face red with anger. "Damn those stupid, selfish—"

Banner forgot that she was leaving for Wenatchee, against her will, forgot Sean, forgot the impervious, irritating man beside her. "Katherine! What on earth—?"

Snow was gathering on Katherine's nose and her eyelashes and on the brim of her stylish, feathered hat. "The Territorial Supreme Court overturned the legislature's decision!" she raged. "Suffrage, they say, is unconstitutional! Can you believe it? *Unconstitutional!*"

People were staring at Katherine, albeit with affectionate amusement.

"Mother," intoned Adam. "You have an audience."

"I don't care!" Katherine retorted. "And what are you two doing here, anyway?"

"Banner is leaving."

Some of the high color drained from Katherine's elegant cheekbones. "*What?*"

Banner flung a furious look at her husband. "I'm not going to Wenatchee!" she informed him. "The minute I get off the steamer in Tacoma, I intend to vanish!"

Adam had obviously not considered this possibility; he looked both angry and taken aback. And the word he said turned more heads than Katherine's diatribe about the territorial high court.

"Now look what you've done," Banner said smugly. "You've made a scandal, Adam Corbin."

He bent until his nose was within an inch of her own. "Oh, that was nothing, O'Brien," he hissed. "If you want a scandal, I'll show you a *scandal!*"

"Do let's get in out of the snow and wind," Katherine broke in, suddenly the diplomat.

Adam nodded. "Certainly," he said. "As soon as O'Brien *boards the steamer,* Mother, I'll see you home."

Banner thrust out her chin and folded her arms. She had the imperious Adam Corbin over a barrel, and she knew it. "I'll write you from wherever I decide to go, dear," she said indulgently.

Adam advanced on Banner, backing her down the wharf. Both of them knew that he couldn't spare the time it would take for him to escort her to Wenatchee, and there

196

was no other way he could be certain of her obedience. "You little—"

"You could still let me stay with your woman, you know."

A swear word echoed out over the water.

"Are you afraid we'll compare notes?" pressed Banner. She was at the end of the pier now; another step and she'd be jellyfish bait.

Adam's face was fierce, and his eyes glittered with blue fury. "Get your—get into the carriage!"

"What will you do if I refuse?" exulted Banner sweetly, well aware of the many witnesses claiming baggage on the wharf and boarding buggies and carriages ashore.

"You don't want to know, O'Brien!"

"Oh, yes, I do," she sang back, enjoying her advantage.

The imposing shoulders moved in a shrug. But then Adam lunged at her, grasped her around the waist, and flung her up over one shoulder.

Mortified, Banner kicked and struggled, but Adam simply strode toward the Corbin carriage, hauling her like a grain sack, apparently oblivious to the amused townspeople all around them.

Gaining the carriage, he wrenched open the door and hurled his wife inside, watching impassively as she rolled across the vehicle's muddy floor in a ball of indignation and green woolen.

Katherine shifted in her seat and looked out the window, failing to notice the spectacle in a very studied way.

Adam said something to the carriage driver and then got inside, just as his disgruntled, blushing wife was rising from the floor. He halted her progress by catching her arm and flinging her, face down, across his lap.

Banner could literally feel his hand, poised over her derriere, and she closed her eyes against its inevitable descent.

"Good heavens, Adam," Katherine interceded crisply. "This is barbaric! Have you lost your mind?"

"Yes," he said, and then his hand made sharp contact with Banner's bottom.

Freed from the odd inertia that had possessed her before, Banner cried out, more in outrage than pain, and struggled. Her reward was a second swat, and this one stung.

"Adam Corbin," sputtered Katherine, over the uproar. "If you strike that dear child again, I'll stop this carriage and get out!"

"It is a long walk home, Mother," Adam replied. And then he wrenched Banner's skirts up until her drawers were showing and the cold wind was biting her buttocks through the cloth.

Absolutely stunned by this affront, Banner shivered.

"Cold, my dear?" Adam drawled.

Banner was writhing now, and twisting, trying with renewed desperation to escape. "Yes!" she shrieked.

"This will warm you," he assured her, and then he spanked her in earnest.

She stood facing the parlor fire, a small, rigid bastion of indignation. "Don't you come *near* me, Adam Corbin," she muttered, without sparing him so much as a glance.

Against his better judgment, Adam chuckled. God, how he loved her, needed her, wanted her. "Why don't you sit down?" he teased.

"Why don't you drop dead?" she retorted.

Adam remembered her shapely, upturned backside and his mother's delightful umbrage and chuckled again. "You were the one who insisted on finding out what I would do, Shamrock. Now you know."

Banner whirled to face him, clover green eyes snapping, chin high. "How dare you strike me that way? And in front of your mother, for heaven's sake! I've never been so embarrassed in all my life and my—my *drawers* were showing!"

Adam grinned, delighting in the beruffled memory. "Defy me like that again, Shamrock, and they'll be around your ankles."

Rich color surged into her face, but she swallowed whatever she'd planned to say and nodded almost meekly. Adam was still puzzling over that when she kicked him, hard, in the right shin.

He bellowed in mingled rage and pain, and Banner fled, quite wisely, for her life.

She was kneeling in a chair beside the bedroom fireplace when he reached her, peering at him over the back with wide, wary eyes.

"If you send me to Wenatchee," she said, "I'll run away."

The thought terrified Adam almost as much as the danger Sean Malloy could be to her. He masked that by making a complicated business of undoing the string tie at his throat, opening his shirt. "Do you want to leave me so badly as that, Banner?"

Slowly, she shook her head, and her hair was a magnificent Titian mane, catching the firelight and making it a part of itself. "I don't ever want to leave you," she whispered.

And when Banner slipped out of the chair and stood before him, his breath caught in his throat. She was wearing only a camisole and a pair of drawers.

She lifted her chin. "Are you sorry for what you did?" she asked.

Adam swallowed. "No," he answered, after a long time. "Are you sorry for defying me?"

She smiled, the temptress, knowing what she was doing to him, reveling in it. "No," she replied.

"Fair enough," he said, more moved than he'd ever been by her saucy, brazen beauty. "Come here."

Miraculously, Banner came to him. The yielding, primitive scent of her made Adam's groin grind. He lifted her, carried her back to the chair where she had awaited him, draped her tenderly across his lap.

But this time was quite different from the other, for Banner was facing him now, her succulent breasts rising and falling beneath the gauzy lace and ribbon of her camisole, her green eyes dark with sultry mischief. She slid one hand inside his shirt, tangled her fingers in the coarse matting there, set fire to the very marrow of his bones.

And, with the other, she untied the ribbons that secured her drawers.

Adam moaned as she guided his hand inside and sheltered it in the still hidden silk. Her knees fell wide, her head tilted back. She closed her eyes, and a soft, savage whimper of contentment passed her parted lips.

He enjoyed her gently, watched in wonder and love as she rose and fell in the ancient rhythm of passion. And yet, even as Banner arched her back, cried out, and then fell, shuddering, back to his lap, he had the distinct impression that it was he who had been seduced, he who had been loved and comforted and appeased.

Banner slid from his lap, like a shimmering mermaid sinking back into a magical sea. Her fingers came to the already straining buttons of his trousers and gently undid them.

That heated, needing part of him sprang toward her; she laughed softly and welcomed it with a kiss that caused Adam's very soul to buckle within him.

"Please . . ." he whispered raggedly.

She kissed him again.

An almost convulsive spasm jolted Adam; he spoke in fevered, nonsensical words.

Banner chuckled and tormented him mercilessly with her tongue.

Adam writhed, frantic, and she delighted in him, ruthlessly and with greed.

And then Banner drew back, refusing to do more than kiss him, no matter how he pleaded. Playing his game, she recited all the places where she meant to do this to him, interspersing the wicked promises with nibbles.

Something inside Adam, something heretofore untouched, broke free. He cried out his love for her and his triumph.

He'd boasted that he owned Banner, earlier that day. Now he knew that the truth was quite the opposite.

And she was stroking him, soothing him, igniting new fires that might be fiercer than those just quenched. "I love you, Adam," she said.

Adam couldn't speak—breathing was almost more than he could manage. He groaned.

"Ummm," she said.

Adam braced himself. "N-No—" he managed. "Banner—"

She laughed, an imp come to power. "Yes," she said.

He was growing again, aching again, straining toward her even as he considered begging for mercy.

Begging would have been pointless, even if he could have assembled the words, for, that night, there was no mercy in the wench.

Adam was sleeping deeply, just as Banner had intended. She stroked his dark hair, her touch as light as a whisper, and bent to kiss his temple.

"Goodbye, my love," she said.

Adam stirred and snuggled deeper into the bedding, and one of his arms flailed toward the spot where she should have lain.

Tears clouded Banner's eyes as she turned away.

The night was bitterly cold and very, very dark, and had Banner not such a clear picture of the fate Adam might suffer at Sean's hands, she would have lost courage.

It was snowing as she descended the hill; her shoes and stockings were soaked through before she reached Main Street, and her cloak was little comfort, even with its fur lining.

By rights, Banner knew, she should have left the garment behind; it, like the shamrock pendant, had come to her because of her marriage, not through honest effort.

Approaching the hotel where she had lived so briefly,

Banner shifted her medical bag from one hand to the other and lifted her chin. She'd left all her other clothes, hadn't she? She'd left the fur muff that Katherine had given her at Christmas, the snow-glass from Jeff—her wedding ring.

Banner thought of Adam, sleeping in the warm bed at home. With him, she had left her heart and her spirit.

Climbing the hotel's rough-hewn board steps, she imagined him waking up, finding her gone. Would he be furious? Would he hurt as she was hurting now, as she suspected she would always hurt?

Banner paused at the sturdy doors of the hotel, closed her eyes for just a moment. Adam would rage when he knew she'd left, and he might feel a measure of pain for a time, but his woman would comfort him.

That thought gave Banner the impetus to open a door, march to the registration desk, and ring the bell for service.

Banner did not sleep at all that night, partly because she could not lie still long enough, and partly because she was afraid. Suppose Sean had already been released from jail? Suppose the clerk, who had obviously recognized Banner, had gone up the hill to report her presence in the hotel to Adam?

The steamer arrived at seven-thirty the next morning, and Banner was the first to pay her passage and get on board. It wouldn't have mattered where the craft was bound for—she was thinking strictly in terms of "away"—and the vessel was well out on the sound when Banner consulted her ticket and learned that she was on her way to Seattle.

Even before he could bring himself to open his eyes and

confirm the fact, Adam knew that Banner was gone. He knew that she wasn't just downstairs, talking with Maggie or cleaning instruments in the surgery—she was *gone.*

A spinning, howling storm of grief engulfed Adam. Where should he look first? And what would he do if he never found her?

Adam opened his eyes, forced himself out of bed, to the washstand, into his clothes.

The ring was lying on the bedside table, along with the small drum Banner had given him at Christmas. He touched the toy, took the wedding band up, turned it in his fingers.

Good riddance, O'Brien, he thought.

And then he sat down on the edge of the bed and wept.

Seattle was a virtual frenzy of activity; men shouted on the wharves as the steamer docked, Indian women sold baskets and beads, Chinamen hurried along the wooden walkways bordering the harbor, small under their burdens of firewood, laundry, or salted fish.

Banner drew a deep breath, walked purposefully to the base of the pier, and sat down on a snow-dusted whiskey barrel to ponder the days, weeks, and months ahead.

Had she traveled far enough? How long could the small amount of money she had be expected to last?

All around, whistles shrilled and bells clanged and people greeted each other. How lonely Banner felt, knowing there was no one there to hug her and shuffle her into a warm carriage and ask solicitously how the voyage had been.

A tear slid down Banner's cheek, and she dashed it

away, bumping her nose with the corner of her medical bag in the process. "Drat!" she sobbed.

"Banner?"

She stiffened, looked up.

Before her stood Jeff Corbin, his blue coat sprinkled with glistening flakes of snow, his eyes warm and more than slightly suspicious as they scanned the length of the wharf and then came back to Banner's face.

"Where's Adam?"

Banner shrugged.

Hands wedged comfortably into his coat pockets, Jeff tilted his head back, searched the sky with a curious sort of interest, then dropped his gaze to his sister-in-law again. "You ran away, didn't you?"

"Yes," admitted Banner miserably.

"Why?"

"He—" she thought quickly, desperately—"he beat me."

Jeff laughed. "Adam? Try again, Banner. I'd sooner believe that he stepped out of a second-floor window and flew around the house."

Banner's toes were numb inside her wet shoes, and she was hungry and tired and heartbroken. And now, of all the people in the Pacific Northwest, for heaven's sake, she had encountered her husband's brother.

How bad could one person's luck be?

"He did beat me," she insisted, somewhat lamely. "He turned me over his knee and—"

Jeff's mouth twitched. "That I can accept."

"Thank you very much," pouted Banner, who was near tears and at the end of her very shaky resolve to be strong.

Jeff crooked one arm toward her. "Come on. We'll get something to eat and discuss my brother's tendency toward brutality."

Banner knew that he was mocking her, but she was too disspirited to rise to the challenge. "I won't go back to Port Hastings," she said, even as she rose from her seat on the whiskey barrel and took the captain's arm.

Ten minutes later, Jeff and Banner entered the busy, clamorous dining room of an expensive hotel.

"Are you staying here?" Banner asked, hoping to guide the conversation away from Adam and her reasons for leaving him.

"I slept here last night," Jeff said, as a pretty waitress minced and fretted at the table side, trying her best to win the captain's attention. Finally the girl went away. "We came into port yesterday," he finished.

Banner's stomach grumbled inelegantly, and she fixed her eyes on the menu. "You left rather suddenly," she said, referring to his disappearance on Christmas Day.

"So did you, I'll wager," he retorted. "And you didn't tell my brother you were going, did you?"

Banner looked up. "Of course I did," she lied.

"You did not. If you had, you wouldn't be here now."

Too hungry to argue, Banner simply shrugged.

The waitress returned, first with coffee and then with plates laden with savory roast beef, boiled potatoes, and green beans.

Banner ate hungrily and tried to plan another escape. "Are there—are there personal facilities here?" she asked, when her plate was empty.

Jeff looked amused. "Of course," he said, nodding

toward the lobby.

Banner dabbed at her mouth with her napkin and tried to look innocent. "If you'll just excuse me for a moment?"

Again he nodded. There was a languid flow to Jeff's movements as he sat back in his chair and folded his arms.

Banner stood up and walked sedately to the doors leading into the lobby. Her ruse was only partial; she did need to find the conveniences.

She was washing her hands when she remembered that she'd left her cloak and her medical bag in the dining room. How was she to recover them without confronting Jeff?

She was still pondering this dilemma when she opened the door and stepped out into the lobby.

Jeff was there, holding Banner's bag and cloak and grinning indulgently. Clearly she had not fooled him for a moment. "Ready?" he said.

"Give me my things!" Banner hissed.

He looked down at her shoes, the damp hem of her skirt. Concern and amusement mingled in his face. "No," he replied flatly.

Banner was tired of dealing with immovable, officious, overbearing Corbins, and she said so in no uncertain terms.

Jeff only shrugged and took her arm in a grasp that was at once painless and totally inescapable. "You're not going anywhere," he said. "Except to my room, where you will have a hot bath and some sleep."

"Your *room?* I will not!"

"Yes, you will. Your clothes are wet and you're obviously exhausted."

"You plan to tell Adam that I'm here!"

"Excellent guess, Mrs. Corbin. Adore you though I do, my first loyalty is to my brother, Adam's interests are my interests, and I'll be damned if I'm going to let his wife walk out of here and catch her death of pneumonia."

"If you take me one step further, captain, I will scream."

"And I will politely explain to all these onlookers that you are my bride, suffering from a state of imperiled virginity. They'll believe me, Banner."

They would believe him, Banner knew that. Their sympathies would lie with Jeff, not herself.

"You don't understand," she pleaded, as he ushered her up the wide, carpeted staircase. "I can't face Adam. I can't go back!"

Jeff smiled at a portly gentleman in the upper hallway and dragged her on. "He loves you."

They reached a door with a huge brass 7 affixed to it, and Jeff drew a key from the pocket of his coat. Banner grew desperate.

"Adam has a woman!"

Jeff pushed her inside the spacious, well-furnished room. "Maybe. Then again, maybe not. In any case, sweetness, you're not leaving this room until you've talked with him."

"I told you that he beat me!"

The captain arched one sandy eyebrow. "I'm beginning to understand what prompted my brother to violence. There is a tub in there, through that door," he said. "Get out of those wet clothes, take a bath, and get into bed."

"I'm not one of your crewmen, *captain!* Kindly stop giving me orders!"

"Kindly stop giving me guff."

Banner thrust out her chin and gauged her chances of getting around the massive barrier of this man's body and escaping. They weren't good.

"When Adam finds out that you made me stay here, he'll thrash you!"

Jeff laughed. "He'll thank me. You're the one he's going to be mad at."

"Please, Jeff."

He turned away, his hand on the door knob. "Get some rest, Mrs. Corbin. I'll be back in a few hours." Jeff paused, tilted his head in her direction. "One of my crewmen will be outside, in the hallway, so don't try to leave."

Beaten, Banner lowered her head. She flinched as the door closed and the key turned in the lock.

The messenger hailed Adam as he came out of the court-house. "I've got a telegraph letter for you, Doc!"

Adam grasped the message, his hands trembled slightly as he ripped away the envelope. Please, he thought wildly. Please.

The words printed on that weather-dampened bit of paper made his heart leap within him: "Banner here with me, in Seattle. Capitol Hotel. Bring her across? Jeff."

Adam laughed, dizzy with relief, and handed the messenger a five-dollar gold piece.

"Wanna send an answer?" asked the boy, staring at the coin in his mittened palm.

Adam dictated a brief reply and ran to his buggy.

Stoically, Banner Corbin stripped off her wet clothes and hung them over a screen that stood in front of a small, ornate ivory fireplace. Then, after commandeering one of Jeff's shirts for a wrapper, she went into the bathing room and began filling the tub.

As she removed the shirt and stepped into the water, she remarked to herself that the Corbins certainly traveled in style. There wasn't even a boiler affixed to this tub, at least, not one that she could see, and yet the water flowed hot from the spigot.

The bath was comforting; Banner had not realized how cold and tired she was until she settled in to soak.

When the water grew tepid, she got out, dried herself with a soft towel that smelled of naphtha, and drained the tub. Moments later, crawling between cozy flannel sheets, Banner yawned and thought that, if a person was bound to be held prisoner, there were certainly worse places for it.

Jeff laid the key on the bar and grinned. "Number seven," he said.

Adam lifted his glass in a weary, wry salute. "Thank you. Is she all right, Jeff? Where did you find her?"

"One question at a time, brother. Banner is fine, and I found her on the wharf, sitting on a barrel and looking like an abandoned urchin. It took me half an hour to get her to tell me why she'd left you, and even then she wouldn't say much more than 'he beat me' and 'he has a woman.' "

Adam took up the room key, dropped it into his pocket. "I didn't beat her, and I don't have a woman." He paused, took a sip from his whiskey, and then explained about Sean Malloy and Banner's reasons for fearing the man.

"Good God," Jeff breathed when his brother was finished. "What are you going to do?"

"I don't know. I can't be with Banner every minute—it just isn't possible. The only sane thing to do is send her away somewhere, until Malloy moves on. The trouble is, ever since I woke up this morning and found her gone, I've felt as though somebody scraped my insides out with a blunt scalpel."

Jeff nodded. His eyes were musing, and a grin lifted one corner of his mouth. "There is one other solution. It's a little unethical, but what the hell?"

"What—"

Jeff chuckled, gave his brother's shoulder an affectionate slap. "Just go upstairs to your wife, big brother. I'm setting sail for Port Hastings."

Chapter Ten

Francelle's father looked pompous and blustery, as usual. Banner was subdued, staring into her wineglass as though she expected a banshee to rise out of it, and Adam seemed restless, irritable.

Jeff grinned and turned his attention to his dinner.

"It's a shame, that's what it is!" barked Senator May-hugh, who never missed a chance to run his mouth.

"You're speaking of the decision about suffrage, I hope," put in Katherine, softly venomous.

"That, too," conceded the senator, reddening.

"Papa's upset about the crimping," Francelle chimed. "We were talking about it on our way over here tonight. Think of it—men being *shanghaied,* in this day and age!"

Jeff watched in wry silence as Adam's head shot up. Blue eyes met blue eyes, and the air seemed to crackle.

"You're a man of the sea, Jeff," boomed Mayhugh. "What do you think of the practice?"

"Crimping?" Jeff fought down the wide grin that was tugging at both sides of his mouth. "Terrible thing, just terrible."

Adam stiffened, frowned thoughtfully. "When do you sail—captain?"

"Midnight," answered Jeff, with a lift of his glass.

"Where is Malloy?" Adam demanded, his eyes boring into his brother's broad back.

Jeff turned from the liquor cabinet in the cabin of the *Sea Mistress,* a brandy snifter in his hand. "In the hold," he answered.

"Son of a—"

Jeff glared. "Gratitude is a wonderful thing," he remarked.

"Gratitude! Do you realize that you could go to prison for this? Suppose the revenue people decide to examine your cargo?"

"It's all legal. No Chinese nationals, no Canadian rum, no contraband of any kind."

"Except for Sean Malloy."

Jeff grinned, lifted his shoulders in a shrug. "The chloral hydrate won't wear off for at least twelve hours. If we sight a cutter, I'll have the bastard dumped in a bunk and tell the inspectors that he had himself a fine time on Water Street before we sailed." He paused. "He did, as a matter of fact. Went straight there after he got out of jail."

"And your men picked him up."

Jeff raised his glass and grinned again. "If I'd known it

was this easy, I might have turned to a life of crime years ago."

Adam laughed, in spite of himself, but he saw the ache behind his brother's mirth and knew it for what it was. "You'll let me know when Malloy jumps ship?"

"I don't plan to grant him shore leave in the near future, but if he gets away, I'll send you a wire."

Adam went to the door, looked back over his shoulder. "Jeff?"

"Yo."

"Take care, all right?"

"You, too. And look after Banner."

Adam nodded. There was more to say—so much more—but he didn't know how to begin, so he stepped out of his brother's cabin and into the gangway leading to the deck.

As he closed the door, Adam heard Jeff's brandy snifter shatter against a wall.

Katherine Corbin watched surreptitiously, and with no little amusement, as her daughter-in-law sat down on the edge of the bed and winced.

"Was Adam angry, Banner?"

Banner looked up, nodded. A revealing blush rose from just above her bodice to pulse in her face. "He was very angry," she replied.

Katherine could well envision the scenario that must have taken place in that Seattle hotel room. She'd been through a dozen like it, with Daniel, though the circumstances had been different.

Daniel. Lord, just the thought of him made her heart

213

contract, even after these five years without him. He had died, but Katherine's love for him had not.

"I should have warned you," she said, sitting down beside Banner, on the bed, and patting her hand. "The Corbin men have been spanking their women for centuries. Unforgivable as it is, they go right on doing it."

The lovely green eyes widened. "What makes me the maddest," Banner confided, in bemused tones, "is that I still love Adam. What's the matter with me? Am I deranged? Perverse?"

Katherine laughed. "If you are, I was too. Once, Daniel and I had a terrible argument—Adam and Jeff were just babies then—and I put every stitch of clothing that man owned in the middle of the road and lit a match to it all!"

Banner's eyes were the size of saucers. "What happened then?"

Katherine giggled at the memory. "The blaze could be seen from Mt. Rainier, I'm sure!" she said. "And Daniel was in a fine rage, I'll tell you that. I'll never forget the way he stomped on his Sunday shirt, trying to put out the flames!"

"Weren't you frightened?"

"*Frightened?*" Katherine laughed again. "Banner, I was terrified! But I didn't want him to know that, so I made matters worse by shouting out that I meant to take the boys and leave him forever."

"What did he do?"

"Mercy," breathed Katherine, shuddering to recollect it. "He came storming into that cabin, my Daniel, mad as sin. He threw up my skirts, pulled down my drawers, and blistered me. Maggie was passing by—bless her heart, she heard me screaming and thought the Indians were having their way with me. She rushed in with her husband's shotgun and there I was with my face as red as my bottom. I wanted to fall through a crack in the floor."

Banner giggled, and some of the confusion drained from her wonderful, tired eyes. "But you loved Daniel too much to leave him?"

"Yes. Truth to tell, the only real injury was to my pride, and when Daniel made love to me, I didn't have any pride."

Banner nodded, and there was a touching look of empathy about her. In hushed tones, she recounted the hotel episode.

The story was quite similar to Katherine's.

Silver fire played over Banner's breasts as Adam kissed one and gently fondled the other. It felt good—so good—to lie in his bed again, to feel the weight of his body on hers and be flung skyward by his insatiable loving.

She whimpered as he pinched one nipple into an obedient pout. "Did—you know that your father—used to—spank your mother?"

Adam chuckled, sampled the nubbin with a searing tongue. "I remember it well," he said.

"It's an—aberration—"

He took suckle, languidly, crooning as she rose to him. "Terrible, terrible—I'll try to—break the habit."

Banner thrust him away suddenly, powerful in her fury. "You'll have to do more than *try*, Adam Corbin! I'm not a child and I won't let you treat me as though I were!"

He considered her seriously. "All right, O'Brien," he

215

said, at last. "You're an adult, and a doctor, and I'll trea you accordingly. But I want something in return."

"What?"

"A promise. Banner, if you really want to leave me there isn't much I can do to stop you. But don't—please—don't sneak off like that again. If you must go, *tell* me, foi God's sake. You can't begin to imagine the things tha went through my mind—until I got to the courthouse anc made sure Malloy was still in his cell, I thought he migh have taken you somehow."

"I-I'm sorry, Adam. I thought you would know—wher I left the ring and the drum—"

"I did, on one level. But on another I was scared. More scared than I've ever been in my life."

She traced the strong, taut line of his jaw with a tendei finger. "There is still Sean. What are we going to do, Adam?"

"For the next few weeks—maybe months—he won't be a problem."

"Why?"

"Because he's been shanghaied."

Banner gasped. "Jeff?"

"Jeff," confirmed Adam, with a sigh. "Sometimes my brother takes a rather direct approach to a problem."

Despite her misgivings and fears, Banner giggled. "He does, doesn't he? It seems to be a family trait."

Adam's lips were back at her breasts, teasing, asserting a gentle dominance. "Speaking of direct approaches . . ."

"Ummm," replied Banner.

Banner awakened in a merry mood. She and Adam had

216

reached a new level of maturity in their union, it seemed to her, and for a time, at least, there was no danger of encountering Sean.

As she went down the back stairs, to get her morning coffee, Banner was congratulating herself on how perfect her life was, how wonderful.

And Maggie was scowling as she washed dishes at the sink. "That fool," she muttered. "Damn, stupid, cussed *fool*."

Some instinct turned the lining of Banner's stomach brittle. "Maggie, what is it?"

Maggie flung one stricken look at Banner and swallowed her diatribe. The motions of her arms were swift and fierce as she went back to scrubbing a skillet.

"Maggie," insisted Banner.

"None of my business what Adam Corbin does," fussed Maggie, her tone terse and cryptic.

Banner ached, and all her happiness wafted away like powder flung into a high wind. After all they'd said and shared, Adam had gone up the mountain again.

"I'm going to follow him," decided his wife. "This time—"

But Maggie shook her head vigorously. "He's been gone over an hour. And there are dozens of trails up that mountain—he could have taken any one of them."

"You're the one who said I should follow Adam the next time!"

"I wasn't thinking," retorted the housekeeper angrily. "There are wild animals up there, and wandering Indians. You wouldn't be safe by yourself."

"Wild animals!" Banner scoffed. "It's winter. Bears

217

hibernate in—"

"Ain't just bears!" broke in Maggie. "There's mountain lions, too. And bobcats."

Banner wasn't listening; she was trying to decide what clothes to wear and which horse to ask for at the stables. Adam had an hour's start, but his team and wagon would leave tracks in the deep snow. Eventually, she would find him.

"Banner Corbin . . ." Maggie threatened when the younger woman turned and bounded back up the kitchen staircase.

Though it was but a hill when compared to the looming Cascades and craggy Olympics, that mountain was high. It was cold out, and there were strange sounds coming from the thick woods. Wrapped in woolen scarves and an old coat she'd found at the back of Adam's wardrobe, Banner rode staunchly on.

The dappled gray mare she'd saddled herself was slow as it labored up the steep trail, nickering and tossing its head and stopping to nibble whenever there was a patch of grass peeking out of the snow.

Finding the trail had not been as easy as Banner had expected; there were tracks of every sort on the paths that scribbled up the mountains like veins. Once she'd had to turn around and backtrack more than a mile, realizing that the parallel lines she'd been following were too close together to have been made by a wagon or even a buggy.

As she progressed, slowly, uncertainly, up the treacherous face of that mountain, Banner Corbin wondered if she wasn't making a disasterous mistake. Suppose she found Adam and his woman and her suspicions became

218

wounding realities?

Suppose there was a cozy cabin, with smoke billowing from its chimney and snow trimming its windows? Suppose there were children playing in the dooryard?

Banner shook herself. Adam had said there was no woman—repeatedly. But he was obviously keeping a secret, not only from his wife but from everyone else, too, and she had to know what it was.

Annoyance and a sting to her pride gave Banner the strength to go on. She had told Adam about Sean and her first marriage, however belatedly. Why was he refusing to shed any sort of light on this mystery of his own?

In the dense woods to Banner's right, an owl hooted, and something scampered through the thorny blackberry vines along the trail, startling the little mare, causing it to dance and throw back its head. A new snow began to fall, slowly filling the hoofprints and the tracks of Adam's rig.

Banner was cold. And scared.

What if it turned out that she wasn't following Adam at all, but some mountain man or miner? What if she froze to death and no one ever found her body?

In the distance, an unseen creature emitted a chilling, keening sort of cry. The mare grew very nervous, her eyes rolling, her teeth on the bridle bit.

"Easy," pleaded Banner, who was no rider as it was and every bit as frightened as the horse. "Easy, now . . ."

The beast was in no state to be mollified. In a sudden burst of high spirit, it reared, flinging its stunned passenger into a thicket of nettles and hazelnut bushes. Before Banner could get free of the thorns and whiplike vines and scramble to her feet, the horse was trotting back down the mountain, its reins dragging on the ground.

"Stop!" Banner screamed, hopelessly, her breath making a white cone in the frigid air.

The horse ran on, of course, and Banner wedged her hands into the deep pockets of Adam's old coat. "Dogmeat!" she yelled after it.

Now, the woods seemed more oppressive than ever. It was almost as though the giant Douglas firs took one step nearer every time she blinked her eyes.

Banner looked up the mountain, then down, trying to decide which way to go. Her hand closed over something in the pocket of the coat and she drew it out, needing some small task to keep her panic under control.

The item was a business card: "Miss Lou, Room 4. *Silver Shadow*. Always a gentle welcome."

Banner sat down on a snow-covered tree stump and cried without shame. The snow fell faster and harder and the trail gradually became smooth. Sniffling, the doctor prepared herself for certain death.

Nearer now, the beast that had frightened her horse away gave a shrieklike growl.

Banner would be torn to quivering, bloody shreds; she just knew it. The creature was coming closer and closer and, whatever it was, it meant to make a meal of her.

She squared her shoulders and waited as bravely as she could.

One hour passed, and then another. The temperature had fallen, and the snow was so dense that Banner couldn't see more than a few feet. It would certainly be a mercy if she froze before the animal reached her—

"*O'Brien?*"

Death must be very close now; Banner was hearing Adam's voice, feeling the strength of his arms beneath her knees and under her back. Euphoria, that was it. She'd read that people felt euphoria when they were about to die of exposure.

"God damn it, O'Brien," snapped the voice of her final fantasy. "If you die on me, I'll never forgive you!"

It was so real, this death-dream. Banner could feel the roughness of a heavy coat against one cheek, smell the scent that was Adam's alone. There was even a jostling motion, a sensation of being carried.

But then there was nothing.

Heaven. Somehow, Banner had bypassed the flames of hell and the darkness of purgatory and been admitted to heaven.

She was warm, so warm, and cosseted in something soft. "I'm divorced," she said, to the nearest angel, who was a vague and shifting shape beside her.

The answering chuckle was oddly familiar and too gruff and sensual to be divine.

Banner's hazed vision cleared at last, and she gasped. Beside her, looking haggard and more than a little annoyed, stood Adam. She was lying in a bed, completely naked, and there were quilts draped over her in smothering layers.

"Where—"

"Be quiet."

Adam went to a flickering fireplace nearby, brought back a mug of something hot and sweetly fragrant.

The brew was a mixture of coffee, sugar, and rum, and

Banner lifted her head to sip it, Adam holding the cup.

"You were following me, weren't you, O'Brien?" he drawled, in a voice that was at once tender and demonic.

Banner fell back to her pillows; it was too hard to hold her head up. Tears rose up in her eyelashes, slid down her face in stinging trails. So there *was* a cabin. And Adam obviously knew his way around the place, felt at home.

"Is this your bed?" she whispered.

"It belongs to a friend of mine. Sleep, O'Brien. We can talk later."

"Where is she?"

An exasperated sound echoed in the warm room. "Who?"

"Your—your friend." Banner's eyes closed, weighted by her weariness. The covers were being tucked beneath her chin, the mattress shifted as Adam sat down on the bed.

Suddenly, Banner was cold again.

"Sleep, damn it," Adam rasped.

"I can't—too—c-cold—"

There was a thumping sound—boots striking the floor? Banner didn't know.

But then Adam was beneath the covers, beside her. He was fully clothed and warm, so wonderfully warm.

Though she was comforted, physically, Banner wept within herself. This was Adam's bed, that woman's bed.

She didn't belong here.

The snow was deep and still coming down. Adam Corbin frowned, took another draught from his coffee cup, and cursed the blizzard that might well force him to betray a secret he had literally guarded with his life.

O'Brien stirred in the bed on the other side of the cabin. She would awaken soon, fit again, after her long rest, and start asking questions.

Adam thought of how she'd scared him the day before and regretted his promise not to treat her as a child. At the moment, he would like nothing better than to drag her across his knee and raise blisters on her bare backside.

He smiled. Well, maybe there was *one* thing he'd like better.

Adam took a step toward the bed and stopped himself. This was no time for passion—Banner had nearly died the day before. Thank God, she hadn't, he thought.

He went back to the window and studied the ceaseless snow, wishing there was some way to get word down the mountain that both he and Banner were safe, wondering if it was really warm out in the shed, as Lulani assured him it was.

Banner opened her eyes. The interior of the cabin was filled with shifting shadows and the scent of something savory cooking.

She yawned. "Adam?"

The voice that answered was feminine. "He is with—he is not here. You will eat?"

Banner's heart wedged itself into her throat and pulsed there. She could make out, though just barely, the slender figure standing at a tiny stove across the room. "You are his woman," she said, in a lifeless voice.

223

There was a hesitant silence before the answer came. "Yes."

Banner wanted to die. He'd lied. Adam had *lied.* "I am Adam's wife," she said woodenly, drawing her knees up and wrapping her arms around them.

"Yes." The woman drew nearer. "Adam has spoken of you."

Adam has spoken of you. The words were uttered so flatly, without rancor or indignation of any kind. Didn't the woman care? Was she so much in love with Adam that the betrayal didn't matter?

Banner ached. It was entirely possible. Hurt as she was, she herself had yet to entertain the idea of leaving Adam. "This is your bed?" she muttered, overwhelmed by her pain and yet inviting more.

"Yes. You are hungry?"

Banner studied her husband's mistress; she was tall and probably Indian—her hair and skin looked dark—but given the poor light, she could discern little more. "No—thank you."

"You will love him?" the woman asked, in a peculiar, flat cadence. "You will treat Adam well, always?"

Treat him well? If he'd been there, the reprehensible scoundrel, Banner would have clawed his eyes out of his head. She burst into loud, unceremonious tears.

The woman patted her shoulder. "*Mesatchie*—much bad to hurt so much. Sleep, eat. Tomorrow, go back to town."

Having said these mysterious things, the woman moved about the cabin, gathering things, stoking the fire on the hearth, humming as though she had not been put out of her bed by her lover's wife.

224

Finally, she brought a wooden bowl brimming with stew to the bedside, extending it with both hands.

"I can't eat," Banner informed her, grinding her forehead into her upraised knees.

"Need to eat."

"No."

There was a soft clatter—Adam's woman had set the bowl on the floorboards beside the bed—and then Banner was alone. The winter wind howled around the sturdy walls of the cabin and rattled the windows.

She tried to get out of bed, found that she was weaker than she'd thought, and fell back to the mattress. How many times had Adam betrayed her, here, beneath these very covers?

A cry of mingled pain and rage rippled itself from Banner's throat just as the cabin door opened and Adam came in, carrying firewood in his arms.

"What's the matter, O'Brien?"

Banner shrieked again, bent to grasp the bowl of stew, and flung it at him. "Liar!" she screamed. "You filthy *liar!*"

He seemed unperturbed by the attack, and he strode toward the fireplace and dropped the wood on the stone hearth. "What are you talking about?"

"Your woman! She was just here"—a great shudder rocked Banner Corbin—"you bastard—you bastard—"

Adam came to her, caught her bare shoulders in weather-chilled hands, shook her hard. "Stop it, O'Brien! You don't understand!"

Banner began to laugh, convulsively, hysterically, like a madwoman she'd seen in a hospital once. "I *saw* her—I talked to her—"

"O'Brien!"

The maniacal laughter turned to raw, soul-splintering sobs. "I hate you, Adam. I hate you!"

Banner had expected anger, denials, anything but what actually happened. Adam drew her very close, held her. "No," he pleaded, "No."

She struggled in his arms, at once repulsed and drawn. "Let me go—don't touch me—"

Adam refused to release her. "That was Lulani that you saw," he said softly, reasonably. "I told you that this cabin belonged to a friend of mine, and it does. It's Lulani's."

"Your mistress!" Banner burst out, into the Adam-scented woolen of his heavy coat.

"No. *My friend.*"

"Friend!"

"Yes."

"I despise you. Let go of me—don't ever touch me again!"

"Take a deep breath, O'Brien, and stop being such a barley brain. Do you think I'd be stupid enough to bring you here if Lulani was my woman?"

Banner quivered. She didn't know what to think about anything anymore. She could only feel, and what she felt was raw, ceaseless pain.

"It w-was too far down the mountain and I was f-freezing. What else could you do, besides bring me here?"

He made no answer, but he pressed Banner back into the bed, and that, in itself, seemed to be a reply.

"Where will she sleep, with me in here?" Banner demanded, sniffling.

"There's a stove in the shed—she's staying there."

226

"How accommodating of her!"

Adam drew away from the bed. "I'll get you another bowl of stew," he said, with hard-won patience.

"I won't eat it!"

"Yes, you will," he replied flatly. There was a rattling sound, the clink of a kettle lid, the click of a wooden spoon.

"Are you ashamed of Lulani? Is that why you keep your visits to her such a secret?"

Even in the dim, dim light, Banner could see his shoulders tense. "Of course I'm not ashamed. She's a good friend—one of the best I've ever had."

"Then why don't you talk about her?"

Silence.

"Adam."

He came to the bedside again, thrust a spoonful of stew into Banner's gaping mouth. She spat it at him.

Adam caught her jaw in a hard grasp, forced it open. "Do that again, O'Brien," he rasped, "and promise or no promise, I will drag you out of that bed and paddle you within an inch of your stubborn, suspicious little life!"

The next time the spoon came to her mouth, Banner ate. She had to. But she didn't have to be cordial about it.

"Does she satisfy you?"

Adam's face was taut, wan in the light of the dancing fire. "Did Sean Malloy satisfy you?" he retorted.

The words struck Banner with the impact of a physical blow. Tears smarted in her eyes and fury ran wild in her veins, heating her blood. "Yes!" she lied, wanting to hurt Adam the way he had hurt her.

Adam closed his eyes for a moment, and when he

227

opened them again, they were the eyes of a cruel stranger. "And he taught you well, didn't he? I suppose I should be grateful to good old Sean."

The room swayed with the force of Banner's anger; her heart leaped and her eyes flared and her hand came up to strike his face.

But Adam caught her wrist in a harsh grip and stayed her. "Don't," he warned in a low, gruff voice.

And then he forced Banner to eat every last smidgeon of the stew in her bowl, bite by bile-raising bite.

Much later, when he joined her in the bed, naked and strong, she turned away from him with an eloquent flouncing motion.

Adam wrenched her back. "Lulani is not my woman," he seethed. "You are. And you will, *by God,* behave as such!"

Banner gathered the spittle in her mouth and spewed it at him.

With terrifying speed, he was upon her. His hands held her wrists, stretching them above her head, his thighs were like granite upon hers. His ink-blue eyes glittered and his teeth were bared, like those of a beast pushed to fury.

"Spread your legs, O'Brien," he growled.

Banner glared at him, hating him, loving him. Worst of all, wanting him. Even now, with all she knew, forces inside her commanded her to receive him. "Go to hell!" she hissed.

"Hell is where you are, O'Brien," Adam bit out. "And where you're not, paradoxical as it sounds. But you're my wife and this is one thing you will not refuse me!"

Banner began to struggle and writhe beneath him,

weeping in her fury. He would have her in Lulani's' bed—
she couldn't bear it. She couldn't!

"Go to her and l-leave me alone!"

One of Adam's knees parted her legs; she could feel the
warm, fierce strength of him at the portal of her womanhood, commanding, not to be denied. He held her wrists in
place and slid down to take slow, deliberate suckle at her
right breast.

Banner groaned and ceased her fighting.

The coupling was a savage one; Adam and Banner battered each other in their ferocious, reluctant passion, both
fevered, both moaning. The peak was reached in a
straining tumult that forced hoarse cries of intertwined victory and defeat from their throats.

Adam seemed determined to subdue Banner, and from the
set of his face, she decided that he hated her.

"Are you warm enough?" he demanded as he climbed
onto the frigid wagon seat beside her, settling the heavy
bearskin lap rug over his legs as well as hers.

"Cozy," she said in tones of sugared acid.

The snow had stopped, but the weather was brutally
cold that morning. Almost as cold as the expression in
Adam's eyes. "If you're planning to leave when we get
back to Port Hastings," he intoned, "one word of warning:
Don't."

The buckboard, drawn by two sturdy horses, was
moving away from Lulani's cabin. It was hard traveling in
the deep, crusted snow.

"As far as I'm concerned," Banner answered, chin high,
"leaving would only be a formality. You are not my hus-

band anymore, you are simply a man who assaulted me."

Adam laughed, low in his throat, and with a discouraging lack of amusement. "Assaulted you, is it? I can still feel your heels pressing into the small of my back, O'Brien. Who assaulted whom?"

"I hate you!"

He smiled coldly. "I know," he said, and his hand came, brazen and strong, to her thigh, beneath the questionable shelter of the lap rug.

"Stop that!"

Adam was drawing up her skirts; they rose slowly but surely to her waist. "When will you learn?" he sighed.

Banner squirmed, helpless, as he reached inside the heavy flannel drawers she'd worn for warmth. "Stop—don't—"

Adam laughed again, his fingers already working their wicked magic. "Stop? I wouldn't dream of it, O'Brien. I want to watch you hate me."

Banner trembled; a blush rose in her face. It was torture, that's what it was—unconscionable, scandalous torture. So why did it feel so good?

"I d-do hate you—I *swear* I do!"

"I can see that," Adam drawled.

Banner's breath was coming in quick, fevered gasps now—her knees, with this man traitors to her good sense, were parting. "Oh, God—I beg of you—"

"Stop?" The word was breathed, not spoken.

"Damn you!"

Adam gave no quarter; his thumb plied her to passion skillfully, while his fingers conquered her. "I was damned the day you came into my life," he answered.

Banner's head fell backward, her eyes closed. Her heart was racing, and a brutal, despairing heat was building inside her. The jolting and shifting of the wagon, as it was pulled over the trail, intensified the wild sensations Adam was stirring inside her. "Oh," she panted, in her desperation, "Oh . . ."

Adam laughed. "Say you belong to me."

Banner gasped at the sweet power of his thrust and stubbornly, blindly shook her head.

"Say it, Banner."

The world crumbled apart, in flaming pieces, as Banner finally obeyed.

They arrived in Port Hastings at sunset and were greeted joyfully by Maggie and Katherine. There had been no great disasters during their absence, but a number of people had left word that they required the services of a doctor.

"Go to bed, O'Brien," Adam snapped, in the welcome warmth of Maggie's kitchen. "I'll make the rounds."

Another time, Banner might have argued. Tonight, she was too tired and too bewildered, and she gave in without a fight.

But as she climbed the back stairs, much in need of a bath and a long rest, her cheeks flamed and her pride smarted. If Adam Corbin thought to enjoy her favors this night, after all he'd done to make her despise him, he could think again.

Summarily, without troubling Maggie for help, Banner moved the necessary belongings from Adam's room to the guest chamber at the opposite end of the hall. That done, she bathed, draped herself in a heavy flannel wrapper, and marched past her husband's door with resolve and flaming cheeks.

In her own room, self-appropriated but hers for at least this one night, Banner locked the door and stumbled to bed. She was asleep almost before she'd drawn the covers to her chin.

Adam fully intended to be unfaithful. O'Brien thought he was every kind of a rounder anyway, so by God, if he had to have the pain, he was going to have the pleasure.

"You look like hell," commented Bessie, sitting back on the bed and crossing her shapely legs at the knees. "How about a drink?"

Adam leaned against a bureau and folded his arms. She must be freezing to death in those net stockings and that skimpy satin thing with the laces up the front—what the devil was it called?

"Bourbon," he said, at length.

Bessie stood up, poured the requested refreshment. "Isn't Red giving you what you need?" she crooned.

Adam's stomach turned within him. O'Brien was giving him what he needed, all right—and a lot that he sure as hell didn't. But he'd be damned if he was going to discuss his wife with this whore.

Bessie came to him, held out the drink. If his silence bothered her, she didn't let on.

"It's been a long time, honey," she said.

The bourbon curdled in the pit of Adam's stomach "Yeah," he said, scowling into his glass.

Bessie's hands came to his shoulders, familiar, skillful

"Don't worry—Bessie remembers what you like."

Adam shrugged free of her, turned away. There were business cards on a table nearby, and he took one up, reading the gilt script, not comprehending a word. Bessie might remember what he liked, but did he? All he could think of was Banner and the way she could fling him beyond death and then resurrect him again.

Idly, for something to do, Adam tucked the card into the inside pocket of his suitcoat.

Bessie stood behind him, wrapped her arms around his waist. "She'll never know," she assured him perceptively. "And I promise it will be good."

"It might be good," Adam rasped, in exasperation, as he freed himself again, "but it would be stupid as hell. I've got to go home."

Bessie was pouting as he handed her money; it was the first time he'd ever paid her. "It was going to be a wedding present!" she protested.

The irony of that made Adam laugh gruffly as he strode toward the door. "Thanks anyway," he called, over his shoulder, as he left the room.

Banner Corbin slept through the night, though not soundly. She half-expected Adam to come pounding at the door, at any time, or even break it down.

Her rest was a shallow and unsettled one, and toward morning she dreamed that Adam and Lulani were making love in the cabin's solitary bed.

Neither of them even cared that Banner was outside, in the wind and snow, freezing to death.

Chapter Eleven

Humming, Francelle Mayhugh sat down at her desk, smoothed the skirts of her best dress, and uncovered her typewriting machine. Beside her was a stack of notes and letters, all scrawled in Adam's nearly illegible hand.

He came into the office as she was struggling over a dry treatise on someone's gall bladder. Francelle remembered all the delicious gossip Marshal Peters had recounted the night before, at her father's dinner table, and felt a surge of wild and glorious hope.

"Good morning," she sang.

Adam scowled at something on the wall behind her, as though she were transparent, and ran one hand through his hair. He clearly hadn't had a restful night; for all his grooming, there were shadows under his eyes and his mouth was taut with strain.

"Have you seen my wife?" he snapped, for all the world as though he was accusing Francelle of hiding the hussy somewhere.

"No," said his secretary, with dignity. "If you don't know where she is, how would I?"

Adam looked ominous for a moment, then sighed. "How indeed?" he rumbled, and then he went to the little stove in the corner and helped himself to the coffee that was always ready but never appreciated.

Francelle stiffened in her chair. "Marshal Peters came to dinner last night," she said, cautiously.

Adam lifted his coffee mug, offhandedly disdainful. "Hurray," he said.

A flush blossomed in Francelle's cheeks. For a man

whose wife might have a spare husband, he was a cocky soul. "The marshal was telling Papa and me about that Irishman—Mr. Malloy?"

To her carefully hidden satisfaction, Adam stiffened. For once in his life, he was noticing Francelle Mayhugh and listening to her, too. "What about him?"

Francelle shrugged. "He's a ne'er-do-well, according to Cam Peters. A drunkard and a brute."

Adam looked dangerous now. "And?"

"And," dared Francelle, rising from her chair in a burst of righteous wrath, "he claimed to be married to your wife!"

A muscle corded in Adam's neck. "So I've heard," he said, in a tone that was no less unnerving for its softness.

Francelle was stunned. So stunned that she lost her composure and forgot her carefully rehearsed speech. "You *know?*" she cried. "Doesn't it bother you at all, Dr. Corbin, that you might be wedded to a—a bigamist?"

"Banner is divorced, Francelle. While it really isn't any of your concern, I would appreciate it if you would pass that fact along to Cam Peters, your father, and all the other slobbering gossips in this town."

Francelle sank back into her chair, wounded. She had expected Adam to denounce his marriage, rage for a while, and eventually come to her for solace. She had *not* expected this staunch defense of a woman who didn't deserve him.

"Strange," she said recklessly, "that Mr. Malloy disappeared right after he made the claim that he and Dr. O'Brien were married to each other. Isn't it strange?"

Adam finished his coffee, and only the slight movement

235

of a muscle in his freshly shaved jaw betrayed his annoyance. "Why are you boring me with all this, Francelle?"

The answer to that was complicated and painful to consider, so Francelle swallowed it. "I just thought you should know what is being said about your—your wife, that's all."

"Thank you," Adam said, with an acid grin and a half-bow, and then he was setting aside his cup, taking up his bag, leaving on his endless, infernal rounds.

When the door closed behind him, Francelle laid her head down on her arms and wept because Adam didn't know that she loved him and probably wouldn't care if he did. What a good wife she would have been to him, if it hadn't been for that shameless Banner O'Brien, who could not be content with one husband but had to have two.

Banner felt tired and very weak. "Good morning, Francelle," she said with a sigh.

Francelle glared at her. "Good morning!"

"Is Adam gone already?"

The girl nodded, assessed Banner, and smiled mysteriously as she went back to her work.

Banner poured coffee and made her way back to the office. It was probably better that she hadn't had to confront Adam today; she was in no mood for an explosion.

At his desk, she took up a text on the constitution of the human foot and began to read. If there were no patients for her to see, she could at least learn something new.

"Doctor?"

Banner looked up to see Francelle in the doorway. "Yes?"

The girl was fairly bursting with malicious amusement. "There is a woman here to see you."

It was rare for a patient to ask specifically to see Banner; most of them preferred Adam. She stood and straightened her skirts before following Francelle into one of the two examining rooms.

"Hello, Mrs. Corbin," smiled Bessie, the prostitute who had shown such interest in Adam that first day, on board the *Silver Shadow*.

Banner sensed a challenge in the mundane greeting, but she returned the woman's smile all the same. "What can I do for you?"

"I've got a sore throat," said Bessie, her eyes oddly veiled even though they were fixed on Banner's face. "And my chest hurts, too."

Banner went to the door—perhaps she'd just imagined that this woman had not come about an illness—and asked Francelle to please fetch her bag.

After an annoying delay, the girl brought the requested item and Banner drew out her stethoscope. "Have you been coughing?"

Bessie smiled as she underwent a brief examination. "No."

The woman's lungs sounded healthy to Banner, and when she inspected her throat, she found no cause for any sort of discomfort. Frowning, she stepped back from the table where Bessie sat and folded her arms.

"Why did you really come to see me?" she asked.

"I wanted to tell you something."

"What?"

"Your husband came to me last night."

Banner reeled, inwardly at least. Outwardly, she was composed. Disbelieving. Even magnanimous. "Is that so?"

"Yes," replied Bessie firmly. "If you don't want to take care of him, there's plenty of us that will. But I like you, Red, and that's why I'm here. I want to help."

Banner said nothing; she was too busy remembering how she had moved out of Adam's bedroom the night before.

"You don't believe me, do you?"

"No," lied Banner.

Bessie's lush mouth formed a pout. "Then you just look in the inside pocket of the coat Adam was wearing last night, darlin'."

"Get out!"

The woman stood, studiously arranged her gaudy, fur-trimmed cloak. "I could tell you how to please your man," she said, in a singsong voice that made Banner's blood pressure shoot heavenward.

"Thank you very much, but I think I know how to do that. Will you please leave?"

Bessie swayed and swung to the door. "You won't have to ask me again, sweetness—I got manners. Just remember to look in that coat pocket."

When the door had closed and she was alone with yet another grief, Banner lowered her head. Now she knew why Adam had not come to the guest room the night before, in one of his fine and typical rages. He hadn't been at home.

Perhaps he hadn't even known about his wife's grand gesture of defiance, or cared.

Banner took a few minutes to compose herself and then

marched past a smirking Francelle to take up the book she'd been reading. She wouldn't enter Adam's bedroom again—she wouldn't. Not until he'd apologized and stopped seeing Lulani once and for all.

But the coat was there—she knew it was—and it pulled at her like a magnet at shavings.

Finally, because she knew she would have no peace if she didn't, Banner left the office, climbed the stairs, and opened Adam's door.

The coat in question was easy to find; it had been flung down on the foot of the bed, which was neatly made.

Even as she determined not to, Banner went to the coat and reached into the inside pocket. There was a card there, like the one she'd found in another coat, on a day when she'd been sure she would die, alone on a snowy mountain trail.

She read it with tear-blurred eyes: "Bessie Ingram. Room 8 *Silver Shadow.* Discretion assured."

When she could move again, Banner let both the card and the coat fall to the floor. Then, with dignity and dispatch, she moved the rest of her things out of Adam's room and into her own.

Adam knew what had happened before he lifted the coat from the floor or read the half-crumpled card that lay beside it. Despair ground in his stomach and clawed at the back of his throat.

He was damned now, he thought, as he sank to the edge of the bed and braced his head in his hands. If O'Brien didn't believe that Lulani wasn't his woman, she wasn't going to believe that he hadn't slept with

239

Bessie Ingram, either.

Adam swore hoarsely and rubbed the nape of his neck with one hand; there was a fierce headache spawning there.

After a time, he rose to his feet again, went to the wardrobe. It was as he had suspected; Shamrock's things were gone.

He sighed. He could go to her, drag her out of the guest room and back here, where she belonged, but what good would that do, really? He could not force her to love him, and that was what he wanted from Banner above all else.

The house was dark when Adam went back downstairs, an hour later, to take refuge in his office. If he couldn't sleep, he could at least read. Failing that—it would be hard to concentrate on the printed word, he knew—he could, in that quiet setting, sort out his tangled thoughts and emotions and come to some workable decision about O'Brien.

In his small study, Adam lit a lamp, fell into the wooden desk chair, and assessed the books lining the shelves with disinterest. Banner's name pulsed around him like the beat of a giant heart; he loved her, he wanted her, she was upstairs now, in a cold bed. A bed from which he had been summarily barred.

Infuriated, he plundered the deep bottom drawer of his desk for a bottle and found one. Adam kicked his feet up, unscrewed the lid of the high-proof whiskey, and drank.

With each swallow, his thoughts became more muddled. Adam began to consider what a truly unfortunate bastard he really was, with his stupid secret and his love for a woman who would spit stew all over him and fling the romantic skill of her former husband into his face at the slightest provocation.

He lifted the bottle again; the firewater scorched his throat and roiled in his troubled stomach.

"Adam."

He lowered the bottle and studied O'Brien, wondering if she was really there or if he had conjured her somehow. "Umm?"

"What are you doing?"

She was real, all right. And on the warpath, judging by the scornful and wifely looks she was hurling his way. "Drinking," he said, and the word was oddly difficult to form.

"I can see that. You should be in bed."

Adam arched an eyebrow and grinned. "I should indeed, madame. However, I'm not."

"Obviously."

He laughed. "I'll go if you will, O'Brien."

Banner folded her arms across the bodice of her blue flannel wrapper, tossed her head toward the bottle, which had drifted wide of his body, though he was still holding it in one hand.

"Why don't you just put a nipple on that and take *it* to bed?"

Adam frowned at the whiskey. "I think she's making inferences about my emotional maturity," he confided to the amber liquid.

"And you call yourself a doctor!" harped O'Brien, her voice piercing the lining of Adam's brain. "What if someone fell ill? Some help *you* would be!"

Adam knitted his eyebrows together and studied O'Brien's outraged and fuzzy countenance solemnly. "I'd send you," he said.

"Go to bed, Adam."

"Oh, no. Too cold. Too lonely."

"No doubt. Lulani is too far away to warm you, but you could always go to Bessie. After all, discretion is assured!"

Adam laughed, which was odd, because he felt so broken and so miserable.

"What kind of name is Lulani for an Indian, anyway?" fussed O'Brien, looking flushed and rumpled and damned appealing.

"Lulani is not an Indian," Adam muttered. "She is Hawaiian."

Now what the hell had made him say that? He brought the whiskey to his mouth and drank, to keep himself from telling the rest.

"Are you going to stop visiting her?"

Adam set the bottle down with a thump, lowered his feet to the floor, rubbed throbbing eyes with the fingers of one hand. "No."

O'Brien whirled and stormed away, and it was all he could do not to call her back and tell her everything.

One week passed, and then another. Adam did not come to the guest room even once, nor did he try to lure Banner back to his bed.

On the twenty-second of February, he went off to the mountain once more. This time, however, Banner made no attempt to follow.

"Why do you stay with him?" asked Melissa softly, her round, crystal-blue eyes trained on her sister-in-law.

Banner ignored the question, at least momentarily. How

242

could she answer, when she didn't know herself? "Are you feeling better?" she hedged, tucking Melissa's covers and refilling her teacup. "It's a pity your visit had to be spoiled."

"I'll be better tomorrow," Melissa said with a brave lift of her chin. "That's the only good thing about cramps. They do go away."

Banner flinched. Cramps. When was the last time she had had cramps, or even a flux for that matter?

Melissa frowned. "Banner? What's wrong?"

"Oh, *no!*" whispered Banner, pacing now, wringing her hands. "No, no—"

"Banner!"

She stopped, faced her sister-in-law. December. Banner had not bled since December, the week before she had come to Port Hastings from Oregon!

"I'm all right," she lied, to still the alarm in Melissa's eyes.

"You are not all right," insisted the girl, setting aside her cup with a rattle. "Banner Corbin, you tell me what is the matter, right now!"

Banner fell to a seat on the foot of Melissa's bed. She was estranged from her husband, a husband she had been making halting, painful plans to leave. There was gossip about her and about Sean—who might return at any time. And now there was a very good chance that she was pregnant!

"I think I'm going to have a baby!" Banner wept, covering her face with both hands.

Melissa was there promptly, offering a hug and a tearful, "Oh, but that's wonderful, Banner! Everything will be all right now—"

Banner howled. All right? How could everything be all right when Adam was probably making love to Lulani at that very moment and Sean wanted to kill her?

And it had been hard enough supporting herself, given the attitude most people took toward a woman doctor. What would it be like trying to earn a living for a baby and take proper care of it in the bargain?

"Banner, don't cry," Melissa pleaded, holding her, rocking her like a child. "If Adam won't care for you, Mama and Jeff and Keith and I will. We're your family now."

"You're *Adam's* family."

"Well, we'll side with you anyway!"

Banner was not comforted. All the love in the world would not sustain her, if none of it came from Adam.

Determined to spare O'Brien and the rest of his family his black mood for once, Adam bypassed the house when he came down from the mountain and went to the *Silver Shadow* instead.

A few drinks, a good steak—he'd feel better soon.

Striding up the boarding ramp, Adam considered Bessie and the singular relief she offered. God knew, with O'Brien sleeping in another bedroom and making it clear that she'd sooner couple with a gorilla than him, he could use some female consolation.

The saloon was brightly lit and a little too loud for Adam's tastes, but he went to the bar, thinking how damnably *married* he was. Had it really only been two months since he'd been able to come into Temple Royce's establishment and take his pleasures in good conscience?

The *Shadow* was crowded that night; there was music and a blond wisp of a girl with dark, empty eyes was singing on the stage. Adam bought a drink and moved closer, trying to hear her.

Instead, he heard Cam Peters, the marshal, who was sitting at a nearby table, a drink in his hand, the center of attention.

"I knew one man wouldn't be enough for that one first time I laid eyes on her," Peters boomed. "No sir. Nobody needed to tell *me* there was fire enough in that redhead to scar a man for life!"

Adam's hand tightened around his glass; he read the worn signboard beneath the stage methodically, in an attempt to settle his mind: Fancy Jordan. She Sings. She Dances. She Does Magic.

"I shouldn't look the other way, I guess," Peters prattled on, blithely unaware of the man standing just behind him. "It's agin the law for a lady to have two husbands, even if one of 'em *is* a Corbin."

Stewart Henderson was at the table, too, and he lifted a glass in a gesture of agreement, spoke clearly without the wires that had held his jaw in place. "Mr. Royce wanted to bed her, but she was already—"

Cam Peters broke in with a lewd chuckle. "Two husbands!" he marveled. "I reckon there'll be more'n one man in line if she decides she needs a third!"

Adam closed his eyes. "Stop," he said, in a low, rumbling tone that somehow managed to still Fancy Jordan's tremulous little voice and every other sound in the saloon in the bargain.

Peters whirled in his chair and fear worked in his grizzled, ordinary face. "Adam! Jesus, I didn't know you were—"

Adam set down his drink, grappling with the murderous rage inside him. "That was obvious," he said.

And his body seemed to be acting independently of his reason; he approached Peters, clasped his lapels in aching fists, wrenched the man to his feet. "Go on, Cam," he said, in a deadly undertone. "Tell us all about my wife and her two husbands."

"Christ, Adam—"

"Talk. You know so much about the subject."

"I ain't got nothin' to say!"

Some measure of sanity returned. Adam released the marshal, watched as he sank back into his chair with all the decorum of a jellyfish.

The girl on the stage began to sing again.

Adam went back to the bar and his drink, which held no appeal for him now. He didn't want a steak, he didn't want a woman.

He most certainly didn't want to hear Fancy Jordan sing.

Wishing to God that he'd never met Banner O'Brien, let alone married her, he gathered the last of his strength and went home.

The marshal shifted from one foot to the other, looking both reluctant and angry in the thin morning light. "I'm afraid you'll have to come down to the jail with me, Mrs. Corbin," he said.

Banner reeled, cast one look at Francelle, who was suddenly very busy at her typewriting machine. "Jail?" she

246

echoed, certain that she couldn't have heard correctly.

"It's agin the law to have more than one husband," pontificated the marshal.

Banner felt color rise in her cheeks. "I don't think you understand, Marshal. Sean Malloy and I were divorced—I have the papers to prove it."

"I'd like to see them," retorted the lawman.

"I-I'll just get my bag."

"Fine, Mrs. Corbin. That's fine."

Banner hurried into the office, pushed aside papers and books and a yellow envelope that rested on the desk. For such a brilliant man, Adam was certainly slovenly, she thought. And where was he now, when she needed him to tell the marshal that she was his wife and no one else's?

She found her bag and wrenched it open, reaching into the side pocket where she kept not only her divorce decree but the papers proving that she was a doctor and the certificates from both her marriages.

The diploma from the New York Infirmary was there, as was the certificate binding her to Adam Corbin. But her divorce decree and the license bearing Sean's name were gone.

Banner shivered. The papers couldn't be gone—she never took them out of this bag. Never.

"Doctor?" prodded Marshal Peters, from the office doorway. "You find them documents?"

Slowly, resigned to a dismal fate, Banner shook her head. "They were here—you must believe me—"

"I'm sorry."

Banner closed her eyes briefly, drew a deep breath, and turned to face the constable. "S-Someone has taken my papers." Adam, perhaps? Had he been that desperate to be free of her, now that she refused him his marital rights?

"Sure they have," said Marshal Peters. "Now, if you'll just come along with me."

Banner swallowed a sob of terror and frustration. Then she lifted her chin, collected her cloak, and walked out of the office with dignity.

Fifteen minutes later, the door of a musty, close little cell closed behind her.

There were no other prisoners being held anywhere in the jail that day, Banner could be grateful for that, at least.

In a daze, she paced the sawdust floor, wondering if Adam had brought her to this. Heaven knew, he could have found those papers in her bag easily enough. Who had better access to her things than he did?

One tear rolled down her face. Adam hated her, and he was unfaithful and callous and wholly immovable, but she could hardly believe that he would do something so base and underhanded as this. Had he wished to dispose of an unwanted wife, after all, there were certainly easier ways.

And yet, what did Banner really know of Adam? He was handsome, he was a brilliant physician with almost unerring instincts, he was a gifted lover. He liked cream in his coffee and wore spectacles when he read and he distrusted all politicians.

Realizing that these unrelated things constituted almost the whole of her knowledge of her husband, the father of her child, Banner wept.

Adam was cold, tired, hungry, and irritated, and he came to a lurching halt when he saw his mother racing across the backyard toward him, her skirts knotted in her hands, her face murderous in the twilight.

"Where in the devil have you been?" she demanded.

Adam had been in an isolated farmhouse most of the day, as it happened, delivering a particularly reluctant baby, but he did not feel disposed to explain. Stubbornly, he faced Katherine in silence.

"Banner is in jail!" she cried, boiling over.

Adam felt as though someone had just rammed his middle with the butt of a log. "*What?*"

"That idiot Peters came and took her away—she's been charged with bigamy! *Bigamy,* mind you! I offered to pay any bail but—"

Rasping a swear word, Adam whirled back toward the stables and his buggy. This, he knew, was his payment for embarrassing Cam Peters on board the *Silver Shadow* the night before. And when he got his hands on that squirrely . . .

Katherine was scrambling along at his side like a small, furious puppy. "Cam wouldn't set bail and he wouldn't let me see Banner even for a minute!" she complained, intensifying Adam's headache and the swirling sickness in his gut.

"Damn it, she has divorce papers," he spat. "Why didn't she show him those?"

"Cam says she didn't have any documents," replied Katherine breathlessly, as her son began to rehitch the tired horse and the muddy buggy in the dense shadows of the barn. "He did show me a marriage certificate, signed by Banner and some man named Malloy."

"Sean," breathed Adam, hating.

"Sean? Adam, who—"

"I haven't time to explain it now," he broke in, leading the nickering horse outside, the buggy jolting along behind. He could have reached the courthouse faster on horseback, but he intended to bring Banner back with him, and she'd be in no condition to ride double.

Despite the encumberance of the small vehicle, Adam reached the courthouse within minutes.

And Royce was there, of all people—looking genteel and solicitous as he squired a dazed Banner down the stone steps.

Adam leaped out of the buggy, strode toward them, half-blind with anger. "What the—"

Temple Royce smiled and held up one hand; with the other, he gripped Banner's elbow. "You've done enough, Adam," he said. "Please, let us pass."

Adam's eyes sliced to Banner's face and a thousand questions hammered in his mind. Why had Royce succeeded in freeing his wife when Katherine had failed? Why was Shamrock staring at him that way, as though she only vaguely remembered him?

"Give me my wife," he said.

"I'm afraid there is some question about whose wife Banner is, Adam. And she's in my custody until some determination is made."

"The hell she is!" rasped Adam, reaching for Banner, feeling gut-jarring pain when she huddled against Royce as if to seek his protection.

"Haven't you done enough?" asked Royce smoothly, his eyes raking Adam's face. "Look at the woman! She's terrified—I'm not sure she even knows you!"

It seemed to be true—O'Brien's eyes were wide and vacant and she was shivering, holding on to Royce's arm with both her hands.

"Banner," Adam ventured, holding out his hand in a gentle gesture.

She shook her head, hid her face in Temple's handy shoulder. "No," she said. "Please. Leave me alone."

Adam was nearly apoplectic now; it was impossible to separate his fear from his anger. "What the hell is going on here?" he rasped.

Royce shrugged, cradled Banner with one arm. "All I know is that Banner has been accused—quite wrongly, I'm sure—of bigamy. The moment I heard about it, of course, I came and persuaded Cam Peters to free her—in my custody."

"Why did he release Banner to you?"

"When he wouldn't turn her over to your mother?" finished Royce, smiling cordially. Benignly. "That's simple, Adam. She was very overwrought at the prospect of going back to your house. Marshal Peters tells me that the poor dear blames you for her arrest, as a matter of fact."

"*What?*" The bullet-sharpness of the word made O'Brien bury her head in Temple's coat again and shiver.

"O'Brien, look at me."

She looked, though not willingly, and her green eyes registered fear all right.

"I wouldn't do a thing like this to you," Adam breathed desperately. "You must know that."

Banner did know him; he could see that now. It was good to have at least one terror dispelled. "I won't go home with you," she said.

251

Adam tilted his head back and drew a ragged breath. The night air was cold, crisp, promising snow. "Where *are* you going, Banner? To Temple's bed?"

As Adam had intended, she broke free of Royce's tender hold and flung herself at her husband, scratching and shrieking and spitting like a cat.

He caught her wrists and held them. "That's it, O'Brien. Fight."

Tears poured down her face. "I hate you!" she hissed. "I'd rather sleep in *any* bed than yours!"

"I love you, too, dear," Adam replied calmly. "Thank Mr. Royce for his kind attentions and we'll go home."

"Now, just a—" protested Royce, a bit lamely.

Adam smiled at Banner, loving her, rejoicing in the return of her spirit and her fire. Even her hatred was better than the quiet, catatonic despair that had possessed her before. "Sorry, Temple," he said, and then he swung Banner up into his arms, where she damn well belonged, and hauled her to the buggy.

It was rather like trying to carry a mother mountain lion away from her cubs.

"Peters will take her back into custody!" warned Royce, who was, no doubt, less concerned with that prospect than the spoiling of his plans to offer comfort and solace to the nubile transgressor.

Adam was busy, taking up the reins with one hand, struggling with Banner with the other. Still, he managed a polite nod for his old and respected adversary. "Good night, Temple. And thanks again."

Royce bellowed an obscene response and hurled his fancy beaver top hat into the slush and mud at the foot of the courthouse steps.

Banner hated Adam Corbin. *Hated* him. And, as he flung her unceremoniously onto his bed, she almost hoped that he would make love to her, so that she could hate him even more.

He began undressing her, as a gentle father might undress a troublesome child, undoing buttons, pulling off shoes, rolling down stockings.

"Don't you dare try to make love to me!" Banner whispered, her cheeks flaming.

"I wouldn't dare," replied Adam, with a half-grin and a lift of one eyebrow.

"You're afraid of me?"

Adam drew her camisole up over her head and, tossed it aside, apparently taking no more than a clinical interest in her exposed breasts. "Terrified," he said.

"Stop mocking me!"

He ignored her, untying her drawers and pulling them down."

"It's been a long time," Banner reminded him, her tones testy and somewhat petulant.

"Ummm. Too long." Adam found a flannel night-gown—one he had damned as virginal and threatened to burn, time and time again. He tugged it over her head.

"I won't let you make love to me!"

He chuckled. "Your virtue is safe for tonight. I don't go to bed with jailbirds, O'Brien."

Banner flailed her arms, but they were bound up in the sleeves of the nightgown. "Good! You needn't make any advances—"

Adam pushed her back onto the pillows, covered her with the blankets, kissed her forehead dispassionately. In another minute, he'd be wanting to hear her prayers.

"Sleep. We can talk in the morning."

Banner reddened. Here she was, protesting and protesting, and he wasn't the least bit ruffled. "Don't you want me?"

Adam laughed. "I want you."

"Then—"

"Sleep." He was moving toward the door now.

"Wait!" Banner gasped.

Adam paused, looking indulgent, his hand on the knob. "What?"

"You d-didn't have me put in jail, did you?"

The magnificent face contorted, ever so slightly, despite the maddeningly benign smile curving Adam's lips and veiling the expression in his eyes. "Of course I didn't. But, since you never believe a word I say, I'll spare you the customary heated denials."

Banner colored profusely. Maybe she didn't believe him when it came to Bessie Ingram or Lulani, but she knew he was telling the truth now, where her arrest was concerned.

"I wouldn't really have gone home with Mr. Royce," she said, to offer an olive branch.

Adam's jaw tightened, and a blue fire sparked in his eyes, turning them savage. "Why should I believe that, Shamrock?" he drawled. "You were clinging to his arm as though you expected me to murder you in the street!"

So, he was capable of jealousy. Banner smiled inwardly, thinking that turnabout was, indeed, fair play. "It's all very innocent, Adam," she chimed. "Temple is my friend."

The emphasis on the final word struck Adam with a satisfyingly visible impact. He staunchly maintained that Lulani was his "friend," so let him wonder about Banner's association with Temple Royce. Let him wonder about the nights they'd spent apart, as she wondered.

"Temple is very handsome, don't you think?" she threw into the dangerous conversational void.

"Actually, he doesn't excite me," retorted Adam, in a biting, sardonic hiss.

Banner shrugged and lowered her eyes. This was a stupid, childish game she was playing, and she was too tired for it. Too broken and needing and afraid.

"Do you think I'll have to go back to jail?" she whispered.

"No," replied Adam flatly, opening the door.

Banner's heart surged into her throat. She couldn't be alone now, not tonight. "Don't go, Adam," she said. "Please, don't go."

Adam closed the door again, came to her slowly, as though he was trying to restrain himself every inch of the way. He sat down on the edge of the bed, traced the outline of her cheek with one slightly unsteady finger. "O'Brien," he said, and for all its softness, the word was like a cry for help. "I've needed you—I've wanted you—"

"And have you loved me, Adam Corbin?"

He closed his eyes, and some unreadable emotion moved in his fine, arrogant features. "Yes," he rasped.

Banner took up one of his hands, brought it to her beflanneled breasts. "That night in the cabin, when I said that Sean sat-satisfied me—I didn't mean it."

Slowly, as if against his will, Adam's hand began to move upon her, kneading her. He opened his wonderous eyes, and she saw torment in their depths. "I know," he said.

"He n-never did anything but hurt me."

Adam's fingers were drawing at the cloth-sheltered nipple now, causing it to rise to attention like a little soldier. "Bare this for me," he ground out.

Banner obeyed, undoing the nightgown, pulling it aside with both hands. Her breasts were plump peaks, proud and firm and overladen with weeks of passion.

A soft, desperate sound escaped Adam as he swept his eyes over this waiting wealth, hungering. "Banner . . ."

Gently, she cupped her hand at the back of his magnificent ebony head and drew him down to suckle.

Chapter Twelve

Adam's breath caught in his throat when he saw the telegraph message half buried in the clutter on his desk. How long had it been there, unnoticed? Why hadn't Francelle brought it to him, personally, when it was delivered?

He ripped open the envelope too fiercely; the message inside was torn. Swearing, Adam reassembled it. It was not the half-expected warning from Jeff, letting him know that Sean Malloy had jumped ship. Banner was safe, for the moment at least.

Bracing himself against the desk with both hands, Adam read the paper again. It was some sort of sales message; he crumpled it and tossed it away.

"Adam?"

He looked up, saw a flushed and discomforted Francelle standing in the office doorway. "Yes?"

"Is Banner—Mrs. Corbin—all right?"

Adam sat down, entwined his fingers, settled back in his chair. "Why do you ask, Francelle?" he countered evenly, though he suspected that he already knew the answer to that.

"Well—she *was* arrested and—everything. I was just wondering—"

"Where are the papers, Francelle?"

Damning color flooded the girl's face. She'd taken Banner's divorce decree all right, along with the certificate proving she'd married Sean. Probably Francelle had given the latter to Marshal Peters, in a burst of good citizenship, and either hidden or destroyed the former.

God, if she hadn't been a child, and one of Melissa's closest friends in the bargain, he would have throttled her where she stood.

"What papers?" she asked finally.

"I think you know 'what papers,' Francelle. You gave the marriage certificate to your father, didn't you? And he, being a worthy sort with a love of the law, rushed it over to Marshal Peters. Since everyone knows that Banner is married to me, it was a clear-cut case of bigamy, wasn't it?"

"I didn't take any papers!"

"Francelle."

"I didn't have anything to do with any of this!"

"Where are the divorce papers, Francelle?"

She lifted her chin, looking at once defiant and prepared to run. Her throat worked, but she said nothing.

Adam was calm, quiet. And furious enough to wring her fetching little neck. "Who else had the opportunity, my dear?"

Her lips trembled. "Why—why, *you* did."

Adam sighed. "All right. I can question your father—it's doubtful that he'll lie to me, Francelle."

Francelle lowered her head, recovering. When she met Adam's gaze again, however, her eyes were overly bright and her cheekbones glowed red. "You believe Banner, don't you?" she marveled. "You believe her when she says she was free to marry you!"

"Of course I do. Don't you, Francelle?"

The child was groping within herself for an answer when Melissa suddenly swept in, through the other door, her blue eyes fierce.

"I want a word with you, Francelle Mayhugh!" she snapped, ignoring her brother, backing her childhood friend up against a bookshelf. "Banner told me about her missing divorce papers and I want to know where they are!"

Francelle looked like a rabbit, forced into a thicket by a snarling, tireless predator. "I didn't—I mean—"

The spectacle was gloriously amusing; Melissa pressed her straight little nose almost to Francelle's and closed in for the kill. "You give those documents *back!* If you don't, Miss Francelle Mayhugh, your own papa won't know you by the time I'm through!"

Francelle burst into tears. "I did it for love!" she cried, like a road show heroine.

Adam lowered his eyes, at once amused and sympathetic. He should have guessed how Francelle felt, he supposed, but the thought had never crossed his mind. Not much had since O'Brien had come into his life and turned everything upside down.

"You had no right to do that to Banner," Melissa replied, more gently. "Francelle, my sister-in-law spent almost a full day in that horrible jail cell, and she could have been sent to prison! How would you like to have a baby in the territorial *prison,* when you hadn't even done anything wrong?"

A shock went through Adam—he heard nothing more of the conversation. A *baby.* O'Brien was going to have a baby?

He shot out of his chair and raced back into the main part of the house, shouting his wife's name at intervals.

It was to be a restful day, a day off from rounds and patients, and Banner was looking forward to it. She was, in fact, sitting in Maggie's kitchen with Jenny, sipping tea and chatting.

"*O'Brien!*" The word rang through the great house, like a bellowed curse.

Jenny's lips quirked, and she exchanged a knowing look with Maggie. "What did you do now, Banner?" she teased.

Banner trembled as she set aside her cup, rose from her chair at the table, smoothed her skirts, and then resolutely sat down again. What was she doing, rising to attention like some soldier about to be upbraided by a visiting general?

The kitchen door clattered against an inside wall as it was flung open, and then Adam filled the chasm, glowering. "You're pregnant!" he accused, as though she had just been found guilty of some heinous crime.

Jenny giggled. "You can never fool a doctor," she said, as she and Maggie vanished from the room like so much smoke.

"Behave yourself," Banner said to Adam in crisp tones, as she squared her shoulders and lifted her chin.

Miraculously, Adam did subside a little; he sank into the chair opposite her own and ran one hand through his hair, looking distracted. "When?"

"If you mean to ask when the baby is due," Banner said, "Then the answer is September. If, on the other hand, you meant—"

"Shut up, O'Brien."

Banner swallowed, realized that her hands were gripping each other with such force that the knuckles ached.

"September," her husband said, musing. And then a slow grin creased his face and crinkled around his wonderful eyes. "September!"

"Yes," teased Banner, more at ease now. "It comes after August and before October."

Adam's grin faded, and she knew that he was thinking of Sean. Though they seldom mentioned the threat of his return, it was always there, like the mountain. Like Lulani and that woman on the *Silver Shadow.*

Adam's hand came to hers, closed over it, warm and rough and strong. "Shamrock, I—"

Banner drew back, hurting again, poisoned by her own thoughts. She had almost forgotten, in the lingering heat of last night's lovemaking, what a disaster her marriage to Adam Corbin really was.

"Don't," she whispered, closing her eyes.

She heard the chair scrape as he stood up, knew that he had turned away from her. Probably he was thinking that his own life had been easier without Banner O'Brien. She'd been nothing but trouble, after all, with her supposed extra husband and her quick, quarrelsome tongue.

"I'll hire another doctor," he said.

Banner's eyes popped open; she stared at the immovable expanse of her husband's muscular back. "What did you say?"

Adam turned, grasped the back of his chair with both hands. The knuckles were white with force. "You'll be busy, O'Brien. And in case you're thinking of arguing this, let me just say that no child of mine is going to be dragged through Indian camps and brothels just so you can go on practicing!"

"No child of yours? Isn't this my baby, too?"

"You're damned right it is, *doctor,* and you're going to behave accordingly!"

In that moment, Banner felt as though she'd lost everything—her husband's love and fidelity, her pride. And, now, her career, too.

"Don't do this to me, Adam," she pleaded, in a soft, defeated whisper, for she knew that he could. Under the law, in fact, he could throw her into the street and keep the child to raise as he pleased. She had no legal rights at all, where her marriage was concerned. "Y-you don't know how hard I worked—how difficult the male doctors made things—"

"I think I do," Adam argued in a recalcitrant hiss. "But the risk was inherent, wasn't it, O'Brien? After all, you're a woman."

Fury displaced Banner's resignation. "Like Jenny said, you can't fool a doctor!"

"Very funny." His gaze rose, meaningfully, to the ceiling over their heads; their room was directly overhead. "But you're a woman first, Shamrock—I can swear to that."

"I'll leave you if you make me give up medicine entirely," she warned, clamoring to her feet, overturning her chair. This time Adam Corbin was not going to sway her with his forceful manner or his lovemaking!

"Not with my child inside you, you won't."

Banner closed her eyes, opened them again. The room dodged and undulated around her. "It's my baby, too," she reminded him again, softly, sadly. "And if I want to take my child and leave, I will."

"Wrong."

Banner swallowed further argument; she had been foolish to fling down that particular emotional glove in challenge, to tip her hand the way she had.

"Couldn't we come to a compromise?" she asked, reasonably.

"What sort of compromise?"

"Just some of the time, Maggie could look after the baby. And I could still work in the hospital . . ."

Adam sighed and his grip on the chair relaxed a little. "O'Brien," he began, in a low, measured voice, "We've never really talked about having children. I just assumed that you wanted a family as much as I did. Was I wrong?"

Tears welled in Banner's eyes; she bit her lower lip and shook her head. "You weren't wrong," she said.

"But you want your practice, too."

She nodded.

Adam rolled his eyes heavenward, then glared at her again. "Don't we have enough problems without this, O'Brien? Isn't it enough that I always have to be listening, always have to be looking over one shoulder, expecting Malloy to come out of the woodwork and hurt you? Maybe kill you?"

"There are things I don't like about this marriage, too, you know!" Banner cried suddenly. "Like Lulani, for instance!"

"That again."

"Yes, that again! How dare you try to strip me of everything that matters to me, Adam? I've lost my pride—I've had to watch you ride off to visit that woman every three weeks—I've had to lie alone in bed and know that you were on the *Silver Shadow* with—"

Adam broke in with a muttered swear word and, "That does it, O'Brien. That's it. Get your things and put on your warmest clothes, because we're going up the mountain right now!"

Banner gaped at him. "What?"

"I want to show you exactly what I've been hiding."

"Why can't you just tell me?" Banner retorted, amazed and off-balance and suddenly not so certain that she wanted to know his blasted secret at all.

But Adam's eyes strayed to her stomach, and Banner knew that he was remembering the child, reconsidering. "I can't tell you, O'Brien—I have to show you. But—"

Not knowing whether to plead against the trip or for it, Banner simply stood still, in silence, and waited.

"You'll have to do as I tell you," he said, after a long and visible deliberation. "For once, Shamrock, you'll have to obey."

She nodded, unable to speak now, even if she had chosen to.

Adam was about to say something more when the sound of a distant blast rattled the windows and even shook the floor beneath their feet. He swore and bounded out of the kitchen at a dead run, closely followed by a frantic and suddenly vocal Banner.

"What was *that?*" she cried, holding up her skirts to keep from tangling her feet in them and falling.

"The mill," rasped Adam, loping through the walkway now. "I'd say a boiler exploded."

"My God!"

They reached the office; Adam was ransacking a cupboard for emergency supplies, dropping things into his bag.

"Let me come with you!"

He impaled her with a look that did not inspire rebellion. "No. You'll be needed here. Fill as many tubs as you can find with the coldest water possible. Have Maggie and Mama and everybody else you can find help you."

Banner did not question him now. If a boiler had exploded in the mill, as he surmised, there would be burn victims. She turned and raced back into the main house, shouting for Maggie and Mrs. Corbin and Melissa.

It was a blessing that Jenny was still there, for many hands were needed, and Francelle was no help at all, hovering in a corner of the ward as she was, muttering something about papers.

The men from the stables were summoned, and they busied themselves with the task of unbolting the tub in the bathing room upstairs, while Maggie scrambled for wash-tubs stored in the attic. Jenny and Melissa set themselves to pumping water.

Banner laid out vials of morphine and sterilized the needles of syringes, all the time imploring Francelle to make herself useful by seeing that the sheets on the ward beds were smooth and clean.

When words failed, she stomped over to the girl, grasped her shoulders in both hands, and shook her. "Francelle, listen to me! There has been an accident. There will be injured people coming here. Damn you, stop your blithering and *help me!*"

"I didn't mean to get you into trouble," sniveled Francelle. "I'm sorry—I'm sorry—"

"Francelle!"

"Do you think A-Adam will hate me?"

Banner drew back her hand and slapped Francelle, with all the force she could muster. "Get busy!" she screamed.

The men from the stables came in, carrying the tub from upstairs. Dismissing Francelle, Banner ordered them to start hauling in water and blocks of ice from the icehouse out back.

They obeyed without question, and Banner scrambled to check the bedsheets herself, since Francelle had wandered off somewhere, mumbling and holding her smartly slapped face with one hand.

The beds, as Banner had expected, were clean.

But there were only eight. What if there were *dozens* of casualties? Where would they put so many people?

Banner resolved the dilemma quickly and raced up the stairs, where she pulled clean sheets from the linen cup-

265

board at one end of the hall. By the time the first of the wounded arrived, by wagon, every bed on the second floor, including her own, boasted fresh linen.

There were five men in that first group, some of them unconscious, some writhing, one shrieking in pain.

Working like demons, Maggie and Banner cut away the men's clothes and ordered those that were awake and suffering lowered into the waiting tubs of ice water stationed in the aisle of the ward.

People began to arrive from other houses—Temple Royce was among them—bringing ice and blankets and a stoic willingness to help.

Another load of wounded men came, and Banner was aware of Adam's brisk presence and the terse cadence of his voice. Even though she was too busy to so much as look up from her work, she was comforted.

With Jenny and Melissa and Katherine, she carried in fresh water and carried out stale. She administered injections of morphine and supervised the placement of those patients who could bear to be lifted out of the tubs and put into bed.

And over all this was the fierce, far-off roar of the lumbermill, consuming itself.

Twilight came and the sky was still a hellish, crimson color, snapping with sparks. Four men were dead, and more than a dozen would wish for the same respite before they began to recover.

Adam Corbin turned from the window in despair, sought Banner with his eyes. Finding her, he found hope.

She was working with one of the patients, her beautiful

cinnamon hair rumpled and falling from its pins, her dress splotched with God knew what.

I love you, he said to her, without speaking.

She looked up, smiled wanly, and her lips moved in silent answer.

Adam was buoyed by the exchange; he went back to his own patients—those upstairs, in the family beds.

The days ahead would be long ones, difficult ones. Ironic as it seemed, he would need O'Brien more as a doctor than he ever had as a wife.

Keith Corbin stopped short, amazed. There were people sleeping all over the dining room floor—Melissa by the sideboard, Maggie near the kitchen door, Adam and Banner under the table.

"Are we being evicted?" he demanded, spreading his hands in the predawn light.

His mother muttered something and sat up in the windowseat, yawning. "Keith?"

"What's going on here?"

Katherine yawned again and gestured for him to lower his voice. "There was an explosion at the mill yesterday," she explained. "Do be quiet."

Keith felt his eyes go round. "Are all the beds full? That many people were hurt?"

Katherine nodded. "You could have chosen a better time to come for a visit, I'm afraid."

"Actually, I came about the orchards," her son replied, smiling, despite everything, as he watched Adam stir and cup Banner's right breast in one hand.

Katherine had followed his gaze, and she cleared her

throat in soft reprimand. "Keith."

He chuckled and shrugged his shoulders. "At least something is going well, it appears."

"That is a rash judgment if I've ever heard one." Katherine rose from the windowseat and stretched. "I'll make some coffee—if we can get past Maggie, that is—and tell you just how 'well' everything has been going."

"Bigamy?" gasped Keith, a few minutes later, in the quiet sanction of the kitchen. "I don't believe it!"

Katherine cupped her hands around her coffee mug. "Of course you don't believe it—it isn't true. That's a good thing, too, because Adam and Banner have troubles enough without that."

Keith sighed. "He's still making those trips up the mountain, isn't he?"

She nodded. "Will you talk to him, Keith? Jeff isn't here, of course, and I know Adam wouldn't listen to me, but he respects you, and you might be able to reason with him."

Keith was close to Adam, but he had his doubts about getting his older brother to confide anything concerning those mysterious and regular pilgrimages of his. "I've tried before, Mama," he said. "So has Jeff. We even started to follow him once."

Katherine arched one eyebrow. "Oh? What happened?"

"Nothing. At least, nothing my masculine pride would allow me to recount."

"He was angry," guessed Katherine.

"Two of Jeff's teeth were loose for a week afterward," reflected Keith. "And I may not be able to father children."

Katherine looked horrified for a moment, and then

268

chuckled. "Speaking of children, Melissa tells me that I'm about to have that grandchild I've been aspiring to for so long." Her smile faded away. "If Adam doesn't drive Banner away before it's born, that is."

"So. My brother is his usual impossible, domineering self it seems. I suppose he wants Banner to forget her practice until the child is old enough to vote?"

Katherine blanched at the word; the defeat of suffrage had been a blow to her, and Keith was sorry for bringing the subject up, even inadvertently.

"I think that's part of it," his mother responded. "But I suspect that Adam just wants to keep Banner under this roof as much as possible, not because he wants to thwart her, but because he hopes she'll be safe here."

"Safe?"

"From Sean Malloy, her first husband." Katherine went on to tell an amazing story, culminating in the appearance of Banner's divorce papers, her arrest, and the vicious gossip that had arisen from it all.

"Where is Malloy now?"

Again, Katherine arched a brow. "I suspect that he's with Jeff—an unwilling passenger on the *Sea Mistress,* if you will."

"Jeff *crimped* him?"

"I think so. He was very pleased with himself, it seemed to me, the night he sailed. And Mr. Malloy hasn't been seen since."

"Good—good heavens. Has Jeff lost his mind? He could be imprisoned for that!"

Katherine's shoulders rose in a weary shrug. "Tell your brother that. Good Lord, Keith, I wish your father were alive. He'd know how to straighten all this out."

Keith grinned gently. "What's this? You're admitting that Papa—a mere *man,* if you please—could manage a situation where you couldn't?"

"I'm not big enough to get Jeff and Adam by the hair and knock their heads together," said Katherine crisply. "Believe me, I'd like to."

"It wouldn't help, you know. They have rock skulls— both of them."

"And rock fists," said Adam, from the base of the back stairway, "so watch what you say, little brother."

Keith returned his brother's weary grin. "Join us," he said smoothly. "We were just talking about you."

Adam went to the stove, helped himself to coffee. "So I heard. What brings you over the mountains, pastor?"

"Divine guidance, it would seem. From what I've seen, you could use a little help."

Adam lifted his cup. "You're right. I could."

Katherine stood up, slipped quietly out of the room, by way of the same stairs her son had just descended. Adam took her chair.

"No," he said flatly, in tones made of grit and weariness.

"No what?" Keith retorted.

"No, I'm not going to tell you why I go up the mountain every three weeks."

"Who asked?"

"You would have, at Mama's urging. Believe me, Keith—you're better off not knowing."

"Is Banner?"

Adam's jaw took on a familiar, formidable angle. "This has nothing to do with my wife."

270

"It does if you're betraying her, Adam. She has a right to expect fidelity from you."

"I quite agree."

"Do you want to lose her, Adam? Is that it? Can't you stand being happy?"

"I don't want to lose her—I *won't* lose her."

"You could. She's a proud woman. A doctor. How much of this do you think she'll take?"

"I expect Banner to trust me."

"On what basis, Adam? Your word?"

"That should be enough, don't you think?"

"In most cases, yes. But not this one. And Mama tells me you're planning to force Banner to give up her practice. Are you?"

Adam's spoon rattled in his cup. "Maybe. I want my child to have a mother—not a crusader who passes through on occasion, between victories and defeats."

Keith sat back, folded his arms. "We're not talking about Banner now, are we? We're talking about Mama."

Adam shrugged, but made no verbal response.

"We're grown now," Keith reminded him. "All of us. Why should Mama hover around, waiting for one of us to need her? She was here when it mattered, Adam, and so was Papa."

All the familiar walls were locking into place; Adam's expression was closed, unreadable. What in hell was he hiding, behind all that hostility and rock-jawed silence?

"Adam."

He bounded out of his chair, this eldest brother, and turned away, flinging the remains of his coffee into the sink, setting aside the cup. "I have patients to look after," he muttered, and then he was rousing Maggie from her position on the other side of the door and striding into a day that would probably be only slightly less hellish than the one that had gone before.

Banner hardly had time to notice that her stomach was rounding in the days and weeks to come—there was simply too much work to do. The ward was full, but enough patients had recovered that the family was able to return to their own beds.

Eventually, Keith returned to his orchards, Katherine went back to her political pursuits in Olympia, and Melissa took up her college courses again. Francelle, in the meantime, had taken a train back East, where she intended to enroll in finishing school.

Although Banner's divorce papers had mysteriously reappeared in her medical bag and there was no more mention of putting her back in jail, there was much talk, she knew, about the questionable morals of Adam Corbin's redheaded wife. On the rare occasions when Banner went into the shops of Port Hastings, women ignored her and drew aside their skirts when she passed.

Though she would not have admitted it for anything, Banner was deeply wounded by this communal rejection.

And if that wasn't bad enough, Adam continued to make his regular trips up the mountain. He didn't offer to take Banner with him again, and she didn't ask—something in his manner precluded that.

There was little she could do, it seemed, but abide. If the days were difficult, the nights were heavenly—preoccupied and uncommunicative as he was, Adam had not permitted her to leave his bed again. And she had not wanted to. Shamelessly, stupidly perhaps, she clung to the one thing in her life that seemed to work.

And in April, when the trees were awakening and the grass was peeking out from under the snow, the wire came. Banner knew only that it had originated from Portland, Oregon—she dared not open it.

Adam was on the mountain, and when he returned, late that night, he looked so tired that Banner didn't have the heart to harangue him about Lulani or recite the rather dull events of the day. She forgot all about the telegraph message lying in the middle of his desk.

In the morning, however, she remembered, and she was alarmed to see the yellow envelope where she'd left it the day before. Somehow, in his hurry to be off on his endless rounds, Adam had failed to see it.

Banner took the missive up, turned it in her hands, set it down again. Why did it disturb her so? Probably, this was only a greeting from a friend.

The name scrawled on the front was Adam's, not her own. Banner turned away and went on about her business.

There was a rock-hard, aching knot on the side of Jeff Corbin's head, and it smarted like hell. So did his pride, for that matter.

Blast, what a fool he'd been to turn his back on Malloy, even for a second.

Hands in his pockets, Jeff walked steadily toward the *Silver Shadow*. He'd warned Adam; that was the important thing. And the idea of going home and explaining how he'd come to on the floor of his cabin on the *Sea Mistress*

273

was singularly unappealing.

Right now, he wanted half a dozen drinks and maybe that many women, and he didn't want to think about how Malloy had gotten the jump on him. Tonight, at least, the *Silver Shadow* was definitely the place for Jeff.

Adam hadn't wanted to go out; he would have preferred to remain in bed with O'Brien, sated by her singular witchery, sleeping. Only Maggie had rapped at his door and said he was needed on Water Street—there had been another brawl, no doubt—so there he was, walking out, approaching the buggy someone had been thoughtful enough to hitch for him.

Strange, though, that it was at the end of the front walk, instead of at the surgery door, as usual. And there was, it seemed to Adam, an odd slant to the way it sat on the spindly-looking wheels.

He yawned and shook his head, trying to clear the sleep from his brain. He would drive to Water Street, finish up there as soon as he could, and when he got back, he would awaken O'Brien and have her well.

Adam grinned, tossed his bag onto the seat of the rig, and stepped up onto the foot rail. He had several favorite methods, when it came to waking up O'Brien, and considering them was pleasant indeed. Maybe he would—

But then there was a sudden, explosive pain in his head. He went tunneling backward, through a star-speckled, tubular universe.

Jeff saw the buggy and frowned. "Adam?"

There was no answer, no sound, but for the shifting of

the patient horse and the spring songs of the crickets, and frogs.

Jeff shrugged, staggered a little, and opened the front gate. If the rig was still out front, Adam wasn't in bed yet. Maybe they could talk for a little while and he could get something for his blasted headache—

The ward and the offices beyond were dark, and so were the parlor and the kitchen.

Jeff was about to go upstairs when someone pounded at the back door. He lit a lamp, opened the door.

Jenny was there, looking wide-eyed and anxious. "Where's Adam?" she demanded. "I knocked at the surgery door—his buggy is out front—"

Jeff stiffened, whirled to bolt through the darkened house at a dead run. Jesus, how could he have been so stupid? *How?*

"Adam!" he bellowed, leaping off the porch, racing across the lawn. He nearly landed on his brother when he vaulted over the stone fence. "Oh, God. *Adam.*"

Adam stirred on the ground, groaned.

Jeff was kneeling beside him, trying to assess the damage in the thin moonlight. "Adam?" he breathed.

Adam's right eye was swollen shut, his lip was slit, and blood was pouring from a gash in his right temple. "Yo," he managed, after a painful struggle.

"Lie still, will you?" Jeff pleaded. "I'll get Banner."

"No—don't get—O'Brien—don't—"

Jeff turned to look at a stricken, shivering Jenny. "Go upstairs and find my sister-in-law. I'll try to get Adam inside. Jenny, *move!*"

The girl started and then stumbled back toward the

house, already shouting for Banner.

"Damn you," Adam groaned, writhing on the ground.

Jeff swallowed the emotions that were grinding in his throat and scalding behind his eyes. "Is there a circus in town or what?" he bantered, in his desperation and his pain. "You look like you just went ten rounds with the trained ape, big brother."

Adam tried to sit up, fell back down. "Christ," he breathed. "It—hurts—"

"I know. D-Do you think it's all right if I lift you?"

Despite everything, Adam gave an agonized chuckle. "Not unless—you want to—see my ribs come—through my shirt."

"What shall I do, then?"

"Get something—hard—flat—a door or something. P-Put me on that."

Banner was scrambling across the lawn now, her hair flying free, like fire in the night, her finely sculpted face in shadow. She sprang over the fence in much the same manner as Jeff had, though he hadn't, of course, been hampered by a nightgown and a wrapper.

"Adam!" she mourned, in a small, strangled voice, sinking to her knees in the muddy April grass, touching his face, moving deft and knowledgeable hands over his rib cage.

"O'Brien—go to bed—I'm—"

"Don't you *dare* tell me that you're all right!" hissed Banner, "I've got eyes in my head! Jeff, bring me—"

Jeff was on his feet instantly, relieved and scared and ready to do whatever Banner told him to do. "I know—a door," he answered, and as he ran to rip the first one he

276

could find from its hinges, he heard his sister-in-law scream into the darkness.

"I'll kill you for this, Sean Malloy!"

They carried Adam inside on the door of the downstairs coat closet, Jeff and Jenny and one of the men who had come from the stables to investigate the disturbance.

Adam's injuries seemed infinitely worse in the light, and Banner despaired even as she tended him.

He was strong, Adam was—so strong. But he could barely lie still on the examining room table long enough for an injection of morphine. "The ribs, O'Brien—"

"Hush," she said, withdrawing the needle from the inside of his forearm. "I'm a doctor, too, remember?"

"Ummm, O'Brien, it hurts. It hurts—"

Banner spared a moment to kiss his bloodied forehead. "I know, darling. But I'm here and I'll help you. Please, just lie still."

He laughed, but the sound was a raw gurgle. "Would you really—kill for me—O'Brien?"

"Gladly," she replied, in all truth, as she cut away his shirt with scissors taken from a drawer in the table. "Can you tell me what happened?"

"S-someone—inside the buggy—"

"Did you see him?"

"D-Do I look like I s-saw him, O'Brien?"

While Jenny and Jeff looked on, Banner assessed the cut on Adam's lip and the wound beneath his hairline, trying to decide whether to tend these before she bound his ribs. "Is the morphine working yet?"

"No," Adam said, and then his eyes rolled back in his

head and closed.

"Is he dead?" gasped Jeff.

"No," replied Banner crisply, even though inside she felt as though she shared Adam's injuries. "He's asleep, and that's fortunate. Find me a clean sheet, Jeff. Jenny, I need alcohol and some cotton."

It was only after she had stitched and bound her shattered husband back together that Banner Corbin allowed herself to lower her forehead to his and weep for him.

When her weeping was through, she took a firm hold of herself again and accepted the brandy-laced coffee Jeff had brought.

"What now?" asked Adam's brother.

"Now we wait. We hope." Banner lifted her eyes to the darkened window and silently cursed Sean Malloy to burn in hell. Had it not been for that, she would have added, "We pray."

Jeff swore. "I sent the wire," he seethed. "Damn it, didn't he get the wire?"

Banner had not forgotten the unopened yellow envelope lying on Adam's desk; it had been engraved into her brain for all time. "It came."

"Then—"

"Adam didn't see it. Jenny?"

The girl came forward; her brown eyes were wide and there were tear streaks on her face.

Banner reached out to touch her friend's shoulder. "You came here to get help, didn't you?"

Jenny nodded. "M-My mother—she told me there is smallpox in the village. They will use the steam hut and Adam told me—told me—"

"That you must come to him if that happened," Banner finished for her. She turned to look at her tall, very pale brother-in-law. "Jeff, can you look after Adam? Make sure that Sean doesn't get in here and—"

"*No*," Jeff spat, in a bellowlike whisper. "If you think I'm going to let you go traipsing off to the Klallum camp in the middle of the night, with that madman prowling around—"

Banner squared her shoulders. "Stop talking like a husband, Jeffrey Corbin. Adam would want me to go."

"The hell he would! He'd never forgive me if anything happened to you, and I can't say I'd blame him. So here is the plan, Mrs. Corbin. Sit down and listen."

Knowing that an argument would be fruitless at this point, Banner found a stool, drew it close to Adam, and sat down.

Chapter Thirteen

Sean rested his forehead against the rough-barked trunk of a fir tree, breathing deeply. Banner's threat pulsed in his mind and his soul, echoing. Aching. *I'll kill you for this, Sean Malloy.*

After a time, he looked up. From where he stood, he could see the lights of that massive, fancy house. His breath evened out a bit, and he smiled.

Corbin was bigger than he'd thought. If he hadn't hidden in the buggy the way he had and caught that bleeding rounder in the face with the side of his boot, it might have been himself lying on the ground.

A sudden and intense ache stiffened Sean's shoulders

and knotted his gut. He'd have killed the bastard, that he would, if it hadn't been for the captain coming along when he did. It would have been a mistake, killing Adam Corbin, considering the plans he had for him and for Banner.

So Banner would kill him, would she? Sean laughed as he started back down the hill, toward Water Street, keeping to the darkest parts of the road and even slipping through the occasional back garden. She'd killed him already, putting him into that stinking prison the way she had, taking money for his freedom, denying him for that fancy man and his bed.

On Water Street, it was said that Adam Corbin kept a mistress and visited her regularly. And still, the story went, he could have Banner whenever and wherever he wanted, her yowling for more like an alley cat.

Rage shifted, cold and raw, within Sean's tormented spirit. Why was it that she'd willingly give herself to the rich man, even knowing about his woman, as she surely must? When he himself had strayed, she'd refused him her bed.

Sean smiled. Her refusals hadn't mattered much to him, had they? He'd had her anyway, and roughly, and he would have her again.

After all, she was his wife.

He found Royce in the appointed place, behind one of the boxhouses on Water Street.

"Well?" drawled the captain of the *Jonathan Lee,* his features hidden in shadow until he struck a match to light a cheroot.

"He's hurtin'," said Sean.

"But not dead?"

"Not yet." Sean paused, folded his brawny arms. His hands still ached to finish his work, to close around Corbin's throat and squeeze. "Tell me something, Royce. What do you have against Corbin?"

Royce's features looked chiseled in the crimson glow of his cheroot's tip. "Adam? Not much, really. Our association is marked by a sort of scathing indifference. It's Jeff I'd like to see stretched out on a slab."

"Why?"

"Let's just say that we're—competitors, Captain Corbin and I. He'll come after you, you know. And that's what I want—one chance at him."

Sean considered the weeks he'd spent crewing on the *Sea Mistress,* against his will, and the rage moved in him again. He hadn't been mistreated on that ship, that was true, but he'd been shanghaied all the same, and that was something a man couldn't overlook.

"It won't be easy, handlin' that one," he observed.

"I'll have help, Malloy. You just draw Jeff Corbin into my reach, and I'll settle your debt and my own, too."

"That leaves the doctor and me wife."

Temple's shoulders stiffened in the darkness. "Wait a minute. I'd like nothing better than to drop Jeff's head into the sound, tied up in a sack, and I don't really give a damn what you do to Adam. But the woman—"

"The woman is mine, Royce. Mine to deal with."

"Hold it, Malloy. Bedding Banner is one thing, but killing her is another. And she isn't your wife—not anymore."

"She is."

281

"No, Malloy. I've seen the papers—the daughter of a— er—friend of mine showed them to me. Banner divorced you in New York, several years ago. Her marriage to Corbin is legal."

Divorce? Banner had dared to divorce him, defying not only her rightful husband but God Himself. "I don't believe it!"

"It's the truth, Malloy. Corbin's within the law when he beds the woman, and bed her he does."

Sean considered killing Temple Royce where he stood; given the man's size and build, it would be easy. But he needed a way out of Port Hastings, a place to hide until it was time to strike again. "What the hell do you mean by that?"

"You've heard the talk, Malloy, just as I have. One of my girls tells me that Adam all but took her in one of the hallways on the *Silver Shadow*, Christmas Eve. It was the night they were married, in fact."

A headache grasped the nape of Sean's neck like the claw of some giant beast. "They ain't married—not in the eyes of God."

"God doesn't seem to mind much, Malloy. And Adam Corbin has the look of a man well-serviced. I suppose she—"

"Why are you doing this? Why the hell are you telling me these things when you know—"

In the fetid gloom, Sean saw the flash of Royce's even teeth. "I want you to be angry, Malloy. Mad enough to kill."

"I'm that, all right. And it's you I'll be killin', Royce, if you don't stop talking the way you are."

"You won't do that. I'm all that stands between you and a long stay in the territorial prison, and we both know it. You killed that redheaded whore, Malloy, and then you assaulted a leading citizen. If you weren't leaving here tonight, on the *Jonathan Lee,* the Corbins would have your ass on a platter before sunrise. That family is close, Malloy, and they look after their own."

Everything Royce had said was true, and Sean offered no argument. "You want something more than the captain's head in a bag, don't you, Royce?"

The nod of the dandy's head was almost imperceptible, but his words had all the impact of a sledge hammer. "I want a turn at Banner," he said calmly.

Sean closed his eyes, reminded himself that he needed this man, for the time being. "She's me *wife*," he breathed.

"She's *Corbin's* wife. Let me have her for one night—just one night—and then, as long as you don't kill her, she's yours."

"Aye? And how will you know if I kill her or not?"

"I'll know, Malloy. And if anything happens to that woman, I'll have you hunted down and dealt with in a manner that isn't pleasant to think about, let alone endure."

At that moment, Temple Royce's real plans were as clear to Sean as if they'd been written across the night sky in stars. He meant to have his vengeance on Captain Corbin, dump Sean himself over the side of the *Jonathan Lee,* and with the fancy man dead, have Banner for his own. Not just for one night, but until he tired of her.

Sean chuckled to himself. Royce's idea, as it happened, wasn't so very different from his own. There were varia-

283

tions, of course, but not many.

"First," Jeff went on, as Banner sipped her potent coffee, "I'll get some of my crew to stand guard here, look after both you and Adam. Jenny and I will go to the Klallum camp and put a stop to this steam hut business, whatever it is."

Banner looked at her unconscious husband. He would have to be moved from the examining table to one of the ward beds. "The Klallum won't listen to you," she said to Jeff, at reflective length.

"Maybe not, Banner," Jeff retorted. "But you're not going near the place. If Malloy didn't get you, the smallpox would."

"I am immune to smallpox," reasoned Adam's wife. "I've treated it before."

Jeff looked quietly explosive, and his eyes swept over the battered, carefully mended form of his sleeping brother. "I can't believe you would even consider leaving Adam now," he marveled angrily. "Damn Malloy and everything else—don't you care about your own husband?"

"You know I do!" cried Banner, shooting off the stool, upsetting her coffee and spilling it down the front of her wrapper. "Jeff, Adam would want me to go!"

"Bull," replied Jeff.

They moved Adam into the ward in stiff silence, the three of them, by means of the same wooden door he'd been carried inside on. Until his ribs had a chance to mend, in fact, he would remain upon it.

"Take care of my brother," Jeff ordered in a terse

284

whisper once they'd covered Adam and put the special railings on the sides of his bed into place. "Lock the house," he added, on his way to the outer office, "and don't let anyone in except me."

"Jeff!"

He was gone.

Banner fell into a chair, her eyes fixed on Adam. How broken and vulnerable he looked, lying there. Suppose Sean did get in somehow? Suppose—

"It's true, Banner," whispered Jenny, breaking into her thoughts. "You can't leave Adam now. Not if you love him."

"Do you think I *want* to?" hissed Banner, trembling in her shock and her weariness and her outrage. "Good God, Jenny, do you seriously think I want to turn my back on him even for a moment, let alone go 'traipsing off,' as Jeff put it, to some Indian camp?"

Jenny lowered her eyes.

Banner regretted speaking so sharply, and she gentled her tone. "I want you to tend Adam for me, Jenny—please. He should sleep through the night, but if he doesn't—"

"What? You're—you're leaving *now?*"

Banner stood, bent to tenderly kiss her husband's forehead. "Yes, as soon as I'm dressed. If I wait, I'm sure Jeff will stop me."

"Banner!"

But she was already tearing herself away from a man she couldn't bear to leave, rushing through the walkway to the main house. When Banner returned, fifteen minutes later, she was fully dressed and carrying a rifle from a cabinet upstairs.

"Sean Malloy is a big ape of a man," she told a wide-eyed Jenny in flat, matter-of-fact tones. "He has light, curly hair and hazel eyes. If he comes into this ward, shoot him."

"Sh-Shoot—" stammered Jenny, trembling again.

"Dead," confirmed Banner. And then she hurried out into the night, where the April wind lashed at her skirts and the fear of Sean Malloy tore at her heart.

Appropriating a horse was easy—the stable hands had evidently gone to bed, for the dark, shadowy barn was empty. Banner didn't bother with a saddle; she needed only a bridle and the gentle, intrepid beast that usually drew Adam's buggy.

Light was gathering, gray and weak, in the eastern skies, when she rode over the ridge and down into the heart of the Klallum camp, the handle of her medical bag looped over one wrist.

There was smallpox here, all right—Banner could smell it niggling under the other odors of fish oil and dung and wood smoke. The squaws went about their early morning work, making a wailing sound as they moved, barely sparing a glance for Banner in their loud grief.

Near the infamous steam hut, a hot fire was burning, and large stones were being heated in the embers, to be carried inside.

She slid from the horse's damp, heaving back and raced toward the scene, stumbling on loose rocks and upraised roots as she went. "Stop!"

An old woman looked up from the blaze, keening mournfully, as the others did. Then, with placid movements that made a ludicrous contrast to her cries, the squaw took up a red hot stone, using bits of tanned hide to shield her hands, and started toward the hut.

Banner searched her mind for a viable word of Chinook, but all she could remember was *kloochman*—"woman" or "wife."

"This is bad medicine!"

The squat woman waddled to the doorway of the hut, pushed aside the buckskin covering, stooped to go in. There was a loud sizzling sound as the stone was dropped into ice cold water.

Clearly, the Klallum, weren't going to listen to Banner the way they did to Adam; except for the old man striding toward her, the tribe seemed bound to ignore her completely.

"You must stop this now!" she enjoined the emissary, who wore white man's trousers and a buckskin shirt. "This is very bad medicine—"

"Doctor's *kloochman?*" asked the elderly man, somewhat archly. "Where Big Doctor?"

Banner sighed, drew a deep breath, brushed a tendril of dark red hair back from her forehead. "Big Doctor is very sick."

The man spoke loudly, to be heard over the cacophonious grief of his tribe. "We have sickness here. Death. Big Doctor come, make better."

"Big Doctor cannot come," Banner argued patiently. "I am here to help you, but you must make that woman stop carrying those stones into that hut!"

The Indian man spread his hands. "Do this to kill bad *tamanous.*"

Tamanous. Now there was a word Banner recognized.

"The disease your people are suffering from does not come from an evil spirit—it is a virulent bacteria." A virulent bacteria.

Banner could almost hear Adam laughing at her choice of words. Are you addressing an Indian, O'Brien? he would say, Or an assemblage of medical students?

She was comforted, just by imagining that Adam was beside her now, sure and strong and full of gentle irony. "There is no bad *tamanous*," she began again. "Not at the moment, anyway. I am Big Doctor's *kloochman*. I make better."

The Indian looked skeptical, even testy. "Fire-hair go home to own lodge. *That* make better."

Banner flushed. "I will not go home until you stop what you are doing! I—"

The woman came out of the steam hut then, carrying a limp, half-dressed child in her arms. She marched toward the frigid waters of the sound, and Banner stumbled after her, grappled for the tiny, sore-covered form she held.

"Stop—give me that child!"

"Kill bad *tamanous*," muttered the squaw, tears rolling down her wide red face.

"*No!* Don't you see—it's the *child* you'll kill—"

Banner's words were broken off by the crack of a rifle shot, as was the wailing of the tribeswomen. The squaw stood stock-still, and the only sounds in the next few moments were those of restive horses and the tide on the nearby shore.

Slowly, Banner turned to face what she knew she must—the cold, quiet rage of her brother-in-law.

He looked like a giant, Jeff did, sitting atop his great,

dark horse, and his breath came in ominous plumes from his nostrils, giving him a satanic appearance. The leather of his saddle creaked as he bent to replace his rifle in its scabbard and then dismount.

With him were two other men, probably crewmen from the *Sea Mistress,* but they remained on their horses, watching the peaceful Klallum with wary eyes.

The tribe seemed to know Jeff, to be in awe of him as they were of Adam. The man Banner had been arguing with was the first to rush toward the imperious, rock-jawed visitor, babbling in petulant Chinook, but the others followed, adding their own unintelligible complaints to the uproar.

Jeff answered them in the jargon, his fair head towering above their dark ones.

At some order from him, two very young braves caught Banner's arms at the elbows and began propelling her toward one of the long wooden lodges she had been so curious about during her first visit here, with Adam.

She was too stunned and frightened to protest in earnest, but she did fling one look back over her shoulder and see that Jeff was striding along behind, through the waves of annoyed and chattering Indians, his face set and hard.

Banner was flung past a mangy bearskin that served as a door and into the close, smelly darkness of the structure. There was a firepit in the center of the dirt-floored lodge, but the embers glowing there gave off very little light.

Outside, there was another swell of angry voices, Jeff's among them, and then the bearskin moved and she knew that he had come in.

"What the hell do you think you're doing?" her brother-in-law growled, keeping his distance.

"I had to come," said Banner, with tremulous dignity, straightening her cloak and squaring her shoulders. "How is Adam?"

"What do you care?"

"I care a great deal, Jeff Corbin! Adam is my husband, and I love him very much!"

"I can see that," mocked the captain, in a sardonic drawl. "No doubt he'll be thrilled to learn that you've left him to walk into the middle of a smallpox epidemic! Banner, the Klallum have been a peaceful tribe for generations, but you have them ready to take scalps and wear warpaint—"

"You make it sound as though I insulted them!"

Jeff drew nearer, to stand at the edge of the firepit. The crimson light moved on the planes of his face, giving him a forbidding, pagan look. "They *are* insulted, Banner. The chief, in fact, wants you properly beaten."

Alarm leaped in Banner's throat, and she retreated a step. "Beaten?" she echoed.

"I wouldn't do that, of course—though I can't speak for my brother. Adam may be moved to violence when he hears about this."

Banner was still reeling from his earlier statement. "They sent you in here to *beat* me?"

"Or otherwise subdue you. You see, Banner, things are quite different here. Brothers share their women. Therefore, I have as much right to deal with you, in their view, as Adam would."

"You—you wouldn't . . . ?"

"Of course not. But we're going to have to make them think I did. Which will it be, Banner? Do we convince

290

them that I'm beating you, or—"

Banner blushed and hugged herself, snapping, "Well, we're certainly not going to pretend that we're making love!"

A grin lifted one corner of Jeff's heretofore taut mouth. "Darn," he said. "I *knew* you'd choose the beating."

"This is ridiculous! I came to try to avert disaster, not stand in this wretched, smelly lodge and playact! Don't you understand that those—those people out there are parboiling *children* in that hut of theirs? And do you know what they'll do after that, *captain?* They'll plunge the poor little things into the water!"

Jeff shook his head slowly, smugly. "No, they won't. I told them that Adam had threatened to conjure up a very big, very bad *tamanous* if they proceeded, and they believed me."

Banner sighed. She had tried to reason with the Klallum, to no avail. But one word from Adam—even secondhand—and the purpose was accomplished!

Jeff seemed to be reading her mind. "Does it matter what made them stop, Banner?"

Slowly, she shook her head. "There are still patients to see to—"

"I'm afraid not, Banner. While the Klallum might let you help if Adam were here, they're not about to permit it now. The medicine man is raising hell."

It seemed that Banner was to be thwarted at every turn. A tear slid down her cheek and her knees quivered, as though they might give out. "Well, then," she sighed, with resignation, "let's go home. I want to see Adam."

Incredibly, Jeff was removing his belt. He chuckled as

291

Banner's eyes widened, then indicated a shadowy heap of something near the lodge's rear wall.

"Timing is all, Mrs. Corbin," he said. "Every time I strike those hides with the belt, you holler."

Color ached in Banner's face. "Oh, Jeff, I couldn't—"

"It's that or the real thing, sweetness. In another minute, the chief and half his braves will be in here, demanding that their honor be satisfied."

"*Honor?* What honor is there in beating a woman?"

Jeff shrugged. "None. The right or wrong of it is irrelevant, Banner—and things could get very nasty if we force them into insisting."

"Y-You mean they'd—they'd want to watch?"

"Or participate."

Banner closed her eyes. "Let's get it over with, then," she said.

Jeff shouted something probably, a severe reprimand, in Chinook, and the belt struck the hides with a hard *thud.*

On cue, Banner shrieked.

"That was pretty good," remarked Jeff, in a whisper, "But you're supposed to be suffering, not finding a mouse in the potato bin!"

Banner recalled what Sean had done to Adam, and this time, when she cried out, there was much pain in the sound.

Twice more, Jeff assaulted the hides, twice more Banner whooped in theatrical agony.

Finally, her brother-in-law caught her elbow in his hand and started toward the door of the lodge. "Keep your head down," he ordered in a brisk undertone. "And try to look submissive and meek."

"Eat a root," Banner whispered back. "There is a limit, you overgrown—"

"Banner."

The Indians were waiting, their dark eyes avid, their faces full of grim satisfaction. Suddenly, Banner found it very easy to lower her head and look as though she'd just been soundly disciplined by her husband's brother.

In a way, she had.

Adam had prevailed upon the stable hands to move him, board and all, to his own bed, according to Maggie, and he was looking wan and impatient and very angry when Banner reached him.

"O'Brien," he began in a low, ominous rumble.

Banner sighed and tried to rub away the headache that was pulsing beneath her wind-chapped temples. "Not now, Adam. Please."

He subsided slightly, intertwined his fingers on top of his neatly bound rib cage. The bruise on his eye was an angry purple, and the stitches in his lip and on the side of his head looked garish against his paper-white flesh. "What happened?"

"I tried to stop the Klallum from using the steam hut."

"And?"

"And they wouldn't listen to me. They listened to Jeff, though—of course." Banner put down her bag and began untying the ribbons that held her cloak closed. "As for the patients, I wasn't allowed to go near them. Jeff and I had to go through this whole charade in the lodge—" She paused, blushed profusely. "We had to pretend that he was beating me."

Adam chuckled.

"It isn't funny!" cried Banner, incensed. "Adam, there are sick children in that village!"

"Don't worry, O'Brien. I had Jenny wire a friend of mine, in Providence. He's coming over as soon as he can make steamer connections."

"A doctor, I presume?" Banner retorted dryly. "And a man, no doubt."

"Oh, Griffin is both," said Adam. "I can depend on him to set things right in the camp."

Banner hurt, inside and out. "As you can't depend on me, I suppose?"

Adam looked annoyed. "Oh, I can depend on you, all right, O'Brien. If anything is going well, you'll botch it for sure. What the hell were you thinking about, running off in the middle of the night like that? What if you'd found yourself face to face with Sean Malloy?"

"I didn't, so why make such a fuss now?"

"Because I love you, O'Brien," he snapped. "Because I need you. Because if Malloy or anybody else hurt you, I don't know what I'd do!"

She came to the side of the bed, knelt, touched Adam's battered and fervent face tenderly. "You're the one who has been hurt," she said, and tears smarted in her eyes because she could not take his pain and bear it herself.

With great effort, Adam brought one hand to her cheek, smoothed it with a gentle thumb. "Get some sleep, Shamrock. You look exhausted."

Obediently, Banner rose, undressed to her camisole and drawers, and started to curl up in a big chair, meaning to cover herself with a knitted blanket and sleep there.

"Here," Adam argued softly, sternly. "Beside me."

Banner came to the bed, crawled in beside her husband, careful not to jar him. Within minutes, she was sound asleep.

The room was shadowy and still when she awakened, shooting upright, her breath hot and raw in her throat, her forehead beaded with perspiration. Sean had been there, standing at the foot of the bed, mocking her, threatening.

Adam groaned beside her, and the sound brought a rush of bittersweet reality. She fell back to her pillows, dizzy with relief: she'd been dreaming. Only dreaming.

"O'Brien?"

"My name is Corbin," Banner argued, only half teasing.

"Yes," grumbled Adam, "But if I called out 'Corbin' every time I wanted you, forty-three people would answer."

Banner giggled. "I suppose you're right. How do you feel, by the way?"

"Terrible. How about you, Shamrock?"

"Scared—I feel scared."

"Don't. Nobody is going to hurt you."

"It isn't myself I'm worried about, Adam. Sean is a brutal, ruthless man."

"Do tell."

Banner giggled again, but this time there were tears in the sound. "What were you thinking about, to let Sean take you by surprise that way?"

Adam laughed. "All the things I meant to do to you when I got back to our bed. The next thing I knew, the side of his boot was in my face."

"That's Sean. He'd probably be afraid to fight you in a

straightforward fashion."

"Salving my wounded ego, are you, O'Brien?"

"Does it need salving?"

"Yes. I feel like a damned fool, and a weakling in the bargain."

Banner raised herself on one elbow, carefully, so that she would not cause Adam pain by the motion. "You're neither a fool nor a weakling, Adam Corbin," she said.

"No?"

"No."

"And you don't regret marrying me?"

Banner kissed his cheek. "Only when you order me about and tell me that I can't practice medicine after our baby is born."

"Ah, yes. Well, I've had second thoughts about that, as it happens."

"What? Ordering me about?"

"Never. That's fun and I won't give it up. Spanking you was fun, too, but alas, that's a thing of the past, isn't it?" He paused, chuckled at the blush in her cheeks. "All those ruffles. I did like pulling down your drawers, O'Brien. What I've had second thoughts about is your practice."

Banner stared at him, trying to read his face. "And?"

"You're a good doctor, O'Brien—you proved that the day the sawmill blew up. I couldn't have gotten through that particular crisis without you."

When she started to speak, Adam laid one finger to her lips, silencing her, and went on.

"I still want you to be a mother to our child, Shamrock. That's your job—not Maggie's or anyone else's. By the same token, you don't have to hover around the little character every moment of the day, either."

"It wouldn't be good if I did, Adam—not for the baby or for me."

"I know. I'll help where I can"—Adam reached out, circled the nipple of one muslin-covered breast with a teasing finger—"but there are some things I'm just not equipped to do, O'Brien."

"And there are some things you are in no condition to do," she reminded him, gently pushing his hand away. "Is it true that you wouldn't take the breast when you were a baby and had to be nurtured on clam broth?"

He chuckled and the hand returned unerringly. "Amazing but true. Have you no mercy, Shamrock? No compassion? You could make me forget my ceaseless pain, you know."

"Poor Adam."

He pulled a wretched face. "O'Brien, I'm trying to appeal to your better nature."

"My better nature says that you need another injection and lots of sleep—not passion."

"Damn your better nature then. Pleasure me."

Banner climbed cautiously out of bed, found her bag. "Some people enjoy morphine, I've heard."

"Malloy broke my ribs, damn it, not my—"

Banner lit a lamp and filled a syringe in the light. "Stop cajoling; it doesn't become you."

"Neither does—"

"Adam." Banner dabbed his upper arm with alcohol soaked cotton, pumped the air bubbles out of the syringe, and administered the injection.

"Woman, you have no heart."

"No conscience, in the bargain," rejoined Banner.

"And you call yourself a doctor!"

She patted the fading evidence of his desire. "Sleep well," she said, to the both of them.

"Wench."

Banner bent, tenderly kissed Adam's swollen mouth. "I may be a wench, but I love you."

"Prove . . . it."

"I just did. Good night, darling."

The reply was an inelegant snore.

Adam's friend from Providence arrived the next morning; he was a very handsome, serious-looking man, and Banner liked him, despite his brusque manner. In the space of only two days, he had the smallpox situation in the Klallum camp under some control, though he agreed with Adam that the most that could be hoped for was that the malady wouldn't spread through the entire tribe.

To prevent this, he had the infected patients moved to a hastily constructed lodge well away from the rest of the village, where they were attended by the few members of the tribe who had had the disease and survived it.

It seemed very unfair, to Banner, that the Klallum would accept such sweeping dictums from Dr. Fletcher but not from herself, and she said so, fervently, after Adam's friend had returned to his own town and practice.

Adam was grumpy, already tired of being confined to the house. "Don't harp, O'Brien," he snapped. "The central issue here is that the problem has been dealt with, for the time being. I don't see that it matters whether you settled the matter or Griffin did."

Banner had no argument to offer, so she forced a smile to her face and bent to kiss Adam's forehead. "Is Jeff still out looking for Sean? I haven't seen him since before Dr. Fletcher arrived."

A storm was gathering in Adam's arrogant features. "How the hell would I know?" he bellowed.

Banner's heart crumbled within her; she'd been more emotional lately, more prone to hurt and anger and all manner of inadvisable feelings. She gave one great, blubbering sob and made to leave the bedroom.

But Adam caught her hand in his and held on tight. "I'm sorry, O'Brien. I'm sorry."

She sat down on the edge of the bed; now that Adam couldn't hold her close, due to his injured ribs, she felt bereft and broken much of the time. "It's all right."

"No, it isn't. The truth is, O'Brien, that I'm scared. You're in danger and God knows where Jeff is—"

Banner touched his lips with a soothing finger. "Nothing has happened to him. Jeff is strong, and he'd make short work of Sean Malloy if the need arose."

Pain surged in the weary indigo eyes. "The way I did?" he barked.

"Jeff will be careful, Adam," Banner said quickly. "And he has his crew with him—the men from the *Sea Mistress.*"

Adam made an impatient, exasperated sound and turned his head away toward the wall.

"Adam?"

He opened his eyes, squinted. O'Brien was asleep beside him and the room was dark. "Jeff?"

His brother fell to sit on his heels at the bedside, keeping his voice low. "I found Malloy—or, at least, I know where he is."

"And?"

"According to the scuttlebutt on Water Street, he's in Seattle, hiding out in some roominghouse on the Skid Road."

"Water Street?" Adam drew a deep breath. "That's Royce's turf. Has it ever occurred to you that this might be a trick of some kind?"

Jeff's shoulders moved in an easy shrug. "I'm not afraid of Royce."

"Maybe you should be. He hates your guts, little brother. Remember?"

"I'm not very fond of him either, as it happens. Right now, I'm only interested in Malloy, and I know my way around the Skid Road."

"Yeah. I'm the one who had to dip you in kerosene after your last visit. Be careful, Jeff—please."

Jeff grinned, tilted his head to one side. "When am I anything but?"

"Too often. And Jeff?"

His brother was standing up again, his face in shadows. "What?"

"We can't spare you, so keep your eyes open."

"I will," Jeff promised, and then he was gone.

Adam closed his eyes, but sleep was elusive. He kept thinking of Malloy and Temple Royce and how they might be in league with each other, drawing Jeff into some kind of snare. After all, both of them had their grudges— Malloy because he'd been shanghaied, Royce because he'd been feuding with Jeff long enough that it was an ingrained habit.

He awakened Banner.

She curled close to him, like a sleepy kitten. "What is it, Adam?" she yawned. "Are your ribs hurting?"

"No."

"Your stitches?"

"No."

"If nothing hurts, why did you wake me up?"

Adam laughed and sought her hand, guiding it. "I didn't say nothing hurt, O'Brien."

She laughed, tugged at him gently, reveled in the rumbling groan the motion elicited. "You are very wicked, Adam Corbin."

"And desperate, too. Please, O'Brien."

"I'll go downstairs and brew some clam broth," she teased. "Would you like that?"

"You know what I'd like, you little wretch."

Banner giggled, but then she sat up and drew back the blankets that covered them both. Cool air washed over Adam, doing nothing to quell the fierce heat rising within him.

"I love you," she said, and one kiss fell upon him, to be absorbed like rain failing on parched ground.

Adam gasped and instinctively arched his back. The resulting pain in his rib cage brought a sheen of sweat to his upper lip, his chest, his forehead.

Banner instantly drew back, hesitating.

"Oh, God, O'Brien—I need you."

"You mustn't move," she said. And then there was another kiss.

"I promise I won't—oh, God—move a muscle."

It was a hard promise to keep, for lying still, under the circumstances, was a blissful, blinding sort of hell. Banner's hair tumbled over Adam, like coppery silk, and the scent of it made him crazy. "O'Brien," he said, unable even to entangle his hands in that rich cinnamon mane. "O'Brien . . ."

The name was a chant, conjuring magic of a brutal sort, and Banner rewarded it with fire.

Adam dared not move, though the ancient instincts commanded it, and his resistance made the pleasure keener. His voice became a senseless, growllike sob.

Banner laughed and bit him softly, and suddenly his mind and soul splintered, their fragments flung in diverse directions, as sweet release came. It was a very long time before he drifted down from the arch of the rainbow to settle in and sleep.

Adam's dreams were pleasant ones, fraught with blue-eyed, redheaded children and the ring of O'Brien's voice. Toward morning, he felt a velvety nipple brush his lips, seeking sanction.

He took suckle greedily, even in his half-sleep, wondering what it was exactly, this intangible nectar that he drew from Banner's full, sleep-warmed breasts.

Inwardly, as O'Brien whimpered in her giving, Adam shrugged. Whatever it was, it sure beat clam broth.

Chapter Fourteen

The figure moved, slender and fleeting, at the edge of the woods. Banner left the task of unhitching the horse and buggy she'd taken on her rounds to a stable hand and walked briskly toward the line of trees.

The soggy ground was soft beneath the soles of her shoes, and the grass was wet with the rains of May. It had been a month now since Sean's attack on Adam, and her husband was almost fully recovered.

Today he had even seen patients in his surgery, though his ribs were still bound and his movements were slow and cautious.

Best of all, as far as Banner was concerned, there had been no more trouble from Sean.

She paused near a fallen log populated by small creatures and busy insects and raised her hands to her hips. "Lulani?" she called.

There was no answer, but for the call of an annoyed bird.

"Lulani! Come out here!"

The boughs of a small pine tree shifted, filling the fresh spring air with the scent of Christmas. Wisely, Banner kept her distance.

"Lulani?" she ventured again.

The woman did not show herself, and her voice was tentative. "Where is Adam? He is well?"

Banner closed her eyes for a moment; she was past jealousy now, loving Adam as she did, and though she was not resigned to sharing him, she had pity for this woman who must have been waiting and worrying all these weeks.

"He was hurt very badly, but he's recovering."

"Hurt? How?"

Banner sighed. "Adam was beaten, Lulani."

There was a silence. "This is true? Adam lives?"

"Yes. Lulani, is there anything you need?"

"Need Adam," came the steady reply.

Banner suppressed a sudden and unladylike need to delve into that bristly pine tree and throttle her husband's mistress with her bare hands. Perhaps she *wasn't* past jealousy, after all. "He is my *husband*, Lulani!"

"Adam has said this. You will send him soon up the mountain, please?"

"I'm sure I won't need to send him," lamented Banner. Adam had been casting anxious looks in the direction of that mountain for days now, and his mood, of late, had hardly been conducive to marital bliss. "Doesn't it bother you, Lulani, to share him with me?"

The question hung, unanswered, in the air, which was well because Banner instantly regretted asking it. After almost a minute, she realized that Lulani had gone and gave up her vigil.

Banner found Adam standing stiffly beside his desk, trying to comprehend the system of organization his wife had engineered.

Banner interlaced her fingers. "I just saw Lulani," she said.

The papers in Adam's hands wafted down to the surface of his desk, and his jaw took on a formidable angle. "What did she say?"

It was hard, so hard, not to shout and cry and demand fidelity from a man who was not prepared to give it. "She has been waiting for you to come to her," Banner said evenly.

"I'm not surprised," said Adam distractedly. "It's been weeks."

Banner blushed and lowered her eyes, struggling with

the rage and pain that rioted within her. "Yes. Weeks."

"O'Brien."

She kept her gaze fixed on the floor. "What?"

"Look at me, please."

She couldn't, not now. Didn't Adam understand that? It was all she could do to stand there, the way she was, with her broken pride all spiky and swollen in her throat. "I don't want to," she replied.

"Very well. I'm not sure I'd care for the expression I would see in your eyes anyway, Shamrock."

Banner's gaze lifted swiftly, of its own accord. "I have not complained," she reminded him, and her tones were calm, even though there was color flaring in her face.

"No. You've been damning me as a rake and a rounder, though, haven't you?"

"I've been tending to you, Adam Corbin! I've been fetching and carrying and putting up with your impossible temper! I've been—"

Adam smiled, his eyes dancing in his gaunt face. "You certainly have. Actually, I guess I should be flattered that you think me capable of bedding another woman."

"F-Flattered?" sputtered Banner, infuriated.

He nodded. "Flattered," he confirmed. "As I believe I told you once before, it would take a greater man than I to stray, O'Brien."

Banner lowered her eyes. It *wasn't* the first time Adam had implied that her love left him too drained to seek solace elsewhere, and she didn't know whether to be insulted or pleased.

"Tell me why you stay with me, Shamrock, when your opinion of my integrity is obviously so low. Is it the child?"

"Partly. But I would stay even if there were no baby."

"Why?"

Banner thrust out her chin. "Because I am weak!" she cried, angry because he'd cornered her. Again.

"Weak?" Adam chuckled. "You? Try again, O'Brien."

"It is my cross to bear that I love you, Adam Corbin. Against all good sense and reason, I might add!"

He came to her, lifted her chin with one hand. "Yes. But love seeks its own purposes, doesn't it?"

Banner swallowed, cast about desperately for a more suitable subject. "Have you heard from Jeff?"

"Yes. He met a woman in Seattle and we probably won't see him again until Christmas. O'Brien?"

"What?"

"Kiss me."

"I absolutely will not!"

"Not even if I promise to take you with me to the mountain tomorrow?"

Banner stared up at him, searched his dear, infuriating face. "Tomorrow?"

"Tomorrow. It's time this mystery was laid to rest—at least where you're concerned. But you'll have to help me carry the secret from then on, O'Brien. And be forewarned—it isn't an easy thing to live with."

"What—"

Adam touched her lips with his, lightly, teasingly. "Tomorrow, O'Brien," he said, just before his mouth claimed hers.

The sky was a clear blue and the wind was warm. As Banner sat in the high seat of the buckboard, she could

306

almost be happy that the truth was to be known to her at last. Almost.

But familiar worries stirred the butterflies in her middle to full flight. If Adam presented her with a second family and a long, poetic discourse on his feelings for Lulani, she wasn't going to be able to bear it.

And even if it turned out that her husband had been faithful, by some miracle, the secret might still be a bitter and wounding one. Adam had warned her that once everything was finally made clear, she might well wish that she'd never found out at all.

As Adam lifted the reins of the buckboard, he searched her face, and she saw the crushing weight of what he knew in the depths of his eyes. "You can still change your mind, O'Brien," he said.

Banner squared her shoulders. "I'm going with you. Are we going to sit here in the barnyard all day?"

He laughed and brought the reins down and they were off, winding and jolting up the face of the awakening mountain. Again and again during the long and uncomfortable ride, Banner marveled at the raw beauty surrounding them. The memory of a meadow strewn with bright orange wood lilies and wild daisies would sustain her, as would the fierce, complex love she felt for the man beside her.

After some time, Adam finally brought the wagon to a stop in a clearing. There were still traces of snow here, and the wind was brisk, lashing at Banner's skirts as her husband helped her down from the seat.

"Aren't we going to the cabin?"

"No," replied Adam, suddenly very busy with the horses

307

and wagon.

"Adam."

He paused, searched the azure sky, with its thin, patchy clouds, and sighed. "O'Brien, I—"

She went to him quickly, took his arm. "Whatever it is, Adam, I'll—I'll try to understand."

Adam stiffened, and the motion of his lips was only a mockery of a smile. "Oh, you'll understand, all right. You'll understand. Just remember, O'Brien—you can't ever tell anyone. Not Mama, not Jeff, not anyone. Understood?"

"No!"

"It will be," he said, and then he stepped away from her again, and his shoulders were taut beneath his shirt and lightweight coat.

Banner ached for him, for Lulani, for herself. But she waited in brave silence.

Finally, Adam lifted his hands and cupped them around his mouth and shouted, and the word that echoed against the sky and the mountainside itself shocked Banner Corbin to the center of her being.

"*Papa!*"

"My God," breathed Banner.

Adam shouted again, and the sound echoed well into forever.

Banner took Adam's arm again, pulling. "Adam, your father? Your *father?*"

Agony rose in his dark blue eyes, old and consuming and well-entrenched. "Lulani is Papa's woman, Banner. Not mine."

"But—"

He lifted his hands to his mouth again, bellowed, "Damn you, Papa, show yourself or I swear to God I'll come looking for you!"

There was a rustling sound in a patch of brush and blackberry vines on a hillside. "Go back!" shouted another voice, masculine and filled with the same pain Banner had heard in Adam's. "Take the woman away!"

"No!" roared Adam. "This is my wife! She's carrying your grandchild! Don't you want to meet her?"

The answer was a swear word that might have been heard in Port Hastings, so heartily was it expelled. But there was more commotion in the blackberry bushes, and small rocks began rattling down the slope.

Banner huddled against her husband and waited. Dizzying images whirled in her mind: Katherine, grieving. A big man stomping on his burning Sunday shirt. Jeff, Keith, Melissa, all certain that their father was dead.

"How could he do this to them?" she whispered.

"You'll see," Adam replied in a hoarse undertone. "Don't go near Papa, Banner, but please don't recoil either."

"Recoil? Why would I—"

Just then, the man appeared. He was tall—taller even than Adam—and his shoulders must have measured an ax-handle across. His hair was dark, his eyes a pale, crystalline blue, like Melissa's eyes, and Keith's.

But his face and hands were so horribly misshapen and discolored that Banner drew in a swift breath and stiffened.

The monster-man paused at a careful distance, his eyes raking his son's defiant frame. Neatly avoiding Banner, the azure gaze swept to the goods piled in the bed of the wagon. "Did you bring the medicine for Lulani?"

"What do you think?" Adam snapped, his hands wedged into his pockets now, the physical breach between himself and his father remaining unbroken. "Papa, this is my wife, Banner."

Banner's heart constricted as the big man's eyes came to her face, reluctant, braced for revulsion. "H-Hello," she managed, automatically holding out one hand and taking a step toward him.

Adam immediately caught hold of her arm and wrenched her back. "O'Brien," he barked, "you were telling me the truth when you said you went to medical school, weren't you?"

Taken aback and more than a little confused, Banner sliced one questioning look at her father-in-law, noted the swollen, distorted face, higher on one side than on the other, the webbed fingers and deformed hands, the patches of discolored pigment in his skin.

Dear God, it couldn't be—not here, not now. Not in these modern times.

"Leprosy," said Adam.

Banner shook her head in useless denial, unable to help herself. Tears slid down her face. "Oh, dear God."

Daniel Corbin scowled at his son. "Are you happy now, boy? Or will you be dragging the rest of the family up here, too, for a good look at the old man?"

"Shut up, damn you!" Adam yelled, his face fierce with love and pain and anger. "You know I won't do that!"

A corresponding pain softened the hideous face. "There's going to be a baby?"

Somehow, Banner gained control of her whirling emo-

310

tions and managed to speak intelligently. "Yes, Mr. Corbin. In September."

Daniel smiled. "September," he reflected.

Adam turned away suddenly, ostensibly to unload the goods they'd brought. But Banner saw the meter of his grief in his shoulders and shared it.

"I love your son, Mr. Corbin," she said boldly, shading her eyes from the sun with one hand.

Daniel laughed, keeping his leper's distance, memorizing the wife of his firstborn son with gentle eyes. "Good. Adam's needed a woman for a long time."

Lulani came out of some hiding place and linked her arm through one of Daniel's. Seeing her clearly for the first time, Banner took note of her flowing, raven-black hair, her nutmeg skin just beginning to wrinkle, her compassionate brown eyes.

"You have not been lost on the mountain again, Mrs. Adam?" she asked, one side of her mouth rising in a smile.

"No." Banner smiled back, very much aware of Adam and the great clatter he was making as he unloaded things from the back of the wagon. "Thank you, for sharing your cabin that night—"

Lulani nodded and then they both disappeared, she and Daniel, two exiles confined to the heights of a wooded mountain.

After a moment of preparation, Banner approached her husband. "Adam," she said softly, "I'm so sorry."

An angry sound ripped itself from his throat, and he ceased his needless stacking and restacking of the crates to turn away from her.

"Was there really a boating accident, Adam?"

He tilted his head back, was silent for a time, in his struggle to compose himself. "Yes. Wasn't that convenient? It provided me with a way to deceive my family, lie to my mother. . . ."

Banner wanted to hold Adam, but she knew she had to wait. "Daniel contracted the disease in Hawaii, didn't he, Adam? When he went there with Jeff."

Adam ran one arm across his face, his back still turned to Banner. "Yes."

"Did he know before he left the islands? Is that why he brought Lulani back with him?"

At last, Banner's broken husband faced her. "Papa didn't develop symptoms for several months after he got back. He'd been—involved—with Lulani during the visit. When we decided he had to live up here, he asked me to write to her and I did. She came to be with him."

"It must have been hell for you—knowing."

"It has been. Can you imagine what this would do to my mother, Banner? To Jeff and Keith and Melissa?"

Banner bit her lower lip, nodded. She knew. And she well understood Adam's reasons for guarding this secret so strenuously. Katherine would have refused to be separated from Daniel, no matter what—at worst, she would have contracted leprosy herself, at best, she would have been almost completely isolated from the rest of the world.

As for Adam's brothers and his sister, they would have had to choose between their good health and their parents.

Too, the authorities would have gotten wind of the situation, eventually, losing no time in shipping Daniel Corbin off to the remotest leper colony they could find.

"Weren't you afraid, Adam? Afraid of being infected?"

"Most people are immune to leprosy, O'Brien. You know that."

So, he hadn't feared for himself. Well, that was typical. "Your mother and the rest of the family—especially Jeff—they were exposed, weren't they?"

Adam nodded, his throat working. "I used to have nightmares, O'Brien. I'd see their faces sliding out of place, their fingers growing together—"

"Adam, stop. Stop."

His eyes were fierce and broken as they came to her face. "You wanted to know my secret, O'Brien. Here it is—ugliness and all."

Banner swallowed. "Adam—"

He was pacing now, back and forth on the carpeting of dried pine needles and tatters of dirty spring snow. "You've been exposed yourself, O'Brien—that night in Lulani's cabin—why do you think I was so goddamned mad at you?"

Banner stopped him, with both her hands and all the strength she could summon. "I don't have leprosy, Adam!"

He shuddered in her grasp, a cry of raw grief rising from his middle to rattle in his throat. "O'Brien," he mourned, groping for her.

Banner held him close. "It's all right," she whispered, weeping. "It is, I promise."

"All right!" Adam raged, shuddering again, his face ravaged. "Damn it all to hell, O'Brien, it *isn't* all right! What if—what if you—"

"Hush. I haven't contracted leprosy, Adam." She lifted her hands to his face, soothing him, loving him. "Cry, my darling," she said. "You're a man, not a rock. Cry and I'll

313

cry with you and we'll go on from here, together."

The splendid indigo eyes were bright with tears. "You'll stay with me, O'Brien? You won't leave me?"

"Not ever."

At this assurance, Adam gave way to his grief. He wept in her arms, like a shattered child, his sobs raw and deep and terrible to hear. Holding him, Banner cried, too.

When they had both recovered some composure, Adam touched the tip of Banner's nose with a gentle finger. "I need you," he said.

Banner gulped, sniffled, dashed away the last of her tears with the back of one hand. "Here?" she whispered.

And Adam threw back his head and gave a hoarse shout of laughter. "I promised my father food, medicine, word of the family," he told her, when he could speak. "Not lewd entertainment."

Banner colored gloriously and stomped one foot. Inside her, there was a feeling of coming home after a long and difficult absence. "Adam Corbin, I didn't mean—"

"You did, too. You wanted to do it in the wagonbed, didn't you, O'Brien?"

"No!"

"It's not a bad idea, really," he mused, raising one hand to his chin and pretending to ponder the prospect, to measure the space in the now-empty wagon with his eyes.

In a fine fit of fury, Banner Corbin bunched her skirts in her hands and stomped to the wagon, where she pulled herself, with some difficulty, up onto the seat. "I swear I'll take up these reins myself and leave you behind, Adam Corbin, if you don't apologize to me this instant!"

Considering his, still-tender ribs, Adam swung easily

into the seat beside her. "All right," he said. "I'm sorry that you wanted to molest me in the wagonbed, O'Brien."

"I wanted to—Adam Corbin, you beast! I wanted to do no such thing!"

Adam's hands rose brazenly to her breasts, cupped them beneath her lightweight cloak. "You suggested it," he reminded her.

"I did—not!" Banner's breath was burning in and out of her lungs, and her heart was careening about between her backbone and her rib cage. "For heaven's sake, stop that!"

Adam lowered his hands, assessed her wryly, and took up the reins. "Are you wearing your drawers, O'Brien?"

Banner flushed as the wagon began the winding, rattling trip down that mountain road. "Of course I am!" she cried.

"Liar," retorted her husband, and when they'd rounded the next bend he stopped the team, wound the reins deftly around the brake lever, and turned to her.

Once again, Banner Corbin was caught in an untruth.

They loved fiercely in the hard bed of that wagon, Adam sitting up, Banner on his lap. And their urgent cries hammered at the spring sky, painting a brazen rainbow there, in colors that were visible only to them.

"How could you do this to me?" Adam teased when it was over and they were both breathing evenly again.

Banner was still joined to him, her skirts fanned out around her like a flag of surrender, and she moved to free herself. "You wretch—"

Adam caught her at the waist with both hands, held her firmly in place. "There I was, minding my own business, and you compromised me. How will I face a kn

315

world, O'Brien? I'm tainted—"

"You're crazy," Banner interrupted, her head falling back, her eyes closing, her breath quickening again as she felt him swelling within her.

He nuzzled her exposed breasts, flicked at one nipple with his tongue. "Do you know how good you taste, O'Brien?"

Banner moaned. "Stop it! We've got patients. . . . we've got to get back home."

"Umm-hmm."

"Adam!"

He took suckle at her breast, languidly, lifting her with his hands, lowering her. The rhythm of his passion and her own was building again; the entire universe pulsed in unison with it.

Banner was gasping now. "Oh," she whimpered, riding the thrusts of his need even as he feasted greedily at one breast. "Oooooh . . ."

Banner's triumph came before his, in a blinding, spinning rush. She shuddered upon him, convulsed, and was still.

And as her vision cleared, she saw the smoldering in his eyes, the age-old plea. She rose until she was almost free of Adam, fell back again, taking satisfaction in the passion that moved in his face as she did so. His head fell back and he closed his eyes, totally vulnerable, surrendering. A low, lingering growl rose from his throat as Banner worked her excruciating magic, pausing now and then to tease his lips with a breast.

Adam's hands came to her hair, groping, and his head moved back and forth in sweet delirium.

Banner brought him swiftly, mercifully, to his own fierce victory.

Lulani found her man in the shed where they stored firewood, his head down, his great shoulders moving in suppressed grief.

"Daniel?"

He stiffened, dashed one hand at his great, misshapen face, which was beautiful to Lulani, unbearably beautiful. "Leave me," he said.

She stood fast. "You think now of the woman, Katherine?"

Ever honest, Daniel nodded.

There was no rancor in Lulani, no jealousy. Only a need to comfort and sustain. "It is I that have loved you, Daniel," she reminded him.

He turned to her, smiling suddenly, his eyes bright with the evidence of his pain and his love for a woman he could not have. "My son—my son has a fine wife now, doesn't he, Lulani?"

Lulani returned his smile, but she would wait to touch him; when he was ready for that, she would know. "Yes. Banner is brave and good, like Adam, I think."

"And strong," said Daniel. "And Adam—Adam was always strong, Lulani. Even as a baby. By the time he was four—*four*, mind you, he was telling Katie and I that he'd be a doctor one day."

There were times when Daniel needed to speak of his children; Lulani knew that and respected it. "The others?" she prompted gently.

Daniel was laughing and weeping, both at once. "Jeff is

317

as tough as Adam, though he never had the need to hide his feelings the way his brother does. And Keith. Keith is funny and gentle and yet I've seen him get the best of his brothers time and time again. He was the youngest, and they were always surprised when he prevailed against them—a little David felling two Goliaths."

"And the girl," urged Lulani, loving this man of hers, ignoring, as best she could, the unrelated pain that made fire in her middle. "Tell me again of your small princess, Daniel."

Daniel lowered his head. "I miss her the most, I think," he breathed. "I miss my baby most."

"Yes."

The light blue eyes seared her face suddenly, their vision clear even in the dimness of that shed. "You're hurting again, Lulani," he scolded with tenderness. "Come. I'll give you some of the medicine that Adam brought."

Daniel's arm felt heavy and warm and good around Lulani's shoulders. "I have loved you, Daniel Corbin," she said again, as they left the shed for the bold spring sunshine outside. "When I am gone—"

Daniel held her very close as they walked. "Where do you plan to go, Lulani?" he teased, falling back on the game that kept them both sane. "Down the mountain to find yourself a man as handsome as me?"

"There is no man as handsome as you," replied Lulani with merry resignation. "So I must stay here."

But they both knew that Lulani could not stay. One day soon, she would die—the meter of her pain told her so, as Adam had—and Daniel would be alone.

. . .

318

They entered the house through the kitchen, Banner and Adam, weary and love-sated and grim over their shared secret.

"There is no hope for Lulani?" Banner whispered as Adam touched the coffee pot with the fingertips of his right hand. "None at all?"

Adam flinched, reached up over the stove for two cups. "None. She has a cancer, Banner, and it's a miracle that she's lived this long."

Banner watched with aching eyes as her husband filled the cups, brought them to the table where she sat. "What will your—what will he do, without her?"

"I don't know, Shamrock."

"He loves her, doesn't he?"

Grimly, Adam nodded. "She's all he has."

Banner lowered her eyes, as well as her voice. If anyone overheard their conversation, the results would be disastrous. "Didn't he love your mother?"

"I was waiting for that question," replied Adam, without anger, as he stirred sugar into his coffee. "You're wondering why he ever got to know Lulani in the first place, aren't you?"

"Yes."

"Rest assured, O'Brien, adultery doesn't run in my family, like quick tempers and blue eyes."

Banner lifted her cup, welcomed the warmth of it against her trembling hands. "I'm sorry for thinking that you were unfaithful, Adam," she said distractedly. "But—"

"But things looked pretty bad, didn't they? Let me tell you something, O'Brien. I *did* go to the *Silver Shadow* one

319

night, with every intention of betraying you."

Banner stiffened. "And?"

"And I couldn't bring myself to touch the woman. All I could think about was you."

Banner saw that he was telling the truth. "I thought . . . all those nights—"

"All those nights, O'Brien, I was either in my office or tossing on my lonely bed, fighting an urge to crawl to your door on my hands and knees."

The image made Banner chuckle. "That will be the day. No one could bring you to your knees, Adam Corbin."

His eyes were serious, faraway. "You could," he muttered.

Banner swallowed, discomforted by the very vision that had amused her a moment ago. "Tell me about Lulani."

Twilight was gathering at the windows, darkening the room, making the great house feel empty and cavernous. Where was everyone, anyway? This was the dinner hour, and the place was usually full of activity then.

"I don't know much about her," Adam said with a shrug. "The voyage to Hawaii is a long one, and Papa was never the sort to go without a woman for months at a time. He was always faithful to my mother before that, as far as I know, but Lulani was close by and Mama was far away."

"Would you do that, Adam? Would you find someone else if we were apart for some reason?"

"Academic, O'Brien. We're not going to be apart."

"We could be. One never knows what the future holds. Would you take a mistress, Adam?"

He looked down at his cup, running an idle finger around its rim. "I'd like to say no, O'Brien, but the truth is

320

that I'm not sure."

Banner was indignant, but she did respect Adam for the honesty of his answer. Who knew better than she did how very deep this man's needs ran, and how fierce they were? She would go on loving him, with all the power and fire in her, and hope that he never had to seek solace with another woman.

"When the baby makes me big—" she mumbled miserably.

"You will be even more beautiful than you are now," Adam finished. "I'll want you, O'Brien. Believe me."

Before Banner could overcome the lump in her throat and respond, a loud cry from the other side of the house shattered the mood.

"Adam!" screamed Maggie. "Adam, come quick!"

Adam's chair overturned as he bolted from it, and neither he nor Banner paused to right it again.

"Thank God you're home—I didn't know." Maggie was sobbing and wringing her hands before the gaping front door. "Thank God—"

Adam pushed past the housekeeper, drew in a sharp breath, fell to his haunches on the porch. "Get my bag, Maggie," he breathed.

As Maggie hurried off to obey, Banner stepped forward, looked through the doorway, and cried out softly.

Jeff lay crumpled on the porch, his face bruised almost beyond recognition, one of his arms at an impossible angle beside him. He was breathing, but unconscious.

"Sean?" Banner wondered aloud, her heart breaking for this cherished new brother.

"Maybe," Adam bit out, his fingers gentle at the pulse

point beneath his brother's right ear.

"Who else would do a thing like this?"

Adam didn't bother with an answer; Banner had not really expected him to. When Maggie came back with the bag, she was immediately sent away again to get one of the men from the stables to help carry Jeff.

Jeff had been beaten savagely, and he groaned in delirium as Adam and Banner set his broken arm and cleaned the cuts on his face. Lying on that hospital examining table, he looked more like a small boy than the widely known captain of a clipper ship.

"Who did this to you?" Adam demanded, his hands busy, the moment his brother's eyes flickered open.

Jeff tried to speak and couldn't.

"Where did it happen?" Adam persisted.

"Water Street—I was on W-Water Street—"

"Don't make him talk now!" Banner hissed, pushing a lock of Jeff's sweat-dampened, blood-crusted hair back from his forehead.

"Royce," Jeff managed, smiling weakly up at his concerned sister-in-law. "The chicken egg—he's still mad—about the—goddamned egg."

"What egg?" Banner demanded, her eyes on Adam now.

Adam was turning away, washing his hands at the basin, drying them with a towel. "When we were kids, Temple Royce was Jeff's best friend. One day, we got into the henhouse and an egg fight ensued."

Even in his pain, Jeff chortled. "God, Papa was furious."

Adam surveyed his brother with a sort of grim amusement. "I remember. He dragged you off to the woodshed,

322

and we could hear you howling from inside the house."

Jeff grinned. "Yeah. And when he was—done with me—he came after you. You didn't yell." He paused, frowned. "How come you didn't yell?"

Adam was bringing laudenum from a glass-fronted cupboard. "I didn't want you or Papa or anybody else to know I was hurting, that's why."

"All this started over an egg?" marveled Banner.

"The one Jeff threw happened to have a dead chicken inside it. It struck Royce in the forehead."

Banner grimaced to imagine the stench, the disgust. "Still—"

"Temple started throwing up," Jeff recalled, with a slow grin. "And we—laughed at him."

"You've been feuding all these years over something as silly as that?"

"That's right," confirmed Jeff after swallowing the laudenum Adam had spooned into his mouth.

"I don't believe it!" Banner hissed, appalled.

"Believe it," said Adam, running his hands over his brother's rib cage one last time to make absolutely sure that it was sound. "Royce retaliated—I forget how—and then Jeff paid him back. They've been enemies since that summer."

"That's childish!"

Adam shrugged. "All feuds are, O'Brien, and most of them start over something small and stupid."

Jeff's eyes closed, rolled open again, dazed and unseeing. "I c-couldn't find Malloy."

The tautness in Adam's features made Banner fear that he'd forgotten that feuds were childish and stupid. "Was

Royce actually there when this happened, Jeff?"

"Yes." Jeff's voice was a gurgling rasp now; he was incoherent and the laudenum was taking effect. "W-Warning—he said it was—a warning—d-don't go after him, Adam—it's a trap—"

"I don't give a damn," replied Adam, and then he was turning away, leaving his brother to Banner's care, knowing, damn him, that as a doctor she could not leave a patient to follow.

"Adam!" she pleaded. "Adam, wait!"

The door of the examining room slammed, and then the door of the outer office.

"Fool," Banner sobbed, covering Jeff with a blanket. "That stubborn, stupid, arrogant fool!"

Just then, Katherine burst into the room, still wearing a hat and her traveling clothes, her face pale and pinched. "Maggie said that—" Blue eyes fell to Jeff's inert frame, filled with tears. "Oh, no—"

Jeff began to writhe on the narrow table; it was clear that he would have to be moved into the ward and placed in a railed bed. "Adam—" he said.

"Hush," whispered Banner, trying to soothe him.

Katherine was at her son's side, pulling off her gloves, searching Banner's face. "What happened?"

Briefly, Banner explained.

"And Adam has gone to find Temple, hasn't he?" asked Katherine when the story had ended, closing her eyes. "That idiot! Doesn't he know that that's exactly what Temple wants him to do?"

"Sean had some part in this," muttered Banner. "It's my fault—all of it. It's my fault!"

Katherine fixed her daughter-in-law in a gaze that left no doubt of her authority. "Don't let me hear you say such a thing again, Banner Corbin. It's nonsense and I won't listen to it.

"Now, go out to the stables and get Walter and that boy that helps him. We've got to move Jeff."

Drying her eyes as she went, Banner hurried off to obey.

Chapter Fifteen

"Banner?"

She sat up in bed with a start, opened her eyes. Adam was standing over her, his face gaunt in the pinkish-gray light of dawn.

"Is Jeff—"

Adam shook his head. "Jeff is fine. He'll be as obnoxious as ever, in a day or so."

"I wanted to stay with him, but Katherine—"

Adam sank to the edge of the bed, couched his head in his hands in a weary gesture. "I know. Don't worry—she took good care of him."

Banner reached out to massage taut, tension-corded shoulders, knew a quiet joy as Adam began to relax. "Did you find Mr. Royce?"

"No. But I will."

"Adam . . ."

He made a groaning sound as Banner worked more of the fierce hardness from his muscles. "If you're going to tell me that I should overlook what happened to Jeff," he muttered, "don't bother. I can live with the beating I took, but what they did to my brother is another matter."

325

"They? So you do think that Sean was involved, as well as Temple Royce?"

"Yes."

"Why do you suppose they brought Jeff back here the way they did, instead of just killing him?"

Banner's fingers were moving on the sides of Adam's neck, kneading away some of the fury that was knotted there. He moaned and rolled his head.

"They worked him over—left a lot of marks—but they obviously didn't want Jeff laid up for long. It was, as he said, a warning."

Banner lowered her hands and shifted until she was sitting beside her husband. Her throat ached and she lowered her eyes to hide the tears glistening there. "If it hadn't been for me, none of this would be happening. I should have known that Sean would find me—"

Adam caught her face in both hands and forced her to look at him. "Stop it, O'Brien. You're the best thing that's happened to this family in years, and I, for one, would rather take a thousand beatings than lose you."

"Jeff and the others might not feel the same way," replied Banner, her lower lip quivering. "I wish I'd never come here, never brought all this trouble—"

Adam broke off her anguished ramblings with a fierce kiss; even as he maneuvered her onto his lap, his tongue invaded her mouth, heralding the thorough possession to come.

Banner's nipples became hard buttons beneath the thin, gauzy cloth of her camisole. And as Adam had no doubt intended, all thoughts of their problems fled her mind.

After a time, Adam positioned her on the bed, her hips

at its edge, her legs dangling over the side. Deftly, he stripped her of her drawers and her camisole. She moaned and flung her head back and forth in a pagan fever as he knelt at the silken altar to worship.

"The gossips say you howl for me," he said, his voice muffled in the quivering softness that awaited him so eagerly.

Half-wild, Banner gasped, "You aren't exactly—impassive—yourself!"

The punishment for this small defiance was one tormenting kiss. "Some rumors are true, aren't they, O'Brien?"

Heat surged through Banner; her knees did not need the tender pressure of his hands to part them further. Still, though, she denied him the answer he wanted.

Idly, he tongued her. "Admit it, O'Brien. This time the gossipmongers know what they're talking about—don't they?"

Banner's back arched in a spasm of pleasure. "Yes," she conceded, breathless. *"Yes!"*

Adam's throaty chortle was triumphant, and his fingers came up to ply Banner's aching nipples as he enjoyed her.

Frantic, hands clawing at the bedclothes, Banner allowed her fierce pride to give way to a fiercer passion, and she relinquished the raspy cry of triumph and surrender that she had tried so hard to stifle. And as she drifted back down, onto the piercing pleasure that waited to hurl her into the skies again, she smiled.

There was no denying it; the gossips were right. She *had* howled for Adam Corbin, and she wasn't ashamed.

. . .

Jeff was fully dressed and pacing the ward when Banner arrived, summoned by a worried Maggie.

"Get back into that bed this instant!"

Jeff faced her and brought his imperious, aristocratic nose to within inches of Banner's. "No!" he yelled.

"Yes!" Banner shouted back, noting the white strain in his face and the way he held his splinted arm close to his body in an unconscious attempt to shield it.

"It's been *three days,* Banner!"

Banner lifted her hands to her hips, as immovable as her brother-in-law. "I don't care," she said firmly. "*Get back into that bed.*"

Jeff turned away, sat down on the edge of the bed in question. "Bring me a woman and I will."

"Jeff Corbin!"

He smiled thinly, and with heart-wrenching effort. "Just one woman?" he wheedled.

Banner blushed. "You are completely impossible."

He laughed and fell back onto the mattress, clearly spent by the brief and fiery exchange. "I'm glad you think so," he said, and two seconds later he was asleep again.

Banner smiled and shook her head and, on impulse, bent to kiss her brother-in-law's bruised forehead. "Idiot," she said fondly, just before she went off to search the examining rooms for Adam.

She did not find him, but standing at the windows and worrying about where he might be, she caught sight of a familiar, brawny frame at the edge of the woods. Daniel?

Quickly, her heart in her throat, Banner found her cloak and draped it across her shoulders as she ran outside, across the backyard, toward the woods.

"Daniel?" she cried, coming to a stop when she reached the line of thick trees. "Daniel!"

He came out of the foliage, his wonderful, hideous face contorted, frantic. "I didn't want to come here—I couldn't—"

Banner went to her father-in-law without fear, caught his thick arms in her hands. "What is it, Daniel? Tell me what's the matter."

"Lulani," he managed, in a choking voice, his anguish rising up around them both like a separate entity. "She's—she's hurting so much—"

Banner was already turning away, her mind racing. "Wait here, Daniel," she called to him. "I'll get some horses and my bag."

"Hurry!" pleaded Daniel.

Banner found her bag immediately, filled it with supplies plundered from Adam's cabinet, and raced outside again. On the wall outside the surgery door was a large slateboard and chalk that Adam used to advise callers of his whereabouts.

Under his almost illegible scribble, she wrote one word: mountain.

The old man who worked in the stables saddled the two horses Banner demanded without question, though his eyes were full of suspicion. No doubt, he would recount this episode to Adam the moment he saw him, but that didn't matter.

Sean grinned, glad that he had resisted the urge to follow Banner when she left in such a hurry. She'd taken two horses instead of one. Did she have a lover hidden away somewhere?

No matter; Sean couldn't think about that now. The fancy doctor was whirling away from the slateboard fixed to an outside wall of the house, running toward the stables at a speed Sean wouldn't have thought possible, considering the working over he'd taken.

Sean forced himself to wait until Corbin had come out of the stables again, mounted on a dancing black stallion. If he followed too quickly, or too closely, he would be seen, and he was damned if he wanted to deal with Adam Corbin now, without the element of surprise in his favor.

Once a few minutes had passed, Sean lumbered into the saddle of a horse he'd borrowed from Royce.

Royce. He smiled again as he prodded the animal into a leisurely trot. He'd wanted to be in on this, Temple had.

And to hell with him. This was Sean's battle, and he wasn't going to let anyone else have a piece of it.

Banner stumbled out of the cabin, her bag forgotten. "Daniel," she said to the man who waited with slumped shoulders beside a tree. "I'm sorry. I'm so sorry."

There was no sound from Daniel, no outward indication of his grief.

"Adam will be here soon," Banner whispered, feeling a need to comfort this man who had already suffered so much loss and pain. "I left word for him and I know he'll come."

Though Daniel did not turn to face her, he spoke at last. "Lulani won't hurt any more."

"No. She's resting now."

"I loved her."

330

"I know, Daniel. I know."

He rounded on her, his deformed face bright with tears. "I loved my Katie, too, but I couldn't live with her—I had to leave."

Banner nodded, her throat tight. "You needn't explain to me, Daniel."

"I don't want you to think that Adam will be like me— that he'll betray you the way I did his mother. He's strong and he's good, my son."

"Yes," said Banner. "But so are you, Daniel, or you couldn't have made the sacrifices you have."

Somewhere in the trees, a bird sang a lonely song. "Go back, Banner," Daniel said. "Go home now. My son will be furious if he finds you here."

Banner thrust out her chin. "I'm going nowhere, Daniel. Adam *will* be angry, but he'll need me and I intend to stay."

Daniel looked back at the cabin where Lulani was, still now. At peace. "Adam is a good husband? He doesn't beat you?"

Banner swallowed. "No, he doesn't beat me."

"Well, he might, if you're still here when he comes. You've taken a foolish chance, Banner—I should never have come near you, brought you here—"

"I know that. You came to the house for Adam, not me. How long did you stand out there in the woods, Daniel, waiting for him?"

The big man shrugged. "An hour—I don't know. I was about to walk up and knock on the door when you saw me and came out. I'm grateful to you for your help, Banner."

Her eyes fell to the loamy, spring-warmed earth. "I

331

wasn't much help, I'm afraid. Lulani was gone when I reached her."

Daniel nodded, and there was a vacant ache in his blue eyes. "I'll sit with her," he decided aloud, and then he was stumbling away, leaving Banner alone with a thousand thoughts and feelings.

Driven by these, she went to the edge of a nearby cliff, where a sturdy, gnarled old tree leaned out into open space, like a circus performer defying gravity. A sob rose from the core of her spirit as she considered Lulani's passing and the terrible void it would leave in Daniel's world.

Suddenly, her elbow was caught in a wrenching grasp and Banner found herself being spun around. Adam's face was terrible to behold.

"What the *hell* are you doing up here, O'Brien?"

Tears burned in Banner's eyes, blurring her vision. "It's Lulani," she broke in, almost choked by her despair. "Adam, L-Lulani's dead!"

Adam closed his eyes, swayed a little. "When?" he asked, after a long interval.

"I don't know exactly. She was gone when Daniel and I got here."

"Papa—how is he?"

Banner wiped away her tears with the back of one hand. "He's shattered, Adam."

Adam lowered his head, nodded. "He'll die without her, Banner."

Banner wrapped her arms around her husband, held him. But her words of comfort were stopped in her throat when she looked past his shoulder and saw Sean striding toward them, a rifle in one hand.

At his wife's gasp, Adam turned, but it was too late. The butt of Sean's rifle landed in the middle of his face with a dull thud. He folded to the ground.

Scream after scream rattled through Banner, but she couldn't utter a sound. She fell to her knees and reached for Adam, but Sean twisted his hand in her hair and wrenched her cruelly back to her feet.

"What good is he to you now, Banner?" he hissed. "Can he part your thighs now? Can he make you beg for his—"

"Stop," pleaded Banner, closing her eyes.

Sean flung her away so that she sprawled on the ground. With one massive, meaty hand, he hauled a half-conscious Adam to his feet.

Banner watched in mute horror as her husband came out of his daze and braced himself to do battle with a man who had every intention of killing him. Sheer hatred sustained Adam, visible in every line of his body.

Blood streamed from a cut over his eyes, but he seemed oblivious to it, to Banner, to everything but the smirking giant he faced. "Put down the rifle, big man," Adam breathed, holding out both hands, beckoning. "Let's see how well you can do in the daylight, one to one."

Sean swung the rifle around, pressed its cold barrel hard into Banner's right temple. "Don't come any closer," he said.

Adam froze. His gaze sliced, murderous, to Banner, who still sat on the ground, and then back to Sean. "If you hurt her," he said evenly, "I'll pull your spinal cord out and wrap it around your neck."

Sean paled, but the rifle was firmly in place, and his free hand was working at the top button of his trousers. "She was never that good when I had her," he said. "Let's see what you've taught her, Corbin."

Banner shrieked, suddenly vocal in her terror and her revulsion, and a hideous, answering cry came from the direction of the cabin.

Three people turned to stare as Daniel came raging toward them, bellowing like a madman, waving his crippled arms in the air.

He must have looked like a monster to Sean, a fugitive from some drunken nightmare. Banner watched as the color drained from Sean's broad face, as he dropped the rifle and stumbled backward in blind fear, his mouth and throat working.

Daniel reached him and flung himself upon him before anyone else could move. Sean screamed as both men tumbled over the cliff.

The world seemed to shift and shimmer around Banner in the following moments, like a heat mirage. She was aware that Adam raced to the edge of the cliff, looked over, grasped the gnarled tree to keep from falling.

At the same moment, Jeff arrived, his horse lathered and panting. He dismounted, stumbled over to Banner, hauled her to her feet with his good hand. And all the while his eyes were on Adam, who still clung to the tree at the brim of the cliff. "What happened here?"

Before Banner could even summon the breath to answer, Adam threw back his head and roared, "*Nooooooo!*"

Jeff strode to his brother's side, drew him away from his perilous position by the cliff. "Adam! Adam, for God's sake—"

Banner held her breath as Adam flailed free of Jeff's grasp and shouted, "Look for yourself, damn you! Look for yourself!"

Pale, Jeff looked over the cliff's edge, swayed. Had Adam not grabbed his arm and flung him away again, he would certainly have fallen.

He jerked free of his older brother, staggering, searching the cliff for a way down over it. "No," Jeff sobbed, as he found what he sought and made his way down a steep natural path, pebbles sliding beneath his boots.

Banner went to the tree as Adam stumbled after his brother. Below, Sean and Daniel lay far apart on the lethal rocks, both of them still.

Banner turned her head and fought down the bile that rose in her throat. They were dead, both of them.

When she dared to look down again, Jeff was kneeling beside his father, reaching for him.

Adam caught Jeff at the shoulders, pulled him back. His words rose to Banner on the warm spring wind. "Don't, Jeff. Don't touch him."

Something primitive moved through Jeff's formidable frame, lifting him back to his feet, giving him the power to turn on Adam in his fury. "You *knew!*" he bellowed, thrusting his good hand into his brother's shoulder. "God damn you, you bastard, *you knew!*"

"Jeff—"

Jeff seemed almost maniacal in his anger and his pain. He shoved Adam again and Adam stumbled backward, not raising a hand to defend himself.

"I'll kill you!" Jeff wept, bitterly, brokenly. "I'll kill you, Adam—"

335

Banner took her brother-in-law at his word and scrambled for the rifle Sean had dropped. In another moment, she was grappling down the same steep path Adam and Jeff had taken. Sharp rocks scraped open her knees, her elbows, the side of her face. Still, she kept going, clutching the rifle in one numb hand.

When Banner reached the bottom, Jeff was still trying to prod his brother into a fight. But this was no good-natured brawl in the front yard, no game.

"Hit me, goddamn you!" the younger brother roared.

Adam did not lift his hands. The wound in his head was seeping blood, and his face was crimson with the stuff, but he seemed unaware of that, unaware of everything but Jeff's pain.

"I'm sorry, Jeff."

"*Sorry?* You're *sorry?!* My God, Papa was alive all this time and you knew it and you stand there and tell me you're sorry?"

Adam wiped some of the blood from his face with the cuff of one shirtsleeve. "Yes, I'm sorry."

There was a spasm of fury in Jeff's face. He muttered a vicious word and lunged at his brother, closing his unhampered hand around Adam's throat. "You lied—all these years—"

Adam displaced his brother's hand easily. "I had to lie, Jeff. Papa wanted that, and he had good reason to."

"No!"

At this point, Banner cocked the rifle, as Adam had taught her to do one day when he was still recovering from his last confrontation with Sean, and pointed it squarely at Jeff's head.

"Touch my husband again," she said quietly, "and I'll kill you where you stand."

Jeff did not even seem to see Banner, but he was deflated all the same. He sank fluidly to his knees, his hand over his face, his weeping a sound that she would never forget. She lowered the rifle as Adam crouched before his broken brother and drew him into an embrace.

They had to talk now, and weep together; Banner left them to that, laying down the rifle and making her way back up the cliff path alone.

After a very long time, Adam and Jeff came up, too. Their faces were cold and closed, and neither of them seemed to know that Banner was there at all.

Working together, in strained silence, they managed to bring the two bodies up from the base of the cliff. After that, they buried Daniel and Lulani beside each other and then dug another grave for Sean.

By the time this gruesome business had been completed, it was well past sunset.

For the first time, in Banner's hearing, Jeff spoke to his brother. "The cabin?"

"It has to be burned," replied Adam. "I'll do it."

Jeff shrugged, his face expressionless, and turned to stagger toward his horse, which had been grazing nearby. After risking one look at Adam, who nodded, Banner followed her brother-in-law.

"Jeff, wait," she pleaded softly.

He stiffened beside his horse, the reins in his hand, but he did not turn around or speak.

"Adam did what he had to do," she told him, her words soft, but firm, too.

"Yes. He stole five years that I could have shared with my father."

Banner closed her eyes. "Your father had *leprosy*."

"He was still my father," Jeff retorted, and then he swung onto the horse's back, and the flames from the rapidly ignited cabin glowed on his face like the light of hell.

Quickly, she caught hold of the horse's bridle, desperate to stall Jeff somehow, to keep him from riding away from his brother now. "H-How did you happen to come here when you did, Jeff?"

"I saw Malloy follow Adam away from the house," he answered, his eyes fixed on some unseeable distance. "Goodbye, Banner."

Defeated, Banner let go of the bridle. "Goodbye," she said.

Banner went back to Adam slowly, trying to deal with her own feelings so that she could then help with his. She thought of Sean—she had not loved him, but she had not wished him dead, either. She hoped that he would find peace now.

Adam's gaze was fixed on his rapidly disappearing brother, and the light of the blazing cabin flickered on his face and the broad, blood-smudged expanse of his chest.

Banner found water and a cloth and began to wash her husband's face. "Did you explain?"

"I tried," he said with a ragged sigh, submitting to the washing with uncharacteristic patience. "He won't tell anyone—that's the important thing."

"Maybe you should have told him sooner, Adam," Banner ventured, laying aside the wet cloth.

But Adam shook his head. "The risk of infection was too great. Besides, Jeff isn't the sort to keep a secret—the concept of deception is beyond him."

After that, there seemed nothing more to say. They waited until the cabin had consumed itself and then mounted their own horses to go back down the mountain. The mounts Sean and Daniel had ridden trotted obediently along behind.

Banner sighed. Saints in heaven but it was hot, even in Katherine's shaded garden. And she was so big.

A tear slid down Banner's face and shimmered like a diamond on the marble bench she sat upon. Within her enormous belly, the baby moved like a small, furious gladiator.

It was late August, and Adam had not lain with her since June. Was he really content with the limited pleasures they could offer each other now, or was he making pilgrimages to the *Silver Shadow* as well as rounds?

"O'Brien?" Adam's hands came to her shoulders, gently kneading. "What are you thinking?"

"That I am an elephant," she sniffled, "not a wife."

Adam sat down beside her on the bench and traced the length of her neck with a tender finger. His blue eyes fell fondly, possessively, to her stomach. "You are beautiful, Shamrock," he said.

Banner sighed and wiped her face. "I wish the baby would come," she muttered. "I want to be able to sleep on my stomach again."

Adam chuckled. "I'd like to be able to sleep on your stomach again, too."

Suddenly, Banner sat bolt upright; dampness was spreading around her, soaking her skirts. "My waters!" she gasped. "Adam, my waters—"

Instantly, he was on his feet, sweeping her up into his arms, striding into the house.

All sorts of strange emotions rushed into Adam's throat from some fount in his heart as he looked down at the furious, redheaded infant boy squirming in his hands. Tiny arms and legs flailed, and a strong little back arched.

"Adam?" whispered the mother of this bristling wonder. "Adam—the baby?"

"The baby is fine," he said, surrendering the child to Maggie so that he could tie and sever the birth cord. "A boy with red hair like yours."

Banner should have been resting, but suddenly she was writhing and tossing her head from side to side. "Adam— there's another! Saints in heaven—there's another!"

Adam felt her stomach with both hands, muttered in amazement. Sure enough, a second baby was on its way.

Even in her labor, Banner was beautiful. "I love you, Adam," she said, over and over again. "I love you."

Finally, after much ado, a girl child made a glorious, outraged entrance, wriggling in her father's hands just as her brother had, squalling when her bottom was slapped and her mouth was cleared.

"We have a daughter," Adam marveled hoarsely.

"*We,*" smiled his weary wife, relaxing at last. "I did all the work, Adam Corbin!"

"Twins!" The word bubbled up out of Adam, like a cry of joy, as he went to the other side of the bed to wash his hands. "*Twins.*"

For all her exhaustion and her residual pain, Banner laughed. "Look at him, Maggie! He's swaggering like a rooster!"

"He has the right to be proud," said Maggie in a quavering voice, as she washed and wrapped the two infuriated infants. "And so do you."

Adam dried his hands and bent to kiss his wife's damp brow. "I love you, O'Brien," he said, feeling no shame for the tears in his eyes.

Maggie wrested him aside to place one baby in Banner's arms, and then another. Then she left, and the Corbins set about naming their children.

The boy, it had been long decided, would be called Daniel Jeffrey, but the girl, having come as a complete surprise, posed a problem.

"What was your mother's name, O'Brien?" Adam asked, frowning at the small delight that was his daughter.

"Bridget."

"That's it, then. Bridget."

As if glad to have a name, Bridget Corbin made a cooing sound and settled against her mother's breast to sleep.

It promised to be a very fine Christmas, indeed, with all the family home and concentrating on spoiling the babies as thoroughly as they could, and Banner hummed as she finished putting the examining room in order.

The door opened, closed again.

Banner turned to smile at her husband. "I'm through now, so we can—"

Adam was grinning at her, pressing her against the examining table. Her skirts began to slide upward under the deft guidance of his hands.

"Adam Corbin!"

He chuckled, knelt. Banner felt her drawers slide down over her hips, her thighs, her knees. She made to flee, and his hands locked around her ankles, holding her fast. He lifted one of her feet, and her lacy undergarment was crumpled around one shoe. If she ran now, she risked dragging her drawers ignobly behind her.

His hands caressed the satiny skin of her thighs, widening her stance as they did so.

Banner trembled. Someone was approaching the examining room, she was sure of it. Someone would walk in at any time—

"Adam!"

She felt a coolness as he parted her, braced herself for what would come next.

His mouth closed over her, and her knuckles whitened where she gripped the edge of the table she was leaning against. Beneath her dress, Banner's nipples hardened, chafing. Her face was aflame and her breath was too quick.

Adam chuckled, the sound muffled by her skirts, and menaced her sweetly with his tongue. An incomprehensible heat surged through her, followed by a brutal, grinding release that left her groaning.

Adam blithely patted her bottom, slipped her drawers back over her feet, pulled them up to her waist, and tied the tie. Before aligning her skirts again, he kissed her muslin-sheltered sweetness once, in parting.

"I've got a house call to make," he announced, grinning.

Damn him, he was completely calm, while Banner could barely trust her knees to support her.

"I'm going with you," she said.

Adam shook his head and gestured toward the window, where a dense Christmas Eve snow was falling. "It's cold outside, O'Brien, and I won't be gone long."

Banner put her hands to her face, in an effort to cool her passion-charred cheeks. "If you think you're going to leave me behind, Adam Corbin, and on our anniversary . . ."

Adam rolled his eyes. "I'll be back soon enough to"—he assessed her mischievously—"celebrate. Besides, the babies need you."

"Danny and Bridget are busy holding court in the parlor. I've fed them and they're just fine."

Adam was ignoring her, walking out, crossing the outer office, catching up his coat and his bag as he passed them. Banner scrambled into her own cloak and scurried after him, unhampered by the slight ache in her right ankle that was the result of a fall at that day's skating party.

Adam looked back over his shoulder, heedless of the snow, and tried to seem angry. But a smile curved his lips as Banner fell stubbornly into step beside him.

Center Point Publishing
600 Brooks Road ● PO Box 1
Thorndike ME 04986-0001 USA

(207) 568-3717

US & Canada:
1 800 929-9108